Sarah Quigley was born in New ⬛⬛⬛ Oxford University, and is now ba⬛⬛⬛ numerous awards for her fiction ⬛⬛⬛⬛⬛ fellowships include the CNZ/DAAD Berlin Writer's Fellowship, the Frank Sargeson Residency, and the Robert Burns Literary Fellowship. Her next novel, *Fifty Days*, is published by Virago in 2004.

'Quigley, an award-winning writer and poet from New Zealand, has a blatant disregard for conventional storytelling. Her skill lies in depicting an offbeat world peopled with larger-than-life characters like Lena's sister, a stunning-looking taxidermist . . . entertaining . . . *Shot* is fresh and inventive, originally written, and littered with great scenes' *Time Out*

'It's a testament to Quigley's ability that she moves the story effortlessly between poles of deep despair and riotous humour with great ease . . . subtle and entertaining . . . a book that remains joyously unpredictable throughout' *Venue*

'Quigley has crafted a humorous and intelligent reworking of the American road trip genre. Reminiscent of a Coen Brothers film' *Big Issue*

'Sarah Quigley, whose keen eye for the absurd, revealed in lively ironic prose, also catches the heartstrings' *Irish Examiner*

'Featuring a cast of endearingly eccentric characters, *Shot* is a wry and heart-warming tale of love, loss and discovery' *Waterstone's Books Quarterly* (Faces of the Future)

Also by Sarah Quigley

having words with you
After Robert

SHOT

SARAH QUIGLEY

Virago

A *Virago* Book

First published by Virago Press 2003
This edition published by Virago Press 2004

Copyright © Sarah Quigley 2003

The moral right of the author has been asserted.

A CIP catalogue record for this book
is available from the British Library.

ISBN 1 84408 014 5

Typeset in Electra by Palimpsest Book Production Limited,
Polmont, Stirlingshire
Printed and bound in Great Britain
by Clays Ltd, St Ives plc

Virago Press
An imprint of
Time Warner Books UK
Brettenham House
Lancaster Place
London WC2E 7EN

www.virago.co.uk

1

In the time it took for a bullet to travel through her left ear and into the back wall of the donut shop on the corner of Ellis and Polk, Lena McLeonard remembered her past.

And this was odd because, although by that time she had travelled many miles and traversed most of California in her reluctant search for fame, she was only a few blocks from the small house in which she had grown up. She had tried not to look back, sometimes to such an extent that it felt like a sin. So perhaps it was no coincidence that she had returned there, in the middle of a spring afternoon in the middle of the city of San Francisco, only to step straight into the path of an oncoming bullet.

Wherever you go in the world, she had told an audience more than once, *there you are*. They had roared at this (the truth is often funny) and their laughter, rising from the dark onto the lighted stage, sounded like vast waves rising from the sea. Much the same as the sea-roar Lena now heard, not only in her left ear but also in the centre of her head, which until this point had been filled with the very ordinary sounds of cars and buses and people hurrying into the next hour.

This is it, she thought, as hot blood flowed down her neck and under the collar of her shirt. This is how it feels to be shot.

Her legs were somewhere far beneath her, so she was no longer conscious of the sidewalk under her shiny red shoes. She had put on those shoes that morning in her Los Angeles apartment, already with the thought of San Francisco donuts in her head: thoughts of jelly centres, and of cream, and of icing sugar falling on her wrists like snow. Lena had been addicted to donuts since the age of four, remembered her first taste with more reverence than she later remembered her first orgasm, and this very same Polk Street shop had paved the way to her addiction.

She had got so close! only to be stopped by the trigger-quick finger of someone in a black car with a grievance against the driver of a blue one. Both cars had accelerated away unscathed, leaving Lena freeze-framed there against a sugar-filled window. And—

'This is what it is like to die,' she thought in a conversational tone to herself.

Although she was by now adept at milking comedy from all kinds of situations, she could find nothing particularly funny in this one.

There was screaming, at a distance, and a wailing that could have been sirens – though from what the locals said in resigned voices, the police were more likely to hurry to the final of a baseball series than to an emergency in that dubious area of the city. And it is here in this neighbourhood that our story really begins, although not on this particular afternoon with gunfire blowing like blossom through the spring streets. It all started many years earlier but nonetheless right here in downtown San Francisco, in an area called the Tenderloin – an odd name, but one as familiar to Lena as her own. For she had grown up just a few blocks from the very spot where she was now staggering, shot.

As she lurched there on the sidewalk in front of a fine display of Vietnamese buns and wedding cakes, her own red blood dripping onto her red vinyl toes, an odd thing happened. Her childhood began to reel before her eyes in a series of snapshots, one following the other in a continuous stream as if in the space left by the wake of the bullet.

(freeze frame: a young woman wearing particularly beautiful high red shoes stands on a sidewalk with blood pouring from the side of her head. Although her cupped hands are filling up with that

2

blood, and her body leans at an odd angle, her face is quite calm as if she is thinking of something else entirely. In the window behind her are the streaked reflection of tail lights and a soaring mountain of donuts)

Yes, this is Lena McLeonard, professional comedian, recently shot in the head. This is Lena, thinking of her own imminent death, of routines not written down and truths never met, and thinking most of all about the Tenderloin past.

Stew

The Tenderloin. It's an odd name for a neighbourhood. Some believe it got its name from the shape of the women's legs seen there after dark, poised under red lights on street corners. But others say that any cop unlucky enough to work that beat earned enough in danger money to buy a better cut of meat; and this second explanation is most appropriate to Lena's story.

There was always much meat in the Domanski household (though certainly not tenderloin, or any other kind of steak). This was one of Mrs Domanski's chief occupations: the chopping up of cheap sausage to replenish the pot that sat on the stove of Lena's childhood, day in, day out. (Years later, with startling clarity, this is what Lena sees: the white hands of her mother stirring the stew.)

As you will have noticed, the name of Lena's stew-making mother and also of her stew-eating father was Domanski, and this was the name Lena had been born to. It was Jay who, much later, had told her to change it.

'Backers don't like anything too foreign,' he had said knowledgeably. 'You want something with a bit of class.'

Jay's own background was Italian: he had the eagle nose of his ancestors, and a smell of spaghetti often hung about his head despite the fact that he changed his shirt several times a day (he had never coped well with high temperatures). But in those bubbling stew days Jay was still a long way into Lena's future. He was nothing more than the promised magic mountain in the

3

songs of the playground, certain only while the hot skipping rope whipped the air into circles and feet pounded on the inner-city asphalt. Once the songs were over and elbows were planted back on the scratched tables of Hyde Street Elementary, then every possible Jay in all romantic shapes and guises was forgotten.

For the time being, then, while the chunks of cheap sausage elbowed their way around the pan and the windows steamed, Mr Domanski remained the one and only man in Lena's life. He was her father, after all, and the only one she would ever have, which in a life tending towards disposability is a rare and precious thing. Bankcards can be lost and replaced in the space of a phone call, appliances go up in smoke and it is easier to reach for the yellow pages than for the toolkit. But there is no free-phone number to get yourself another father, should you be careless enough to lose sight of him.

If Mr Domanski's uniqueness weren't reason enough for Lena to love him, there were plenty of other reasons – as many as the juniper berries bobbing in the stew, and as bright. Mr D hardly ever shouted at his children, he never left bristles in the sink when he trimmed his moustache, and sometimes he took time out from work to attend the finals of spelling bees.

The feeling of love was mutual. For Lena was Mr Domanski's only American-born child. In her shining hair he saw the glint of new starts; he saw ten brand-new opportunities in her ten tiny fingernails, and a whole land of opportunity in the small spread of her feet.

'My American Pie,' he would call her, and every time he said the words he felt a rekindling of the bursting hope he had experienced on first arriving in California. Lena could sense this, and through her growing-up years the two of them were bound by it. When she and her father looked at each other there was a secret lifting of their hearts, even as the smell of meat lay heavy on the rubber tree plants and Mrs Domanski stood, herself like a silent tree, stirring the stew and staring unseeingly out at the back alley.

'*Singing bye bye, Miss American Pie,*' sang Mr Domanski.

'*Drove my Chevy to the levy but the levy was dry,*' sang Lena.

Her voice was perhaps her making, a reason for her later success on stage and the key to her undoing. For it was as high and sweet as a bird announcing morning in a land where the air is unsoiled by belching cars, and unsplit by the evils of fluorocarbons.

'Your voice,' said Mr Domanski when he was feeling whimsical, 'it is like liquid honey.' At other times —

'Your voice is like *faworki*,' he would say with meaning. This was on days when he felt it his duty to remind Mrs Domanski that it was a long time since she had served them real food. Food that tasted of nostalgia, that allowed him to sit in a dusty corner of his mind, warmed once again by a coal burner and the attention of his old Nannie Lopuk. For although Mr Domanski woke every day with a determination to embrace America, sometimes his stomach and his heart warred with his head.

'Yes, your voice is pure *faworki*, my little Pie!' he said again, taking off his glasses and wiping them on his waistcoat. 'A person would get in their Chevy and drive a hundred miles – a thousand! – just to hear you sing.'

'What is a Chevy?' asked Lena curiously.

'What *are faworki*?' asked Bella, in a scornful voice.

Bella's real name was Gabriella but like Jay, the looming mountain in Lena's future, she had a horror of anything too Foreign. She was determined to bury her past, and was well on the way to doing it: determination had always been one of Bella's best qualities. With the burden of her East European birth on her shoulder, Bella-Gabriella strode with vigour but also clumsily. Lena watched her now, cleaving through the forest of rubber plants, setting the wooden birdcage that hung from the ceiling into a spin.

'What are they?' Bella demanded again, as she slapped place mats down on the table like a malcontent card dealer.

'*Faworki* are *Chrust*,' said Mr Domanski, acting as a thesaurus rather than a dictionary. 'As you well know.'

Bella made a face and marched off to get the cutlery. Although the floor had been hoovered by Mrs Domanski that morning, Bella had a knack of raising dust; clouds of it rose in alarm behind her, and settled back with a sigh.

5

Lena looked at the wooden bird still reeling inside its wooden cage. She had the oddest sensation

(*a ringing,* sang the bullet teasingly, *a singing ringing reeling*)

and she swayed in her child-sized chair found in the alley out back of Uncle Larry's store. Its fabric arms were stained from old wads of gum which Lena had painstakingly scraped off with a razor blade, and she stared at these stains now, using them to steady herself.

'Are you all right there, Yankee Doodle?' asked Mr Domanski, looking concerned.

Bella looked annoyed. She hated being reminded that Lena was exactly what she herself most wanted to be – and these reminders happened far too often. Even when it had rained for days, even when the front door had been generously splashed with graffiti and needles were found on the doorstep, Mr Domanski remained adamant that immigration was always for the best and that Lena was living proof of this. 'How, when you are offered a new start, could you turn your back on it,' he would ask, 'yet still look yourself in the face?' His grasp of English had remained slippery, meaning he often mixed his metaphors. But he was persistent in his pursuit of optimism, even though it was at odds with the character of his native Poland, and so his frequent question carried its own answer.

'Been into Da's vodka, have you?' said Bella in a mean voice, looking at her swaying American-citizen of a sister.

'Shut your cakehole,' said Lena with dignity. She had learnt this phrase just that day from her best friend Elroy, a seven-year-old African-American who knew far worse insults than this. But as a person of a superior age he had always been protective of Lena.

'Are you ill, my little one?' asked Mr Domanski worriedly.

The truth of it was Lena had just realized, as she watched the string of the birdcage twirling in the ceiling, that she had no idea where she belonged. She didn't feel American, she didn't feel anything, and so she was reeling from anxiety. She grabbed the sides of her chewing-gum chair thinking that it might lift up and fly through the ceiling with her in it, forcing her to circle the earth forever in search of a land she felt passionate about. Oh, how she suddenly wanted that! The passion that her father almost always felt for America, Land of Opportunity, and that Bella definitely felt for America, Land of the Cheap Nylon Stockings, and that her mother Mrs Domanski felt for Poland Past.

'What did you say?' asked Bella, looking interested. 'Shut your *cakehole*?'

'Cakehole?' said their mother distantly from the kitchen, where she stood root-bound by the stove. 'That does not sound a good word.'

'It sounds all right to me,' said Mr Domanski in a deliberately casual voice. Fathers were not supposed to have favourites among their children but sometimes it occurred to Lena, in the moment before sleep, that perhaps she was the one. She did not like this thought; it brought a hot guilty rush as she lay there in the dark and thought of Bella who, though beautiful, was never quite beautiful enough for her own exacting standards, and of their brother Delayed Davey, whose thin neck often evoked protective feelings. Yes, it brought a warm flood of guilt

(*warm and dark,* murmured the bullet, as the blood ran sweetly down inside Lena's ear and out)

and this guilt came now, and to banish it Lena had to speak again. 'Shut your bitchin' cakehole, woman!' she said in a rush, which after all was far more in keeping with the spirit of the absent Elroy.

'Lena!' said Mr Domanski in a shocked voice. 'Go to your room!' His youngest child might be the daughter of Hope and Democracy, but enough was enough.

Lena stood up, relieved. As she picked her way between the hanging pot plants, six years of weighty favouritism rolled temporarily off her thin shoulders.

'Talk about push her pull her,' said Bella, doing one of her lightning-quick changes of sides which were endearing if they were in your favour. 'Give the kid a goddamn break, why don't you!'

'And you can go to *your* room,' thundered Mr Domanski. 'Why

7

can you never show respect for your father like a good Polish girl should?'

'You wanna know why?' bellowed Bella. 'Because I'm not fucking Polish!' She threw down a handful of knives and forks with an impressive clatter and followed hard on Lena's heels.

As it happened, Lena's and Bella's rooms were one and the same thing. Although the Domanskis lived in a real house – one of only three in the entire fifty blocks of the Tenderloin neighbourhood – it *was* a small house, and there was much sharing of space. This meant that, amongst other things, Lena and Bella were required to listen to each other's nightly prayers.

'I pray to belong,' whispered Lena. It was only six-thirty and still light outside, but she hoped that God would be alert enough to tune in at an earlier time than usual.

'I pray to God for a sane and modern father,' said Bella loudly, in a way that was more blasphemous than religious. The walls were like paper and it was obvious that she wanted Mr D, rather than any greater being, to hear her plea.

Lena's toes curled on the carpet. Kneeling there, she agonised for her loud dissatisfied sister and her large defeated father, both of whom (she understood with six-year-old wisdom) suffered from a degree of homelessness in spite of the patched iron roof over their heads.

She and Bella got into their beds, one on each side of the room, and listened to the evening go on without them. They heard the revving of engines in the street and the shouts from the Rec Center across the road. Through the wall on Bella's side came the smack-smack of their neighbour's punch bag in the alley. ('He's a machine,' said Bella admiringly.) And through Lena's wall, not so far from her open face, came the clink of dishes as Mrs Domanski, the uprooted and transplanted, moved her branch arms about in the kitchen, stirring the stew.

Sugar

In spite of Elroy's efforts to protect her from the street, Lena had picked up far worse taunts than *cakehole* in her six Tenderloin years. Taunts that would have silenced even the bellicose Bella, and earned Lena a week of six o'clock bedtimes or maybe even a whack with a gravy-stained wooden spoon. But there was a reason why this particular piece of slang had already lodged so firmly in her small, pale-gold head.

Lena was a cake-lover. Even by this stage her sweet tooth was notorious within the family. Those *faworki* that Mr Domanski had mentioned? Those tender, twisted, melt-in-your mouth morsels of pastry, the mention of which had started all the trouble with disaffected Bella? Well, Lena had eaten hundreds – perhaps thousands – of them in her short life. When a piping hot plateful arrived at the table, the thin paper under them spotted with grease, she could hardly take her eyes off them. She was well behaved, she held back until everybody had helped themselves and her mouth was full of saliva, but after that no one got a second chance. Of its own accord her hand would creep like a small animal back and back to the plate, until there was one lone pastry left and Lena would realize that all those other *faworki* were now in her small rounded stomach, and her buttery fingers would fly to her lips in dismay.

And so it was with the golden apple fritters, sieved all over with powdered sugar donated from Uncle Larry's grocery store behind Union Square. Lena could eat dozens of these apple fritters; although they were large, they were also light and they turned quickly to air under the determined slice of her baby teeth. And so it was – to an even greater extent – on Shrove Tuesdays and St Sylvester's Day, when Mrs Domanski would drop fresh yeasty donuts into a sizzling pan of sunflower oil. Lena would eat three, four, six donuts and would just keep on going, until someone was observant and obliging enough to remove the plate from in front of her. On other non-feasting days, however, she was obliged to go to the shop on the corner of Ellis and Polk, where she would hang around the doorway until Tam Walker noticed her and called her inside.

'Looking for nuthin'?' he would say in a joking kind of way. And he would give her a small paper bag full of nothing: deep-fried zeros, the holes from the donuts about to be stacked high in the window. Lena couldn't wait until she got home to eat these: besides, she knew if she did so that Bella or Mr Domanski would take the lion's share. So she would squeeze onto the narrow ledge in front of the sliding glass windows and start to nibble, and soon the bag would be empty.

The first time she had perched birdlike in the shop, Tam had come out from the back and offered her another treat – or what he considered to be so. Tam with his treacle brown eyes, flecked through with the colour of egg yolks.

'How 'bout this?' he said, holding out a pair of tongs so hot they smoked. 'Was just about to start dicing,' he said, 'and then I thought, hey, my friend Lena would like a piece of this!'

And Lena looked at the rasher of bacon hanging from Tam's hand, wizened as a rat's tail, and she declined. She was polite, she was anxious to please at all times, but even at that age she had an unerring and enviable sense of principles. There was no one for whom she would deviate on this point, not even the kindly king of the deep-fry vats, the master of donuts supreme.

For although she had been born into the heart of the Tenderloin, into an area whose very name reeked of meat, by the age of six Lena McLeonard was already a devout vegetarian. It was as if the blood of those long-ago cattle, milked in Cow Hollow and slaughtered in Chinatown, had seeped into her tiny spidery veins and fostered a strange and instinctive resistance there.

The hen

It was a fine afternoon in the hood, and Lena and Bella were making their way home from school. A wind from the unseen sea had left its shores and was snaking its way through the city, so that Lena's fringe blew back to mingle with the rest of her hair, and Bella's new second-hand skirt swirled like a gypsy's. At the corner of Hyde and McAllister Streets, they were accosted by a girl holding a hen.

'Open your bags!' said the girl threateningly. She was not as tall as Bella – who ever was? – but her shoulders were muscly and her black limbs were covered all over with small round scars.

10

She pushed the huge hen at them in a fierce way.

'Why should we?' said Bella. 'They're not your bags.'

'They will be soon,' said the girl, 'if you don't show me what you've got.' She came closer, fencing them into the corner with her long legs that were darker than the night. Lena had never seen anyone quite so black or so scarred, and as she stood sheltering in Bella's shadow she didn't know which was more mesmerizing and terrible: the girl's black, blemished legs, or the open-beaked head of the hen weaving on the end of its patchy neck.

'Who's the hen?' said Bella scornfully. 'That your only friend, is it?'

'Don't you fucken insult the bird,' said the girl. She shoved it closer, right up to Lena's face so that the shiny beak with its slotted nostrils and the waving pink tongue looked as huge as a dinosaur's. 'Want to see your little sista pecked to death, do you?' said the girl.

'Help,' said Lena faintly. Backing up against the rough wall of the Cambodian grocery store, she pressed her hands flat against it as if, somehow, she might magically absorb its properties: would become tough and graffiti-splattered, could fall with a roar on this girl and her monster hen and flatten them like paper dolls onto the sidewalk. Not surprisingly, this failed to happen.

'Help,' said Lena again.

'You hear your sista, bitch?' said the girl to Bella. 'She wants you to help her. And there ain't no way you're gonna be able to do that, unless you give me' – she peered around the flapping brown fan of feathers, looked at Lena cowering by a crate of root ginger – 'that bracelet,' she said, pointing to Lena's tiny chicken wrist.

Lena nearly groaned, but the hen fixed her with an eye so beady and cold that her throat seized and she was silent. The coveted silver plastic bracelet belonged to Bella, who had spotted it at the very top of a dumpster and had climbed over rotten cabbages and flea-ridden rolls of carpet to retrieve it. Lena's skinny arm had been granted it for no more than the short distance between school and home, and she knew that she was lost.

'Fat chance,' said Bella scornfully. 'We won't be giving you nothing.' (By this it was clear that Bella was also slightly scared, for her English was usually impeccable.)

'OK,' said the girl. 'Then the runt gets it.' She raised her eyebrows in anticipation of a slow death by pecking. The short hair on her scalp moved like a rug. She pinched the hen hard on its back and it gave forth a terrifying battle-scream. 'Die, *immigrants!*' said the girl, and she let the hen go. It flew through the air in a light spray of feathers and claws. And the next second, it was perched on top of Lena's head, its talons digging through her fine hair and into her scalp.

(freeze frame: a small girl outside a shop is topped by poultry. She is skinny legs and small shoulders, she is shrunken sundress, but on her head she has the magnificent finish of a huge tawny hen, wings outstretched like a hat. Small Polish-American girl in the neighbourhood of the Tenderloin, with glorious, beautiful bird on head)

Lena's head finds the hen oddly heavy, like the weight of a wig borrowed from the local theatre. She takes a step: the hen stays with her. She turns as if in a dream to look at Bella, staring at her with her mouth open. She turns back to look at the girl, who has a look of terror and glee on her face. And in the glassy shop front she catches sight of herself and the hen, superimposed against slanting pyramids of oranges and tins of paraffin.

In that instant, seeing herself as others see her, Lena is different. But her sister is not. Her sister, she knows, is the same difficult, belligerent, loyal person as a minute earlier, and so she is about to give up glittering plastic trash to save Lena's life.

'Stop, Bella,' says Lena calmly, and she reaches up with both arms and lifts the hen down. As she does so, she can feel its heart flickering wildly in its rusty breast. 'Finders keepers,' she says, and she walks away on her small sandalled feet, holding the hen in her arms.

Behind her, she can hear Bella and the girl exchanging insults. Then there is a small thud and a piece of root ginger lands in front of her. A shrivelled apple follows, bouncing along in the gutter beside her.

'Run!' bellows Bella, appearing at her elbow.

A plum flies past them, narrowly missing Lena's left ear. *Wheeee!* She feels the thin narrow air-path left in its wake. She runs, holding the hen in front of her with both hands, away from her body so that it won't be jostled or jarred. Beside her Bella runs also, a large dutiful warrior in T-bar sandals.

The cage

'What exactly are we going to do with this?' said Mr Domanski in disbelief.

'I'll rehouse it,' said Lena. 'I promise.' She looked at the hen, sitting balefully in the wooden birdcage, looking like a giant. Its feathers bulged through the sides of the cage, and every movement of its head set the tiny painted parrot swinging on its perch.

'It must be gone by tomorrow,' said Mrs Domanski tiredly. For as long as Lena could remember, her mother had spoken in a tired voice, as if all her energy had been used up in moving her husband and her two oldest children from the creaking grey North to the New World.

'I promise,' said Lena earnestly, to the hen as well as to her parents. She didn't exactly like the hen: although it must have been glad to be removed from the line of duty, it didn't look especially grateful. As she watched it lifted its tail and shat through the bars of the cage onto the bathroom floor. 'I'll go down to the church hall tomorrow,' she cried as she fled to the kitchen for a cloth. 'I'll ask around.'

Because it happened to be Friday it was fish day, but Mr Domanski had forgotten to do a deal with Uncle Larry on the carp.

'I ask you to do one thing,' said Mrs Domanski resentfully. She began lifting ornaments off the windowsill and wiping underneath them, as if sweeping away dust would also sweep away her woes: a life in a land where the sea lay on the wrong side, a husband with memory problems, and children who brought large dirty birds home to a very small house.

'I know, I know,' said Mr Domanski. 'I was preoccupied thinking about the next play, you understand.' He looked hopefully at his wife, though from the start it had been plain that she thought his interest in the local theatre was foolish.

'Friday is my day off,' said Mrs Domanski. 'I will not wear the apron on a Friday.'

'And neither you should,' said Mr D heartily. 'I will sort it out. You wait and see, I will prepare a feast!'

Lena's mouth watered at the thought. Her father was a good cook, and his reputation was such that his Polish eating house on Post Street was often packed to the gills. But there was no sign of anything happening immediately, and she went to her room to do her homework so that the weekend would be free. Mrs Domanski and Bella went to pick out some cotton to mend Bella's old school dress. Davey had straggled out to the alley to play Kick the Can. And by the time they all returned to the living room some hours later, the table was covered in its red cloth and pots were hissing on the stove.

'Fish?' said Mrs Domanski, pleased but doubtful. 'You got all the way over to Larry's?'

'Not fish!' said Mr D. 'I have made *golabki* for you, with an extra-special filling.' Reverently, he carried a steaming tray out of the kitchen. He laid a neat cabbage parcel on each waiting plate and then he called Bella and Davey and Lena and God to the table. After eyes opened again and heads lifted, the rest of the family tucked in but Lena sat and stared, and began to look suspicious. She slipped off her chair and went to the bathroom, and when she came striding back her face was thunderous.

'How could you?' she said in the ringing tones of a judge.

'You found me out,' said Mr D, and he sounded guilty, but nonetheless he took a long drink of milk and continued chewing.

'Mmmm, it tastes good,' said Davey, his fork travelling slowly between his mouth and his plate.

'That's because it's sweet revenge,' said Bella, the memory of flying stone fruit in her eyes.

'Oh Jakob,' said Mrs Domanski reproachfully, and she was the only one to put down her knife and fork. 'She was going to find a home for it.'

Lena stood away from the table and put her hands up to her still unwashed chicken hair. 'I can't eat *that*,' she said. 'I held it in my arms all the way home.'

'Come along,' said Mr D. 'Sit down and try it. *Golabki* are your favourite!'

'*Golabki* means little pigeon,' said Bella with a snort.

'And the pigeon's flown the coop,' said Davey, catching on far more quickly than usual.

Lena backed away. The laughter of her brother and sister flew over her head and out the open window, leaving her unmoved. 'I will eat bread,' she said sternly.

'You'll eat what you're told to,' said Mr D thickly, through a mouthful of bird that had been first fighter, and then hat, and then refugee, and was now just a part of the food chain.

'Sit up at the table now, Lena,' said Mrs Domanski, picking a small bone from between her front teeth.

'No,' said Lena. 'No.' Her voice was filled with such certainty that it rang over the busy scraping of knives and forks, and drowned out the shouting of Mr and Mrs Lopez who lived and fought next door. Her family sat silently as her resounding *No* circled the room several times, sweeping around under the low ceiling until it got caught in the fan. Then, still without a word, they resumed eating and Lena went to the kitchen for a chunk of ryebread and a cup of sauerkraut left over from yesterday's dinner.

This turned out to be yet another gift her father had given her, albeit entirely unconsciously. Not only had he waited to reach the shores of California before penetrating his wife without contraception for the third and final time, thus saving Lena from divided loyalties and the cry of a rejected country at her back. Not only had he (rightly or wrongly) bestowed so much affection on her that she had never felt the draughty fear of not being *the* most loved; not only had he handed down good teeth, a fast metabolism, and toenails that never grew in. Finally, unwittingly, he had saved her from meat.

For that was the beginning of Lena's devout vegetarianism,

caused solely by the fact that on one warm Friday afternoon in her sixth year, her father was thinking of amateur theatrics instead of fish.

Cosmetics

Mrs Domanski had not always been pale and tired. She had not always had a voice like a dying wave on a stony beach, nor had her mouth always twisted as if coming across a herring pickled in excess vinegar.

(*sometimes*, says the bullet chattily, picking up a part of Lena's ear like a conversation piece, *life changes us beyond recognition*)

No, Mrs D had not always been faded – how could she have been, when at the age of eighteen she had won a beauty contest in her home town of Zamosc?

'Your mother was beautiful back then,' said Mr Domanski, somewhat tactlessly. 'She was really a looker.'

And sometimes Mrs Domanski was still beautiful. When she was wheeled from the operating theatre having had Lena's small body cut from her belly, for instance, she had been pale and wan but also as radiant as the snow.

Once Lena grew old enough to listen to her, Mrs D the Beauty Queen used to tell many stories about the chilly white beauty of snow. 'When I won the contest,' she said, 'it was minus twenty-five degrees Celsius, yet there I stood without stockings, without boots. There I stood in my pretty sandals and my manicured feet, in the snow.'

'Did you get a crown?' asked Lena. She stared hard at her mother's soft dark hair, now spun with grey. Briefly a silver tiara appeared, sparkling against the dull wallpaper, only to fall into nothingness when Mrs Domanski tossed her head.

'I got a beautiful crown which I kept until we left Poland,' she said. 'And, also, I got your father.' She didn't sound quite as pleased about the prize of Mr Domanski though, nor did she sound as if she wanted to go on with the story. But she seemed to think it was her duty and so she recounted, dutifully, the details of the train and the boat, the weeks of damp lurching motion and uncertainty, and the moment when, with Davey's sweaty hand clutching hers, she had seen San Francisco, a small empty city washed up on the other side of the Bay like a shell.

'I wanted to turn around and go back to Warsaw,' she said. 'There was too much water, and no snow.'

Since that landfall, a lot of the colour had been taken out of Mrs Domanski. She was like a blossom which had opened early under a frosty grey sky but had closed and shrunk under an American sun. Still, there were times when she came close to pretty again, when she almost matched up to the crinkled photo that Mr Domanski carried in his wallet and pulled out after a few rounds of vodka. And when Uncle Larry came for dinner, when he untied Mrs D's apron and put his big hands around her waist and uprooted her from the kitchen – then, yes, she looked more beauty queen than mother.

'Forget about those local actors you fool around with,' said Uncle Larry to Mr Domanski. 'You should put your wife back on the stage.' He said this admiringly but it was the wrong thing to say, because never for a second had Mrs Domanski wanted her husband to stray from the realm of food – needed by everyone – to the arguably trivial world of entertainment. Now, at Uncle Larry's words, her face closed. As she walked to the kitchen, her discarded apron caught on her nylon stockings and trailed after her as if it had no intention of letting her out of its sight.

'Hey, Lena!' said Uncle Larry, determined to return light to the room. 'Hey kiddo!'

Uncle Larry was not really Lena's uncle, nor Bella's, nor Davey's. He had come out from Warsaw long before the Domanskis had, riding on a promise from the American government that they would keep him safe. It was too late for his teeth – he opened his mouth and showed them the few that Stalin's soldiers had left him with – but by and large it had been good for his business. Instead of sheltering Jews, he now sold them gluten flour and kosher meat and in this way everyone was happy.

'Hey kiddo!' he said again.

Lena looked across at his familiar, ruddy face. 'Yes?' she said politely.

'What's the difference between a chihuahua and yourself?' said Uncle Larry, leaning so low over the table that his moustache rustled on the cloth and salt grains jumped like fleas.

'What?' said Lena, going hot all over. She clenched her hands under the table and prepared to laugh, although she knew Uncle Larry's jokes were no laughing matter.

'The difference,' said Uncle Larry, looking over his shoulder for the return of Mrs Domanski and her former festive self, 'the difference is that the dawg's legs are long enough to reach the ground!'

In her short life Lena had heard many wisecracks about her size or the lack of it, but this was the worst yet. Even so, she managed a small laugh.

'D'you think I've got the star factor too?' said Uncle Larry. 'How about a family act?'

Mrs Domanski returned, but it was clear that her glow had gone for good. All this banter only served to emphasize the spot in which her husband had landed them: in an area where not only was it dangerous to walk home alone, where single females approached cars and displays of fishnet tights jostled with crotchless underwear, but smack bang in the middle of the world of theatre. In Mrs Domanski's eyes, stage lights were almost as bad as red ones.

'Eat up!' she said to the table at large, putting down plate after plate of food. 'I hope I have not ruined my back bending over a stove for nothing.' Although she was trying to be jovial, her voice was flatter than the pancakes she was serving.

Obediently Lena seized up the jam spoon, shook it until a vast mountain of dark red appeared in the middle of her yellow desert.

'Pig!' said Bella, with a trace of envy in her voice. 'You deserve to get fat.'

'Beats me how Lena has any flesh on her at all,' mused Uncle Larry who, in spite of holding the unofficial Bay Area record for the eating of dumplings, still cut a handsome figure. 'A vegetarian Pole is a rare Pole,' he said.

'A weird Pole, you mean,' muttered Bella.

'Oh, Lena takes after her mother,' said Mr Domanski, a cloud of whipped cream swirling on his lips. 'Chicken-boned, the pair of them.'

'I never saw a chicken with such mighty fine legs,' said Uncle Larry, winking at Mrs Domanski.

If Mrs Domanski had not been used to this by now, she might have blushed. When Uncle Larry was still unknown to them all, he had approached Mrs Domanski in a supermarket and asked her on a date. She had shown him the ring on her left hand – 'Looked like she wanted to smack me with it,' said Uncle Larry, who loved to tell the story – and then she had hurried away down the cookie aisle, with stacks of Oreos falling in her scandalized wake.

'I had to buy the whole lot for my store,' said Uncle Larry, with a shake of his well-coiffed head. 'Crushed, they were, just like my ego.' Shortly after this he had met Mr Domanski over a game of dominoes in the Civic Plaza, and Mr Domanski had brought him home for tea. 'Even so I could not keep my eyes off her,' he said, and he appeared to be serious.

While Lena had inherited Mrs Domanski's skinniness, it was in fact Bella who had inherited her good legs and her thick dark hair. (Where Bella's strapping frame and height had come from was anyone's guess.) Yet there was nothing much else Bella-Gabriella had in common with her mother. A lot of the time her behaviour made Mrs Domanski wilt with disappointment – and the disappointment was mutual.

'Mom should wear lipstick,' Bella would hiss. 'She looks real weird when she goes out without it.'

'I think she looks all right,' Lena would object, sitting on the big bed, watching her sister rifle impatiently and patronizingly through her parents' top drawer.

'No,' contradicted Bella. 'No one else's mother has pale lips.'

'Elroy's mother does,' said Lena, trying to be fair.

'Of course Elroy's old lady has pale lips,' said Bella. 'She's a black momma, you shit-for-brains.' Her street talk sounded odd: try as she might, Bella could never quite shake off the Polish lilt of her first few years.

Lena picked at the edge of the tartan rug. If she pulled the brown thread, she noticed, it turned to blue and vice versa. She pulled away in peace for a while and then—

Slam! Bella closed up the drawers, one by one. *Slam slam slam!* Lena winced.

'Nothing!' said Bella dismissively. 'She's completely hopeless.'

That week was close to Christmas, and Lena took a lot of change out of her special savings jar. Because the jar had once belonged to pickles, the coins smelt slightly sharp and sweet as if they were still hung about by the breath of gherkins. She carried an aromatic handful of these coins down to the corner store, and when the twenty-fourth of December arrived there was a long spindly present wrapped in silver foil waiting for Mrs Domanski.

'It looks like a joint,' said Bella under her breath. Recently she had been hanging out with the boys at the Rec Center, and after sessions there she went to sleep heavily and snored. But when the thin present was unwrapped by Mrs Domanski's equally thin fingers, there were no illicit drugs inside.

'It's an eye pencil!' Lena said quickly, in case her mother thought it was meant to be used for shopping lists or thank you cards.

A slight flush came into Mrs Domanski's whey-like cheeks. 'Thank you, my darlink!' she said, and her voice had a lift at the end like sled runners. Every morning after that, for a number of weeks, she applied the pencil. Her eyes looked beautiful but odd, like those of a sea bird rimmed around with black.

'You've made her look worse,' said Bella. 'Not better.'

Bella seemed to be going through a particularly tiring stage. Not only had she begun ordering Lena to look away while she undressed, she had begun a regime of two hundred sit-ups a night which meant that getting rest was very difficult for anyone else around. Lena would almost be asleep, would be drifting over the day like a small light cloud, only to find herself pulled back to earth by Bella's grunting and straining.

'Can't you go and do that in the living room?' she said, almost crossly, peering out from her bed. In the dirty orange street light

Bella looked like a galley slave: lying on the floor, sweating and rising, falling and rising.

'They'll – laugh,' said Bella, her voice squeezing out between her compacting ribs, 'at – me.'

Although Lena sometimes got cross she never laughed, not even at the sight of Bella's large white stomach emerging from her shrunken T-shirt. Every time Bella sat up her stomach disappeared, but every time she lay down it rose confidently towards the ceiling, looking as if nothing would subdue it.

'Like the People's Army,' said Lena quietly, into her warm flesh-smelling blankets. She liked this phrase and she said it several times more, although she did not really know what the People's Army was, or the Red Army, those Communists Uncle Larry referred to with a sneer and a spit. 'It was not all bad,' said Mr Domanski, but Uncle Larry would open his mouth with its great gaps in it and scoff, and it wasn't until he had gone home that Mr Domanski would finish his thoughts.

'At least it was orderly,' he said to Mrs Domanski with his hands outstretched. Those hands, Lena knew, had built many boats back in Poland, and the veins running through his palms looked like small red rivers.

'Not at the end!' said Mrs Domanski. 'Those strikes were your undoing.'

'At least the men wanted to work,' argued Mr Domanski. 'At least they were not spending their days going through the trash cans.'

'Don't forget you brought us here,' said Mrs Domanski quietly. 'Here there are trash cans on every corner.'

'I had no choice!' said Mr Domanski. 'I could not support my men against the government. It was an abominable position for anyone to be in! Insupportable!' He stared at the floor and his face was flushed.

'If we had just waited,' said Mrs Domanski. 'We were so quick to turn our backs.'

'So go back to your homeland,' said Mr Domanski, and he picked up the paper and shook it angrily. 'Go back and see if it still feels like home.'

21

Mrs Domanski went to her kitchen instead. She spent more and more time there, where at least the contents of the cupboards were her own, and her drawers were tidy and hygienically lined with paper. 'Home,' she said, walking across her cracked but clean linoleum, 'home is where the heart is.'

The thing was, it sounded as if her heart was neither here nor in some grey concrete tenement building on the right bank of the Vistula River. Who could tell where Mrs Domanski would ever feel right again? As for the listening Lena – well, she thought that one day she would travel back to Poland alone, or perhaps with a dog at her side to snuff the cold sea air. A Saint Bernard dog with a barrel at its throat, able to seek her out in the snow: or a Newfoundland for her *new found land*. Animals were easier than people, she thought, as she watched her mother sweep and her father sulk; animals didn't expect to be laughed at, or appreciated, or even listened to.

Mr Domanski sat and looked disconsolately at the newspaper, at pictures of shopping centres opening, and a report of a new fast food outlet not so far from his own home-style restaurant. 'Progress,' he said, shaking his heavy head. (He could never let an argument go, even when he no longer knew which side he was on.) 'My God, it is overrated,' he said.

'What is progress?' asked Lena timidly.

'Progress,' repeated Mr Domanski. 'Pah. Progress.' This appeared to be all he could say, and he spat on the floor.

Lena looked in horror at the spit, clear except for a few rising bubbles and some crumbs of biscuit from Mr Domanski's back molars. Quickly, quietly, she went to get some toilet paper to clean it up before anyone could slip on it.

(When Lena managed to spell 'Existentialism' in the spelling bee, thereby winning her class the cup, the entire school stood and clapped her. Even Bella's face, bobbing at the back of the hall high above the others, had momentarily lost its scorn.

'*Extremely* well done,' said Mrs Penney. At such rare times she allowed her students to call her Verity, but this had never come easily to Lena. 'Your progress,' said Mrs Verity-Penney, 'is *excellent*.'

'Progress?' queried Lena faintly.

'Better progress than any student I've had!' said Mrs Verity heartily.

Lena burst into tears.)

Space

As the bullet tore towards her head like a determined bee, Lena moved a fraction to the side. Perhaps, from its dark and secret listening place, her subconscious heard the whine? Perhaps her eye had seen the glinting torpedo coming towards her? Or perhaps it was simply that she was already leaning into the window of the donut shop to see if there were any chocolate-almond sprinkles left for her to buy that day.

Whatever the reason, her slight movement to the right (the experts said later) was what saved her. But her left ear remained in the firing line of that whining, determined, light-and-shade-striped bullet

(*don't think you can escape me that easily*, hissed the bullet, chagrined at having missed the blue car)

and it crumpled like tinfoil, that ear, as the bee-bullet passed. And as her ear folded irretrievably into itself, Lena remembered Davey.

In fact Lena's brother had always been easier to overlook than remember, even when he was in the very same room. There he would sit at the table in the Domanskis' long-ago living room, absorbed in secret work that involved the smoothing of many small squares of aluminium foil. The patience with which he used to smooth out that tinfoil! It drove Bella crazy, and she forbade Lena to help. 'It's pathological behaviour,' she said, and she would drag Lena and her helpful fingernails away from the table. Yet still Lena would save the wrappers of Christmas chocolates, scraping them against a flat surface until the back of her nail was red-hot and the foil was as smooth as the Bay on a calm Sunday in June.

Davey had never been particularly big or particularly small, not Bella-large or Lena-scrawny. He was just middling and the reason that he has taken so long to appear, even as Lena's past careered before her eyes, is his very ordinariness. The truly ordinary are rare in this life; strange habits leap like lizards as soon as front doors are closed on the world. But Davey Domanski was one of those blessed, cursed few who had nothing whatsoever memorable about him. He ate his meals obediently, and he emptied the trash can but only when he was asked to; sometimes he left the toilet seat up and sometimes he didn't. He was like a gap in a row of teeth – the main reason he got noticed was because he was absent.

The one thing about Davey that came anywhere close to a quirk was the slowness of him. He was slow to get out of bed in the mornings, slow to come to the table, slow to anger, and his face was slow to register emotion – if, that is, it showed any emotion at all. Delayed Reaction Davey. That was what Bella, who was good at nicknames, called him, and it became shortened to Delayed Davey and it stuck.

For most of his growing-up years Delayed Davey was extremely quiet, and this was because he was engrossed in making space models. Was it because he had already travelled many miles by land and sea, had toiled over plains patched with ice and across oceans reaching farther than any body of water had a right to? For in spite of traversing half the world, not one of the Domanskis had ever been on a plane, and so as soon as Davey could hold a tube of glue in one hand and a matchstick in the other, he began to dream dreams of the air.

Although the Domanskis were fortunate enough to live in a house with its own four walls, and a ceiling that wasn't someone else's floor, still they found themselves pushed for space. Their house was wedged between two great grey tenement blocks, and the wringer washing machine donated by the church sat in the tiny narrow hallway, plugged into a socket by the front door, because there was no other place for it. There were only two bedrooms in the house and they were full to overflowing, what with Bella and Lena and Mr and Mrs Domanski, and clothes and folded sheets, and canned food for times of earthquake. And so Davey was forced to sleep in one corner of the living room, screened off by a bamboo blind that had begun its days as a yoga mat and had then languished for a time behind the Rec Center before being reincarnated as a bedroom wall. The arrangement didn't appear to bother Delayed Davey but it bothered Mrs Domanski considerably.

'I am concerned what you will do,' she said, 'when you get older.' As she anticipated the very many problems waiting in the future, not all of them relating to space or the lack of it, her voice became as tangled and tense as the wire wool with which she scrubbed the pots. Budding breasts and the start of the Cycle were known to her, were as familiar and as tedious as waiting in a bread-line, but when she looked ahead to Davey's unknown male body and then looked sideways at the flimsy screen, small worry lines appeared between her eyes.

As a concession to his lack of privacy Davey was allowed a portion of the front window all to himself. This made the living room dark but it was clearly worth it, for it seemed that Davey was never happier than when lying in bed, looking far beyond the glare of the street lights to the small white dots criss-crossing the sky like beetles.

'Satellites,' he informed Lena. 'Last night I saw seven.' In the light of morning he looked as plain as ever, and he picked up his spoon in a matter of fact way and began ploughing into his oatmeal. But the handle of his spoon caught the tiny gleam in his eye and bounced it across the table to Lena.

It was easy enough to give Davey birthday presents: all you had to do was find a good clean square of foil, and that could often be wheedled out of Uncle Larry or scrounged from the corner store. Davey's ongoing project, which seemed to have lasted for years, was a perfectly recreated model of the Vostok 3KA-2.

'That boy shows an unhealthy interest in the Russians,' complained Uncle Larry.

'It will pass,' said Mrs Domanski. 'One day he will be a rocket scientist and they will ask him to enter NASA.' Although she tried to sound positive, her voice was as hollow as a chocolate egg. For how likely was it, really, that a small Polish boy from an immigrant neighbourhood would ever penetrate the prestigious gates of America's space elite?

'He can always change his name,' she said as if in answer, though no one had asked her a question. (Already she was thinking like Jay, although at that time Jay had not even set foot inside the Domanskis' home.)

'All boys are space crazy,' said Mr Domanski comfortably.

Their words and their divided, restless loyalties flew over Davey's unheeding head. 'I'll need to borrow one of your dolls for launch day,' he said to Lena, blowing on a join to make the glue set faster.

Lena bit her lip. She never considered not meeting Davey's large demands. But which of her dolls could she possibly sacrifice?

'They sent a dog up there too, those Ruskie bastards,' said Bella, taunting her. 'There goes Bluey.'

Lena felt sick and she pushed away her milk. It was many months before she realized that the Vostok Project was so large-scale, she would have outgrown her dolls before they were called up for astronaut duty. In the meantime Davey continued to collect materials, raking through gutters and trash cans with a commendable thoroughness.

'Anyone would think you were off the street,' said Mrs Domanski disapprovingly, 'instead of coming from a decent home.' As the months matured into years and Mr Domanski showed no sign of giving up his interest in the theatre, she seemed to be increasingly concerned about the decency of their home.

Unperturbed, Davey continued his scavenging. In spite of Mrs Domanski's thorough cleaning, an odd smell rose from behind his screen, far worse than the familiar scent of milk put out to sour. When Lena peeked into the annex one day she saw thin silver lines trailing from the window ledge and off the end of the bed, looking like a fall of bright rain. In fact it turned out to be strips of foil hung out to dry.

'I have to rinse them in the bathroom sink to get the pork fat off,' says Davey, not noticing Lena's shudder.

26

And this was what was most memorable about slow, average Delayed Reaction Davey: his intense and unwavering passion for silver foil, and for what it might become. When he talked of rockets his face became radiant, and sparks flew from his fingertips. When he stopped he was just plain old Davey Domanski again, slightly freckled from the fickle San Francisco sun, slightly pinched from the fog.

The launch

Although Mrs Domanski's thought patterns foreshadowed those of Jay Antonelli, Jay himself was still a long way in Lena's future. So far in the future that, by the time he met Lena, she had been funny for over eleven years. That is to say, it was eleven years since Mr Domanski had put her on stage, Mrs Domanski had objected, and a roomful of people had found her so amusing that there was no going back.

Ever since starting The Polish Sausage in the premises of an old factory canteen, Mr Domanski had had stars in his eyes. They had been partially put there by his involvement with the nearby amateur theatre where, happily, he carried about large pieces of scenery and sat in the wings dishing out forgotten lines to forgetful actors. But such gratification was not immediate enough and so he set to work on his own plans – plans he had carried with him all the way from Poland – for what he called a supper club.

'It will be like the grand old clubs of Warsaw's heyday!' he said excitedly. 'I will offer the complete night out. A good dinner guaranteed to stick to your ribs, followed by some first-class cabaret.'

Bella rolled her eyes. 'The future,' she said scathingly, 'is in television.'

'Well, why not television?' said Mr Domanski. 'Why not indeed?' His enthusiasm soared to the low roof, only to fall with a crash as he considered the practicalities. 'No, we do not have the money for that,' he said decidedly. 'At least, not at the moment. But we do have room for a song and a dance!'

The Polish actors from down the road, already regulars at The Sausage, became almost as enthusiastic about the idea as Mr

Domanski. Most of them were unemployed and searching for some way to fill in the windy days and fog-ridden nights, but Jani and Gabbi – twin brothers from a tiny village in the region of Lodzkie – were completely and utterly passionate about theatre, and they saw Mr D's plans as an extension of their own.

'We will start a new fringe movement,' enthused Jani. 'Right here in the Tenderloin!' He was safely married to an American waitress and so was more buoyant than his brother, who was forever looking over his shoulder for the men in uniform.

'The neighbourhood needs us,' agreed Mr Domanski. 'Here there are not enough jobs, but too many needles and cunts!' With a beam, he slopped an extra-large serving of stew onto Jani's plate.

'Oh,' said Jani, looking slightly startled. 'Thank you.'

Gabbi gnawed on the skin around his fingernail as if he were making a difficult decision. 'That word you used,' he said eventually. 'It is not such a good one.'

'Which word is that?' asked Mr Domanski, rolling another dumpling out of the pan onto the side of Gabbi's plate.

'The one that followed "needles",' said Gabbi. Faced by Mr Domanski's blank stare he dropped his knife, and as he bent to pick it up he quickly mumbled the word into the carpet.

'Oh, *cunts*?' said Mr Domanski in a loud interested voice, making Gabbi flush. 'Does that not mean just a bit of pussy?' asked Mr D. 'Does it not simply mean ladles of the night?'

'Ladles!' said Jani, and he gave a chuckle into his gravy.

'I have heard people talk of *spooning*,' said Mr Domanski, starting to look flustered. 'It is the same thing, no?'

'You must be careful what you say out on the streets,' said Gabbi worriedly. 'If the wrong word is used to the wrong person it can cause much trouble.'

'Don't you worry,' said Mr Domanski, wiping gravy off the counter with great sweeping strokes. 'Nothing will happen to Jakob Domanski. You boys put your minds to entertainment and leave the pimps and the wimps to me.'

Gabbi gave a wan smile. 'We will bring light relief to the Tenderloin, no?' he said, picking up a pork rib.

'That we will, you sonofabitch,' said Mr Domanski, clapping

him on the back in such a friendly way that Gabbi nearly choked. 'The time is ripe.'

'The time is ripe,' echoed Lena, from where she sat on the edge of the bar swinging her pale, spindly legs. 'You sonofabitch! The rhyme is tripe.'

'When you have a family to feed,' said Mrs Domanski every time she heard Mr Domanski's catch phrase, 'when you have a family to clothe, the time is never ripe.' But she spoke resignedly, as if knowing there was nothing to be done but stand aside in the face of Mr Domanski's steamroller enthusiasm.

And sure enough on St Sylvester's Day Mr Domanski made the decisive move. For the first time he stepped out from behind the grill and into the spotlight. The routine he offered up was an odd one: a song of dubious lyrics, accompanied by exaggerated actions performed in the drinking halls of his youth. Neither his wife nor his family had seen it before.

'And I sincerely *hope*,' said Bella, 'that we will never see it again.'

But ripping and roaring his way into the final stanza, Mr Domanski was unheeding of his eldest daughter's scorn. There he stood high on a stool, twirling an umbrella, soaring above the heads of his audience; his stage presence was hardly diminished by the fact that there was a small flake of pastry caught in his moustache. Nor was his fervour dimmed by the fact that his spotlight was a single hundred-watt bulb. He looked straight into its dazzle, and he was hooked.

After this there were regular variety shows at The Polish Sausage, though Mr Domanski was not pressed into repeating his act.

'You may intimidate the other performers,' said Gabbi, biting on his thumbnail.

'That is very considerate of you, Gabbi,' said Mr Domanski, thoughtfully. 'I believe you are right. I must stand aside.'

'Perhaps you could compère?' suggested Jani.

'Compare?' said Mr Domanski. 'But that would encourage unhealthy competition! No, Jani, I will introduce the acts – it is my eating house, after all.'

The next day to be dedicated not only to saints but also to

performers happened to be St Patrick's Day, which that year was preceded by a week of rain. The house steamed up and, behind misty windows, Mrs Domanski cleaned mud off the floors with even more determination than usual. As the festival drew closer and the skies continued to weep, the city became jittery. 'Will St Pat's Day be Mayday?' trumpeted the newsmakers and the spinners of puns. 'Will the weather forecasters rain on our parade?'

Yet Mr Domanski remained cheerful: he had his own plans. 'We have no need for sunshine,' he crowed. Every afternoon he took Lena and Elroy down to The Sausage and kept them there so long there was no time for homework, so that in the mornings they were crowned with paper caps reading, 'I am a D minus citizen of Hyde St Elementary' and they would have to wait until last to drink from the fountain in the hallway at lunchtime.

Mrs Domanski was foreboding from the start – which only goes to show that the old saying 'Listen to your mother' is worth listening to. But then these words rightly belong to the father of the family, whereas Mr Domanski was so excited about his show that he was incapable of listening at all, and would not have had a leg to stand on had he told anyone else to do so.

'It does not seem right to put seven-year-olds on the stage,' said Mrs Domanski. 'To treat them as if they were performing animals.' She brushed specks of green paint out of Lena's hair with a vigour that bordered on roughness.

'Ow,' said Lena in a small voice, but she lifted her limey fingernails and smoothed the worry lines out of her mother's forehead in the same way as she smoothed Davey's tinfoil. 'We're having fun,' she said reassuringly. Had she known what she was letting herself in for, she might have put her small foot down and made Mr Domanski use Davey instead. But Davey had about as much stage presence as a potato, whereas Lena was small and light and danced very well on her bare green feet. Besides, she had a wonderful costume made by Jani's waitress wife, who had sewed like a wild thing in her cigarette breaks.

On the night belonging to St Patrick (and partly to Mr Domanski) The Sausage was packed. A special licence had come through—

'In the nick of time,' said Mr Domanski, whose grasp of idiom was better than his street vernacular. Tonight for the first time he was able to serve Guinness, out of two huge silver barrels placed as far away from the hotplates as possible. Even so, by the end of the night the beer was blood-warm, but by then it didn't matter because the hose protruding from the covers had been in constant use.

'It's like an elephant,' said Bella in fascination and every now and then she would sneak up and stick the trunk in her mouth when no one was looking. After each trip she returned to the family table a little more unsteadily, a moustache of pale fawn foam on her top lip.

The room filled up with revellers, who proceeded to pour gallon after gallon of Guinness down their throats. Mr Domanski and the kitchen hands could hardly keep up with the demand for food, and the vats of oil hissed as they threw in great hand-fuls of potato dumplings and potato *pierogi*.

'Tonight the potato is King!' said Mr Domanski, although he had believed this for the whole of his life anyway.

The *pierogi* in particular were out of this world. That week Mrs Domanski and Bella had made hundreds and thousands of them, spending every afternoon stuffing pastry cases full of floury mash, their onion-eyes streaming just as the windows streamed with rain. When Lena danced in from rehearsals she had been press-ganged into pinching the edges and now, in that hot noisy room, she sat and watched the small crescent imprints of her fingers disappear into other people's mouths.

'Da said I was the best Pierogi Pincher he's ever seen,' she said slightly boastfully to Elroy, who was eating so fast that he could hardly look up from his plate. 'He says it's like I was born to it,' she added.

'So why don't you just go right back to Poland,' said Elroy, spraying small flakes of pastry over Lena. 'Go right on back to stupid Poland if it's so fucken great.' He put his head down again and shovelled another forkful into his already full mouth. He hated it when Lena made out that she was different: as if she hadn't been born right there in the Tenderloin, in the hospital just down the road from where he lived!

31

Lena looked at the top of Elroy's busy fuzzy head, weaving angrily over his plate. 'C'mon,' she said. 'If you eat any more you won't fit into your costume.' She brushed the flurry of white crumbs off his cheeks and took his hand in a friendly sort of way, a small Pole and a tubby African-American uniting in a room full of Irishmen.

And soon they could no longer see those Irishmen, who were fast on the way to getting drunk, or the Polish families doing the same. In less than ten minutes she and Elroy were poised for their debut, standing back to back in the stuffy dark behind the curtain borrowed from Uncle Larry's living-room window.

'Most of my acts have no need for a curtain,' Mr Domanski had said grandly. 'But there is to be an element of surprise in this particular play.'

Lena thought about those words afterwards: long afterwards they rang in her ears, and ricocheted around the inside of her head. For in those few minutes following the rise of Uncle Larry's green velvet curtain, she was catapulted into a career that was certainly surprising: one she had never foreseen. Forced into a lifetime of funniness – what sort of legacy was that for the child of Polish immigrants who still held the shadows of history in their eyes?

(*I should have been allowed to remain melancholy*, cried Lena, as her ear was neatly parted from the thin skin on the side of her head, *at least for a little longer!*)

The curtain rose, Elroy leapt away from her like the mad leprechaun that he was, and Lena followed. The frenetic beat of the Irish music – a bootleg recording of a genuine folk band from the Old Country – drove itself into her shin bones in a way that had never happened during rehearsals. She felt the blood-swell of the audience, smelt their sweat and their eagerness to be dazzled, and she was inspired.

For minutes on end she jigged. She was hardly aware of Elroy jigging beside her, except when one of his sturdy legs lagged and got out of time, and she had to slow her starry steps so he could catch up. She turned, she capered, her green satin cloak flew straight out from her shoulders like a magic carpet. The fast clapping of the audience settled into a rhythm lying just under the ceiling of purple cigarette smoke.

And then, for the *pièce de résistance*, Mr Domanski lit the fireworks. One by one along the edge of the makeshift stage, Catherine Wheels began to twirl. The people at the front tables gasped and their chairs went back with a squeak, but the spinning wheels had been securely nailed into place by Jani and Gabbi. And soon there was a blazing white trench between the Little People and the Real People.

Lena reached out a deft green hand for Elroy and felt his fingers, slippery with body paint.

'Light the sparklers!' she panted, and Elroy did so. Columns of sparks sprang up like flowers from the pots around them.

'Aaah!' said the room, their admiring sigh fuelled as much by sentiment and Guinness as the sight of two small leprechauns standing in a magic circle. The clapping went on and on, the Catherine Wheels spun, and Lena and Elroy stood, framed by fire, in front of a crudely painted backdrop of spotted red toadstools.

'Take your bow!' hissed Mr Domanski from the dark folds of Uncle Larry's curtain.

'You first,' said Lena to Elroy, over the roar and the dazzlement. She stepped graciously back in the circle and watched Elroy, her best friend and co-star, bob up and down in front of her. Mr D clicked off the tape recorder but the applause continued.

Once Elroy had finished bobbing, it was Lena's turn. She sank into a deep curtsy, a move she had practised at home with quick glances taken at her reflection in the night window to check that her back was straight and her leg perfectly extended. Although her heart was still thumping in her chest, she made herself stay as still as possible by focusing on a small gravy stain on the carpet. Evidently this worked magnificently, for another collective gasp ran round the room.

'Lena!' she heard in a tiny hiss.

She straightened up to see Elroy's round black face sweating into his white cotton-wool beard.

'Sister!' he said, wide-eyed. 'Look to your skirt, sister!'

And when Lena did so, she saw something that quite took her mind off her glory. A sparkler had become caught in the green hoops of her skirt, and was fizzing and hissing at her rear end. In other words, her arse was on fire.

If Lena had moved fast before, well, that was nothing. Leaping out of the circle of fire, she fairly flew around the stage. Past Elroy, whose chubby lips were still hanging wide open in astonishment. Past Mr Domanski, who started forward, tripped on the curtain cord, and fell flat on his face on top of the tape recorder. Wild fiddle music started up again, and the crowd rose to its feet.

'Bravo!' they called. 'Let's hear it for the Lubberkin!'

In the front row, Bella's face was ablaze with interest. Now this was what she called entertainment! She said something to her sister-on-fire as she flew past, but Lena had no time to stop. Around and around the crowded room she flew, so fast that her buckled shoes were a blur, and people parted like the sea before her and her fiery bottom.

'Go go go!' they cheered, as if they were at a ball game.

After the third lap, Lena realized there was no escape. There was a certain heat at her rear end which suggested the firework was burning dangerously low. Leaping over Mr Domanski – only now struggling dazedly to his knees – she made straight for the full slop tray on the floor beside the bar and threw herself into it, bottom first. Dirty brown beer launched over her like a tidal wave.

The vanquished sparkler hissed in disappointment but the room erupted in delight. The applause was enormous – far greater than for the dance which had been painstakingly rehearsed for seven days at the cost of school work and domestic peace. Elbows were newly bent in honour of the Sprightliest Sprite, the most Lubricated Leprechaun of the New World.

'Well and truly caught!' crowed Mr Domanski in delight, presumably referring to the reluctance of the Little People to be cornered, let alone wedged safely in a metal slop tray. As his guests surged forward to clap him on the back, he nodded and beamed. 'A great surprise, no?' he said repeatedly. 'We Domanskis, we always have a surprise up our sleeves!'

Lena sat on for a while, her small arse wedged in a channel of warm beer, her buckle shoes splayed out in front of her. She had no particular desire to get up and confront the future. She watched her family accepting congratulations on her behalf. There was her mother, wiping her eyes, looking happier than she had for many months. Even Davey had lost his usual freckled pallor and was gesticulating excitedly with his stubby, chewed fingers.

Eventually, Mr Domanski came to Lena's rescue. He took one arm and Elroy the other. The foam in Lena's eyelashes made it hard for her to see, and she tilted her head back and looked at the room through half-closed eyes, in a unintentionally sultry way.

'You sly dog!' said Mr Domanski. 'To think I nearly ruined your act! Thank the Good Lord for curtain cords.'

'But I didn't—' said Lena.

'Go, take your applause!' said Mr Domanski, his face beaming. 'The people cannot get enough of you.'

It was true, the crowd were reluctant to let her go. 'More!' they cheered. 'Encore!'

Lena's mouth tightened. She put her head even further back so that her red cap sat at a dangerous angle to her head. Enough was enough! Her treacherous skirt swayed at her knees, its hem still decorated with cloudy beads of beer. Giving her waistband a purposeful hitch, she strode back on stage.

'Hell-oooo, Rocket-arse!' the crowd greeted her. 'Hello, Sparkling-bottom!'

Lena held up an imperious hand and waited until there was complete silence before speaking.

'What *exactly* were you laughing at?' she said in a stern voice.

But the crowd laughed again, as uproariously as before. For some reason they seemed to find anything she did, even scolding them, extremely funny.

'A child could have died out there today!' said Lena severely.

35

This appeared to be even funnier. Mouths opened like dark caverns, teeth flashed, and the dark smoky room shook with laughter.

Lena shook her head, and her skirt shook with her, spraying beer over the people at the front of the crowd. 'Give a grown man enough alcohol,' she said, 'and you'll have a child before the night's through.' She didn't think her mother would mind her borrowing this saying, though it was usually said in the privacy of their own home after her father blundered in from a night with the Actors. But her audience would not be subdued: they held onto the sides of their seats and rocked with laughter.

Lena gave up in disgust. 'Obviously you're not in the mood to listen,' she said.

'Oh no!' howled the audience. 'Don't go!'

'Pappy St Hat-trick's Day to you all,' said Lena stiffly. Giving her skirt a final hitch which dislodged the blackened remains of the treacherous sparkler, she marched offstage only to be mobbed by her appreciative family.

'I do feel it was a little dangerous,' said Mrs Domanski, but her eyes crinkled up at the memory of Lena throwing herself backwards into a trayful of beer.

'I didn't mean to!' said Lena.

'Of course you didn't,' said Mr Domanski, winking conspiratorially behind Mrs Domanski's back.

So frustrated was Lena that she almost stamped her buckled foot. 'Elroy?' she said, looking to her fellow performer for support.

'Man,' said Elroy almost reverently, wisps of cotton wool trailing from his chubby chin. 'Man, that was *cool*.'

Lena sighed.

'Cool? It was the best!' said Bella. 'Far better than that stupid dance! No offence, Elroy.'

So impressed was Bella by Lena's daring and her newfound talent that she actually offered to carry Lena's damp and smelly cloak all the way home. Over the next week she was embarrassingly respectful. She offered Lena first bathtime at night, and first pick of chores in the morning, and after the lights went out she lay in bed and reminisced over Lena's masterful debut until Lena became profoundly tired of the whole thing and told Bella to shove it.

After this family life almost went back to normal, except that Lena's place in it was no longer the same. Because of an errant firework and the freakish nature of comedy, she could no longer hide soberly at the bottom of the Domanski family. The world had found her funny and she was expected to be so, whether she liked it or not.

(*That was you, in your seventh year*, whispered the bullet as it floated gently past her, taking some of her head along for the ride)

Feathers

Although Lena's career had begun with slapstick, then, within minutes it had refined itself into a more verbal humour. And this, according to her father, was where her talent lay. Sadly he was right: there was something about Lena's solemn face and her sincerity that made even the most banal joke seem sidesplittingly funny.

'I envy you,' said Gabbi with a sigh. 'There was a time when I thought I might have a talent for comedy.'

'Yes, you've got a future, all right,' said Jani cheerfully to Lena. This too proved correct: Lena's debut at The Polish Sausage was no flash in the pan. Every Friday night following that fateful St Patrick's Day she would take part in Mr Domanski's variety show, and her presence was like a lucky charm.

'That's one smart leprechaun you've got there,' said Jani to Mr D. 'Talk about bringing home the pot of gold.' He and Gabbi took turns at sitting on a stool by the door of The Sausage and checking the other performers off in a red notebook. Actors and singers, comics and puppeteers, mime artists and wannabes poured in from all over the city. On show nights Mr Domanski employed a Swiss flügelhorn player to pull the beers for him so that he could step up to the microphone without a care in the world.

'Welcome to my living room!' he would say with a beam. 'Here we are one big happy family!' His voice, as rich as a prune *pierogi*, rolled around the room. He was a generous host, talking up the most milk-and-water of performances, but his prune voice was at its shiniest and fullest when he introduced the smallest member of his real family.

'Yes, bring on the Little Pole!' the audience would shout.

Mr Domanski's face would break into a smile so huge and happy that there was almost no need for a spotlight. 'Heeeere's Lena!' he cried, to the manner born.

And there she was, every Friday night, ready to take the stage in her top hat and her small glitter skirt reluctantly hemmed by her mother and put on almost as reluctantly by Lena herself.

'If you don't want to do it,' said Bella, watching Lena button up her little red show jacket with the silver sequins, 'then don't. You don't have to, just to please Our Father.' Bella was a Railer, or that was what Mr Domanski always said. Her first instinct was to disagree with things even if later she ended up agreeing with them: it was just the way she was.

'I don't *mind* doing it,' said Lena, who often thought that Railing was a waste of time. 'It's just that I don't see the point.'

'The point!' said Bella in an adult kind of way. 'The point! If it's *point* you're looking for, my little friend, you'll be looking for a long time.'

Bella's sit-up regime had not slackened: on the contrary, she had added a set of weight-bearing exercises which involved the raising and lowering of the body off the seat of a wooden chair. Every morning she would look critically at herself in the mirror, flexing her shoulders and the muscles in her arms.

'Excellent,' she would say to herself, ignoring Lena in an obvious way. 'Excellent, Bella. You will soon have the strength to make grown men cry.'

She came to see Lena perform every now and then, and this made Lena slightly nervous. It was one thing to tell a few babyish jokes in front of regular drinkers and fellow entertainers, but quite another to see Bella's critical face peering out of the darkness, wincing whenever Lena's timing was slightly off or the punch-line was too obvious.

'You've got to *sock* it to them!' Bella would say later, when they got home. 'You've got to get in there and bloody well give them something to laugh about.' Looking fierce, she showed Lena how humour should be delivered: bounding around an imaginary punch bag, jabbing and darting.

As Bella became stronger and Lena became funnier, their mother was becoming increasingly hard to see. The eye pencil had found its way to the bottom of the drawer a long time ago, and Mrs Domanski's red eyelids were now the only touch of colour in her pale face.

'Come down to The Sausage tonight,' wheedled Lena. 'The Actors are going to do a whole set on Poland.'

'Aah, Polska,' said Mrs Domanski, with a wistful smile. Her light eyelashes gave a flutter as if caught in a breeze that had rushed in suddenly from the Russian Steppes. Then —

'Oh, but I can't,' she said, slightly desperately. 'There is so much to *do* around this place.'

Lena looked about her. Floors were scrubbed so clean that she could see a blurred reflection of herself in them. Dishes were neatly stacked on the kitchen shelves, chairs stood stiffly in at the table waiting for dinner.

'Did Davey remember to take the bottles out?' she ventured.

Her mother shrugged. 'Bottles, cans,' she said. 'They are never-ending. Even when they have just been taken out, there are always more waiting to take their place.'

Lena shuffled. 'It would do you good to have a night off,' she said.

Her mother looked upwards. 'Dust,' she said. 'I have not washed the lightshades for the longest time.'

'You shouldn't worry so much,' said Lena gently. 'I don't mind performing – sometimes I even enjoy it. And it's doing Da's business the world of good.'

For a second, Mrs Domanski dragged her attention away from the interior of her house and focused on her daughter. 'Like a performing bear,' she said. 'That is how he treats his children. Your father is no better than a ringmaster.' She turned away, went to the cupboard, and took out the broom. 'Could you go outside and bang your shoes?' she said to Lena. 'You have tracked in a bit of the street.'

Lena went and sat on the doorstep, and counted the traffic for twenty long minutes. She developed a forecasting system by laying down small splinters of glass. White was for taxis, and brown for buses. If the taxis won, it was all right to go on with the show; if the buses came out in front she was being exploited. (White for the bright lights of show business, brown for what Bella would call the shit of parental pressure.) Lena sat and martialled her evidence with a long stick while the afternoon rushed along the road in front of her.

'I will do the step now,' said Mrs Domanski, sweeping up behind her with the broom. 'Oh my Lord, look at all this glass! Still, I suppose it is better than needles.'

Lena sighed. She watched her neat piles of glass that had been growing neck and neck being brushed into the pale blue plastic pan. Now she had no idea what she was supposed to feel! She went to get changed into her sequins anyway.

'Wipe your feet!' called Mrs Domanski. Her voice trailed after Lena, along the hall, past the washing machine, and into the echoing living room. Home was beginning to look like a motel, thought Lena. Even the few ornaments brought out from Poland had been stacked away in cupboards, out of sight.

Collecting her costume from her room, Lena went back out to the main room to call Elroy. 'There's nothing wrong with children being on stage, is there?' she asked doubtfully.

'Hell no!' came Elroy's fat voice down the phone line. 'You think there's any way in the world yo' ma would let it go on if it was a bad thing?'

'That's just it, though,' Lena pointed out. 'It's Ma who's made me think about it.' She loved Elroy – if she were honest, she loved him more than Davey and possibly even than Bella (Elroy always listened to what she said, and was never mean). But sometimes, just occasionally, he let her down in the logic stakes.

'There has to be some reason for entertainment,' she said. 'Otherwise how would it have gone on since Time Immemorial?' The phrase rolled comfortably off her tongue. She might have

40

only been alive for seven years but her trade was made respectable by its immense age. 'Since Time Immemorial,' she intoned again, squeezing the phone receiver between her chin and shoulder so she could pull her spangled tights on with both hands.

'Since the time of the Romans, probably,' agreed Elroy. 'Boy, did those cats know how to party!'

When Bella came in from basketball practice, dripping sweat and wiping her face on her tank top, Lena asked her about this. 'Elroy says the Romans had naked dancing girls,' she said dubiously.

'And not only,' said Bella, critically studying her biceps in the mirror. 'They had boys who sang like girls.'

'Why?' said Lena in horror.

'Because they'd had their weeners chopped off when they were small,' said Bella.

'Bella!' said Mrs Domanski, appearing disapprovingly behind her. 'I do not want you telling tales like that.'

'Why not?' said Bella. 'It's the truth, isn't it?'

The truth was, Bella had become adept at creating disturbances. Not only did she say the wrong thing, not only did she stir the night air with her sit-ups, she had also begun working in a funeral parlour after school.

'Only to get some drug money,' she said. 'Calm down, Ma, I'm joking.'

Since she was paid a pittance for her work – which included the swabbing of bodies, many of whom had been victims of violent crimes – it was obvious that Bella was driven by pure interest rather than avarice.

'Did you know,' she would say over dinner, 'that fingernails keep growing even after massive blood loss? Although you can see from the cuticles just when the stabbing occurred.' Then, while Bella put down her own knife and examined her own nails, everyone else would stop eating for a different reason altogether.

On other days, just when Mrs Domanski had blown to the sofa like a brittle leaf and had momentarily come to rest, when Lena was peacefully colouring in and Davey was there or not, Bella would burst in at the door and the trumpet call of her voice would split the air.

41

'It burped!' she would say.

'What did?' said Mrs D, nervously, tiredly.

'My corpse!' said Bella. 'I swear to God it gave a burp! Just when I sat it up to do its hair.'

At such disturbing utterances, Mrs D would immediately flutter to her feet and resume her cleaning. 'I wish you would not go there,' she would murmur, into the lake-like depths of her linoleum. 'It is not healthy.' Soon the pitted floor was so well polished that it squeaked underfoot, and all because of Bella's interests.

When the hours of her job conflicted with basketball practice, Bella did give up the funeral parlour, but the seed had been sown and something had to take its place. And so it was that Mr Domanski stumbled on the early stages of Bella's new hobby one night out back of The Polish Sausage.

'I had stepped out into the alley for a breath of air,' he told his family the next day, 'and there I found Bella, rummaging in the garbage like an animal!' It was more likely that Mr D had gone out for a quiet piss than for fresh air (he had always found a peculiar pleasure in urinating under a large night sky) but the Bella bit of his story was true enough. She had indeed been head-down in trash: so deep in the dumpster that Mr Domanski had not recognised her and had brought a stick down hard on her wide denim bottom.

'Get the hell out of my trash!' he had said indignantly.

'Ow, shit!' said Bella, emerging red-faced, hanging half in and half out of the skip. 'Shit, Jakob, what the hell do you think you're playing at?'

'Bella?' said Mr Domanski. So astonished was he that he forgot to reprimand his eldest daughter about her language and the disrespectful use of his first name. 'Bella,' he said, 'what in the name of God are you doing?'

'Collecting material,' said Bella. 'But I wouldn't expect you to understand.' She jumped down, landing heavily, and the dead chicken she was holding swung in her hand, its legs pedalling the air as if at any minute it would run away.

'Material?' said Mr Domanski, staring in horror at the chicken

42

which had been thrown out on account of its half-thawed, salmonella-inducing state. 'You are damn right I do not understand,' he said, and he sat down heavily on a trash can and put his head in his hands. 'Satanic cults,' he said. 'I hoped I'd never live to see the day.' He sounded quite unlike his usual optimistic self, almost as if he would cry.

'And you haven't,' said Bella, enormously impatiently. As she had grown older her impatience had grown apace so that sometimes it seemed it would swell so large, she would burst like a balloon. 'Taxidermy, Jakob,' she said briskly. 'I need something to practise on. Now, are you coming home with me?'

'She seemed to think that it was all quite normal,' said Mr Domanski bewilderedly, the next day.

After this incident, most of Bella's spare time was spent at the library hunting out technical manuals, or hanging around the restaurant kitchen on the lookout for carcasses. 'Don't cut the skin like that!' she would say in a horrified voice. 'Get it off cleanly, for God's sake.'

Mr Domanski would give up. 'Do it yourself,' he would say. 'I just want a good fillet. You think I give a damn how I get it out?'

Bella seized up the carving knife, muttering darkly to herself. 'Men!' she said. 'Clumsy oafs.' And in spite of her oversize hands she removed the skin from the rabbit deftly, turning the small floppy body in a respectful way. 'See that?' she said, when Mr Domanski returned from setting out the tables. She held her hands out to display a perfect, naked rabbit: ears intact and paws outstretched, as if all it had done was take one jump too far to find itself on the wrong side of death.

'Yes, yes,' Mr Domanski mumbled. 'Beautiful, I am sure.' There was something about the whole thing that embarrassed him terribly, and he refused to let Bella pester the cooks next door at the Bangkok Grill. 'If I find you with any illegal skins,' he warned, 'you will be seeing that stick again, my girl.'

Bella scoffed. She appeared to be finding plenty of material to work with, legal or otherwise, and her skills grew alarmingly fast. Lena began to dread opening the door of their shared room, and she drew a line down the middle of the floor.

'Nothing is allowed to cross this line in any shape or form,' she said, quite angrily for her. 'No feathers, no claws, no *nothing*. Have you got that?'

Bella hardly looked up. She was engrossed in shaping small waxy eyes for a duck that Mr Domanski had deemed too full of lead shot for his customers. 'Yeah, yeah,' she said. 'Don't get ruffled. Keep your hair on.' She gave a crack of laughter. 'Hah!' she said. 'Hair!' Bella's jokes were rare but when they did emerge they were so bad that Lena wondered how she had the nerve to sit in judgement on Lena's performances, and then dissect them afterwards.

'That sequence about public transport was all wrong to finish with,' she would say, turning her sheets down smartly so they snapped with authority. 'It was useless. Fell completely flat.'

Lying in her small blanket cocoon, Lena would think back to the roars of laughter that had accompanied her offstage. 'Not completely,' she would say, politely. But now that their tiny room was filling up with odd creatures, mounted on blocks of wood scrounged from the builders down on Union Square, she didn't feel so polite any more.

'That isn't my sweatshirt, is it?' she said, peering at the duck's back. Chunks of feathers were missing and the skin underneath appeared to have been patched with brown velour.

Bella had the grace to look slightly uncomfortable. 'It was too small for you,' she pointed out. 'You were starting to look ridiculous, your wrists stuck out a mile.'

'But I liked that sweatshirt!' cried Lena. 'It was my cosy after-school outfit!'

'You looked like a refugee,' said Bella. 'You don't want people thinking you came here on a boat like the rest of us, do you?' She stared significantly at Lena, the fortunate all-American child, but Lena refused to be beaten by guilt.

'You're not allowed to cut up my clothes,' she said furiously. 'I'm going to tell Ma.'

Bella looked flustered at the unexpected challenge. She dropped the wax eye she was working on and it rolled over the chalk line into Lena's half of the room, and lay there staring at the ceiling.

44

'Now look what you've made me do!' said Bella, swooping for the eye. But she was too late.

'Look what you've made *me* do,' said Lena, planting her foot firmly on the eyeball. The squish under her sole made her feel quite nauseous. 'I said no body parts in my territory,' she said. 'And that includes eyes.'

'Oh, all right,' shrugged Bella, and for a second she looked almost submissive. 'I guess I'll just have to start over,' she said.

Lena sat on her bed and scraped the remains of the eyeball off her shoe. She waited until Bella went to the bathroom and then she stepped over to the duck where it sat blindly on its pedestal of treated pine. 'I'm sorry,' she said, giving it a quick stroke. 'Nothing personal.' Under her fingers the feathers felt smooth and cool, but when she shut her eyes she felt the missing patches like scars.

The shutter

Lena's fingers had always been able to tell her things. She was able to thread needles in half-light, untie knotted shoelaces without looking, and fill in jigsaw pieces even when blindfolded by Bella's hanky. Sometimes her hands could tell how things would feel without even picking them up and it was particularly like this with Davey's camera.

When Lena was very small, she had been fixated with this camera. It was a boxy Kodak on a cracked plastic strap, a strap so irresistibly black and grooved that it often made its way into Lena's mouth. When Davey caught her sucking on it one day, he pulled it from her mouth at a speed that for him was both impressive and alarming. As a consequence Lena's front tooth had come loose a long way before time, and had gotten so wobbly that Mr Domanski had had to manoeuvre it out with a handkerchief. (Still, Lena could taste the muffling cotton, and feel the sharp and bloody wrench.) But she had not cried, nor had she complained. For she knew that, if you put a front tooth in a glass of water at night, by the morning you would be quite a lot richer. Perhaps even by enough to buy a Kodak camera of your own.

Yet nothing had happened. No money appeared for, although Mr Domanski was a skilful enough amateur dentist, he had never heard of the American tooth fairy. Lena's tooth had sat on, greying slightly in its water, until one night Bella had gone to the bathroom, stumbled back into the bedroom half-blind from sleep, and swallowed the whole lot.

'No wonder I turned out so mouthy,' she said in years to come, giving her braying laugh.

Lena, on the other hand, had not laughed. She had simply continued to watch Davey sitting at the window, training his tiny lens on the windows of the Rec Center like a sharp shooter. By the clumsy way that he opened the case, by the way his finger fumbled for the red button, she knew that he had no feel for it and her own fingers twitched in frustration. She was not covetous by nature, but she longed to take that camera right away from Davey and keep it by her side for a long time. In fact she had never craved anything so much except the taste of donuts, and after a while she came right out and asked Davey for it.

'You want my camera? No way!' said Davey indignantly. 'Don't you know the history behind this thing?'

Lena did. An old man had bestowed the camera on Mr Domanski before the Domanski family had departed from Poland, for the purpose of capturing the first sighting of their brave new world. But no photographs of San Francisco or the Bay or any other landmark had eventuated, then or ever, because as long as the camera had been part of the Domanski family it had never been loaded with film.

'Film!' said Mr Domanski, as if this were a very odd question. 'What do you think we are made of, Pie? Gold nuggets?'

Lena sighed and watched Davey pointing and clicking in a slow and random way. He had no deftness, no speed. But still he would not give it up, and in the end his camera became a would-be telescope that he trained on the sky, hoping for the wheeling of great galaxies.

'I see more through the lens,' he said. 'I see things differently.'

After he said this, Lena left him to it. For if she knew one thing already, it was this: that to see differently is everything. An escape, a gift, sometimes a burden, but always valuable, and the reason that poets and dreamers wake in the mornings. And so she began to train her eyes to do the job instead. *Snap!* A blink with both eyes, or a wink with one, and in that instant – for an instant – life would be stilled. *Snap!* No one else knew it but Lena could halt traffic more efficiently than any traffic cop, could stop a runner at green pedestrian lights or a cyclist on a steep downhill slope.

Her mind's eye: she had heard this phrase before, but never knew what it meant until now, and now it was all she needed. Sometimes, catching something out of the corner of her vision, she would stop dead.

'What the hell's the matter with you?' Bella would say, bumping into her far more roughly than necessary, to make a point. 'Are your puny legs giving up or what?'

What Lena was doing was holding up the world (while also holding up Bella and any other impatient people behind her). It only worked for a moment and then the world rushed on, and noise and chaos returned. But she became so good at doing this that after a while she pitied Davey, with his clumsy black plastic apparatus. The moments began lining up in her head, storing themselves in a random yet orderly way so she and her mind's eye could flip through them later in bed, with her real eyes closed.

Holding up the world: like a highwayman with a gun, like Atlas with the whole sackload of humanity on his shoulders. Sometimes life seemed like one spinning globe of images to Lena and she could hardly pick which ones to keep.

Lipstick

Polish Independence Day was always, determinedly, celebrated by the Domanskis even though it fell in November when the nights were too chilly to sit out and picnic.

'Why can't we just celebrate July Fourth like everyone else?' grumbled Bella, as she did every morning of every Polish Independence Day.

'The eleventh day of November was an important day for our country,' said Mr Domanski with great solemnity. 'Even if the Germans did come knocking on our door soon afterwards.'

'If you're that proud of Poland still,' said Bella, 'why did you ever leave?'

'Nothing is that simple,' said Mr Domanski sharply. 'The best years for Polska are over. You will understand that one day, mark my words.'

'Mark your words, *why*?' said Bella. She couldn't stand being talked to like a child.

'That's enough, both of you,' said Mrs Domanski, putting down the coffee pot exhaustedly. 'You are on the same side, remember?'

Mr Domanski and Bella looked at each other, looked deep into each other's heart and saw stars and stripes there. 'Humph,' they said at the same time. Bella gave up her challenge, picked up her third piece of toast, and spread it widely with Mrs D's plum jam as if top-dressing soil in a particularly windy country.

'Go easy with that,' said Mr Domanski. 'Leave some for the rest of us, would you.' He took the pot away from Bella and proceeded to spread twice the amount on his own bread. He and Bella sat in identical positions to eat their breakfasts, sturdy elbows on the table, legs apart, chewing stolidly.

That afternoon, when Lena and Elroy burst in the door, they found Mrs Domanski sitting quite still at the very same table, plates and jam and dirty cups in front of her as if breakfast had been only twenty minutes ago instead of eight and a half hours.

'Hello, Ma,' said Lena uncertainly.

'I have not got it,' said Mrs Domanski. Although she looked up at Lena and Elroy, she did not really appear to see them.

'Huh?' said Elroy. 'Hey, c'n we have a sandwich, Mrs D?'

'Don't you ever stop thinking about your stomach, Elroy?' said Lena, quite sharply. Elroy might not have been worried by the sight of an uncleared breakfast table; he had an ordinary mother who swept the floor once a week, and didn't demolish his cushion huts the same hour they were built. But Lena – well, she felt an odd lurch in her stomach.

'Give me a hand, will you, Elroy?' she said, piling up plates, carrying them to the kitchen.

Still her mother did not move. 'I have not *got* it,' she said again, and then she picked up a letter all smudged with plum and held it in front of her eyes, even though clearly she had been doing this for most of the day. 'I have not got it,' she repeated.

And this was all she would say – or variations on it – until Mr Domanski got home that night, earlier than usual because of the Independence Day celebrations. Lena, who had been waiting anxiously by the window, rushed over to him. She grabbed hold of his sleeve. 'Ma's gone strange,' she hissed urgently. 'She's gone all repetitious.'

'Repetitious?' repeated Mr Domanski, uncomprehendingly.

'She's lost something,' said Lena, jerking her head at the table that she had now wiped clean. Out of courtesy she kept her voice low, although it seemed that Mrs Domanski had turned into a statue and could not hear a thing through her stone ears.

Looking concerned, Mr Domanski went over to his wife, removed the letter from her hand, scanned it and then put it down again as if it was of no importance. 'But you don't *need* a work permit, dear,' he said, in a slightly puzzled voice. 'What would you want one of those for?'

He patted his wife on the shoulder in a kindly way, but Mrs Domanski's eyes were as glassy as one of Bella's mangy trophies, and they stared at the wall in the same way. 'I wanted it,' she said, and her voice had a mournful toll to it. 'Oh, how I wanted it.'

Mr Domanski shook his big head. He picked up the letter again, but this time he went and threw it out the window. Mrs Domanski didn't move, but Lena ran over and watched the paper fall. It sliced back and forwards through the chilly air, scudding in to land at the foot of the lamp post where the Lopezes' mangy dog came to investigate, sniffed it, then raised his leg and pissed on it.

'There now,' said Mr Domanski, sliding the window down so decisively that it nearly took Lena's head off. 'That's that out of the way,' he said.

'But I might—' said Mrs Domanski woodenly. 'I might have—'

'You do not need a job,' said Mr Domanski. 'Aren't we enough trouble for you?'

'A job!' said Lena, startled. 'But Da looks after you.' She put her face against Mrs Domanski's, which still felt quite cold and stone-like. 'Doesn't he?' she said.

Mrs Domanski took hold of Lena's hand but absently, as if it were a book of supermarket coupons that she didn't want right then but might hold on to for later. She looked at her husband. 'I have lost my place,' she said.

'Lost your place!' said Mr Domanski, and he gave a laugh. 'You make life sound like a book!' He came over and planted a huge kiss on the top of Mrs Domanski's head. Lena could feel the reverberations through her own cheek as Mrs Domanski's head shook with the impact and wobbled on its thin neck.

'I have nothing to be good at,' said Mrs Domanski, her voice buzzing into Lena's skin.

Lena drew back worriedly. 'You do too!' she said. 'You're good at—' She paused. What was Mrs Domanski good at, apart from worrying? 'You're good at washing,' she said in a hurry. 'You're *primo* at washing.' Using one of Elroy's words helped, made her feel slightly less connected to what was going on.

'Washing,' said Mrs Domanski with a sigh and a laugh. 'Washing.'

'And so you are!' said Mr Domanski. 'The way you wring the shirts without cracking a button! It is nothing short of miraculous!'

A silence fell in the room, and the only sound was the third-hand fridge, burping and shaking in its corner like an old man. After a minute or so Mr Domanski spoke.

'Not one of you needs to worry,' he said. 'Thanks to The Polish Sausage we have enough money to live on and we will never have to go home again.' He stopped and gave a cough. 'Of course,' he said. 'I did not mean to say that. We *are* home!' And he picked Lena up and put her on his shoulders, although she was way too big for that now, and he marched around the living room singing 'American Pie', which he hadn't sung for a long time.

They had their Independence Day dinner (Herring in Sour

Cream, with Apricot Kompot to follow) but it was an odd hollow meal, nothing like a celebration, with conversation like flimsy paper chains that peeled apart at intervals. The following evening, after they had finished their leftovers, Mrs Domanski left the dishes in the sink. She went into the bedroom and shut the door firmly on her children, and when she came out she was wearing a long purple skirt made out of velvet that swept nearly to her ankles. Lena had never seen this skirt before in the flesh – only in photos of long-ago knees-ups in Poland.

'Le-na!' said Mrs Domanski, smartly.

Lena jumped.

'I need to borrow your lipstick!' said Mrs Domanski. It was not a request, it was a command, and Lena hurried to her show bag that hung in its place on the back of the bathroom door.

'Lipstick!' said Bella, her face lighting up into astonishing beauty. 'At last.'

Lena had one only, Lilac Shimmer. The Actors had told Mr Domanski that it was not seemly for small girls to wear much makeup, even on stage. 'It brings child beauty queens to mind,' said Jani, serious for a moment.

'Yes?' Mr Domanski had said eagerly.

'Not a good thing,' said Gabbi, policeman of prudence. 'Only a monster would do that to their child.'

'Of course,' said Mr Domanski hurriedly, though he looked in a slightly disappointed way at the lipstick Jani's wife had donated to the cause of comedy. 'Isn't it a little pale?' he said tentatively, and he drew a silvery stripe of the back of his big hand.

Now Mrs Domanski seized the Lilac Shimmer out of Lena's hand as if she could hardly wait to apply it. 'It is not really my colour,' she said, but she picked up a shining fish-slice anyway, holding it out in front of her on a stiff right arm and applying a layer of left-handed lipstick to her mouth.

'Only our mother,' said Bella under her breath, 'would use a kitchen utensil as a mirror.' But her sarcasm was no more than a habitual hat perched on the top of her head, beneath which her face was alive with interest. What did Mrs Domanski have up her purple-crocheted sleeve?

'Bella, you will stay at home and look after the little ones,' said Mrs Domanski, surveying the long blurred stripes of her face in the fish-slice. 'Where is Davey, by the way?'

'I don't know,' said Bella. 'Am I my brother's keeper?' But when she and Lena looked vaguely around, Davey was less than six feet away, crouched at the table with his feet drawn up on the rung of the chair.

'Calling Davey,' said Bella as a test. 'Come in, Dopey Davey.'

But Davey was poring over a sketch he had done on the back of a K-Mart brochure, examining his pencil lines which darted in and out of the garish patio furniture like trails of ants. In such states of absorption he heard nothing, not even his own name, and his lips continued to move soundlessly, formulating silent equations that transported him far above the San Francisco fog.

'Well, he won't be any trouble,' said Bella matter-of-factly, anticipating a quiet night painting her nails with white correction fluid.

'Where are you going, Ma?' said Lena. She looked in dismay at the smeared mess of lilac that now covered Mrs Domanski's mouth. It seemed to shout, *I used to be someone different*, and Lena's heart was filled with foreboding. She dragged her feet over to the table and sat down heavily opposite Davey.

'I am going to Clara's Ballhaus,' said Mrs Domanski, almost gaily. As she turned from the bench her long crocheted sleeve somehow picked up a teaspoon, which dangled at her elbow like a piece of jewelry crafted by a satirical modern artist with a point to make.

'Clara's Ballhaus!' cried Bella in dismay. 'But that's for sad old people!'

'That's right,' said Mrs Domanski, smiling determinedly. 'Your Uncle Larry is partnering me, and we are going dancing.'

'What about Da?' breathed Lena. And at that moment, as if on cue, they heard the sound of a key in the door, and after that Mr Domanski's usual dramatic gasp as he pulled his stomach in to edge around the washing machine.

'Hello, my dears!' he beamed, bursting into the room. 'I have

52

left The Sausage to run itself for a couple of hours so that I might come home and see my family.' Not one of his family ran eagerly towards him, as he seemed to hope for when making such grand paternal gestures, but then he had movement enough for all of them. On large feet he marched around the room, planting kisses on ears or whatever was closest, and he finished up beside Mrs Domanski, standing like a tall purple stalagmite in the middle of the kitchen.

'Why do you have a spoon in your sleeve, my love?' said Mr Domanski, removing it.

'Ma's going dancing at Clara's,' said Bella in disgust.

'You are?' said Mr Domanski in surprise. 'Well, good for you, my lovely.'

'You do not mind?' said Mrs Domanski. For a moment her face lost all its animation. She took the spoon out of Mr Domanski's hand and carried it to the sink, where she rinsed it several times and dried it carefully with a clean cloth.

'Mind?' said Mr Domanski, sounding slightly puzzled. 'Why should I mind?'

'Oh, no reason,' said Mrs Domanski with a return to brightness. She shut the spoon away in a drawer and her voice pushed its way out into the room through sticky layers of lipstick. 'I am going with Larry,' she said. 'I do not want to go alone for fear of what people would think.'

'*Old, sad* people,' hissed Bella to Lena. 'People who go there to grope other people while they pretend they're doing the tango.'

Lena laid her head down on the scratched table top. Creeping into her left ear came the tiny noise of Davey's pencil as it moved over the cheap shiny brochure.

(*listen close*, says the bullet, quite kindly. *You will not always be able to hear so well*)

'Lena!' said Mrs Domanski, sharply. Her voice sounded more distant than a star, for Lena could hear through one side of her head only. The other, pressed deep into the wood, was tuning into Davey's dreams of escape.

53

(listen closely my lovely, sings the bullet, *for you will not always be able to hear the songs of stars)*

'Don't put your head on the table, Lena,' came Mrs Domanski's faraway voice. 'It is not hygienic.' She swept over and lifted Lena's head off the table as if it was a folded pile of clothes, then she took her hands away and whisked them together as if to get rid of hair germs. 'I'll wipe that,' she said, automatically heading for a cleaning cloth, and all the time her purple dancing skirt trailed heavily behind her.

'For God's sake, Ma,' said Bella. 'Just go, would you?'

'Yes, I suppose I should,' said Mrs Domanski, but she returned to the table and began wiping it in perfect circles, dislodging Davey's outstretched arms as he tried to protect his paper.

'Go and have a splendid time,' said Mr Domanski heartily. He went to the fridge and pulled out some eggs. 'Anyone for a scramble?' he said.

Crustaceans

After this, for many months, Mrs Domanski went dancing. She told them nothing about it but on the day after dancing days she seemed brighter. Her hair stood out in a halo, as if static electricity from the dance floor had entered her body through the soles of her feet and made its way upwards until it reached her head. But the next day her face closed up again and her hair flattened out, and she swept and scrubbed and washed walls as though her life depended on it. She had retreated back into herself and there she would stay until the next Monday rolled around.

'Move that school bag off the bench, would you?' she said, picking it up and depositing it out in the hall before Lena could do so. 'You never know where that's been sitting.' Just as the wrists of some women seem to exude a faint floral scent, Mrs Domanski's carried a whiff of disinfectant with them always.

'How was dancing?' Lena sometimes forced herself to ask. She felt as if someone should venture down the dark stairs to the subject that, for some reason, was never talked about.

'It was fine,' said Mrs Domanski to the floor. Her thin bottom stuck into the air and her arms circled rhythmically out the sides like the twin heads of a polishing machine.

'Don't you want to take Da with you?' said Lena in an almost-whisper.

'Oh, he would not be interested,' said Mrs Domanski, sitting up and pushing wisps of hair off her face. 'Anyway, your Uncle Larry is a far better dancer,' she said. 'I will never forget how your father stood all over my feet in the Beauty Queen polka. They turned black and blue and I had to bicycle to work instead of walking. For days I could not lace up my shoes.'

After this conversation Lena's own feet felt heavy and she scuffed down Hyde Street on her way home from school. As she passed the end of Golden Gate Avenue she peered along the road and could just make out, down by St Boniface's Church, the looped fairy lights of the entrance to Clara's Ballhaus. She used to like looking at the bright red hearts painted on the gates and the plaster cupids strung in the trees, but now that Mrs Domanski had started going there she could not venture again along that road. It was her mother's territory now, she had staked it out as determinedly as a prospector in a gold rush, and even to pass on the other side of the road would feel wrong.

'It's her own special thing,' said Lena, trying to explain to Davey why they now had to walk two extra blocks to get home.

Interestingly, Davey appeared to understand. 'It doesn't do to take the mystery out of things,' he said after a long pause.

'That is it,' said Lena. 'Exactly.' Sometimes she was surprised by Davey and the amount of information he absorbed while appearing to sit as still as a creature under a rock. *Flip!* His tongue would go out, he would digest whatever had flown past him, and later he would disgorge it as a small chunk of wisdom.

They trudged on, taking six hundred or a thousand or perhaps six thousand extra steps to afford their mother some small and temporary peace. And this method worked quite well until one particular autumn evening.

Was it Lena's fault, somehow? Could her light footsteps on the face of the earth be blamed for disrupting its very core? It seemed unlikely but for many winters to come Lena felt a kind of guilt when she looked around the empty chaotic kitchen, and looking back she placed it squarely on those few hours.

'Get over yourself!' scoffed Bella. 'You're not that important.'

But Bella always discounted the mysterious balance of things, didn't seem to notice when her large stride crushed worms into the sidewalk or the edge of her coat dislodged someone's plate from a sidewalk table. Lena, on the other hand, knew that you could never be sure – and sometimes you never found out – just what you had caused by turning down one street instead of another.

There had been no warning. It had been just another day of chilly winds and cardigans, with a slight edge in the air that had less to do with winter than with Mrs Domanski's determination to get to the Ballhaus early.

'The Selection Committee will soon be paying a visit,' she said. 'They will choose three pairs of dancers to participate in the heats for the Interstate Semifinals.'

'To participate in the Heats for the Semifinals for the Interstates for the Nationals,' drawled Bella. 'Gee, that's some knockout process.'

Mrs Domanski smoothed her hair into a professional-looking bun and fixed a small plastic rose behind her ear. Her Monday movements had their own importance, so that Bella's cynicism washed on over her like a final easy-rinse cycle after the hard removal of stains.

'What time is Da due home?' asked Lena. Her math looked more than usually difficult, and Mr Domanski had a tiny calculator that he always carried in his breast pocket.

'I must be gone by six,' said Mrs Domanski, glancing at the clock. On dance nights it was as if she had difficulty hearing anything her children said. 'I cannot wait for him,' she stated.

So, by the time Mr Domanski blew in a good ten minutes after six, his wife had gone and the room she had left behind was still with concentration. Bella was fashioning a coat hanger into a wire frame, Davey was removing the foil seal from the lid of a syrup jar, and Lena had her head in her hands and was staring at columns with so many decimal points in them that her eyes had begun to jig.

'Hello, my little pigeons!' boomed Mr Domanski.

At the sound of his voice, several things happened. Lena quickly took a deep breath, because when her father entered a room there seemed less air to go around. Davey gave a guilty start but continued to peel the seal off the jar (once he had started in on something, he found it impossible to break off in the middle as other people would). And Bella just gave a gusty sigh.

'A bit of quiet, please,' she said, as if she were the parent.

Lena went over and gave her father a hug. Against her cheek his moustache felt rough but comforting. 'Will you have time to help out with some numbers?' she said hopefully.

'I'm only taking the foil this once,' said Davey, though Mr Domanski's attention had long since left him and his petty pilfering there in the middle of the kitchen floor.

'Of course I will give you a hand,' said Mr Domanski to his youngest child. But by the time he had helped Lena herd her decimal points into straight lines, he was getting cabin fever. 'I only came home momentarily,' he said. 'To check on you.'

He strode to the oven and looked inside and gave the sort of sound a walrus would make, if that walrus had hoped to find fish and had instead found none. 'Dancing,' he said in a disparaging voice, even though on Friday nights when his variety show was pulling in the crowds he approved of all kinds of dancing.

'You don't need to check on us,' said Bella in annoyance. 'I'm old enough to take charge.' Picking up a shoebox from the floor beside her chair, she extracted the skin of a dead sparrow and attempted to stretch it over her wire frame. 'Shit,' she said, stretching and pulling. 'The damn skin's too small.'

'Don't you mean—' said Davey. They waited – at least Lena did, while Mr Domanski found a dish of cold sausages in the fridge and crammed a couple into his mouth, and Bella took up a blade and began to make small slits in the sparrow's floppy neck.

'Don't you mean,' said Davey finally, 'that you've made the frame too big?'

Bella stared at him. 'I mean,' she intoned, 'that the skin of the bird is too small.'

'I don't think you should be doing your taxidermy at the table,' said Mr Domanski thickly through a mouthful of cold pork. 'Your mother would not like it.'

'Lucky she's lambada-ing,' said Bella. 'Fortunate she's folk-dancing.' Instantly, her mood lightened. She gave a snort. 'Wonderful she's waltzing!' she said, and next second she was bent double, shaking with laughter over her strands of wire and the tiny limp skin. 'God, I crack myself up,' she groaned.

Lena scrunched her toes up inside her shoes. She hoped Bella would stop soon: she was much better when she was her normal, humourless self. Mr Domanski, perhaps also feeling the embarrassment of bad comedy, went to the radio and turned it on. A surge of Dvorak swept through the room.

'Aaah,' he said, holding up one reverent hand. 'The European masters! Nothing can compete.' He stood for a moment in the middle of the room with his eyes closed. Then he left them.

'The new boy's good with the beer,' he said by way of explanation, 'but no good at grilling.' He stuck his head back into the room for one last fatherly word. 'Don't go out now,' he said.

'How can we?' said Bella to the closed door. 'With only one goddamn key between us?' She stuck her tongue between her teeth and stretched the bird again. 'Better,' she said to it encouragingly. There was a slight cracking noise that sounded to Lena like small bones, even though she knew from past experience that the bird's real, God-given skeleton would already be wrapped in newspaper and sitting in the bin. *Crack!* she heard, and she held her breath.

'Shit!' said Bella angrily. 'Bastard bird.'

Lena switched off the soaring violins and the room fell into welcome peace. She went and lay down on the sofa, stained with spilt Domanski milk and with spaghetti sauce from previous, more dashing owners. She closed her eyes. She did love her father, he almost always came first in her prayers and not just because he was the head of the family. But sometimes, she thought a little guiltily, she loved him better when he wasn't there, raking up the air and spraying crumbs of dead pig from behind his moustache.

'*Go out!*' said Davey, with real urgency. His chair hit the floor with a crash and Lena opened her tired eyes.

'What is it, Davey?' she said, trying to trace back all conversation that had occurred over the past ten minutes.

'I have to!' said Davey. 'I have to go out!' His face was unusually flushed, his eyes almost wide.

'Why, dillbrain?' said Bella. 'It's dark already, and, oh, did I mention about half an hour ago that we only have one key?'

Davey looked obstinate. 'My project,' he said. 'They're taking the science fair down tonight and I forgot to dismantle my project.'

Lena looked at him. She hoped the glint in his eyes was the reflection from the street lamp rather than generated by emotion. 'Surely they'll put it aside for you,' she said comfortingly. But she could hear the principal's voice from several days ago booming in her head. *Any project not picked up by Monday*, he was saying threateningly to the school hall at large, *will be put through the crusher*. She sighed: how could the principal have known that his warning might have come in time for the other kids, but that it would take far longer than a few days to filter into Davey's space-dazzled brain?

Davey looked beseechingly at Bella. 'Come with me,' he said. 'I won't be able to carry the whole shuttle by myself.'

'Can't,' said Bella briefly, not looking up. She had several pins stuck between her lips, making her look like a savage sabre-toothed beast. 'Too much to do,' she said. She pulled a pin out of her mouth and drove it deep into the top of the sparrow's soft head. Lena winced.

'But it took me weeks to make!' said Davey. 'It's the only prototype in the world.' His voice quavered but fortunately he was saved by honesty. 'Well, the only one in the western world,' he amended. 'The Russians probably got there first.'

'I'm sorry,' said Bella, 'but I don't think any of you realize that taxidermy is an Art.' She straightened up and feathers flew on the breath of her importance. 'A misunderstood, much maligned Art,' she said, 'which cannot simply be picked up and put down again because of forgetful little boys.'

Davey bit his lip.

'I'll come,' said Lena quickly. For how could she lie there on the sofa and jeopardize not only the future of space exploration, but also Davey's composure?

'The key,' said Bella sternly, warningly. 'You've forgotten we only have one.'

'We'll run all the way,' suggested Lena, 'and you can let us in when we get back.'

'You'll come?' said Davey, in response to her last comment but one. He looked doubtfully at Lena's small arms, slipping from her T-shirt like thin white ribbons.

'I'm stronger than I look,' said Lena.

'Well, OK,' said Davey finally. 'We'll have to hurry.' And for him he actually moved quite quickly, so they were out the door into the cold night before Lena had time to worry about breaking their word.

'Be careful,' said Bella, who had ordered them to lock her in and take the key with them. 'Don't talk to dealers. If you have to talk to anyone, talk to strangers.' She gave a little crack of laughter before she could stop herself. 'Strangers!' they heard her murmur, as they turned the key in the outside of the door.

'I hope there isn't a fire,' said Davey gravely.

Once they were in the street it wasn't as dark as it had looked from inside.

'We should run,' said Davey. 'Not just because of Bella. They'll be closing the school hall soon.'

And away they jogged through the streets, with the dirty orange sky smothering them like a huge sweater. Was there fog in Poland? wondered Lena as they ran. Did Poland have a continuous fog like San Francisco did, sweeping in and out like the sea? She tried to remember what she had read in the school encyclopaedia under the title *European Environments*, but then a tram streamed in front of them in one long line of lighted carriages and she had to jog on the spot and her thoughts went on hold.

The lights were still on in the school hall, but Mrs Pulver was the only person left. 'Davey Domanski,' she said in a disagreeable voice. 'I was just about to start work on your project.' When she said 'work', though, she meant the opposite because she was bent on destruction rather than creation. As Davey and Lena began carefully dismantling the shuttle, Mrs Pulver tugged away alongside them, ripping down a range of cardboard mountains that were so beautiful they made Lena's eyes water.

'Do they have to go?' asked Lena. She thought they would make a perfect backdrop for any kind of play – perhaps *The Sound of Music*, for which she had a special liking as it had happened on her family's side of the world. But she was scared of Mrs Pulver, whose mouth turned down at the corners even when smiling, and so her question was whispery and became lost in the ripping of cardboard and the sound of Davey's heavy breathing as he pulled out staples with the back of a hammer.

By the time the pull-down was done Lena's arms were aching from reaching up high for tail gates and for the bright silver lights that had glowed in a surreal way as part of the spacecraft, but were now revealed to be the lids off jam jars. A while back Mrs Domanski had been on a constant search for these lids, bending to look under the stove and craning to look on the tops of cupboards, but Davey's talent for vanishing had meant that he was never caught red-handed. No wonder space launches were appealing to him, thought Lena: even at that moment when all the world was watching you, you could sit safely in your capsule and know that in twenty seconds, in fifteen or ten or five seconds you would be gone – *poof!* – in a rush of wind and fire, with no one able to follow you and quiz you about screw-top jars.

'I'm glad we've saved it,' said Lena, dropping her puny arms to her sides and giving them a stretch.

Davey gave a nod, strangely authoritative as if he had captained a mission. 'We've done well,' he said briefly. And then they strode past Mrs Pulver, leaving her struggling with great armfuls of snowy peaks and a slippery plastic Danube under foot.

'Hope she drowns,' said Lena as they ran out the door laden with pieces of space equipment. But once again, as always when she talked about mean people, her voice was so tiny that it rolled under the wheels of the traffic and was gone. Meanwhile Davey was talking to the astronaut's helmet painted in the front window.

'Air pressure?' he was saying professionally and, unlike Lena's, his voice did make it safely across the road: a crackling tinny voice, not usually heard on the streets of the Tenderloin. 'Give me a reading,' he said through his fist-radio as they darted across O'Farrell Street.

Once over the main intersection they slowed up and the urgency drained from the situation, so that Lena was left slightly cold. The wind whined around the corners of the tenements, balled-up paper skittered like rats on the footpath. Up ahead a man was sitting in a car talking out the window to someone wearing a very short skirt and very tall heels.

'Davey,' hissed Lena. 'It's a hooker. You think we should cross?'

The wind wailed and Davey took his time to think about it, so that by the time he answered there was no point. 'No,' he said, as they walked right past the man and the woman and the car. 'No, I don't think so.'

'Oh shut up, Davey,' said Lena, suddenly furious. She had only wanted a quick piece of advice: it seemed that she could never get her family to answer anything directly, not about the time they were due home or safety on the street.

The woman turned her head and looked straight at them as they passed by. There was a smile on her mouth but her lips were drawn back like a dog's, and under the afro wig her eyebrows were huge and thick.

Lena hitched her silver panels more securely up under her armpits and stepped quickly on. 'Davey,' she said, out the side of her mouth. 'I think that was a man.'

'In the car?' said Davey, wandering half a stride behind her.

'No, stupid,' said Lena. 'The one in the skirt.'

'Was it?' said Davey. He sounded a lot less concerned about this than about the tiny tear in the window of his paper cockpit. Perhaps that was the way she should be too? thought Lena. Focusing on the small things instead of trying to get a grip on the whole world?

They walked on in silence, and came to the corner of Leavenworth and Golden Gate Avenue. Here they were so close to the Ballhaus that Lena could almost hear the surging music, and the scrape of her mother's shoes as she whirled forgetfully in Uncle Larry's arms. She sucked in her cheeks.

And then they were past the pawn shop and approaching the lighted windows of Monsieur Vuong. There were people inside, laughing and eating and drinking. These people balanced prawns and precarious snowpeas on the ends of their chopsticks, raised them to their wide mouths. Golden plum wine tilted in their glasses like the plates of the world.

'Oh, no!' said Lena. 'The crabs.'

Always, she hated seeing the lighted tanks placed in the middle of Monsieur Vuong's window. These tanks were filled with lime-green water, and with seafood about to become somebody's dinner. Small fish darted about like iron filings and these were bad enough, but somehow they seemed nowhere near as touching as the crabs. For the crabs had real faces. Their mouths were down-turned as if they knew that soon they would be pulled from their watery home, air-lifted to saucepans and thrown to their deaths. Their small bulbous eyes waved on the ends of their stalks, waved at Lena. *Come save us,* they begged, *oh Eater of Beansprouts and Sauerkraut!* And Lena would have to stifle a cry and walk on.

Now, although she tried not to look, her head turned as if attached to a string. Sure enough, on the bottom of the tank were three large crabs, making for the glass wall in a desperate side-ways crawl. And there was the small lethal net of Barney Vuong, breaking through the ceiling of their water-world, zeroing in through the green weed.

Lena took a sharp breath inwards and stopped in her tracks.

'What is it?' said Davey, coming up beside her.

And at that moment, the earthquake struck.

Gap

Just before Davey arrives beside her, Lena hears a vast space: a space in the spinning of the world. In that vacuum, in that preceding absence of air, the rushing of the streets fades and she can hear horses neigh to each other across the Bay, and dogs beginning to bark. She hears the resonance of church bells about to sound and the thrumming of windows about to break, and a faraway creaking which could be the shifting cartilage of the earth or could be her mother's memory turning and turning to the strains of a Polish waltz.

(freeze-frame: a small girl holding a pair of silver wings looks through the window of a Vietnamese noodle house, looks deep into the faces of three crabs. What does she see in the darkness behind their round eyes, in the gaping of their flat open mouths? Her reflection in the glass window is reflected in the glass tank, and again in the ceiling of water, and her double-triple self looks almost mystical)

In that hearing, listening time Lena also sees. She sees:

herself,

her brother,

three crabs,

and a world on the edge of disaster.

And then everything starts to move.

Maps

It was like a miracle, Lena thought later. Though she did wonder whether God would risk the lives of seven million people to intervene on the part of three crabs.

'Who were doomed anyway,' said Bella afterwards, scathingly.

And this much was true. For as Lena and Davey felt the street roll under their legs and their legs turn to jelly, as they grabbed hold of each other and staggered backwards, the fish tank came hurling out of the window with an explosive force, landing in front of them on the swirling sidewalk and blowing apart. Water and weed sluiced across Lena's feet, and the crabs were lost forever in a maelstrom of ripping asphalt. ('They knew already,' said Lena afterwards, remembering the darkness, and the melancholic mouths.)

'Run!' said Davey's voice, out of the whirling glass and the screaming, and the swaying of lamp posts. And then his hand was pulling at Lena and dragging her along the street.

'Where to?' gasped Lena.

'The church!' said Davey. They ran and stumbled, leaving a trail of space shuttle behind them. People were all around them, also stumbling and running. 'Get inside!' a woman screamed at them from where she had fallen. Her mouth gaped at Lena: a terrified, turned-down crab mouth. 'Get under something!' she yelled again, stumbling to her feet, streaming blood from her nylon knees.

Was this the right thing to do? Lena couldn't remember, but she followed Davey and they left the woman behind. A pedestrian sign showing a picture of running children crashed down beside them, and lights fizzed and popped above their heads. It reminded Lena of the fairy story Mrs Domanski used to tell them, about Babayaga with her steel teeth, and the fleeing children throwing down objects which turned into great chasms and rivers. But here the rivers were made of electric wires, and the cracks in the sidewalks offered no kind of protection. Lena looked down into one as they flew over it and she held tight to the silver wings of Davey's shuttle, for if she dropped them into that yawning space their chances of survival would be even less than at the hands of Mrs Pulver.

Suddenly she and Davey were outside St Boniface's Church, with its huge doors opening and closing like clappers. They rushed on through and fell onto the damp tiles. Lena could feel grit under her cheek and she pressed her face hard down into it. In here the floor was quite still.

'It's over,' said Davey into the dark breathy silence.

'Is it?' said Lena. 'I thought it was the church keeping us safe.'

'It will if there's an aftershock,' said Davey. 'See up there?'

Lena turned her head and looked through the darkness to where he was pointing. High above her were windows of stained glass, gleaming red and blue in the night. 'Yes?' she said, her jawbone moving against the tiles.

'That's Saint Anthony,' explained Davey. 'And Saint Emydius. They protect against earthquakes. It's one of their jobs.'

'Saint Emydius,' repeated Lena. She rolled onto her back so that she could breathe better. She felt as if she could stay there for a long time, listening to Davey explaining the history of saints.

Outside sirens were starting up but they sounded far away and somehow phoney, like the soundtrack to an old and not very convincing black-and-white movie. The noises inside, though very quiet, were much more real. The roof of the church shifted and creaked, and there was a small creeping sound near Lena's ear that could have been the wind whispering under the door.

'How come the saints didn't break?' she asked. The light from outside shone through Anthony's pale cheeks, making him look more ghostly than saintly.

'The lead around the glass,' said Davey. 'It lets the window move without shattering.' He seemed to be answering more smartly than usual, as if the sudden shaking had loosened some blockage in his head.

'You know a lot,' said Lena respectfully.

'Oh, not really,' said Davey in an off-hand voice. 'Just what I read.'

'Do you think it's safe to leave?' said Lena. She sat up and suddenly her responsibilities rushed at her like a pack of wolves out of the stone shadows. 'Davey!' she said in horror. 'Bella – she was locked in!'

Davey stood up. 'It's good she was inside,' he said gruffly. 'You should never go out in the street in a 'quake.'

'And what about Ma?' cried Lena.

'We'll go find her now,' said Davey, picking up his shuttle. Its nose was crushed inwards, like a hard-boiled egg hit with a spoon.

'Your project,' said Lena. 'Your poor project.'

'It doesn't matter,' said Davey. He put up a hand and rubbed at his eyes. 'Grit,' he said.

Lena looked down at the portion she had been carrying. Even in the dim light she could see great rips in one wing, and the

66

foil was scratched and torn as if it had been dragged through many turbulent forcefields. 'We could pretend it was damaged during take-off,' she said hopefully.

They left the church, though Lena wished they could stay a while longer in that huge cavernous peace. They pushed open the huge heavy doors and stepped out, expecting to see a new post-apocalyptic world. But there was Golden Gate Avenue looking quite recognizable, although it was strewn with debris as if a giant baby had had a tantrum and had then been lifted on out of there. Lena, of course, had not seen this part of the street for some time because of having to avoid Clara's Ballhaus – and now, because of a freak event, she had been propelled to its very door.

She looked over uncertainly. A couple of trees lay across the Ballhaus path, and the sign with the dancing couple on it had crashed through the gate so it looked as if the painted woman was kicking her pointed toe right through the wire netting. A group of people were standing outside the door, exclaiming in loud overexcited voices.

'Oh boy,' one of them was saying. 'All I could think of was what a mess my tax is in.'

'You think yours is a mess!' said another man. 'Come to think of it I might have been better off dead!' And he laughed and all the other people laughed along with him in a nervous, exaggerated way.

'Lena,' said Davey, who had been looking, not listening. 'There's Ma!'

Sure enough, it was Mrs Domanski, not with the tax evaders and the laughers, but sitting all by herself under a tree that had been kept upright by its sturdy roots. She was wearing a white fringed shawl that Lena had never seen before and white dancing slippers with tiny white roses on them, and she had her head down, staring at the ground.

Lena ran towards her, leaping over fallen trees like the leprechaun she had once been. 'Ma!' she cried. 'Are you hurt, Ma?'

Mrs Domanski raised her head. Her hair hung in wisps down the side of her face, and there were clean crying lines down her grimy cheeks. 'Hello, Lena,' she said, as if in a trance. She looked unsurprised at the sight of her two youngest children walking out of the middle of a shaken dark night.

'Oh, Mama!' said Lena, and she held on tight to Mrs Domanski's wrist. 'What happened to you?'

'Uncle Larry,' said Mrs Domanski, in a voice bleaker than a wind over an empty lot. 'Your Uncle Larry has found a new partner,' she said. 'He does not want to dance with me in the competition.'

Lena fell silent. This was not at all what she had expected to hear: she had been asking about sore heads or broken bones, and instead she had been handed a broken heart.

'Did you hear?' said Mrs Domanski, and she gave an odd smile. 'I will not be back here again.' She sat amidst the wreckage of the Ballhaus entrance. A plaster cupid fell with a soft thud out of the tree, its cheek coming to rest on her shoe.

Lena bent down and moved the cupid gently to the side. She rubbed at the dirty streaks on Mrs Domanski's satin toes and searched for a joke to lighten the moment, but her head was strangely empty.

Davey came to the rescue. 'We should go home,' he said gruffly. 'We have to check on Bella and Da.'

'Of course,' said Mrs Domanski, sounding relieved to have someone take charge. 'But I could have won that competition, you know.'

Lena saw Uncle Larry come out of the building behind, and look around with a worried look on his face. She took Mrs Domanski's hand. 'Let's go,' she said quickly.

And they went, walking in a line, picking their way down the street towards home. On the corner was a humming hornet's nest of electric wires, with danger tape already fencing it off and some firemen standing around it. 'Careful now, folks,' said one of the firemen courteously, as the Domanskis filed past.

Another fireman eyed up Mrs Domanski's trailing fringes and her grimy rose-toes. 'Nice night for dancing,' he said. There was a small explosion of laughter and Lena, who was bringing up the rear, spun around.

'Do your job,' she said fiercely, 'or I'll do you.'

When Bella heard about this, she was suitably impressed. 'Good for you, Lena,' she praised. 'You see, you don't have to be a wimp-bag all your life.'

Bella was at home alone when they finally got there, sweeping up the remnants of plates. 'I got under the table,' she said. 'Took the sparrow with me.' Ten minutes after they got back, Mr Domanski blustered in. 'The phone lines were down!' he said. His voice held great excitement. 'There I was crammed under the bar,' he said, 'worried out of my brain and I could not call my girls! But it seems that Davey has looked after them. Did you, Davey?'

'I—' started Davey. But with the return to the living room he seemed to have slowed up again, and his leadership qualities had vanished. He stood for a while as if not quite knowing where to start, and then he shrugged his plaid shoulders and disappeared into his annex to check that his mobiles were still hanging.

'How was dancing, dear?' said Mr Domanski politely to his wife. It was odd, perhaps, that his question was not about what had happened in the Ballhaus when the earth had rumbaed: whether the floor had collapsed or the ceiling had crumbled, whether Uncle Larry had done his manly best to protect the womenfolk. But Mr Domanski, too, seemed reluctant to pry into the sequined corners of Mrs Domanski's life.

Mrs Domanski looked at the grimy roses on her shoes, then she bent down and picked up Bella's blade, still covered all over with smears of blood and the tiny fluff of a sparrow's throat. She took off her shoes and, one by one, she used the blade to cut the roses off. 'Dancing?' she said dully. 'Oh, it was much the same.'

She trailed to the bathroom to remove the final traces of her glamorous self. Mr Domanski stood in the middle of the dishevelled room and looked slightly lost until Bella began bossing him around. 'You could fix that Virgin Mary back on her perch,' she ordered.

'And you could clean up the dirt from those plants,' retorted Mr Domanski.

And as quickly as that, in spite of having been uprooted and shaken for minutes on end, the family sank back into their usual ruts. But there was a new restlessness in the house, a feeling of disturbance as if the air had also been shaken up and then reassembled, but not in the right way.

For once in her life, Lena did not help. Letting the others bustle around her, she went across to the shelves and pulled out the family atlas. Sitting in state at the end of the table, she opened up the blue cloth covers that were smeared all over with fingerprints, and she began to look for new countries. Her criteria were small but immovable: no fault lines, no Communism, and no biting ocean winds from either the north or the west.

The choices appeared to be vast and her heart lifted in spite of itself. This is what she would do. She would make enough money from her jokes to take her parents with her, and Bella and Davey if they cared to come. They would move to an entirely unknown country, one where fruit bats hung from the trees like Christmas decorations and the air smelt of new clothes.

The coins

It was two sleeps before the twenty-fifth of December that Lena found Mrs Domanski cleaning in her nightgown. There she knelt on the kitchen floor with her green rubber gloves on, but her feet were bare and cold, and she was whispering to herself.

'Ma?' said Lena, in surprise.

'Quietly does it, Lena,' said Mrs Domanski, quite unnecessarily for Lena's whisper made even less noise than the small strokes of the scrubbing brush on the floor. 'We don't want to wake Davey up,' she said.

The moon shone in the small slit window over the bookshelves, and Mrs Domanski's hair flowed down her back, a sheet of glinting black and grey. She sat back on her bare heels and surveyed the floor, then moved over to where Lena was standing. 'Shuffle over, my darlink,' she said. 'I see a mark there between your feet.'

Lena moved obediently.

'There it is again!' said Mrs Domanski, clicking her tongue with annoyance, following Lena with the scrubbing brush.

'I think it's the shadow from my sleeve,' said Lena, moving to test it out. 'Yes, it is,' she said. She went to the sink and took a drink from the tap, flicking her tongue in and out of the water.

'Lena!' said Mrs Domanski sharply. 'You are allowed to use a glass.'

'I'm having a cat drink,' said Lena, turning off the tap. 'It's more satisfying.' She gave a tiny miaow.

'Sshhh,' said Mrs Domanski, although the two of them were making less sound than Mr Domanski's snores, which were rolling forth from under the bedroom door.

'Why are you cleaning now?' said Lena. 'Isn't it a bit late?' As she spoke, the clock gave a grunt and rolled over on to the hour. 'Two o'clock!' she said in astonishment.

'I do not get enough time during the day,' said Mrs Domanski, and her voice sounded quite desperate. 'There are always chores to do, always the shopping to fetch.'

'But you have all day while we're at school!' said Lena. 'And you don't really need to be here when we get home. We're not babies any more.' As soon as she had said this, she realized it might make her mother feel as though she wasn't wanted. 'Though of course it's always lovely to see you,' she said, sounding like the wife of the parish priest who greeted people after the service.

Mrs Domanski stared away, her eyes blank in the moonlight. 'You are not babies any more,' she repeated, dropping the brush into the bucket with a small deep splash. 'That is true. You are not babies.'

Lena stood on one foot and then the other, trying to keep them off the cold wet floor. 'Would you mind,' she ventured, 'if I went back to bed?' She didn't want to be rude but she had a show the next night and she thought she should get some sleep.

'Go!' said Mrs Domanski but, as Lena tiptoed past, she grabbed hold of her heel.

'What?' said Lena. 'Have I trodden dirt on your floor?' And she looked anxiously behind her.

'Come here,' said Mrs Domanski, and she pulled Lena down into a hug. 'My little Lena,' she said. 'My littlest one.'

Lena could feel the hard bones of her mother's chest against her own flat one. She rested her forehead on Mrs Domanski's arm, just for a moment, and there caught in the short hairs were tiny bubbles of soap which shone in the moonlight like miniature space helmets. Puffing gently along her mother's arm, she watched the suds pop in a row into nothing.

'Oh, Ma,' she said, out of affection and worry. 'Oh, Ma.'

'Go to bed now,' said her mother, and she patted Lena slightly awkwardly on the head.

In the morning neither of them spoke about what had happened, not even when Davey dropped his toast in slow motion on to the spotlessly clean floor where it landed in a smear of hot butter and crumbs. Lena looked on in horror but—

'I was going to clean that floor today, anyway,' said Mrs Domanski in an expressionless voice.

Lena had little time to think about anything after this, for Christmas and New Year were upon her and they were her busiest times. There were shows to give, a whole row of them, and because of the festive mood of her audiences she hardly had to try before she had them in fits. They lay there across the tables, shoulders shaking and hands clutching huge mugs of beer, and they called her back again and again when she tried to leave the stage. She was the spirit of Christmases past, she was an elf, she was Santa and Mrs Claus, and most often she was herself, Lena Domanski, entertaining the masses.

Occasionally, as she had admitted to Bella, she would lose the point of what she was saying. But when this happened she would look over at Mr Domanski and see his face shining with pride. 'See?' he would be saying to the person next to him. 'See that? That's my Pie.' And then Lena would turn to the crowd again, would place them back in the palm of her small, slightly sweaty hand and finish the act. It was the least she could do for such unconditional love.

After the show, after the tills had been balanced and the lights turned off, she and her father would step into the cool foggy night. 'Look, there's Coit Tower!' said Mr Domanski, though there was no way in the world he could see Telegraph Hill so many miles off, all the way past Chinatown and Nob Hill. As for Lena, what with the bleariness in her eyes and the night mist, she could hardly make out the tops of the lamp posts. But she hated to disappoint.

'I get your drift,' she said, which was something Bella said when she didn't really understand but didn't want to admit it.

'When they built Coit Tower they painted murals inside,' said her father. He peered at Lena. 'You know what murals are?' he said.

'Long skinny paintings?' said Lena.

'That'll do,' said her father. 'Anyway, in one of those murals someone drew a hammer and sickle.'

There was a pause. Their footsteps sounded loud in the midnight street. Mr Domanski looked expectantly at Lena but she was busy with an experiment that involved inhaling the clammy air through her nose and then exhaling it through her mouth.

'You know what a hammer and sickle is?' asked Mr Domanski.

'I think so,' said Lena in a nasal voice. Breathing like this was interesting: it made a kind of snort that sounded like a pig.

'They scrubbed that drawing out before they opened the tower,' said her father. His voice sounded very odd, even heard over Lena's snuffling pig breath. 'Years ago, this was,' he said. 'Even all the way over here, they knew what the hammer and sickle could do.'

'Look, we're nearly home,' said Lena, relieved, and she rushed on ahead, feeling slightly guilty without knowing why.

By the time they got in on those nights the rest of the family was in bed, but Mr Domanski and Lena were often giggly due to what Mr Domanski called 'The Hype After' and Lena called 'Showdown'. They had to have hot chocolate made with water to settle themselves down, which meant they were even later getting to bed, and Lena would wake late in the mornings.

By the time she had straggled up and into the living room, Davey was usually out of the house and Mrs Domanski would be cooking whatever speciality was required on that particular day, for feasts came thick and fast as the old year gave way to the new. As for Bella, she would be wrist-deep in an animal, although not the one she had had her eye on.

'I wanted the turkey,' she said in a growly voice. 'It was a fine specimen.'

'It was dinner,' said Mrs Domanski tiredly.

On the sixth day of January, there were no arguments over who got to do what with the food; this was Epiphany, and it was traditionally a donut day. Even Bella, who baulked at her family celebrating European traditions when they should be acting like Americans, allowed this one.

'Donuts *are* America,' she said, even though everybody knew her approval was largely won by her stomach rather than her principles.

As for Lena, there could be no better treat. On Epiphany mornings she always woke to find a lightness in her limbs, and when she looked outside the winter sun was spreading sugary rays on the sidewalks.

On Epiphany that year Mr Domanski decided to close The Sausage. 'I have worked twenty days in a row,' he said. 'Today I wish to take my family to the park.'

'I'm not coming to the park,' said Bella, but she said it in a testing kind of way. When Mr Domanski said that certainly his oldest child was to come, that she was part of the family whether she liked it or not, Bella went to get her hat and coat. 'Just this once,' she said, and she took a minute to tidy her menagerie of stuffed animals, putting a hare recently saved from a stew in pride of place at the front. Lena had long since been forced to move all her books off the shelves, for Bella liked to keep not only her taxidermy work there but also her growing collection of shoes.

'My footwear collection will soon be legendary,' she said now, gazing fondly at some rope-soled platform shoes picked up for a song at the church fair.

Lena looked at the turquoise cowboy boots whose toes were so pointed that even half of Bella's foot wouldn't fit into them. 'But they're all unwearable,' she said. She didn't mind the display; in fact she had a weakness for shoes, and she hoped one day to own a high shiny red pair like the ones Elroy's mother wore to church. But unlike Bella she was not a collector at heart, and having to carry a notebook at all times so she could write down jokes that might never be used made her feel heavy inside.

'Who wants to wear them?' said Bella scornfully. 'That's the whole point, you philistine. You don't *wear* art.'

'All you really do is slice up dead animals and pull other people's dirty sneakers out of the trash,' pointed out Lena, who was becoming tired of Bella and her artist's pose.

'Child,' said Bella in a cutting voice. She turned away from Lena and began slicking Vaseline on her lips to make them shiny.

'Would you girls please put your best feet forward?' called Mr Domanski from the other room. 'My day off will be over before we have even left the house.'

Lena rummaged in the cartons under her bed to find something to read, bypassing her joke books because this was a day off for her as well. When she emerged into the living room with her bag packed, she found Mr Domanski standing in front of Mrs Domanski, looking uncertain. More and more often this was his stance, as if his wife were a cow of uncertain nature who might or might not be herded in the desired direction.

'I think you should come along with us,' he was saying, but his voice lacked its usual conviction.

'And I have told you that I do not have the time,' said Mrs Domanski, quite decisively for her. But she stood in front of a wall stained yellow with cooking fumes and looked as if she might vanish right into it. 'I have the *paczki* to prepare,' she said, with a shrug.

'Always the house!' said Mr Domanski, trying to be expansive. 'Can it not spare you for a few hours?' He took a step towards his wife and almost reached out for her, but at the last moment his hand fell to his side.

Mrs Domanski turned away and began to mix water and yeast in a bowl. Her elbows stuck out of her dress awkwardly, the bones pressing against the skin.

'Do come, Ma,' said Lena persuasively. 'It's all sunny outside.'

'You go and enjoy yourselves,' said Mrs Domanski, bending down and hunting for a tray in the cupboard under the sink. Her voice sounded muffled, creeping backwards out of the dark cupboard as if it would rather have stayed in there.

'I guess we will,' said Mr Domanski. He turned away and his moustache looked very bristly. 'Davey?' he said. 'Hurry along! I would like to get to the park before the sun goes down.'

In spite of Bella's pretended reluctance and Mr Domanski's uncharacteristic quietness, it was a good day out and the sun was, in fact, heading for the horizon by the time they all started for home. Bella had met a boy by the drinking fountain, an Italian boy she had seen at the Rec Center but had never talked to, and so she had spent most of the afternoon lying coolly on the grass, not looking at him.

'He's smiling at you, Bella,' Lena had hissed. 'I think he wants to come talk to you.'

'I said *don't look*,' said Bella. She spoke fiercely with her face shoved into the wintry grass, but Lena could see a small secret smile on her mouth. When they got up to go and the boy had mooched off in the opposite direction, Bella strode out ahead looking pleased with herself.

'What's he called?' asked Lena, running to keep up. 'That boy?'

'Oh, some wop name,' said Bella off-handedly.

'Bella, please,' said Mr Domanski reprovingly. 'I do not like those terms.'

'His name is Jay,' said Bella. She walked on faster, with great springing steps.

'Wait up, would you,' complained Davey. He was bouncing his ball as he walked, one bounce to every step, which made him even slower than usual. All the way home he brought up the rear, several lamp posts behind striding Bella and running Lena and bumbling Mr Domanski.

As they arrived at the door of the house, the street lights came on. 'Make a wish,' said Bella, stepping aside for Mr Domanski to unlock the door.

'I wish—' said Lena. But there was too much to say.

'I know what I wish for,' said Bella, shutting her eyes tight for a moment and stumbling over the mat.

'My wish is that Ma will have made us *hundreds* and *thousands* of donuts,' said Davey greedily. And then they were in the room.

The *paczki* were there all right, lying on a tray in pasty splendour, lightly snowed over with flour. Beside them on the bench stood the sunflower oil and the salt and the sugar, all in a neat row. But the kitchen was empty.

'Maaa?' bellowed Bella hungrily.

A meat loaf sat browning in the oven and the table was laid. It was like a scene from the mystery of the *Marie Celeste*: no sign of life, and the ship's captain nowhere to be seen.

'Maybe she has stepped out to see Uncle Larry,' said Mr Domanski doubtfully. Lena felt equally doubtful, remembering the look on Mrs Domanski's face as she had sat amidst the ruins of plaster cupids. It had reminded her of the way their cat had looked, lying dead but whole in the road after being hit by a delivery truck: slightly aggrieved, slightly surprised, mortally wounded. ('A waste,' Bella now said about the cat, with taxidermist's hindsight.)

The meat loaf browned and then blackened in its dish. Still they sat and waited, and then Mr Domanski lost patience. 'We will eat,' he said. 'We are as hungry as hunters after our big day.' He carved the loaf and shining rounds of egg fell cleanly onto the plates. 'Eat, drink, and loosen your belt!' he said, pouring himself a tiny measure of vodka to celebrate not only Epiphany but the fact that he was home with his family instead of at The Sausage.

'Now say that in Polish,' said Bella shrewdly.

'Oh, piffle!' said Mr Domanski, looking flustered. 'I would not fill your heads with such rubbish.'

Bella gave him a sly look. '*Jedzcie, pijcie,*' she began, before remembering that she had no interest whatsoever in returning to her cold Polish roots. She shovelled a large mouthful of meat loaf into her mouth and began chewing vigorously.

Lena ate the roasted onions and the potatoes from around the side of the dish. She could detect but tried to ignore the taste of beef and pork fat. Every now and then she glanced longingly over at the far better second course: the fat round circles of yeasty dough, ready to be cooked, still rising.

'Could you fetch some water, Lena?' asked Mr Domanski. 'A

jug for the table, please.' Although he bossed Bella around and often overlooked Davey, he was unfailingly polite to Lena: she was, after all, his star attraction.

Lena wiped the onion grease away from her mouth and went to the kitchen. Her foot skidded on the linoleum, she fell against the bench, and her elbow caught the baking tray. Donuts leapt through the air like flying saucers: some fell to the floor and promptly sank.

'Elephant feet!' said Bella from the dining table.

'I slipped,' said Lena with dignity. 'I was not *clumsy*.' She bent to pick up the donuts, and also the piece of paper that had made her slip in the first place. 'It's a note from Ma,' she said. And as she looked at the handwriting she began to shake, so much that she had to sit down on the floor amongst the fallen donuts.

'What is it?' said Mr Domanski sharply. He came over and snatched the note out of Lena's hand, not politely at all. For a minute there was complete silence in the room: the only sounds were the bright hum of the fluorescent light, and Bella's stomach giving a loud gurgle. Then Mr Domanski went back to his chair and sat down, so heavily that it seemed as if he weighed twice as much as usual, and the chair cracked underneath him.

'Where's Ma?' said Bella. 'What does she say?'

'She has gone,' said Mr Domanski simply. He picked up a discarded crust of bread and mechanically began to chase the stray breadcrumbs around his plate. Neatly, he shovelled up the crumbs and the grease and placed them in his mouth.

'Gone?' said Bella with alarm in her voice. 'Gone where?'

'She has returned to Poland,' said Mr Domanski. Although his teeth were covered with parsley, he retained a strange dignity. 'It is Our fault,' he said, as if he were royalty. 'We have not made her happy.' Without another word he left the room and they heard the front door bang.

Bella began to cry, Davey kicked the table leg repeatedly with his foot, and Lena sat completely still on the floor. She pressed her back against the kitchen cupboard which was where she last remembered her mother. The flat hardness against her shoulder blades helped a little.

'She might come back,' she offered. 'If we wrote to her.'

No one spoke. The rhythmic banging of Davey's foot continued. Tiredly, Lena got to her feet and gathered the donuts up off the floor. There was no dust on them, no hairs or specks, and this was hardly surprising as the floor had probably been cleaned several times that day. Yes, the donuts were pristine but they had lost their lightness.

'What next?' said Lena to herself. What was the right thing to do, she wondered, when your mother had left the dinner in the oven and gone to Poland?

'Oh, oh, how could she?' wailed Bella, though it was unclear whether she was more horrified at the loss of Mrs Domanski or at the thought that anyone would voluntarily return to Warsaw.

'I will cook the *paczki*,' decided Lena, and very carefully she poured the oil into a deep frying pan and heated it on the front element. As Bella fretted and Davey kicked, Lena let a small drop of water fall into the pan and watched it leap and hiss.

'Who will get the coin, I wonder?' she said aloud, as she lowered the donuts one by one into the oil. 'Who is the lucky person who will get the prize?'

She fished the donuts out of the pan and drained them on newspaper. They were flat like river stones and lay heavy in her hands, but she took them to the table anyway.

'Eat,' she urged. 'Eat to keep your strength up.'

Bella stopped crying and Davey's feet became still, and the three of them sat quietly around the table, munching dutifully. Outside, the fog licked at the windows with a long grey lizard's tongue and suddenly—

'I have the coin!' said Davey, and he spat it into his hand.

'But so do I!' said Bella, and a dime dropped from her mouth like the girl in the fairytale who spoke in diamonds and toads instead of words. And as they ate their way through that plate of Epiphany donuts, they discovered there was a coin in every single one of them. It was as if their mother, feeling guilty at leaving them, had decided to bestow parting gifts on each and every eater.

'The change from her airline ticket, no doubt,' said Bella wryly. 'How kind.' Clearly she was already on the road to recovery.

Lena ate stolidly on. The fleshy dough in her mouth was a kind of comfort, though it was tinged through with the blood-taste of metal. 'We'll keep one for Da,' she said, and she put the last donut aside on a paper napkin with a longing look.

Just as they were clearing the table, Mr Domanski returned. He blew into the room, hung about with the chilly breath of the fog, full of recriminations at himself and at Mrs Domanski, and at Uncle Larry whose money had funded the airline ticket for the escape.

'He said he thought it was for rent payments,' he said, spinning indignantly in the middle of the room like a top. 'As if I would let my wife borrow money to pay our bills!' But there was a lightness in his voice that seemed odd in view of the fairly dire circumstances. Perhaps he was relieved that Uncle Larry had turned out to be behind a shop counter in the heart of San Francisco rather than on a plane heading for Central Europe?

'She will change her mind,' said Mr Domanski. 'When she sees the state of Polska, oh yes, she will come back.'

But as the New Year took hold and the days stacked up into months, Mrs Domanski sent letters but no hint that she would return. In spite of Mr Domanski's predictions, Warsaw seemed to agree with her: she was staying with her cousins, and looking for work, and there was more animation in just one of her Polish postcards than there had been in a whole day of her Tenderloin conversation.

'I would like Lena to come and stay with me,' she wrote. 'When I have earned enough money I will send a ticket.' In the mean-time, though, she sent a photo and sometimes when Mr Domanski was at work Lena pulled this photo out from the kitchen drawer and studied it closely. Behind her mother's smiling face were some blurry trees that looked nothing at all like Californian palm trees, and over her mother's left shoulder was an old stone church looking very different from St Boniface's. As Lena put the photo away, she couldn't help giving a defeated sigh. She would never go to Poland now: she had wanted to *discover*, not to follow.

And so it was that, by the time Lena reached the age of eight, the Domanski family had been depleted by a whole twenty per cent. After Mrs Domanski's departure some white hairs grew above Mr Domanski's ears, and sometimes one of the children would cry at night. But gradually the thin gap left in their ranks closed up and over, and life went on.

The kitchen always seemed empty after that, but the living room became newly chaotic. It filled up with tinfoil satellite models and the stiff dead carcasses of lambs, and nothing ever got cleared away. Mr Domanski put in even longer hours at The Sausage, although sometimes he would bring the books home with him so he could spend quality time with his family.

'Expansion,' he said to Lena, gesturing to the piles of curling yellow accounts. 'For a country it is not always a good thing, but for a small business there is nothing better.'

Looking back on it, Lena thought this was when her childhood proper dwindled to an end – if, in fact, she had ever really had one. For although so small at birth that she slept the first three months in a cereal box, she had also been born as old as the hills. And she always took her responsibilities seriously.

So there goes Bella, hunched over a pile of feathers and bones. There is Davey scratching at the heads of matchsticks, and Mr Domanski sighing over his mountains of bills. And in the middle of it all is the tiny figure of Lena, trying against all odds to be funny.

2

In the time it takes for the bullet from a .38-calibre Colt Python to raze neatly through her ear, Lena McLeonard sees her present. She thinks fleetingly of her past, it flies through her head in a jumbled second (something about fireworks, something about fog, something about dead birds and a kitchen floor). And then, because this second may well be one of her last, Lena McLeonard sees her present in its entirety.

She has been shot

She has moved away from the city of her childhood, from San Francisco, refuge of the hip and the homeless. And she has relocated not so very far down the coast to a dry and dusty city, a vast city, a city that sprawls in the shadow of the great white sign on the hill. Yes, she lives in Los Angeles, City of the Stars, which is just as it should be because she, Lena McLeonard, is firmly entrenched in the professional world of show business and has been for many years now.

But she has been shot

She – that is Lena McLeonard – is an adult, with an adult relationship and an established (albeit comedic) career. She cohabits with her manager, Jay Antonelli, who is also her lover, who also happens to be the boy eyed up by her sister Bella beside a drinking fountain in the cold sunny environs of a San Francisco park, on the very same day that Lena's mother flew away to Poland and never came back again.

She has been shot, she has been shot!

She has changed her last name. She is no longer Lena Domanski, she is Lena McLeonard, and she lives with Jay Antonelli (her roommate, her bedmate, her sister's ex-boyfriend) in the City of Angels, where the sound of gunfire is as common as the clatter of garbage cans and the Santa Anas blow down from the eastern mountains and the grit swirls in the hot and shameless air. And she thinks she is happy here, though at times she misses the shadows of San Francisco Past.

And her ear shatters

She has been shot in San Francisco, though her home is in Venice Beach, in the City of Los Angeles, in the state of California. She has been shot here in the Tenderloin, the district of her childhood, the most dangerous district of a safe city where she has always felt immune. This is Lena McLeonard, here she is, shot in the head in San Francisco Present in the middle of spring.

and the bullet hisses and a window explodes and the blood soars

She is a good comedian with good red shoes, she is heading for the donut shop but is about to fall. She is a good comedian who over the past two decades has learnt many things, but not necessarily how to survive a shooting and so she will fall.

She has practised timing but has known it since birth, she has perfected routines until she could perform them standing on her head, she can grab comments thrown from the dark and juggle them like oranges, she has learnt all these things

and the blood falls

she has learnt to be contemporary and relevant and professional
and funny

and the bullet sings and the afternoon shines and the sun is red

and now (she thinks with startling clarity)

she might have to learn

to be dead.

3

In the time it takes for Lena McLeonard to see the perfect donut
and be shot in the head, she anticipates her future. She realizes,
in that small whining second, all that is wrong with her career.
Mainly, that she has never found comedy funny.

After a part of her ear is embedded along with the bullet at
ankle height in the wall behind Tam Walker's counter, Lena falls
to the ground. She staggers left and right, she clutches at her
head, and then she topples on to the sidewalk like a drunk collaps-
ing on a subway platform under the weight of too many whiskies.
She might have learnt from this moment of clumsy grace had
she pursued the art of slapstick, were she still in the habit of
running around with her arse on fire to amuse the public. But
long before this she has been pushed into another sort of comedy:
by Mr Domanski, by Jay Antonelli, by the need to make a living.

Perhaps life is not to be laughed at? thinks Lena McLeonard
now, as she lies on the sidewalk compressing her future and
waiting to die. Or perhaps (she thinks as she lies there, minus an
ear but within reach of the best chocolate donuts in town), perhaps
it is one monumental joke?

Jay would have no doubts on the issue. Always, unequivocally,
he has regarded life as a comedy mine, has dug assiduously into
its depths to come up with gems for Lena. Yes, from the moment
he took Lena on (as girlfriend, client, and potential winner) Jay
has been deadly serious about comedy.

'You'll have to change your name, you know,' he says, when it becomes clear that a sparkling career in stand-up can no longer be avoided.

'I've already changed cities,' says Lena, though this is not a change she has minded so much: there is a certain novelty about living in a place where oranges hang heavily on patios in the middle of winter. But the decision to give up the Domanski title seems an altogether more significant thing.

'Domanski's no good for show biz, honey,' says Jay practically. 'It's a newcomer's name.'

'But everyone's a newcomer,' objects Lena. 'Relatively speaking.' This is one of Lena's favourite sayings, she has picked it up and made it her own just as most people pocket a phrase or two in their way through life. *Relatively speaking.* It is a good phrase for Lena because she has carried this ability with her since she was a child: an ability to see things balanced and to see them whole.

About the newcomer issue – she is right, of course. A third- or fourth-generation Los Angeles resident is as rare as the tooth of a hen. Since Lena has moved to the suburb of Venice Beach and moved in with Jay, she has met all kinds of people. She has chatted to bag ladies and tramps, has seen the sons of Presidents weeping on stoops and the chairmen of multinational corporations roller-blading into trees. The boardwalk in front of her apartment throngs with familiar and unfamiliar faces, and everyone speaks to everyone else because here there is a looseness in the air. But although many of these people have lived in Los Angeles for ten or fifteen or twenty years, in high-rises with pools or on a park bench – well, not one of them has ever spoken of the city as home.

'Relatively speaking,' Lena says again, 'I belong as much as the next person.' Although she states this strongly in a spray of organic bagel crumbs, she is not sure if she completely believes it. Poland and her mother have often been felt tugging at her sleeve, and sometimes her pale skin flinches away from too much Californian sun. But she feels she has a point to make.

Jay doesn't listen to her reasoning, relative or otherwise. Because he has lived with Lena for almost ten years, her phrase has no impact anymore, no *punch*. In this Jay and Lena are not unusual; there are quite possibly hundreds and thousands of couples who talk over breakfast every morning only to see their words melt away unnoticed like brown sugar into oatmeal.

'People want American glamour,' asserts Jay. 'It's not enough to be a star, you've gotta be an All-Star.' His large fingers tap away at the keyboard of the computer, churning out sample Lenas for promotional purposes.

Lena has a strange and sudden urge to preserve her tenuous link to Poland, in spite of the fact that the country has only ever had a negative effect on her life. Putting a permanent chip on her sister's shoulder, driving her father to become the Marin County Small Businessman of the Year, not to mention stealing her mother away so early in life! Reaching out and reclaiming Mrs Domanski – yes, that was pretty bad. Seducing Mrs D so thoroughly over a number of years that she never has made it back to San Francisco: swallowing her whole into a newly commercial Polish world. (In recent photos Mrs Domanski's hair is jet black once more, and her lips are brightly painted. 'I am helping Poles feel good about themselves,' she writes, as if her work is in international relations rather than for a Warsaw cosmetics company. 'I am allowed to take home free eye-shadow samples,' she writes. It is obvious that she feels equally good about both these things.)

In spite of all this, in spite of Mr Domanski's comments on its declining morality and rising crime rate, in spite of being insulted by Bella and ignored by Davey and avoided by Lena, now Poland lays its head on Lena's shoulder and speaks to her in a meek and milky voice. *Don't give up on me*, it says. So that when Lena replies to Jay's suggestion there is a sudden unevenness to her voice, as if it is being lifted at the edges by a Baltic breeze.

'Well, what about your own name?' says Lena Domanski to Jay Antonelli, attacking as she has been attacked. 'Your own name doesn't sound as if it's straight off the Mayflower,' she says.

'This is true, honey,' says Jay thoughtfully. His large shoulders, which will almost certainly run to fat if he ever stops lifting weights, rise in a shrug. 'But at least Antonelli *sounds* glitzy,' he says. 'It sounds LA, if ya know what I mean. While Domanski on the other hand, well, Domanski sounds kind of Eastern Blockish. Kind of Tenderloin.' He pauses. 'No offence, honey,' he adds.

This is Jay's favoured phrase and he uses it often: *no offence*. A truth lies at the heart of it: he never does want to cause offence, whether he is criticizing your ancestry or the levels of your mike. And so Lena submits – without offence, and with a sigh – and Poland also sighs and walks away with its head hanging to take its usual back seat in Lena's family history.

'Here,' says Jay generously, offering up a random volume of the phonebook to Lena. 'Pick.'

Lena opens the book and points with closed eyes, with a pencil.

'McLeonard!' approves Jay. 'That's a fine choice. Very American.' And he sets the paperwork in motion and Lena finds herself one reluctant inch further along the road to a professional comedy career, one step closer towards establishing a profession out of something she has only ever considered a diversion at best.

'McLeonard!' says Bella scathingly, when she hears what Lena has been persuaded into. 'Hoots, mon. Are you going to do your routines in a Scottish burr from now on?' But then Bella is always scathing, to various degrees, when it comes to Jay. For of course Jay was once Bella's before he was Lena's, and separation from someone can sharpen the eye to a razor's edge.

Occasionally Jay refers to that long-ago day when, in the cold San Francisco sunshine, he bounced his basketball beside a drinking fountain on the edge of a park and was marked out by Bella.

'I remember it clear as day,' he admits to Lena, one Sunday night after they have spent an uncomfortable weekend visiting Bella in San Francisco and are driving somewhat uncomfortably home. 'She had this coon tail hanging at her belt,' he says, 'like a girl version of Davey Crockett. I thought she was kinda weird.'

'But you ended up dating her,' points out Lena, with a hint of accusation in her voice. There are certain things she loves about Jay: the way he carries a shovel in the trunk of his car so he can bury other people's roadkill on the side of the highway; the way he rips into sleep, a snore revving in his throat like a stunt man gunning for the barrier between consciousness and dreaming. But there is the odd moment when Lena cannot forgive him, first for being attracted to Bella and then for rejecting her. At these moments she feels both jealous and protective of Bella, and so she must move a little away from Jay, shuffling her body towards the car door.

'I did ask her out,' confesses Jay. 'I most certainly did, I admit it. I couldn't get my head around the dead animal thing, that's the truth of it.' He looks over at Lena, sitting in the passenger seat with the shadows of pylons marching over her face. Her small nose is pressed against the vibrating window and she looks as though at any moment she will jump from the car and roll away like tumbleweed into the uncomplicated desert. 'Besides—' he says.

'Besides, what?' says Lena nasally. The vibrations from the window run up one nostril and out the other, and in spite of her conflicted feelings she begins to laugh.

'Well, I kinda liked the little quiet one,' says Jay. He takes one of his sausage hands off the wheel to stroke Lena's face but, because of his clumsiness and the movement of the car, his finger almost ends up in her left nostril. Lena laughs and sighs, and sighs again. Managed, that's what she is. Jay does not understand her, but he knows how to manage her.

The rabbit

It had not really been a case of Jay jumping ship from the large and beautiful Bella to small Lena chugging quietly in her sister's wake. In fact it was years after the drinking fountain episode that Jay and Lena had set eyes on each other again – years after those odd dinners in the Domanskis' front and only room, when Bella was uncharacteristically demure and had cleared plates from the table without being asked, and Mr Domanski had warmed to Jay and offered him the ultimate token of acceptance (a shot glass of top-quality schnapps). After a couple of months Jay had sloped off into the sunset behind the Rec Center and had never called again, but before that who knew how far he and Bella had gone? Lena had always been hesitant to ask whether her boyfriend had ever had sex with her older sister, although sometimes at the height of orgasm, with her back arching and Jay shuddering inside her, she felt like crying out: *and have you been inside my Bella too?*

There was one Tenderloin night in particular (though this is another thing she has never discussed with Jay, even as she lies in the curve of his armpit and inhales the satisfied smell of his post-coital Marlboro). It was the night when Mr Domanski had gone to bed exhausted from the opening of a second Polish Sausage on Columbus Avenue, and Bella had smuggled Jay into the bedroom. No lights had been switched on and Jay had only stayed an hour or so, but to Lena it had seemed like an eternity. Lying in the dark, she had squinted over at Bella's bed through slit eyelids, at a heaving mass of sheets and blankets. Soon she had put her pillow over her head and pulled up her own blankets so that she, too, was a sheet monster in a lumpy bed. Even so she could hear more than she wanted to: laughing and groaning, and then what she thought – what she hopes – was Bella saying she didn't want to, and that Jay had gone far enough. And this last memory is what Lena clings to when she sees the sometime-look on Bella's face, as Bella looks at her younger sister, the Comedian, and at her own ex-boyfriend (now the Comedian's live-in manager) and tries to be positive about their relationship.

'It's not a problem,' says Bella, when Lena broaches the subject. 'So maybe I was hurt when I first heard.' She lights a cigarette. 'More amazed than hurt, really,' she says. 'I mean, you're quite attractive, but Jay – well, he's hardly a pinup.' Bella is often mean when wounded. She is like one of her own stuffed animals come to life, a fox or a ferret that, although it has been caught and cornered and might even have a mangled paw, still flies at its trapper with a snarl.

'Jay's OK,' says Lena mildly. 'Maybe a little overweight.' She glances at Bella's husband Ken who is sitting reading the *Wall Street Journal* under the raised paw of Bella's prize grizzly. As Lena watches he folds a just-finished page into a small tidy square and places it in a metal clip; by the time he reaches the sports section, the day's news will be compacted into a neat wad the size of a pack of playing cards.

Bella sees where Lena is looking. 'Oh, I *know*,' she says, and she puffs a mouthful of smoke over Lena. 'I *know!*' She raises eyebrows at her small pedantic tax-officer of a husband, whose moustache is so rigorously tended that it is clipped almost to extinction, and then she and Lena shriek with laughter. Bella is redeemed by her objectivity: after she has blown hurt and scorn out of her like a testy volcano, she is more clear-sighted than anyone else Lena knows.

'Jay can do good things for you, honey,' she says to Lena, suddenly turning kind. 'He can make you a star. Whereas me?' she says. 'Well, I'm better off getting tax breaks.'

Perhaps it had been professional interest that made Jay notice Lena again all those years after their first meeting, in the middle of the Tenderloin Street Festival. Though he says it was personal, that Lena's small quiet face had stuck in his memory.

'One look,' he says, 'and you jumped right back into my mind again.'

Lena had been persuaded into performing at the festival by a group of puppeteers who wanted to stage a rap routine. 'You're a veteran already, Lena!' they cried with enthusiasm. 'You've gotta help us out!' And although Lena felt almost constantly tired at that time, having seen Bella through an abortion and her father through the opening of a third restaurant, and having heard that very week that her mother had been appointed CEO of the Pretty Poles Cosmetic Company – well, she firmly believed in taking theatre on to the street. Besides, the puppeteers were right, she was experienced; for she had now been on stage once a week, every week, for over a decade.

'You were eighteen when I saw you again,' says Jay. 'When I spotted you as Rapper Rabbit.'

'I felt like sixty,' says Lena, feeling again the weight of the rabbit head that had almost made her sink to her knees.

'You stood out a mile!' says Jay who, at that time, had been a professional organizer of street parades. 'You were great,' he says, with reminiscent admiration.

'I was all right,' corrects Lena. Although her memory is often erratic, although it stacks away images randomly like a hoarder with a large attic, when it comes to her performances she remembers each and every one. For when Lena steps in front of an audience, her eyes become sharper and her hearing more acute, and her sense of the ridiculous heightened.

'When I saw your face under those floppy ears—' says Jay.

'With my eyes in slits because the headdress was so tight,' says Lena.

'All I noticed,' finishes Jay, 'was that it was little Lena Domanski, and she was still cute.'

And what exactly had Lena noticed as she had jumped down from the platform with her cotton tail bobbing behind her, and had spotted Jay Antonelli emerging from the crowds? What had she seen in the palm of Jay's big hand, outstretched to grasp her paw? Perhaps, for a second, she had seen herself as she used to be, in the days when Mr Domanski still considered her small enough to come home for, and Mrs Domanski still promised to return to them with a purse full of Polish currency.

'I knew right away that I could make you a star,' says Jay solemnly.

Lena is in no way a star, though Jay quite possibly considers her one, and Mr Domanski and many of her other non-related fans are adamant that this is so. She is in no way a star, although she has played the Red Salon on Sunset and has had gigs at the Comedy Store, treading the same boards as luminaries such as Robin Williams and Whoopi Goldberg. But then Jay and her father have always reached for the lowest apple on the tree, whereas Lena looks away up into the dazzle of a never-ending sky and knows. Even before her acquaintance with a bullet, she has realized she will never reach the tiny shiny apple of perfection at the top of the tree. Who ever does? And so she has remained slightly detached, slightly indifferent, and less than serious about the whole strange phenomenon that is comedy.

Pick-up

By the time the ambulance men arrive, blood is seeping around Lena's head. She has an awareness of the movement of that blood, imagines it spreading under her hair like a bright pillow.

'A cushion of concrete,' she murmurs.

The men pick her up, carefully, and they ask her about medical insurance (for they are as careful of their jobs as they are of the shot and the wounded). Then they load her into the back of the van. 'Don't try and talk, lady,' one of them says. 'Looks like it's just your ear but it could be more.'

'My ear,' says Lena vaguely. 'My pillow of air.'

'You want air?' the men ask her, and they connect her to an oxygen tank. 'You want a pillow?' they say, and they lay her head down with its ragged side to the roof. Before they start to bandage Lena hears the siren shrieking, but by the time they are rushing through the mean streets of her childhood she cannot hear anything at all except the whoosh of her pulse.

Jay is called and is sufficiently concerned to leave a very important talent-spotting session in LA and rush up the coast to her bedside.

'But why were you in the Tenderloin, honey?' he says perplexedly. 'Why were you here in San Francisco?' The hospital chair is too small for him, his bottom is wedged between the metal tubes and his thighs bulge out the sides.

'I wanted to check out a stage,' says Lena. She barely moves her lips but still her bandaged head hurts. 'I wanted to have a show for old time's sake,' she says in a tiny voice. 'For charity.'

'For *charity*?' Jay is astonished. His large hands, spread wide, create shadow wings on the bright linoleum. 'But we're not in the business of charity, Lena,' he says. If it were not for the fact that Lena has been recently shot, it is likely that he would be far more direct with her, even annoyed; and Lena feels momentarily grateful to the gun-toting guy in the black car who has made her into a vulnerable person, one not to be shouted at.

'Clara's Ballhaus,' she explains. 'The creditors want to close it down.'

'Clara's Ballhaus?' says Jay. He stands up and his head bangs the fluorescent light, setting it swaying wildly. Lena begins to feel nauseous, in spite of all the drugs that have been pumped into her to avoid exactly this.

'Clara's Ballhaus?' says Jay again, sounding just like the

93

outraged Bella on that long-ago night when Mrs Domanski first went dancing. 'That old dump on Golden Gate Avenue?' he says, pacing back and forwards on Lena's tiny curtained-off piece of floor.

Lena feels even worse. 'I need rest,' she says, and it seems that, even as she considers ditching her career, her timing remains spot on. For as if on cue the anorexic nurse with the fiery red hair appears and comes to Lena's rescue.

'Visiting hours are over,' says the nurse, pulling the curtains back with a stick arm and exposing Jay and Lena to the rest of the ward. 'Kiss her goodnight now,' she orders.

Jay does so and his lips feel far too wet on Lena's cheek. They remind her of slimy blood, and the remains of her ear slipping down the side of her face. 'I think I'm going to throw up,' she says, and she does, all over the side of the bed and into her water jug.

'Try to give me some warning next time,' says the nurse in a scathing voice. She has her own problems to deal with: the gnawing in the pit of her stomach, the persistent seduction of meal trays and of chocolates stowed in bedside cabinets. She has no sympathy for someone who has to deal with straightforward physical pain, even with the possibility of a skin graft in the days to follow.

'I'm sorry,' says Lena faintly.

The Pope

Sometimes Lena thinks she has spent her life apologizing, though usually for other people rather than herself. In the days when Jay was taking control of her stand-up career, he and Mr Domanski had often fallen out and Lena found herself defending her father even when she didn't entirely agree with him.

'You've gotta get away from those terrible jokes your father likes,' Jay would say critically. He and Lena often sat in the original Polish Sausage in the long Tenderloin afternoons, discussing possible routes to success. Mr Domanski, on the other hand, was already successful, whatever Jay might think of his sense of humour. But his particular success was not measured by cheering crowds, nor by glowing reviews in entertainment magazines; it had taken on the shape of no fewer than five Polish Sausages, including one with sea views in Bodega Bay and one with vinyl upholstery in the glossy neighbourhood of Nob Hill.

'Those Mr Domanski jokes!' said Jay, rolling his eyes.

'You mean the ones about the Polish cars,' said Lena with a sigh. 'And the Pope.'

'Those are exactly what I mean,' said Jay, biting his bottom lip with teeth that were as big as a horse's and slightly stained with nicotine. Considering that he and Lena were sitting in the place where Lena's career had begun, where her father had lain prostrate in a drape in front of a roaring crowd, any criticism of Mr D seemed like treachery. But still Lena waited to hear Jay's suggestion.

'You need to come across as brainier,' he pronounced. 'A little more *cele-bral*.'

Much as Lena liked this word with its overtones of festive days and of colourful plates dusted with powdered sugar, she felt dutybound to correct Jay. 'I think you mean cerebral,' she said tentatively.

'You *see*!' said Jay. 'You really are smart! You know more than me, and I'm your manager!'

Now it was Lena's turn to bite her lip, and she did so because Jay's managerial status was still a sore point with Mr Domanski. It was true that her father still pressured her to trot out old jokes about Polish institutions like the Maluch car, which one in a hundred audiences might understand. For better or for worse, though, it was her father and not her manager who had first shunted her onto the conveyer belt to fame.

'I'm sorry, Jay,' she began. 'But—'

Mr Domanski burst in through the restaurant doors. For a moment he stood framed against the bright white day like a handsome cowboy, but once the doors had swung shut behind him and the room had regained its dimness, he was simply a large man with iron grey hair and dubious taste in jokes who had nearly let his wife die of homesickness.

'Lena, my Pie!' he beamed, and he came over and pulled up a chair. 'I have been seeking on the Internet,' he said, 'and I have come up with a whole stable of new jokes for you! Just wait until you hear them.'

Jay stiffened in his chair. It was possible that his habitual uneasiness around Mr Domanski stemmed partly from the fact that he had come close to penetrating a teenage Bella, with only a thin wall between Bella's father and himself. But now there was even more at stake: now Mr Domanski and Jay were like professional rivals, like coaches wanting gold for the same athlete but holding vastly different ideas on training.

'Da,' began Lena, 'I don't—'

'Have a listen to this!' said Mr Domanski, and he pulled a crumpled piece of paper from his equally crumpled jacket.

Lena sighed. For some reason when she was around Jay and Mr Domanski, she never seemed able to finish what she wanted to say. Yet how could she resent this when they were the two men she had chosen to love?

'Here I go,' said Mr Domanski, and he tapped at his Adam's apple as if it were a microphone. He cleared his throat. 'Why is the Maluch blessed by the Pope?' he asked.

Lena stole a look at Jay. His face was set and she gave a tiny inward flinch. But—

'Why?' she said, obligingly, against her will.

'Because it is so small—' said Mr Domanski, but he couldn't finish, and he began to slap his thigh and gasp with laughter. 'Because—' he spluttered, 'because—'

'Because it's so small you can't have sex in it?' said Jay calmly.

Mr Domanski's laughter stopped. 'You knew it already?' he asked, looking crestfallen.

'I guessed it,' said Jay.

Lena laid her head down on the scratched formica table. She looked along the wavy lines scored by someone's long-ago fork and they seemed to stretch into infinity.

'First, you see,' said Jay, 'you would have to explain to the audience that the Maluch is a type of Polish car.' His voice was loud but patient; he never let himself forget that this was the man who had fathered the woman he loved, the man who had impregnated an unwilling Mrs Domanski to produce the talented, drooping comedian in front of him now.

'Explain the Maluch? Piffle!' said Mr Domanski. 'I could do that in my introduction. That is not a problem.'

'No offence, Mr D,' said Jay, 'but intros are a waste of time. Besides, one-liners are on their way out. Think Pogo, think Kosta the Greek, think Nutty McNasty!'

'Think who?' asked Mr Domanski. His voice, so robust on arrival, was becoming thin and plaintive like gravy strained through a fine-mesh sieve.

'You've gotta be more celebral these days,' said Jay with authority.

'Cerebral,' said Lena, raising her tired head off the table.

'You see?' said Jay triumphantly. 'Lena agrees with me.'

Lena was no longer sure whom she disagreed with more. But being cursed with an innate politeness she kept her mouth shut and simply hoped that one day she might get to finish a sentence.

Speed

The skin graft happens. Because of Clara's Ballhaus, because of the long-reaching arms of the past and the retrospective nature of responsibility, Lena is transported to a medical centre in Los Angeles where she will have skin removed from her inner thigh and sewn to her head. The thought is disturbing: a fusing of epidermal layers never intended to meet. But then the very way in which she had been born – her mother's belly sliced open and herself lifted out like a slippery oyster removed too soon from the darkness – well, that had not been exactly natural either.

'It could be worse,' says the surgeon who has been assigned to her case. 'The ear isn't all that important. Not the external cartilage part of the ear.'

Lena would like to disagree. She thinks of all the other body parts that could be parted with far more readily. What about the spleen, only making its presence felt when it ruptures and floods the body with muddy fluid? What about the appendix, that useless organ that could easily be left out at the early stringing together of the chromosomes? Who wants their appendix? Who wants their tonsils? Lena lies in bed and mentally auctions off body parts.

But the ear! The most valuable ear, which is able to pull off magical tricks, can offer the sea through the cup of a shell. The ear, which can draw sound from the deepest silence, can detect unease under confidence and infidelity in a husband's whisper. Who could possibly believe the surgeon when he says that any part of the mysterious, wonderful ear is disposable? Lena cannot, but she has no time to state her disbelief. The surgeon is busy, he is a small and busy man, and his mind has already rushed on to other things.

'What will it look like?' Lena asks him instead. 'Afterwards?'

For a straightforward man, the surgeon looks strangely shifty. 'Oh, don't worry about that yet,' he says. 'We've got a lot of ground to cover first.'

'You're lucky they can use your own skin,' says the woman in the bed next to Lena. This woman has been waiting weeks for a skin graft, while all the time the walnut-coloured cancer creeps slowly down her neck. 'I'm on a low-priority list,' she says. 'That's the problem with living in fucking California.'

'What is?' asks Lena. Random gunfire is a problem, she thinks. Pollution is a problem, and police corruption, and the way that the city steals water away from the desert flowers. But she doesn't think that the woman in the next bed is particularly concerned about any of these as she lies there wilting in the tepid hospital air.

'What's the problem with California?' asks Lena again, politely.

'Not enough skin to go around,' says the woman in a voice rough and scratchy with resentment. 'Too many fucking movie stars wanting new fucking faces.'

Lena listens until the woman falls silent, and then she turns her head on the pillow, away from problems of the state towards her own. What are they? First, she is already tired of hearing how fortunate she has been: an assertion pushed at her daily by doctors and therapists and priests, and by those odd emotion-specialists determined to restore people to happiness even when those people have lost significant parts of their bodies like toes or penises or hands. (However many times you might be told you are lucky, the telling does not automatically bring belief.)

The second problem looming over Lena is that her head is still bandaged, still wrapped around and around like an Egyptian mummy, and this makes her uneasy. She has never liked lurking in the wings, would always rather get out on stage and front up to an audience however cold, and now she would prefer to see whatever damage the bullet might have done to her.

(*how could you think I would hurt you*? protests the bullet in a wounded voice, as it is dug out of the wall of the donut-shop by the gloved hands of a forensics expert)

But Lena has been hurt. She has been physically hurt by the rushing silver bullet, and shortly she will undergo further pain all in the name of damage control.

'You won't feel a thing,' the surgeon assures her. He has come up to the ward to consult: that is he is here to spend a minute, or two at the most, talking to Lena (though soon he will spend hours bent over her inert body). 'Skin grafts happen every day round here,' he says. 'Piece of cake.'

'Do you think you could show me,' says Lena diffidently, 'where the skin will be taken from?'

'From your behind,' says the surgeon. Or does he say, 'From your behind?'

Lena assumes the question mark is there. 'No,' she says, giving an answer which may not have been asked for. 'No, you must take it from somewhere else.'

The surgeon looks slightly surprised. For how could he know that Lena's smooth buttocks are sacred, have never been smacked even in play or in sex? 'Fine with me,' he shrugs. 'It's easier for us to take the skin from your thigh anyway.'

'Us?' echoes Lena. She has no idea how many people will be swarming around her body: ants on an anthill, birds around a carcass still warm from a bullet in the head. But this query is one query too many for the surgeon. He is a small man, a quick and a skilled man, a man of action. Indeed, it is these traits that have attracted him in the first place to a world of sharp blades and snapping rubber gloves. He has not become the success he is today by being patient, and he is not about to lose his success because of one small Polish comedian lying in a questioning bed.

'I'll come and see you afterwards,' he says, sewing up the conversation neatly and quickly. He gives a nod: his head is small to match his body, and his short hair lies close to his scalp. With lightning fingers, he fills in a few figures on Lena's chart and is gone.

Lena expects to see him the following morning when she is wheeled into surgery, but instead there is only an anaesthetist in a pale green gown.

'You're late,' snaps the anaesthetist.

'Sorry,' says Lena. Her voice is slightly smudged from the pill they have given her to calm her nerves.

'Not you,' says the anaesthetist, and he smiles at her. Against the bright fluorescent ceiling he is both angelic and demonic: his hair sticks up in spikes, and his youthful skin looks good enough to touch. 'I was talking to the orderly,' he explains gently.

'Oh,' says Lena. Her eyelids droop in disappointment. There is a small part of her that would like to be reprimanded by this man with his firm yet tender hands. He is monitoring her weight and her well-being, after all, so why not her tendency towards tardiness?

'You weigh nothing,' he says. His hands take hold of her wrist, move the hospital bracelet gently up her arm. Is he about to slip a ring on her finger?

'What's your name?' slurs Lena, made bold by the unfamiliarity of the setting and the fact that she is no longer aware of her own feet. 'What are you called?' she says. But it seems that she has not spoken for no one turns to look at her, both the disorderly orderly and the calm seductive anaesthetist looking instead at the chart. Where has her voice gone? she wonders in drowsy alarm. Has it fallen on the floor, is it about to be trampled by the rushing buffalo feet of—

'Jay?' she says. Her voice has returned, though it sounds like a frog croak in that bright flickering pond of a room.

'I'm here!' booms Jay. 'I got caught in traffic!'

'Quietly now,' says the angel. 'We're about to go under.'

'You're coming too?' croaks Lena.

And then, with a quick thank you for not sending her alone into the river Lethe, Lena forgets. She forgets her CEO mother and her entrepreneurial father, forgets her bumbling bedside manager and the speeding black car and the smell of burning tyres and burnt flesh. She forgets that she doesn't have a one hundred per cent belief in what she is doing, that she has been feeling increasingly reluctant to extract the funniness from life and *get it down* in a little blue book.

Daughter, sister, girlfriend; funny woman, lover of donuts, and victim of a drive-by shooting. This is Lena McLeonard, leaving consciousness behind her and her body in the hands of the gods, the angel, and the short dancing surgeon.

The cat

Shortly after moving to Los Angeles and moving in with Jay, Lena had found a cat crouched on the median strip between life and death. There it was, perched on a barrier in the middle of the 405, and who knew how it had got all that way down a concrete bank, under a wire-netting fence and across four swarming lanes of traffic?

Lena McLeonard, having recently changed her last name, was still reeling from the task: from the seemingly unnecessary red tape, and the supposedly necessary paperwork.

'This is America, honey,' Jay had said practically. 'They wanna keep track of what happens to their citizens. It's only right.'

But who had kept track of this all-American cat with its hair ruffled up around its neck as if, not so long ago, a collar had been removed? Somebody had wanted this cat to go back into the melting pot but, fortunately, in the moment before it had dived in and was lost forever it had been spotted by Lena Domanski (still getting used to McLeonard) in her rear-vision mirror.

She had swerved onto the hard shoulder, had swerved to a halt and put on her hazard lights. She had got out of her car and run and dodged between many other cars and many long thundering trucks to get to that small shabby grey cat.

(*so you've faced death before, have you?* says the bullet in an interested voice, as it is loaded into a plastic bag and into the front seat of an unmarked police car. *So you know what death looks like?*)

She had picked up that cat, had Lena McLeonard, and then taken the same hazardous journey back to her car. For nights afterwards when she lay down to sleep she went hot all over with remembered fear, because even as she was doing it she had known that she could be killed.

'Shit, honey,' said Jay, disapprovingly. 'You could have been arrested.'

Much later, once her horror at running barefoot on the Interstate had subsided, Lena was able to work Jay's comment into a routine. But although she looked back on that day as her first real brush with danger, she needed only to see Mitchell's ears flick towards her to know that she had had no choice.

'*Mitchell?*' says Bella, though after sharing a bedroom with Lena for fifteen years she is never as surprised at Lena's actions as she likes to make out. 'What sort of a cat name is Mitchell, for God's sake?' she says.

'A purr-fect name,' says Lena, hamming up something she feels quite serious about.

Bella groans. 'It's a white trash name,' she says, and then she puts on a head teacher's voice. 'You can take the comedian out of the Tenderloin,' she intones, 'but you can never take the Tenderloin out of a comedian.'

In a way Bella is right, though not in the way she thinks. It probably is the Tenderloin, and its violent, extraordinary, razor-edge streets, that have made Lena think normality is not such a bad thing. Mitchell is about the most ordinary name she can think of and so she bestows it on her new grey cat, wishing calm for him, hoping he will forget the dangers of his past.

Yet in spite of her efforts Mitchell turns out to be slightly odd: completely loveable, but odd. Quickly, he becomes a well-known character in Venice Beach, and he blends in perfectly with all the other characters there – the chainsaw juggler, the old woman whose dachshund rides in a pram, and the musical Mexican who straps his guitar into a baby seat on the back of his bicycle. These people are naturally drawn to Mitchell, a cat whose favourite food is cucumber and who will regularly walk twenty long blocks to sit and look at the Santa Monica Pier. When one or other of these characters brings Mitchell home to the door of the apartment, Lena will invite them in for a beer or a glass of milk.

'Do you have to encourage them?' says Jay. 'Those people?' Taking off his jacket, he spreads the trappings of his respectability around the room: cellphone, tie, briefcase, shiny shoes. A boy from a bad hood made good.

But Lena suspects that, after his highway experience, Mitchell's nine lives must almost be up. So she continues to invite the juggler into her kitchen, where he deposits his chainsaw politely under the table and stays to share a salad bowl with Lena and Mitchell.

And after a while Lena begins to realize something. Normality is something that other families have, like Thanksgiving dinner or a regular Chinese Takeout Night. Whereas what does she have? She has a sister of startling beauty who is six foot two and stuffs dead animals for a living. She has a brother who has spent most of his adult life in a deserted hangar building satellites out of scrap metal. Her father: makes a living out of the cuisine of a country he professes to despise. Her mother: has made a small fortune out of false eyelashes.

Perhaps a renunciation of all that is ordinary is a good place to arrive at? thinks Lena. Perhaps then you are better equipped to deal with anything life might throw at you, one random day in a well-remembered street? For if you are born with a sweet tooth, say, or a particular instinct for danger – well, there is not always a lot you can do about it.

The bucket

Although hours of Lena's life are sliced away in surgery like meat from the bone, the professionals do a good job of splicing the loose ends together again. When she wakes in a narrow bed in the recovery ward she feels surprisingly healthy, although she is slightly concerned about what she might have said under the blue haze of the anaesthetic.

'Yes, you came out with some good material,' says Jay in a considering, managerial way. Being Jay, it is unlikely that he would joke about this.

He is allowed to take Lena home, after she has lain for twelve hours next to the woman who is being eaten up by basal cell carcinoma and resentment. He lifts her into the car, and then he lifts her out of it, and he carries her over the threshold of their apartment like a bride. Lena feels as if she could walk, for her leg has been bandaged into stiffness, but she lies unprotestingly on Jay's shoulder and stares at the side of his neck. There is a patch of stubble under his jaw that he has missed in his morning shave: perhaps he too has been worrying about Lena's now uncertain future?

The Venice Beach apartment shared by Jay and Lena is a restless kind of place. Ocean winds rush in off the balcony and get trapped inside: the air bangs around looking for an escape route, picks up the pages of magazines and flips them over. It has always been like this, but since Lena has been away the house has got out of control. Windows stand open and could have been open for days; curtains blow, paper blows. And on every surface the dirty dishes have gathered like flocks of birds.

'Do you feel like eating?' asks Jay doubtfully. 'Do you want something to eat?'

Yes, Lena does. She is ravenous, having eaten nothing good since well before the shooting, and never having had her vision of light, toothsome, chocolate-sprinkled donuts realized before being struck down in the street.

'Soup!' she says, and she slurps noodles from a takeout carton, tilting the box to get the last salty drops. 'And wontons!' she cries, crunching through the golden layers into steaming shredded cabbage. 'Vegetarian,' nods Jay. He sounds pleased with himself for remembering that she doesn't eat pork, even though he has lived with her for over nine years.

That night Lena wakes screaming. Her body, helped out by shock and pills and intravenous fluids, has held off the pain for as long as possible but suddenly it has become tired of being besieged. It opens its gates. *Here I am!* it calls in a defeated, yet proud voice. *Here I am!* it trumpets to the waiting hordes, and it gives itself up to memory.

The leg is the worst – that leg offered up so readily to save the smooth creamy expanse of Lena's left buttock. Her head, with its alien skin sewn tightly to its side, hardly hurts at all: and this is most ironic, for it is her head that was the troublemaker, that craved a light dusting of donut sugar on its mouth and so moseyed forth into the shining wasp-path of the bullet.

Since then that head has been pandered to, fussed over, made up to until now it sits almost smugly under its bandages. But her leg, that had been quietly enjoying its red vinyl point of contact with the pavement, had then been hit hard by that same pavement. It has been shovelled into a van, lugged about from hospital to hospital and city to city, and then defiled in a most unexpected manner. Drawn all over in purple pen, decorated with a thick-rimmed round-edged square in preparation for its sacrifice. Had the registrar practised on paper in the staffroom? 'Quiet now,' he might have said in a joking way to his colleagues as he slurped on bad coffee. 'Quiet now, I'm practising my squares.'

But it has been no joke for Lena's leg, which has had its thin thigh-skin removed by a surgical potato peeler and then lifted in layers onto a troublesome, not very streetwise head. Now the leg is grieving, smarting, ready to make trouble itself. It wakes Lena up, and she screams.

The night outside is warm, and the wind breathes seductively on the curtains. *Come away*, it whispers, and it beckons – to Lena? to the indecisive curtains? – to venture out on to the balcony. But Lena cannot even walk to the bathroom, let alone across the room. Besides, she has no time for external seductions; she is being taken over, raped, by the cellular makeup of her body. All she can feel is the hot, quick slice of metal fingertips into her leg.

'Oh, Jesus!' says Jay in panic, leaping out of bed. 'Oh Lena! Oh Jesus!' He runs around the dark room and trips over the base of the very lamp he is looking for, so that it crashes full-length on the floor like a tree in the forest.

(*like your father trying to save you from the firecracker*, laughs the bullet in a slightly mean way, as it is slapped down on the table of a police laboratory. *Remember?*)

But all Lena can remember is the sharp and shining sound, the whine past her ear which seems so real that her head cowers away in anticipation of something that has already happened.

'Oh shit! Oh Jesus!' says Jay. 'Can't you stop screaming for one second, Lena?' He flips the main light on and stands on one foot. 'My toe,' he says, looking at the blood in a horrified way. His foot dangles from his elevated leg and his cock, which for some reason is erect, sticks out at an odd angle due to his lopsided stance.

'Are you OK?' says Lena, even as sweat pours from her bandages and runs down her face in small desperate rivers.

'I'll probably lose the nail,' says Jay, sticking his bottom lip out. He is losing his erection at any rate; it is subsiding fast as he stands there naked under the bright light, peering at his stubbed toe.

Lena rocks in the bed like an old woman in the throes of grief. 'Jay,' she says, 'get me a bucket, would you?' She thinks she might faint from the pain although she has never fainted in her life, not even when caught in the middle of an unexpected shootout.

'Sure, honey,' says Jay, and he catapults into action again, running this way and running that. 'Under the sink, Jay,' he says, giving orders to himself as if he is one of his own acts. 'Go get the bucket from under the sink.'

Lena grits her teeth, bites back nausea with the determination bred into her by a long line of stoical Poles. 'I will not throw up,'

106

she says. 'You will be all right.' The second reassurance is to her leg for which she feels an odd sympathy, even though it is giving her a hard time.

Jay is back. 'A bucket!' he says, and his voice has the same flourish as when it says, 'The Great Lena McLeonard!' He places the bucket in her arms like a bouquet of flowers, and the not-so-great Lena McLeonard plunges her head into stale plastic and throws up noodles, and wontons, and the fortune cookie that had already warned her *You have a surprise in store!* This is no worse, she tells herself as she rears back from the bucket, than the first time on stage. This is no worse (she thinks, gasping and streaming) than being seven years old and naturally pensive, and having the burden of comedy thrust upon you.

At last she lies back on the pillow but her turbaned head is too large, too bulbous, to allow rest. 'Could you get me some towels?' she says to Jay. She swallows two large orange painkillers and wills them to travel fast and efficiently to her leg. 'Help is on its way,' she promises, and she lifts the bedclothes and looks weakly but encouragingly at her thigh, wrapped in its many layers of crepe.

'There you go!' beams Jay. He seems to believe that the worst is now over and, cheerfully, he steadies her unsteady neck with the towels. 'I'll leave this here,' he says, bringing her the empty bucket and propping it on the bed beside her, 'though I'm sure you won't need it.' He lies down beside Lena and goes to sleep, and she lies there flanked by his large naked body on one side, the bucket on the other.

She feels odd, empty. The light has been switched off again and in the wall opposite her the four inset glass tiles, bought from a scrap dealer named Mikey Mike down in South Central, glow dimly silver. In their four-square silveriness, those tiles tell Lena that it is 2 a.m. outside, that old men are sleeping sound in doorways and surfers might still be riding the waves. How long until I can be out there again? wonders Lena. How long until I will step back on a stage?

Panic rises in her throat. There is no clear path into the days ahead, she can see no farther than the wall and the uncompromising shape of the glass tiles. Jay gives a loud snore and the bucket rocks and tilts on the bed, a strong smell of disinfectant rising from its open mouth. Jay snores again.

'Jay,' whispers Lena, hoping he will turn on his side.

There is a small silence, and she feels hopeful. She swivels her head on the hard brick-like towels. There is such a loud snore that the bed shudders and Jay wakes himself up.

'How are you?' he says instantly. The ability to wake fast is something he prides himself on. Once, while he slept outside a tent at a festival in the desert, his pocket had been picked but he woke so fast that he managed to grab the guy's hand before it was even out of his pants. 'I pushed his head into the shit bucket,' he nods, at dinner parties where it is preferable not to know the details of desert ablutions. And now it is the same: he bounds from sleep to wake in a second. 'How are you?' he says, although his throat is still clogged with dreams.

'What were you dreaming about?' says Lena restlessly, enviously. The pills have stopped the pain but nothing will take away the future which stands threateningly, blurrily, at the end of the bed. She waits for Jay's answer and hopes for an interesting one, or at the very least a good lie that will give her something to think about until morning.

'Um, a bus,' says Jay. 'I think.' He sounds blurry, as if any minute he will head back into sleep.

'Oh,' says Lena. 'Right.' She tries not to feel abandoned, but lying there on her rough towels she dreads the lonely hours spent in her own head.

'Lena,' he says after a few minutes.

'What?' she says, and eagerness leaps in her voice.

'I've just remembered what I was dreaming about,' mumbles Jay.

'What?' she says again, and she turns towards him.

'Soup,' he says. 'That was it. Leek and potato soup.'

The bird

The days that follow are as shifting as sand on the beach. Lena loses track of time and looking back she cannot see any footprints, even though her way has been slow and laborious. Jay cancels all gigs: he is still her manager, after all, and this is his job. Lena's job is simply to wait, wait for the day when the bandages will be taken off her head and her leg. But she suspects that after this life will look stranger and more unfamiliar than ever.

On one of those shapeless mirage days, long before she can walk, she hears Bella's voice in the other room, and then Jay's.

'But I told you we'd be OK,' Jay is saying. There is the usual unease in his voice that comes from having abandoned Bella, albeit many years ago, so she has ended up marrying a small fastidious tax inspector who makes people leave their shoes at the front door.

'She *is* my sister, Jay,' says Bella. Even from a distance her voice sounds belligerent: it strides through the living room, squeezes under the bedroom door and plants itself squarely on Lena's floor, looking around for her.

Lena lies quietly under her flat blankets. The only obvious sign that she is there is her leg, which swells under the covers like a huge fungus.

'She's your sister and she's my girlfriend,' says Jay. 'You think I'd let her go wanting? You think I'm gonna neglect my own girl-friend?' Always, someone ends up claiming Lena. Lying in her hiding place under the covers, she feels tiredly glad that Mr Domanski is in Warsaw on one of his periodic crusades to bring home his glamorous wife; if he were around now he too would be on the doorstep, staking out a portion of Lena's sickbed.

'No, Jay,' says Bella, and her footsteps become louder as she heads for Lena's door. 'But you don't think I'm going to let my sister get shot in the head and not come see her, do you?'

Then she is bursting into the room, followed by a resentful Jay, and she is kissing Lena and staring in fascination at Lena's bandages. But it doesn't take long for her to get down to the busi-ness at hand. She has brought Lena a present.

'It's a wild turkey,' she says, a glimmer of pride showing under her stern professional exterior. 'I found it on a road trip we took up to Pacific Grove. It had been hit by a car but there were no external injuries, thank God.'

'Thanks, Bella,' says Lena, trying to sound grateful. Having once shared a room with Bella's passion she is almost used to it, but still she avoids looking at the glassy eyes and the stretched membrane around the beak.

'It's worth a lot of money,' says Bella importantly. 'I could get four, maybe five hundred dollars for that.'

Jay lifts the bird by the claws and hangs it upside down. His hands look huge, they dwarf the thin scratchy talons. 'Gee, thanks,' he says. 'You shouldn't have.'

Bella snatches it away from him and smoothes the breast feathers back into place. Lena lies in the bed, concentrating on keeping her breathing smooth so her head doesn't hurt.

'You could put it up there,' says Bella, deliberately turning her back on Jay and pointing to the ledge in front of the tiles that are now Lena's diffused view of the outside world. 'Those tiles are a bit posey, don't you think?' she says. 'They don't really go with the rest of the house.' And now she does look over her substantial shoulder at Jay. 'No offence,' she says, challenging him at his own game.

'None taken,' says Jay easily. But when Bella has gone, after much loud conversation and many loud condolences, he gives a derisive snort. 'So the tiles don't go with the house,' he says incredulously, 'but a dead turkey does? A bit of a freak, your sister.'

Lena imagines Bella roaring back up the coast, singing loudly, the waves crashing way out somewhere beyond her large left elbow. 'She's all right,' she says, guardedly. It is one thing for Lena and Davey to roll their eyes at Bella's behaviour but when it comes down to it, no one else is a Domanski.

'She could have brought us real Wild Turkey,' grumbles Jay, and he goes through to the living room to fix himself a drink. 'That would have been more sensible.'

Lena's depleted ear is itching badly under its bandages, the skin cells on the side of her head scrambling for new places like kids on the first day of school. She grabs a chopstick off the bedside cabinet and sticks it up under the hot layers.

'Don't you dare,' says Jay, coming back into the room. 'You want the doc to chew you out?' He takes away the chopstick and the remains of last night's takeouts, and leaves Lena with a glass of lukewarm water.

Although the room is now empty, it still feels full: the air has been dishevelled by Bella's questions, and by Jay's hints about working on some new routines as soon as the doctor has given the all-clear. Lena pulls the sheet up to her chin and peers over it at the turkey, which is propped against the balcony doors. Its small pointy face is turned away from her, it presses yearningly against the glass as if wanting to swoop out into the air for one last fly.

'Taxis,' Lena informs it, 'means movement.'

The turkey stands firm, its face averted from her.

'And *derma*,' says Lena in a small voice, '*derma* means skin.' She slides down in the bed. Her joints are sore and achey from too much lying around, and there is a bedsore on her smooth left buttock. But no amount of discomfort can distract her from the side of her head, from the movement of her own membrane, the constant crawling of skin. Particles of that skin have been blown through the bright Tenderloin air, carried by the misplaced anger of other people and by the wind. Small pieces of it are still buried deep in the wood of Tam Walker's wall; large chunks have been moved about by medical experts, transported and transplanted by white-gloved hands.

'Taxi-dermy,' sings Lena in a small hopeless voice. '*Taxi, dermy*.'

The turkey slips sideways and falls heavily onto the carpet. Although it is a big bird, the thud sounds small in that shifting, restless room.

Stitches

'So what do you do for a job?' asks the surgeon as he tilts Lena's head back. Lena can see her throat shining in the reflective towel dispenser on the wall, like that of a bird about to burst into song.

'What do you do?' the surgeon asks. He appears not to like waiting for answers: after all, he can have a scalpel in his hand a second after barking for one.

Lena is wondering whether to correct him. She does nothing,

has done nothing over the past weeks except lie in bed eating vast quantities of Chinese takeouts and looking at a stuffed bird. And after this, once the surgeon has exposed her new and different self, she will walk from the medical centre on to the vacant street and she will have no idea where to go. She is without tracks, in front of her or behind: she is an animal looking low over a snowfield into an alien sun.

'I'm a comedian,' she says eventually. She thinks she might as well say what she once knew.

'A comedienne!' says the surgeon. He says this – it is certain – with an *en en ee*, just as his wife will go by the title of Dr Mrs. 'It takes all sorts,' he says, cutting deftly into the huge wad of bandages that has become Lena's head. 'We sewed this to your own skin,' he says. 'Keeps it nice and tight.'

There is a moment of silence as he bends over Lena, and Lena looks behind his small round glasses and his competence, and thinks for a moment *you could save me*. Yes, it is possible that this man could pull her back into a well-regulated world where being a doctor is a serious job, where performers are slightly unusual and therefore often live in Venice, and there is a place for both. *You could save me*, she breathes to his tight top lip, with its small sheen of concentration.

In a sense, though, the surgeon has already saved her, as she lay spreadeagled in a gown on his operating table. And it could be this that makes Lena's stomach suddenly lurch. She has been observed unconscious, with her face as immobile and quiet as that of an ice-preserved mummy pulled from the insides of a high mountain. The surgeon has seen too much without her permission, and Jay sees too little, and everything must be different from this point on.

'So you're an actor?' confirms the surgeon, slicing and pulling. There is a succession of tiny tugs on the side of Lena's head, and a barely discernable needling.

'I guess you could say that,' she says. 'Though mainly I do myself.' Shaking starts deep inside her; she can't tell if it is laughter at what she has just said, or fear.

'You'll have to keep this covered up for a while,' says the

surgeon, ignoring what he doesn't understand. He stands beside Lena, looking long and hard at his handiwork. 'You could wear a hat for a while,' he says. 'That wouldn't be a problem, would it? People expect that sort of thing from theatre types, after all.'

Lena feels saliva choking her, swallows just in time. The surgeon's crotch is right beside her: neat trousers, pleats and tucks. With one quick movement of her hand she could cripple him for minutes on end. 'A hat?' she repeats in a small voice. 'I guess so.'

'Lena McLeonard?' It is Jay's voice, booming from the waiting area like the call of a bull. 'Is Lena McLeonard here?'

'My boyfriend,' explains Lena, although as she stares more intently into the white glare of her future Jay is already beginning to fall behind her. 'He's been parking the car,' she says.

'Perfect timing,' says the surgeon. For a man who shows little emotion, he sounds almost relieved. And then Jay is in the cubicle, although Lena is not yet allowed to raise her head and must flap her hand by her side like a performing seal.

'We've just removed the wrappings,' says the surgeon, as if Lena is a Christmas present. 'You might like to have a look.'

Now Jay's crotch is also beside Lena. His hips are a lot larger than the surgeon's, although both have rather pear-shaped bodies for men.

'Hi, sweetie,' he says to Lena. 'Let's see the damage.' There is a second as he leans over Lena and she can hear his heavy, slightly asthmatic breathing. Then he gives a loud groan. 'Oh, shit,' he says. 'Ohhh shit.'

The surgeon calls for a nurse: there is a quick squeaking on the linoleum floor. 'Are you all right, sir?' says the nurse's voice in a concerned way.

Jay gives another loud groan. 'I think I'm gonna faint,' he says. He is hurried from the cubicle, and Lena lies still. She can hear Jay moaning on the other side of the curtain. 'I'm sorry,' he is saying. 'It was a bit of a shock.'

Lena thinks she had better ask for a mirror. She has always realized the good sense in plunging straight into cold water rather than lingering on the edge. 'I need to see,' she says.

113

'Of course you do!' says the surgeon heartily. He infinitely prefers decisiveness to fainting. 'Now, it may look a bit messy,' he says, 'but I can assure you that in a few months you'll hardly notice it.'

Still lying on the bed Lena holds the glass up, King-Lear-like. Her eyes slip to the edge of her face, look sideways at the side of her head. Will there be misted breath on the mirror, indicating that her old self is still alive?

No mist, except that which grows in front of her eyes. Her ear – where her ear used to be – is a mottled, glazed mass of skin.

'Turkey,' she says, almost as faintly as Jay. Because this is what the skin graft reminds her of: of the stuffed offering lying on her bedroom floor, of the roasted basted carcass that Jay's mother insists on bringing over every Christmas. ('But Ma,' says Jay, picking greedily at the pinpricked skin, 'Lena doesn't eat bird.')

'I'm sorry?' says the surgeon, who has picked that moment to fill in a chart. 'What did you say your last name was?'

'Domanski,' says Lena in a quavering voice. She sees that her hair has been shaved away from around the graft: the greasy, brown, unreal, un-Lena-like graft.

The surgeon is clearly bothered. 'That's not what it says here,' he argues. 'It says McLeonard here. What's it going to be?'

'My name is Domanski,' says Lena. She puts the mirror down on the bedside cabinet and sits up without waiting for permission. She knows there is no turning back now: her former life has been incinerated along with the scraps of her old skin.

'It's the feminists,' says the surgeon, with a tinge of annoyance. 'They've made life a whole lot more complicated for all of us.' He crosses out Lena's past identity with a more than necessary vigour.

'What about my leg?' asks Lena, since the surgeon appears to have overlooked this.

'The bandages are too caked on for us to move them,' he says. 'You'll have to soak them off in the shower.'

Lena reaches down for her boots. 'Thank you for your trouble,' she says to the surgeon, and she means it: this is not a safe place for the uncertainties of irony, this flimsy green cubicle with its waving fabric walls.

'You're welcome,' says the surgeon automatically, but he looks surprised. The disproportionate nature of what he and Lena have meant to each other is perhaps unfair. While he will be carried around forever on the side of Lena's head, she can be crossed off his list of duties and instantly left behind him.

But before he leaves the cubicle, he puts a hand on Lena's shoulder. 'Goodbye, my friend,' he says. 'I hope you will be better soon.' Which seems an odd thing for a doctor to say but perhaps it was out of his hands all along, success or otherwise relying on such random factors as the elasticity of Lena's skin and whether the Colt Python had been powerful enough to fire a fast clean shot.

And this is the last time Lena is to see the surgeon, though from time to time she thinks of him playing a round of golf, putting the winning shot with a club funded by her medical insurance company. She sits on alone in the cubicle, wearing her hospital gown and her boots. To have her feet clad makes her feel stronger: she is ready to march into the future! But as she sneaks another look in the mirror, her hands grow a little sweaty.

Salt

Mr Domanski returns from Poland empty-handed – that is, without his wife – and is on Lena's doorstep the very next day.

'My poor Pie!' he cries when he sees Lena, and suddenly Lena is almost crying too, even though she has survived Bella and the turkey, and Jay's near-swooning, and her mother's letter extolling the virtues of cosmetic surgery.

'Oh, my Pie,' croons Mr Domanski. 'Shot!' He gathers her into his arms and she breathes in his familiar smell: spicy meat, and cheap spicy aftershave, and an odd sourness that could be the dairy products he uses for cooking or could simply be the whiff of damp clothes left for too long in the washing machine.

'It was all in a good cause,' says Lena, speaking into his neck. Is she referring to the doomed Ballhaus, or does she simply mean that, with just a few more steps, she could have been biting into the most toothsome donuts in the state of California? Slightly desperately, she takes a last breath of her father's skin and tears herself away. 'Cup of tea?' she says, going to the fridge and forestalling Mitchell's rush on the vegetable drawer with her foot.

'*Dying* for one,' says Mr Domanski, with a wink. This is an expression he has picked up from the world of stand-up and already, to Lena, it has the staleness of something left behind, but it is none the less comforting because it is what he always says.

'Coming right up,' says Lena, opening the fridge. The rush of cold air makes her one-time ear sting and her eyes smart, and she draws back in alarm.

'Well, I may have returned from Poland without your mother,' says Mr Domanski, managing to make it sound as if this is still a surprising thing. 'But guess what I did bring back for you?' He looks around so furtively that Lena instantly knows what he is about to say.

'Some new material?' she says.

'Bingo!' says Mr Domanski, his head still swivelling, his eyes scanning the room. 'Where's that boyfriend of yours?' he asks. 'Not downstairs doing weights again, is he?'

'He's gone to Ralph's,' says Lena.

Mr Domanski can hardly hide his relief. 'I'll read you a few of these,' he says. But just as he snaps open his notebook and clears his throat, Jay walks in with a twelve-pack of toilet paper under his arm.

'Hey hey, Mr D!' he says. 'Back already?' And he beams and claps Mr Domanski on the shoulder because, in spite of their differing visions for Lena, he is really quite fond of his almost-father-in-law. 'Red Stripe?' he says, offering Mr Domanski one warm from the bag. But then he catches sight of the notebook which has been hastily stuffed under the fruit bowl, and his face clouds.

'You've got some new jokes,' he says.

'And they are good ones!' says Mr Domanski, giving up and pulling the notebook into full view again. 'Some wonderful new Papal jokes,' he says, 'just wonderful.' He flips through a few pages, his lips moving silently, and he starts to laugh. Sitting there on his stool like a great grey pigeon, he shakes with laughter. 'Listen to this,' he says through his chuckles.

'No *more Pope*,' interrupts Jay, shaking his head. 'I've told you before, he doesn't work here in California – hell, religion as a whole doesn't work!'

Mr Domanski looks mutinous. 'These jokes would work anywhere,' he argues. 'Humour is a universal language, my son, and the sooner you learn that the better.'

'Here's your tea, Da,' says Lena quickly, though Mr Domanski has already snapped the top off his beer and is gulping it down as if Jay might repossess it at any moment.

'It's irrelevant anyway,' says Jay. 'Lena isn't ready to go back to work yet.' He moves swiftly from the role of boyfriend and provider to manager, which means that he can discuss Lena as if she isn't there. 'Although personally,' he adds, his loyalties divided, 'I think it's time she got back on stage.'

Mr Domanski looks at him. 'You know,' he says, 'you are dead right. Once you have fallen it is important to get right back on that horse.' The balance of sympathies in the room swings like a weathercock in a wind change: Jay and Mr Domanski nod and raise their warm bottles of beer at each other, leaving Lena stranded on the other side of the breakfast bar. Her only ally: a grey cat with static fur and a dull name who is obsessed with cucumber.

'Look at me!' she says then in a loud voice. 'Look!' She pulls her hair back so tightly that it squeaks under her fingers, and her scar shines red and purple in the side of the shining toaster.

'You look just fine, honey,' says Jay reassuringly. 'We can slap some makeup over that in a jiffy.'

'No makeup,' says Lena loudly. 'The doctor said.'

Clearly Jay sees it is high time to approach her: he comes over to her right shoulder and kisses her on the right cheek, avoiding her entire left side as if it is a nuclear dumping ground. 'We'll sort something out,' he says. 'In the meantime, how about a whole new image?' Once again, as if he can't help himself, he turns towards Mr Domanski.

Mr D straightens instantly on his stool. 'What were you think-ing?' he says.

(*yes, what were you thinking?* yells the bullet, as it is placed under a bright light and examined all over. *Putting your head in the way like that and getting us all into trouble!*)

Lena sways and feels nauseous, leans on the bench. Neither Jay nor Mr Domanski notices.

'Tell us your thoughts,' says Mr Domanski to Jay.

'Well, just now on my way home from the store,' says Jay, and his voice becomes expansive, stretching out into story-telling mode. 'Down on the corner by that little spaghetti place,' he says, 'I happened to notice there was a power pole down. Which got me thinking to myself, Lena's a Pole, right?' He looks around for appreciation but gets none. Mr Domanski looks uncertain, and Lena is still hearing the fading roar of a getaway car.

'A *Pole*,' repeats Jay. 'A Pole, get it? So we've changed Lena's last name, but she still looks slightly different, so to speak.'

'Different?' echoes Mr Domanski, his face filling with disapproval.

'Of course,' says Jay, as if he is talking to a two-year-old. 'You know, *foreign*. Not quite right.'

Mr Domanski stands up, looking thunderous. 'You are imply-ing,' he says, 'exactly what?'

'Hey, calm down!' says Jay hastily. 'How about I say exotic – is that better?'

'Exotic,' repeats Mr Domanski, the clouds sweeping over him and away. 'Yes, you are right,' he says, sitting down again and staring at Lena. 'My Pie is exotic.'

'Correct,' says Jay. He looks relieved but doesn't hesitate to press home the point. 'The slanting eyes, the lashes,' he says. 'Well, I started playing around with the whole nationality notion and I thought how about we relaunch Lena as—' He stops, takes a step forward as if positioning himself in front of a mike, and coughs in a stagy way.

'Yes?' says Mr Domanski, his face alight. 'What?'

Lena looks on. None of this means anything to her now: still, she waits with mild interest to see what she might have become.

'Allow me to introduce to you—' says Jay, with a drum roll in his voice, 'the Pole Cat!'

'Oh *yes*,' says Mr Domanski, and there is profound respect in his voice. 'Oh yes, you are right, that is very good indeed.'

'It's sexy,' says Jay, 'it's smart. People will remember it.' He nods, Mr Domanski nods, they both nod, seriously, for several seconds. Lena shifts her weight from one tired foot to another, watches to see when they will turn towards her. At that moment, she thinks, she will tell them of the shift that has occurred inside her damaged head, inside her relocated, repositioned self.

But they continue to nod at each other like wise Mandarins, her father and her live-in manager. Although they are extremely pleased with themselves, there is no glimmer of a smile on their faces. And this is one thing that all of them, Lena included, have in common. It is just as she has always suspected but only recently realized, with a force that had made her reel on the blood-spattered pavement. Comedy cannot be underestimated. It is no laughing matter, being all that humans have between themselves and the fact that, one day, they will put on their red shoes and walk straight into the punchline of their own life. Yes, thinks Lena. Death, sex, comedy: these are all that life is made of.

But even as she watches her conviction leaves her. She is filled with weariness and desolation, and has no energy left to break news of her own. 'I'm going for a sleep,' she says. She leaves what could have been her future to Jay and Mr Domanski, goes to the bedroom and opens every window and door so that cool air floods through the room. Her bed stands in the middle of the flow like a high white island, and she lies on it and is still.

Some time later Jay comes in. 'Lena?' he says. 'Are you OK?' He touches her cheek. 'Oh, that's all right,' he said, and his voice is thick with relief. 'I thought you might have been crying.'

'Hmm,' says Lena non-committally.

'We're just going out for some food,' he says. 'You want me to bring you back something?'

'No,' says Lena.

'You'll be all right?' says Jay.

'Yes,' says Lena.

'Keep up the good work,' says Jay.

This is something that most people don't realize about crying.

If you do it while you are lying down, the tears run down one side of your face only.

Blonde

In the shower, Lena washes the seaweed bandages off her leg. She stands there for so long under the hot water looking at her thigh that even her undamaged skin becomes red and blotched. But unlike the rest of her body, the redness on her leg does not subside. There is a square on her thigh, a determinedly red square that retains its grudge. Small scabs of white hang around on its surface like complaints needing to be addressed. Every morning, Lena forces herself to scratch a few more of these off with her fingernail.

She does several gigs that do not go well, which is hardly surprising considering she has lost all conviction back in San Francisco, somewhere in the middle of the pavement at the inter-section of Polk and Ellis Streets.

'Why don't we try you on warm-up instead?' suggests Jay. (He has never been one to be negative.) 'Just until you get your old form back,' he says, not seeming to realize that Lena's old form has vanished without trace under the squealing tyres of a fast-departing black car.

Warm-up? Lena has never done this. A comedian launched so decisively and brilliantly at the age of seven has no need to start at the bottom of a career. Still, she thinks she might as well do it until she knows where else to go and, dutifully, she works a crowd several nights a week to ease the path of other comedians who have less talent than her and more belief in what they are doing.

'I thought for the Fourth of July Beach Parade,' says Jay with a slightly forced enthusiasm, 'you'd be just right to get the crowd up and running for the Howdy-Dudies.'

'The Howdy-Dudies?' says Lena. 'Aren't they more of a sports set?'

'I thought I'd give them a trial,' says Jay. 'They might be a big success.'

For the next couple of weeks he labours over patriotic and anti-patriotic jokes for Lena, fuelling himself at regular intervals with Red Stripe. Lena looks at the cue-cards he gives her, thinks they could, perhaps, be used to make people laugh if she gives them the spin she remembers from her old life. On the day before the parade Jay brings home a marching girl's outfit: red, white, and blue, spangled all over with stars. When Lena tries on the skirt, it is so short that the neat square of skin on her thigh is clearly visible.

'You can't wear that,' says Jay. He shakes his head. 'Oh, no,' he says.

'I don't mind, actually,' says Lena. Her leg has not forgotten the cutting and the slicing, it still flinches even from her gentle touch. But it is settling down day by day, turning to a dull purple not unlike the colour of the registrar's felt-tip pen; it might not be averse to an outing.

'Absolutely not,' says Jay. Quickly, his eyes dart away from her leg and refocus on his schedule. 'You'll have to wear pants,' he says, scratching his chin and then his balls, still scrutinizing his comedy list. 'Your red ones would do.'

Although it is late in the afternoon the temperature is rising ninety, and the sweat on Lena's top lip tastes like the sea. 'Jay,' she says. 'Do you want to go to bed?'

'To *bed*?' says Jay, as if she has asked him to float up the Ganges or shoot over the Niagara Falls in a barrel. 'What in God's name for?' he says.

'To – you know,' says Lena. She sits sideways on the sofa and then lies with her legs slightly, invitingly spread. Even looking at Jay standing there with his hands stuck down his pants, she starts to feel that she wouldn't mind being between the sheets. 'Come on,' she coaxes. The breeze lifts her starry skirt to reveal the lace knickers that Mrs Domanski has sent her from Warsaw, in lieu of a mother.

'Lena, *really*,' says Jay, sounding more like an old woman of ninety than a red-blooded, slightly overweight male approaching his middle years. 'We've got way too much to do to fool around.' He pulls his hand out of his pants and marches to the kitchen. 'Juice?' he says in a business-like way.

That night in bed, after Lena has been lying still for some time, she feels the mattress start to shake. She is about to reach for the light-switch, perhaps even head for the doorway because the city hasn't had a big quake for a while now, but then she hears Jay groan, very quietly. She lies there and feels the blanket rubbing back and forwards over her shoulder, and the bed keeps vibrating in an uneasy way as Jay's hand moves under the sheets like a small rodent.

Lena bites her lip, feels the already tight skin on her head pull tighter so it is like the taut top of a drum. She listens with her still good right ear through the pillow so that the sounds of Jay's eventual orgasm are muffled and slightly dull. *Like a silencer on a gun* she thinks, and she imagines Jay's semen shooting out underneath the sheet and seeping up through the cotton to dry in the salty air.

'Jay,' she says, after a while.

'Yes, honey?' he says. His voice sounds completely normal: not at all as if he has failed her seduction test that very afternoon and then proceeded to give himself a hand-job.

'Oh nothing,' she says. She lies staring outwards into the dark pool of the room for many hours.

The next day Jay is out of the house early. 'I'll pick up some breakfast from that place on the waterfront,' he says, grabbing his briefcase. 'Make sure you fix yourself some oatmeal, though. It's gonna be a long day.'

In spite of the heat, Lena does make oatmeal. She stirs the pan for a long time and watches the small bubbles rise to the surface. *Change is afoot*, she thinks. She pours milk into her bowl and eats quietly at the table, not reading, just waiting.

At 10 a.m. there is a call from Jay. He is on his cellphone, on the boardwalk, and in the background microphones are being tested and brass instruments are practising snatches of show tunes.

'You ready to go, honey?' says Jay's voice. 'You got the pants hemmed up? Hey, guy, I said *not* on the fucken stage!'

'It's hot for pants,' says Lena. She looks out to the beach, thinks maybe she can see Jay in the distance, a large man with a tiny cellphone attached semi-permanently to his head.

'I guess I'll see you down here,' says Jay. 'Be funny!' He always says this when he signs off, but today it sounds almost like a plea.

Amongst the stalls on the waterfront, Lena finds the trailer where the other, real, comedians are making up and getting dressed and stressing out.

'Oh my god!' one of the female Howdy-Dudies is saying. 'Where the hell is the script?' She looks up at Lena, says hello in a distracted way and then does a double-take. 'Oh my god!' she says again. 'What the hell happened to you?'

Since Lena has a bandanna around her head to shield it from the sun, she knows that the Dudie must be referring to the scar on her thigh. And it would be this way anyway, she knows, because the Dudie herself has such very long, perfect, and utterly unblemished legs. Her skin is not pale like Lena's, is not descended from a land of snow; no, the Dudie's legs are the exact same colour as the treacle that melted into Lena's oatmeal less than two hours before. Neither does the Dudie have a large purple scar emerging from her mini-skirt.

The head Dude rushes into the conversation, perhaps hoping to avoid any further awkward discussion on the topic of disfigurement. 'It's Lena McLeonard, right?' he says quickly. He and his fellow performers have been brought in from up the coast, are used to playing huge cavernous inns with marlin and mooseheads looking on, so today is a pretty big deal for them. As the Dude chit-chats, the staring female Dudie subsides; and Lena nods and smiles there in the hot stuffy trailer.

'So how come you're not mainlining today?' asks the Dude. 'I hear you've got quite a name round here.'

'I did.' says Lena mildly. She puts her bag down, pulls out her silver wig. 'I'm thinking of getting out though,' she says.

'Oh *right*,' says the Dude significantly. Out of where, he doesn't need to ask; like all comedians he knows that stand-up is best spoken of in terms of a cage, a mental hospital, or a deep swampy puddle. 'It's a tough call though,' he says. 'If you're used to being funny it must be kinda hard to stop.' He peers at himself in the mirror, does a few lip manoeuvres to get the laughter apparatus

123

working. 'I drive my family crazy when I'm on holiday,' he says. 'Wisecracks! I just can't help myself.'

Lena pulls off her bandanna and pulls on her wig (carefully, carefully) while the Dude proceeds to tell several of his best jokes. 'Impromptu, those,' he says with a nod when he finishes. 'They just burst outta me on various occasions. My kids loved 'em, so I reckon the crowds will dig 'em.'

'They're not bad,' says Lena, and she gives him a smile because he probably is a good father in spite of the fact that his jokes suck.

The treacle-legged blonde keeps well away from Lena. She applies her many layers of makeup on the far side of the trailer on the off-chance that purple squares might prove contagious. But the smaller blonde is less cautious, leans against the wall and watches Lena adjust the long silver strands of her wig. 'You dance?' she asks. She chews gum with such velocity that her jaw gives off loud clicks and Lena almost shies away.

'I've done some,' says Lena faintly. 'I tap-danced when I was a kid.'

'We dance,' says the blonde. 'We tell jokes, we sing – all-rounders, I guess you'd say. You sing?'

It is time for Lena to leave. She steps out of the trailer into the thick warm air and runs fast down the beach, and faster back. The white tassels of her boots stream behind her, her purple square flashes in and out of her vision as she runs.

The phone

Predictably, Jay is not happy.

'Jeez Louise!' he says. He only uses this expression when he is upset, so upset that he forgets his manager's speak (*coolio! fab!*) and reverts to his Tenderloin roots. 'Jeez,' he says again, throwing down his cellphone and wiping his forehead. 'I thought we'd sorted it out. So why?'

'That wasn't the important thing,' says Lena. 'I did the warm-up, didn't I? And it went fine.'

Jay sits down heavily, springs up again. 'Shit! My phone!' he says, looking worriedly at the display panel. 'Oh jeez.' He pushes some buttons and seems reassured by the answering beeps. Then he looks back at Lena and shakes his head. 'It was unsightly,' he says eventually.

'It might have been unsightly,' says Lena, 'but it was *too hot for pants*.' She closes the bedroom door firmly behind her.

The argument about the skirt leads to arguments on other topics, and after this it is reasonably easy. Lena is forced to fire Jay.

'I have to,' she says, 'or else you'll have to let me go.'

'Let you go?' says Jay, staring. 'What the hell are you talking about?' He really seems to have no idea: he sits backstage watching Lena take off her makeup after a middle-of-the-road variety show and he twists the hat she has refused to wear in his hands, so that it looks more like a felt pretzel than something he has bought to make Lena look good again under lights.

'Well, that's what you do to performers who haven't got it anymore,' says Lena reasonably. 'Let them go, release them, or whatever else managers say when they want to be tactful.'

'But, honey,' protests Jay, 'you're still sexy. A new haircut, a bit of makeup—'

'I've told you,' says Lena. 'No makeup on the scar.'

'Hypoallergenic?' says Jay hopefully. After so many years, he seems unable to break the habit of pushing Lena into the spotlight, while at the same time desperately wanting to hide her away.

'My appearance doesn't frighten audiences,' says Lena, 'as much as it frightens you.'

'Oh, honey, it's not that,' Jay starts gamely. 'It's just—' He stops under Lena's stern eye. 'OK,' he says. 'It is, but hell, I still love you!'

'You might still love me,' says Lena, 'but we're not right for business anymore.'

Jay sucks his cheeks in, then puffs them out. In, out, in, out. 'You mean,' he says, swallowing, 'you don't want to work with me anymore? On anything?'

'I don't want to work anymore, period,' says Lena. She rubs the cosmetic glow off her face with a cotton pad and is relieved to see her own white cheek appear.

'I don't feel funny,' she says with a shrug, and her lips emerge: pale, resolute.

'I no longer want to be a comedian,' she says. And as easy as that, it is done.

The star

Although she is now ready to exit, it is not always possible to depart with the speed and the silence of a Mrs Domanski. Lena has never been one to slide out of duty and, to farewell her fans as well as herself, she agrees to do one last performance. Jay is no longer her manager but he is still full of organizing enthusiasm, and he sets up one last gig at the prestigious Id and Ego club right there in Venice.

'Maybe you could do a set on disability?' he says, sitting at the living-room table with his appointment diary in front of him. 'That's a subject that can be great value if you tackle it right,' he says. Outside the sea is waving blue arms at him but Jay has never taken much notice of the landscape, having founded a successful career on exploiting personalities.

'What about a Venice Beach Special, since it's local?' suggests Lena. 'Take real life, add humour, and stir.'

Jay doesn't hear her. 'Disability, disfigurement,' he says, brainstorming with himself. 'You said something really droll about your operation the other night. Now what was it?' He stares hard at the table, lips silently moving as he replays the last few days of Lena's conversation. 'Shit,' he says finally. 'I knew I should have told you to write it down.'

'I'm not interested in that topic,' says Lena. This is not the whole truth: she is, though she is not yet sure how to use what has happened to her. But she knows the danger of using up material in the wrong way.

By the time she gets to the Id and Ego on the night of the gig, the other performers are already milling about nervously, lending each other lipstick or accusing each other of stealing it.

'Hey, Lena McLeonard!' one of them cries, in an exaggeratedly friendly way.

But Lena has already walked straight on by, and has to double-take and turn. 'I'm sorry,' she says. 'My hearing's not so good right now.' The thing is, she no longer recognizes her name.

The comedian avoids looking at her scar. 'I know,' he says. 'You poor sweetheart.' For a moment he looks genuinely sympathetic, and then his face dissolves into a series of warm-ups. 'Hell,' he cries, 'I'm gonna *slay* those motherfuckers tonight!' His voice gets louder, his actions more exaggerated, as if these things will disguise the fact that he is so nervous he could piss his pants. (Lena once saw a guy do this at a gig in Vegas and has never forgotten it: the small definite outline of the puddle on the tiles, a map of humiliation and lost hope.)

All around the room nerves are stretching and snapping like elastic, but Lena turns her back on them and gives herself a perfect scarlet mouth. There are only two acts before her but by the time she steps out on stage the boards are already spotted with sweat and spit. Lowering her head, she looks out low between the lights. *This is the last time*, she says to herself, and there is a quick pain inside her, a pang, which for a moment supplants the now familiar one on the side of her head.

And then she begins. She mimics every comedian she has ever known, she mimics Los Angeles celebrities and figures from the local circuit and herself as she used to be. *This is the last time*. She uses her last time on stage to say all she has ever felt about the history of stand-up and because she has never cared less, she is spectacular, she is sensational. She is – finally – a star, and she steps off the stage with the glamour of wolf-whistles falling around her.

Jay is ecstatic. He jigs from foot to foot. 'Damn, you were good!' he says, grabbing hold of her.

Lena pulls back. 'I need a shower,' she says hastily. This is true: she is dripping with sweat, and she pushes her hair back and waits for Jay to recoil, but he doesn't.

'We'll take one together when we get home,' he says. Suddenly his lips look very red, as red as Lena's stage mouth, and as he stares at her there is a hunger on his face.

After the show Lena and Jay and the other performers go next door for pizza, where Jay drinks beer and proceeds to tell his version of what is about to happen to Lena. 'No, she's not *quitting*,' he says to the table at large. 'It's just a temporary break.' He shakes his big head. 'God, she's too good to quit,' he says. 'I mean, you saw her tonight!'

Much as Lena would like to leave Jay with his pride, she cannot let this rumour run freely around the red-checked table and out into the night. She also shakes her head. 'Actually,' she says, slightly apologetically to Jay and to the crowd, 'this *is* it. Finale. Curtains.'

Jay gives a loud laugh. 'It's been a real traumatic time for you, honey,' he says. 'I don't think you're in the best state to make decisions.' He turns back to his small but attentive audience; Lena gives a mental shrug and sits back in her seat. 'If I could find the fuckers who pulled that trigger,' says Jay, 'by God, they'd wish they never left home that day!'

More beer arrives at the table, Jay talks on, and Lena retreats, for it is more interesting inside her own head. She thinks of dust, of long dusty roads and lost landscapes: of faces that are not always animated, and bodies that are not Hollywood-perfect. A small noise drops from the dark sky.

'What?' she says vaguely.

'I was asking what you want to drink,' says Jay. He rolls his eyes in mock exasperation. 'Artists!' he says, and he plants a kiss on Lena's scrubbed cheek.

'Oh, anything,' says Lena, 'anything will do.' But she doesn't particularly want alcohol, or soda, or olives on plastic cocktail sticks. Although Jay hasn't realized it yet, she has already left the smeared table: she is heading fast for unknown flatlands, and acres of clean uncharted space.

The newspaper

Missing someone is the strangest feeling. Try describing it and it is like describing the back of your eyelids: flickering, changing, and so much depending on whether the sun is shining outside.

Now try describing this. Missing yourself. It is this that faces

Lena one-time-Domanski, then McLeonard, and now Domanski again. She is free of show business (she is free!). But there is an absence where she used to be. The bullet has carried away not only a part of her ear, but also herself.

As the summer swells and then fades she finds herself drifting. Her only anchor is the occasional appointment at the hospital: the place of the last official and indisputable sighting of Lena. When she steps through the front doors there is a sharp divide between heat and cool-conditioned air, and the shock is almost like a return to reality.

'I have to say,' says the charge nurse, 'it's not looking so great.' She is middle-aged, sensible, and she takes Lena's chin with firm hands and tilts Lena's head this way and that like a hair-dresser.

'I can't tell,' says Lena. 'I don't know how it's supposed to look.' Almost, she is glad to hear someone state the negative truth when most people stare fixedly, optimistically, at her face.

'Of course you can't,' agrees the nurse. 'It's not every day you get a bullet in the head.'

Lena gives a small laugh, but then realizes the nurse is serious, and seriously worried.

'I'll give you the name of a scar therapist,' decides the nurse. She writes a name and number down on the back of a card. 'Are you working?' she says. 'Or can you come anytime?'

'Not working,' says Lena neutrally. 'Just waiting.'

'Isn't that always the way,' says the nurse. 'Five people have lost their jobs this month in Plastics. And they call it restructuring.' She looks tired, as if redundancy would do her the world of good. But still she makes an effort, in her flat voice, to reassure Lena. 'Don't you fret now,' she says. 'You'll look better eventually, it's just going to take some time.'

'How long?' says Lena, picking up her bag, forcing herself to ask.

'Oh, about eight years,' nods the nurse, with manufactured brightness. 'That's how long it takes for the skin to completely regenerate itself. But just think, by then you'll have a whole new covering.'

Patience! warn Lena's feet, as they squeak away from the nurse. Patience, they say, and they carry Lena out into the world where brakes are screaming and jackhammers are pounding and workers swarm in and out of shiny glass buildings. Viewed from the steps of the medical centre, Los Angeles is a heaving anthill of activity and purpose. And Lena? She is a tiny centre of scar tissue and uncertainty.

Because today her feet are taking charge, they carry her wisely to the one other person in the city – perhaps in the world – with patience to spare. They lead her to a bus-stop, to a bus that takes her to Bell. This is the area where her brother, Delayed Reaction Davey, works. Here he has spent the past eight years hanging out in a disused hangar, designing and building his very own satellite. 'I want to bring the prices down,' he says earnestly, sounding like an airline official except the cost he is referring to is that of getting into space.

As always, he is there, working on his prototype in his large and dusty space. Lena sits on a pile of aluminium sheets that creak and crack even under her light weight. After several seconds—

'Careful!' says Davey. 'They could bend.'

Obediently, Lena moves to a beer crate, and through the gloom she watches Davey wander back and forwards between his flickering computer screen and the solid shape of reality. 'I've been trying to crack this all day,' he mutters. 'The son of a bitch doesn't want to be solved.'

Nothing has changed. This is Lena, waiting politely for someone else's attention. And this is Davey, labouring over the smallest of practicalities while vast dreams swirl behind his freckled forehead. They are older, that is all: but at any minute they might hear Mrs Domanski's pale cotton-thread voice reeling them in to dinner.

'I got shot a while back,' offers Lena, by way of updating Davey on her life. 'I was in the Tenderloin for the day and there was a drive-by, and I got caught in it.'

There's a small silence.

'So that's what happened to your ear,' says Davey. 'Isn't that

130

the darnedest thing.' He turns aside from his laptop and stares at Lena.

'Darnedest, why?' says Lena. To tell the truth she also thinks it is pretty odd, but she hopes that Davey's interpretation might shed some light on the meaning of it all – if, indeed, there is any meaning to be found.

'We spend our whole lives in that neighbourhood,' muses Davey, 'walkin' around, talkin' about the bad guys. But nothing ever happens for all those years. Then one day back there, and whammo!'

'I guess we were just lucky,' says Lena. She flips back through the pictures in her head, sees threatening bird-beaks and cigarette burns on black skin.

'Luck?' says Davey darkly. 'Luck has nothing to do with it.' His voice also holds a world of memory: the dark cavern of a church, doomed crabs, and poles crashing down beside weeping dancers. Then—

'Visiting Bella, were you?' he says. 'Is that why you went back to the Tenderloin?'

'No,' says Lena. 'I wanted to set up a gig to save Clara's Ballhaus.'

'There you go,' says Davey. 'Nothing good ever came out of that place, and nothing good came from going back there.'

'But the Ballhaus was what kept Ma going,' argues Lena. 'Otherwise she would have died.'

'She was half dead already,' says Davey. 'She only got a life once she left.' He jiggles his computer mouse so that the screen rushes back, and focuses on his work as if he has said enough for now. His hair has been cut so short that his scalp is visible through the soft bristles.

Lena sits and listens to the trucks outside: dark shapes thundering past the fibreglass doors like racehorses. Here they are in the hub of the aerospace industry: around them stretch hundreds of hangars, harbouring hundreds of Daveys, all with their own secret projects.

'It looks pretty small, your satellite,' she observes.

'Small,' agrees Davey, 'and real light. It'll end up weighing less than twenty-five pounds.' Davey is not like Jay, he is not obsessed with the size of things, which is probably why he is able to remain undaunted by black holes and the concept of an infinite universe.

Lena leans forward and puts her head in her hands, giving her aching neck a break from the weight of past and future. On the paint-spattered table beside her is a pile of newspapers, and on the top of the pile is a full-page advertisement with Davey's pencil hieroglyphics all over it.

DO YOU HAVE THE RIGHT STUFF TO SPEND TWO YEARS ON MARS? the headline asks. IF SO, LET NASA KNOW!

'Davey?' she says, startled into speech again even though she has come to share quietness. 'Are you applying for this?'

It takes Davey a while to answer so Lena has time to read the ad right through. In short warning sentences it speaks of arctic temperatures, of being locked in a module and dressed in a spacesuit and allowed outside for only a few minutes a day.

'Yes, I've applied,' says Davey finally. 'It's my dream job.'

And Lena knows, as she looks at his slow serious face, that he will get it; his entire life has been spearheading towards this point. Davey puts down his tools in slower than usual motion, as if hampered already by gravity or the lack of it, and comes to sit on a beer crate opposite her.

'It's the simulation of a mission to Mars,' he explains. 'It's controlled from a base in Colorado. The only difference is we'll be in Alaska instead of forty-five million miles away.'

'In Alaska!' says Lena. 'The northernmost point of America.'

'That's right,' says Davey. 'There's a twenty-minute radio delay built in so communication's slow, just like a real space connection.'

This really could be Davey's ideal occupation, Lena thinks; there are not many jobs, after all, that come with a legitimised delay between the giving and receiving of orders.

'There's eight of us,' says Davey happily. 'In a twenty-five-foot tin can.' Already he is talking about the mission in the present tense, as if he has been through the selection process and the interview process and is right now settling into a white pod, in the middle of a crater, in the middle of arctic tundra. To a person who is Californian through and through, a person used to long sun and wide blue skies, the prospect would sound like a night-mare. But then these are Domanskis sitting here facing each other in the middle of an industrial estate in Los Angeles and although they may look at home, they have always been slightly different.

Davey sits still, sealed in the same air as seven other people, dreaming of privation in the cause of progress. But Lena – well, Lena is feeling the breath of a cool arctic wind on her neck, and suddenly the shutters lift in her head and she has the clearest picture she has ever had. Instinct fills her body, her hands move involuntarily. *Time to get started*, they say.

The hangar doors rattle as if in a backdraft. There is a pause.

'Does that hurt?' asks Davey suddenly, gesturing to Lena's head.

'Hardly at all,' says Lena. The truth is, she has forgotten all about it.

The key

She has waited a long time, Lena, many long years to use the skill in her fingers. This is partly through a lack of opportunity, but mainly because her quick head has always got there first. Now that her head is convalescing, her hands can finally step in.

She takes a bus across town to the Hollywood Park Casino. But it is no gamble because she knows what she wants and knows that she will find it there, in that place where women start the hot afternoon wearing diamonds but have bare necks by sunset. As she sets off along Prairie Boulevard, the planes coming in to land fly low over her head like geese.

The pawn shop is dark and it has an odd smell, a smell of musty furs and desperation that makes Lena breathe through her mouth. But she goes straight on over to a smeared glass shelf and, within minutes, finds what she is looking for. There is no price tag on it: perhaps it has been here so long waiting for Lena that the shop owner has given up on it.

She carries her find to the counter. 'How much do you want for this?' she asks.

'Let's have a look,' says the owner of the store. He is hardly older than Davey, but in his short lifetime he has seen so much human nature that his skin is ingrained with grey, and there are deep grooves around his mouth. 'Hmmm,' he says. He stares at the camera for so long that Lena knows he has little idea what it is worth, and when he names his price, she is ready with ammunition.

'See here?' she says, turning the Nikon to the light, showing to advantage the deep scratches on its body.

'Sure, it's battered,' says the guy with a shrug. 'What the hell do you expect in a place like this?'

Lena proceeds to show him the tiny fingernail marks around the shutter (which to her make it more desirable) and the frayed strap (which to her gives it character). 'It's not worth that price,' she says, as she feels the camera nestle, settle, into her hands.

The owner is immovable. 'So look somewhere else,' he says, doing this very thing himself. His weary eyes swivel towards the rows of television sets displaying multiple soap stars in multiple satin beds. Although Lena does not have satin sheets or lingerie, she can use her assets with the best of them. She takes off her old hat, throws it on to the counter and into the ring.

'You willing to bargain?' she says, persuasively, firmly, smoothing her hair back.

The guy's eyes are pulled back towards her, fix for a second on her beautiful scarred head which gleams in the flickering TV light. He gives a start.

'You know what?' he says. 'You're right. It has seen better days.' He could, of course, be talking about her head, but it is more likely that he is referring to the Nikon SLR, and his eyes quickly fall away to fix on its scratched and battered form.

'You can have it,' he says. 'Shall I put it in the case for you?' And Lena agrees and relinquishes it, just for a moment.

'You got a tripod?' asks the guy, ringing her money up on the till.

'Not yet,' she says.

'Might as well throw this in,' he says, and he reaches behind the counter and brings out some spidery aluminium legs, which he folds up and places in a long narrow box. 'Have you done much photography before?' he asks Lena, carefully not looking at her.

'Some,' she says. 'I did a night course once, and I've read books.'

'The way you handle the camera,' he says, 'I thought you might do it for a job.'

'Not yet,' says Lena. 'But I will be soon.'

'You'll be OK with this one,' he says, patting the padded case. 'I remember the guy who brought it in now – he didn't want to part with it. Said it'll do anything you want it to and more.'

Lena smiles at him and picks up her hat. 'Thank you,' she says. She is grateful for his kindness and his discounts, although she knew she was meant to have the camera from the moment it lay heavy and relaxed in her hands.

'You're welcome,' he says, sneaking one last look at her. 'You take care of yourself out there,' he says. Although they have talked for less than ten minutes, it is as if he really doesn't want her to deflect any more flying missiles with her head.

Outside, the street is still bright with polluted sun, is so garishly lit that it looks like a B-grade movie set. Lena blinks. She steps into a shadowy doorway that smells of piss and beer, pulls the camera from its case, raises it and twists the lens.

The street rushes towards her. Her head screams, her ear recoils, and her leg shivers although the bases of the buildings opposite are still shimmering in heat.

And then everything stops. The world is made clear and sharp, stilled by the equipment she holds in her hand. There is no rustling shifting audience in front of her, no instructions being whispered from the wings. There is no laughter flying around her head, no bullet shaving chaos from the air. Stillness is here and it is hers, bestowed by the glass and metal box she now holds in her hand.

Coffee

'Where did you say?' says Jay, staring at her incredulously. 'You're going where?'

Lena spins her grapefruit in the bowl with her spoon. Small particles of sugar fly. 'To Alaska,' she says. 'Not for a while, though.'

'But that's a godforsaken place!' says Jay. 'They don't even have malls there!' He shakes his head. 'And what about that twenty-four-hour darkness thing?' he says.

'I'm not going till the spring,' says Lena.

'It's cold all year round,' says Jay with authority. 'You'll freeze.' He strides to the shelves and pulls out a world atlas, the only book he owns. It is important to Jay to know where the next entertainment capital of the world might be, and what climatic conditions to expect when he gets there. 'See?' he says, stabbing at the notes with his finger. 'See what it says? Ninety below.'

Lena shrugs, tucks her feet up underneath her. She thinks of the way that, every time she goes into the street, the side of her head crackles like shiny wrapping paper. 'I've had enough of heat for now,' she says. She spoons out a small sour triangle and puts it in her mouth, while Mitchell watches longingly.

'If you want to get away somewhere, why not Poland?' says Jay. 'That place has really come a long way in the last few years. It's a whole lot better than it used to be.'

Lena has a vision of Mr Domanski shaking his heavy head over the *Warsaw Business Journal* as he reads of multiplex cinemas, and master clockmakers who now peddle medical supplies. 'Some would say better,' she says mildly. 'Some wouldn't.'

'You've never even been to Poland,' Jay rushes on. 'Don't you think you should see it at least once? Considering?' It seems ironic that, having initially tried so hard to rid Lena of her East European taint, he now views it as the safer option.

'I'm a US citizen,' says Lena. 'Don't you think I should get to know my own country first?'

'Alaska doesn't count as America,' says Jay darkly. 'It's weird.'

'Weird is a relative term,' says Lena, master of relativity.

'It's full of outsiders,' says Jay, child of immigrant pasta-makers from Naples. 'Loner types go there,' he says, 'and they never come back.'

'I'll come back,' promises Lena. 'Whereas if I went to Warsaw, who knows what could happen? I might be seduced into a career in cosmetics like Ma.'

'Yes?' says Jay hopefully.

'No,' says Lena.

'Well, Alaska sounds too damn risky to me,' says Jay. 'Anything could happen up there. Hell, you could get raped, or shot even!'

'Shot, you say?' says Lena, with a small laugh. She offers Mitchell some grapefruit off a teaspoon.

Jay looks flustered. 'I didn't think,' he says, with a slight flush on his cheeks. 'No offence, hon.'

'None taken,' says Lena.

'Well, at least you'll be working on something when you get there,' says Jay, seeming a little reassured by this.

'A book,' agrees Lena. 'A book of photos.' She stares a long way out, past Jay's face and Mitchell's whiskers to the white line of the horizon, a narrow negative space between sea and sky. 'A book of loss,' she says, almost to herself.

'Now, that sounds good,' says Jay. 'Yes, I like the sound of that.'

'You do?' says Lena. 'Why?'

'Well, losers are great material,' says Jay. 'The world loves losers!'

'I didn't say—' says Lena.

'Sounds as if it could be a real riot,' says Jay. He takes a loud slurp of coffee, and then puts his cup down with a bang. 'If you got something together fast,' he says, and his voice takes on its managerial tone although it is not yet eight in the morning, 'we could have it out on the humour market by next Christmas!'

'No,' says Lena warningly. 'Not.'

'Think about it,' enthuses Jay. 'We could bring out a new one every holiday!'

'Absolutely not,' says Lena.

And this time Jay hears, though whether he believes is quite another story. He gets up to get a fresh pot of coffee, and when he returns—

'Lena, honey,' he says. 'I'm with you all the way.' He refills her cup almost to overflowing. After the tang of the grapefruit she can hardly taste the coffee, but she appreciates the gesture.

'Thanks,' she says, though both she and Jay know that she would be going ahead with her plans regardless. She puts her feet flat on the floor and the boards under them are as warm as human flesh; her toes unfurl like flowers.

'But Christ,' says Jay, 'I'm gonna miss you.'

'I'll miss you too,' says Lena. She looks at his honest ruddy face and remembers how he used to make her come, one hand on her narrow back pressing her into the bed, the other working energetically inside her. No, it is not Jay's fault that she has had to leave him by the wayside.

'And Mitchell?' says Jay. Now he looks less enthused: he has never really bonded with Mitchell, prefers animals with purposes other than general socializing and the eating of salad. 'Give me a working dog,' he always says, though the closest he has come to a ranch is the farmyard corner at the San Diego Zoo. 'Give me something that can earn its keep.'

'Mitchell will go to Bella's,' says Lena decisively.

'To Bella's?' says Jay.

'Correct,' says Lena.

'Call me crazy,' says Jay, 'but why anyone would want to leave their prize pet with a taxidermist is beyond me.'

They look at each other, Lena and Jay, and they start to laugh. Jay thumps the table and coffee leaps from the pot. They laugh so hard that they fall from their chairs and lie on the floor, and the clock ticks over and the sun gets higher in the sky. And this is a good thing, for once there were two people called Jay Antonelli and Lena McLeonard and they had a kind of love, and no one ever said that love has to end in tears.

The envelope

Because Lena is a child of America, because the powerful men in suits do not wish their country to be viewed as the sort where innocent people can go to buy donuts and return minus an ear – well, because of these things she is awarded a substantial amount of compensation. One morning a letter drops through the door of the Venice Beach apartment, and when Lena opens it the zeros stretch across the paper like astonished mouths.

'My God!' says Jay, in huge admiration. 'It's almost worth getting shot these days.'

Lena goes ahead and accepts the money, although sometimes

she thinks the gesture unnecessary, for the bullet has already provided her with several valuable things. But on other mornings she wakes to find her fingers stuck to the side of her face. The days are not so bad: there are plans to make and phone calls to take, and Jay endlessly wanting to discuss the finer details of his new Lena-less life. But at night, when the pillow takes a soft hold of Lena's damaged head and allows it to rest, then her brain has time to take fright. Eight years is a long time to wait for a healing, even if you are a patient person by nature. So the tears leak out and in the morning Lena must peel the pillow gently away from her face. Then—

Yes, she thinks. *Perhaps I am owed something.*

'But a handout!' objects Mr Domanski. 'If you need money, my little dove, I will give it to you. I am making plenty.' It is true, he is, and with his success has come an added fleshiness so that now his eyes hide away in the folds of his cheeks. Even so, Lena can see the horror in those eyes at the thought of relying on a government for anything at all. 'Don't let them get a hold on you, Lena,' he has always said. 'You will pay for it in the end.'

Now he throws down a warning in the middle of Lena's kitchen floor. 'Think about it carefully!' he says. 'Please tell me you will reconsider.' The gesture he makes with his gold-ringed hand, though, is like someone casting seed on ground that they already know to be too hard for sowing. Just as Lena has a deep knowledge of Mr Domanski, so too does Mr Domanski know his smallest and youngest daughter: newly scarred, long-time stubborn. Didn't he watch over her as a baby as she lay like an apple pip in her cardboard bed? Didn't he pray for her night and morning until she reached the age at which she was supposed to be born? Yes, he knows Lena through and through, and so he suspects his words are futile. And in this he proves correct, for a bubble of anger is welling up inside of Lena.

'Look at me,' she orders.

Mr Domanski looks. He sees her there, slight as a teenager but no longer untouched by life. Defiant in a red T-shirt, she stands in front of him and one side of her head is sleek and shiny, but the other is rough and stubbled like a badly mown field. And in the middle of that field, a scar: as red and as angry as her shirt.

'Look at me!' cries Lena again. She stamps her small foot although it is obvious that Mr Domanski really is seeing her properly rather than simply looking on past (as he sometimes does) for the next opportunity.

'I am sorry,' says Mr Domanski humbly. 'I did not think.'

'I will take the money,' says Lena sternly. 'I have spent my life giving, and forgiving. But I will not forgive the twist of fate that has left me like this.'

'No,' says Mr Domanski, and he looks down at his large feet. 'Of course you should not.' He shuffles on to a stool and accepts a juice, and he heaves a sigh of relief when Lena sits down opposite him and starts talking about other things. He is a strong man and a big one, a man who has extracted his family from the iron grip of a country that he felt no longer loved them and one who has founded a successful chain of restaurants through several lower American states. But when his youngest daughter looks at him like that – well, something in him falls.

Tea

Even before drug money had been counted and missed, even before the gun had been loaded and the car revved up, Lena's looks had not been perfect. Before the streets of the Tenderloin had been staked out and roped off, before she had put on her red shoes and walked into something never meant for her, she had not been drop-dead gorgeous. But then she had never had a problem with this.

'You have such tiny hands,' Jay had said when he first took one of them in his own. 'So delicate. So small.'

'So stubby,' said Lena, calmly.

Jay had looked puzzled. Apart from Bella (who was the exception to every rule anyway) he had always dated girls who would rather bite on glass than confess to their imperfections. But Lena – well, Lena was different. She was philosophical about her uneven looks. She knew that her hair only looked golden in certain lights, that most of the time it was just plain tan. She knew that her nose was smaller than most people's and that this made her cheekbones seem too wide and too high.

'Cosmetic surgery!' she had said to Jay when he signed her up, and she had actually laughed. 'Why on earth would I want that?'

So Los Angeles had left her untouched, had swept around her like the parting of a sea. When she walked on to stage she was like a small cat – light, immovable – and she spun successful jokes out of the side of her slightly crooked mouth. And eventually Jay realized that Lena's indifference was no defence mechanism: everything she said was true. She was telling the truth when she said she disliked peroxide, and that she had no desire for breasts that would draw appreciative stares, and carried with them the minimal risk of exploding at high altitudes.

Now, although Jay would once again be slow to realize it, things have changed for Lena. There are days when she longs for catcalls and wolf-whistles, when she actually wants road workers to put down their shovels at the sight of her and construction workers to drop their tools as she walks by. When she sees billboards featuring unblemished thighs and glossy heads, an ache starts up inside her and she walks fast through the streets as if she can leave it all behind.

(*you mean I've made some difference in the world?* crows the bullet, as it is placed alongside a familiar-looking Colt Python by a satisfied detective)

Yes, just for an hour or two, Lena would like to leave behind the reality of a head shrink-wrapped in skin once belonging to her leg, and a leg looking as if it has been painted on by a child. (*What a terrible scar!* says the blond Dudie, over and over like a badly dubbed soundtrack in Lena's head. *You poor poor sweetheart*, croons the Ego Comedian at Lena's hurrying back.)

Only in Davey's hanger can Lena breathe easy, as she sits and watches him completing his satellite and preparing, like her, for a whole new phase in life. Davey has had his interview, has swum slowly through a roomful of questions compiled by engineers and ex-astronauts and professors to emerge unscathed and successful.

And now he must work as fast as he knows how to finish his satellite. 'I've got someone interested in buying it,' he had told Lena over the phone, and for a second his voice had gone distant so that Lena knew he was giving his confirming nod. 'The head of a research group at Berkeley.'

As he gets closer to completing it, his thoughts are heading north, traversing many state borders towards the final frontier: Mars, or Alaska, depending on how you choose to see it.

'We can fly as far as Fairbanks together,' he tells Lena. 'But after that we'll have to split up. You won't be able to come to the base with me.'

'I know that,' says Lena. She also knows that Davey is not warning, he is simply telling, for he is not remotely worried by Lena hitching a ride to Alaska on his coat-tails. By now Bella would be snarling, prowling her borders, defending her territory. But Davey and Lena have always co-existed peaceably, running side by side through life like trains on parallel tracks, not touching, never swerving closer, every now and then looking over and giving a friendly nod.

'Herb tea?' asks Davey.

'Great,' says Lena, lying on his floor, picking up splinters of fibreglass in her hair.

Davey puts a steaming cup on the floor beside her and there is silence, broken only by his slurps.

'How's the book going?' he asks. 'Got any good shots lately?'

Still lying on the floor, Lena reaches an arm out for her bag. For a second her fingers miss, they grope around in thin air and cannot feel what they are looking for. Then the corners of the camera bag are there: the cold hard shape of reassurance.

'I'm just messing around right now,' she says. 'I haven't seen what I want yet.' She sits up, and then stands up. Most of the time she feels reasonably steady, but sometimes she still needs reminding that she is no longer lying on a sidewalk with blood and grit on her face, staring at death.

'It'll come,' says Davey, and this is all he says. His company – his understated, laconic company – is just right for the state of recovery. In this he is the opposite of Jay, who is hyperbole personified. Jay is no different from the way he has always been, but Lena is finding him newly tiring and every evening she steels herself for his arrival home. The garage door slams below her, the floor of the apartment shakes before Jay is even in the room. And then, when he bursts in, his voice is too loud and his opinions exaggerated. *There is no need for this*, thinks Lena. Life itself is so extraordinary, so unexpected and unruly and over the top, that it seems almost dangerous to encourage it.

When she suggests that she might move out, Jay sounds surprised. 'But there's plenty of room here!' he says. 'Hell, I wish you'd take back the bed. I'm happy to take the couch for a while.'

Lena doesn't want the bedroom back. It reminds her of too many idle hours and too much pain. Besides, she likes sleeping in a room not designed for it: likes having to turn the lights off before she undresses, and creeping under the shutterless windows bent double so as to get to the bathroom. She likes the creaking foldaway bed that seems as if, as any minute, it could flip inwards, enfolding her in its metal arms and suffocating her with blanket love. As she lies there on her back she hardly breathes, and she turns her head quietly when she wants to see the ocean.

But Jay is a problem and is becoming more of one. There is a night when he comes home late, with multiple Red Stripes sloshing inside him; a night when Lena is sitting quietly in the dark wearing only her knickers, watching the huge night clouds rolling over the surface of the sea. As soon as she hears Jay's key in the door she jumps up to look for a T-shirt, but before she can get there Jay has flicked the light on and both he and Lena look slightly embarrassed.

'Sorry, hon,' says Jay, and he flicks the light off again.

But Lena can already hear from his voice that he is not all that sorry, not so sorry that he will just say goodnight and lurch off to bed. Quickly she slips between the covers of her folding bed. Its frame sighs underneath her. *Where have you been all the day long, Lena?* it says gently.

'Y'know what?' says Jay through the dim room. 'I thought you looked really good without the sheets on.'

'Go to bed, Jay,' says Lena. 'You're drunk.'

But Jay's big form comes a few steps closer, and he bends down and aims a kiss at her cheek.

'You're drunk, and you're stoned,' says Lena, moving her head away so his marijuana breath falls on her one good ear.

'C'mon, honey,' he wheedles. 'For old time's sake? We used to light a good fire in our time.' He tries to get on to the bed with her. The frame gives a sharp hiss and collapses in a heap.

'Shit,' swears Jay. Now he is underneath Lena, tangled in sheets, and his foot is trapped between two indignant metal legs.

Silently, Lena thanks the bed. But out loud—

'For Christ's sake, Jay,' she says. 'You know the goddamn rules.' She speaks more sharply than she means to, for her head has hit the edge of Jay's belt buckle. It screams silently to itself, cries like a panicked child, and she puts her hand up to touch it, even though she hardly ever does this.

There is no blood, there has been no blossoming into an instant reminiscent red. But it is sore, and so is she.

'Go to your own bed,' she says to Jay sharply. And he goes, dragging his injured foot behind him.

In the morning, neither of them mentions it. But Jay looks slightly shamefaced as well as hungover, and Lena starts to wear an old baseball shirt to bed – a huge shirt, a giant Giants shirt that used to belong to Jani and then to Mr Domanski and then to Davey, who has given it to her. Swamped in fabric worn by three safe men, she too feels safe. But still she feels cramped by Jay, and his loud and noisy body.

'I take my camera and go out for the day,' she says to Bella, 'but I'm in such a rush to escape that once I get outside I don't even know why I'm there.'

'Tell me about it,' says Bella's voice down the line. She knows, and Lena knows she knows, for she has seen the look on Bella's face when Ken is inspecting the contents of the fridge, when he lays out the root vegetables in neat rows as if he is about to do an audit on them. At such times, Lena has witnessed Bella leaving the kitchen, abruptly, without a word, and heading for her work-room as an animal goes to its hole.

'I've got to find somewhere to stay,' says Lena slightly desperately. 'Just for a few months.'

'Why don't you come here?' says Bella's voice down the line, sounding almost hopeful. 'Revisit the old hood?'

'Oh, I couldn't,' says Lena. It is an instinctive answer but the second she says it, she knows it is true. Because at that very moment, she hears the squeak and click of the neighbour's swing door and her palms break out in sweat and the phone falls from her hand.

(*Squeak!* It is the bullet pretending to shear its way once more through the thin afternoon. *Click!* It is that bullet again, replaying its moment of glory when it connected neatly with the cartilage on the side of Lena's head)

'Oh I couldn't!' cries Lena again, dropping to her knees, reaching blindly for the phone.

'Lena? Lena, honey?' Bella's voice slides out of the receiver and over the floor. 'Lena, are you there?'

Lena picks up the phone and manages to speak. 'Here,' she says faintly.

'Elroy was back in town for a few days,' says Bella, her voice sounding as if it is echoing down a long tube. 'He looked real smart, in a suit and all. He was asking about you.'

'You know what, Bella?' says Lena. 'I've got to go.'

This, too, is the honest truth. Only by trying very hard can Lena say goodbye in a way that will not panic Bella. As the line goes dead, she pictures Bella lumbering purposefully towards her next task: a heap of feathers, a pile of slackened dead skin. She feels so nauseous that she stays on the floor and this is where Jay finds her, much later. Sitting with her back to the cupboards and her knees hunched up, in much the same position as she had sat all those years ago when she first realized that she was a part of her mother's unhappiness, and that she had been left behind.

Blue

'You can sleep here,' says Davey. 'Though you know there's no real bathroom,' he says. 'Only the toilet out in back.'

'That's fine,' says Lena.

'And I arrive early in the morning,' says Davey. 'Sometimes very early.' Once again, he is not throwing down obstacles to deter Lena but is simply dragging them out into the light of day so Lena can see what she will have to hurdle.

'Early starts, fine,' says Lena. She has no problem with either problem, prefers to avoid bathroom mirrors at the moment and likes working in the early morning light.

So she says goodbye to Jay, who is naturally reluctant to see her leave. His big heart would find it hard to let any wounded woman go, let alone one he has been involved with, in both business and pleasure, for nearly ten years.

'You know you don't have to do this,' he says worriedly. He calls her a cab, and he carries her suitcases chivalrously out the door and then brings them back in, feeling that they belong right there in that room. 'Is it because of—' he says, and he scuffs his feet on the carpet.

'The collapse of the foldaway?' says Lena. She reaches out to touch his arm and sparks fly. 'Ouch,' she says. 'Stop scuffing.'

Jay stops. 'Or is it because of—?' he says, and light dawns over his face. He puts up one huge hand and smacks his forehead. 'Oh, shit, Lena,' he says, and his feet look as if they want to raise static again. 'It's because of the twins, isn't it.'

'Don't,' says Lena, skirting around him to get to her bag.

'Don't scuff?' says Jay. 'Or don't even go there?'

'Both,' says Lena firmly.

'Donna and Cindy,' says Jay, as if he can't help himself. 'They're good girls, you know.' Recently he has become more than necessarily talkative about identical blondes he has met on the comedy circuit, and it is possible that his interest is merely professional – certainly he hopes they will soon song-and-dance their way on to his list. But then this is the way that he and Lena started, after all.

146

'You'd like them,' he says earnestly. It isn't apparent to Lena which one of the twin-set Jay himself likes best; it is possible that he hasn't yet managed to tell them apart. But if a Donna or a Cindy – or in a worst case scenario, both – arrives home on Jay's arm one night soon, Lena would rather not be lying there on her prim and narrow bed.

'Let's not get into this,' she says. 'No hard feelings, I promise.'

There aren't, and as she gets into the cab she wonders at how easily people fall away: like icicles, holding on fast through a long hard winter and then dropping in an unexpected instant to the ground. So the cab carries her away from Jay, along hard colourful streets, past concrete playgrounds and through blaring lines of cars. Lena leans her head against the glass and projects herself out of there, out of the noise and the chaos into a silent landscape of snow.

Davey has put a mattress up in the storage loft for her, and when she lies there Lena can reach up and touch the roof. Made of cracked and brittle fibreglass, when it shifts on its steel struts it makes a sound like rain, even though there has been no rain in LA for six months now.

'You gonna be OK up there?' calls Davey, getting ready to leave. 'You won't fall off now?' He lets the heavy doors fall shut behind him, and the silence stretches its long arms through the hangar and settles in for the night.

There is a clear patch in the semi-opaque roof above Lena, and through this she can see the sky like a deep blue second ceiling. As she lies and looks, the colour slowly drains out of the sky, suckled away by the blind seeking night, and for those few minutes before the dark Lena Domanski knows true emptiness.

Boxes

On most of those melancholic fall mornings, Davey arrives before eight.

'I'll try not to wake you,' he says.

'I should be gone by then,' says Lena, and most mornings she is. By the time Davey's beaten-up Ford Fairlane rolls up outside,

147

the kettle is already cool on the Primus stove, the toast crumbs have been swept away, and Lena is on a bus to another part of her vast, anarchic, adopted city. As Davey finetunes his satellite, Lena combs the streets for the damaged and the blemished.

She gets off the bus wherever she feels like it, carries her camera into parking lots and playgrounds, through glamorous empty avenues. She photographs crack addicts in alleyways with plastic bags over their heads, and tired young mothers in tears from the sudden relinquishment of independence. On Hollywood Boulevard she captures old tourists searching for the stars of the past, and impatient twenty-something tourists pushing right on past them. With her camera, she is both invisible and invincible: she can go anywhere.

So before most people have started up their computers or drunk their first coffee of the day Lena's work can be finished. She prefers the clarity of the early morning, the hours before the haze has settled on the city and the features of people have been rubbed into indifference. On her way home the camera bag feels heavier, full of the images she has picked up off the city streets. A limp, the stoop of a back under a heavy school satchel, an anxious or a lonely expression: she carries all these back to the hangar with her.

But although Lena is deliberately, daily seeking out imperfection, sometimes she wishes she did not have to live with it. In the evenings, under the dim grey roof, she examines her leg as it lies against the dingy mattress looking like a sacrificial exhibit offered up in some meaningless urban ritual. The edges of its neat purple square are now stretching and blurring, but even so Lena can sense the anxiety of the new skin which still cannot breathe, grow hair, or sweat. Small white eruptions of panic appear on its surface and it reminds Lena of Bella when she was growing up: not knowing how to do things, not content to wait.

Patience, she reminds it gently. But on those particular nights when she lies down to sleep, it is in the recovery position, one forearm under her aching head, one knee crooked up to her heart. As her images build she sorts them into shoe boxes and stacks them at the foot of her mattress: barrier, retaining wall, shelter.

The first story of loss

It is a clear sunny December day and a woman named Flo is heading down the Interstate 405 to visit her daughter (Amy) in San Diego. There Flo will get some sea air and a change of scene, she will buy some new clothes and revitalize herself, and will return to LA feeling like a different – and a better – kind of Flo.

As she drives, Flo talks on her cellphone to her daughter (Amy) and her daughter is so funny and makes Flo laugh *so hard* that, when she switches lanes, she fails to see the motorbike in the lane right next to her. Because of Flo's lane change, because of her funny daughter (Amy) and her plans for Christmas and her cellphone and her laughing, the guy on the motorbike next to her must brake *so hard* that he almost goes head over arse.

'Crazy bitch!' the guy swears.

The guy on the bike accelerates and catches up with the woman (Flo). So mad is he that he rides alongside her on his Ducati (900 cc) and he reaches into the convertible and grabs a hold of Flo's small, white, fluffy dog. Lifting that dog (Leo) right out of the front seat of Flo's convertible, he throws it into the middle of three lanes of oncoming traffic.

Leo (a Bichon Frise) lets out a series of tiny cries as he is bumped over by trucks, Cadillacs, and an ambulance on the way to another emergency. *Lost: one friend.* Leo's body is squashed on the hot road, and his clean, fluffy white fur, blow-dried only that morning at the Malibu Hound Lounge, becomes marked all over by the track marks of passing tyres.

(freeze-frame: a middle-aged woman with good legs and a good cosmetic surgeon stands in front of an officer of the LAPD. While the gold buttons on the woman's jacket wink at the officer's gold badges, tears are pouring down the woman's face. In one hand she holds her cellphone, with the other she adjusts her false eyelashes. In the background is a small dog, lying on the long shiny bonnet of convertible with its eyes closed. It looks almost as if it is sunbathing)

Animal lovers throughout the state of California put a bounty on the head of the motorbike man. In time that man (Vinny) is tracked down and is fined one hundred and ten thousand US dollars (a sizeable sum for a postal worker living with his mother in a San Jose tenement block). *Lost: a small fortune.*

Vinny is ordered to apologize to Flo but he is not allowed to do this by mail – not even by e-mail, or over the phone. In front of an impartial mediator hired by the state, Vinny must look Flo right in the eyes. He must say he is sorry, and he must buy Flo a brand new Bichon Frise that will never be Leo. *Lost: perspective on all sides, and a whole lot of taxpayers' money.*

Time

'So how did you get the definitive shot?' booms Bella down the phone.

'I was in Davey's car going to pick him up,' says Lena, 'and I just happened to be driving by.'

'Right place at the right minute,' approves Bella. 'Good. Maybe your timing's gonna be better than when you were in comedy.'

'In for the kill, that's me,' says Lena ironically, but as she looks down at the photo she strokes Leo's black-and-white head very gently with her finger.

'Hey, Lena?' says Bella.

'Yep?' says Lena.

'I suppose the body was beyond repair, was it?' asks Bella. She puts Mitchell on the phone so Lena can hear him purr.

As the New Year begins and Epiphany rears its ancient head, Mr and Mrs Domanski exchange their annual letters about reconciliation and get on with their lives. And Davey receives a letter requesting his presence in the desert.

'For preliminary training,' he says. 'Though we're not supposed to tell where – even you, I shouldn't.' He looks a little worried in case Lena might be hurt.

'That's OK,' says Lena. 'I'm not offended.' She is now familiar with reticence, has grown used to grunts and monosyllables and the erratic speech of Davey's hammer. But on the morning that

150

Davey leaves, he looks at her and speaks in a rush.

'We're going somewhere near the Salton Sea,' he says. 'It's OK to tell you, because you don't count.'

Lena takes this as the compliment it is meant to be. 'Don't get lost out there,' she says. 'We've got some travelling to do.'

Davey is gone for ten days. When Lena wakes in the loft, she stretches her legs and arms into an all-day silence. Her head hurts far less now she is away from Jay and his twenty-four-hour cellphone.

('A book of losers!' brays Jay down the phone to a publisher he knows in New York. 'It'll be real funny.'

'It sounds perfect,' says the publisher, dropping ash on his list of upcoming comedy titles. 'God knows we've got enough of the feel-good crap, we could do with some real savagery.'

'Huh?' says Jay, down the phone.

'*Savagery*,' says the publisher, stubbing his cigarette out on a two-dimensional club comedian from Bradford, England. 'That's what we need.'

'Oh no, it won't be a violent book,' says Jay. 'Lena's against violence.'

'Satire,' says the publisher tiredly. 'It's a dying art.')

The second story of loss

With the arrival of January into Los Angeles, Philly Tarantella – one-time giant of the comedy circuit – also comes to the fore. Sexy, successful, arrogant-son-of-a-bitch Tarantella, who got his start in the small clubs of San Francisco and has never looked back. A big man in all senses of the word, Tarantella is renowned for his flamboyant dress sense, and for starring in the longest running sitcom in the history of American television. But recently his ratings have taken a dive, and he plans to stage a comeback through a series of live shows.

At the first gig Tarantella appears to have put on weight. His set is based on his TV character – the character that has failed to hold the attention of either the studio executives or the nation

– and his fans rustle and fidget. They realize Tarantella is no longer compelling; they look to their cocktails for distraction, and twirl their paper parasols. Before he has even finished his set Tarantella is being clapped off stage. 'Milk milk,' his fans chant, making gestures as if they are sitting on three-legged stools. *Lost: adoration of the masses.*

At Gig Number Two Tarantella starts out rowdy and insulting. His audience are unimpressed. ('You're a has-been fella, Tarantella!' one man shouts.) Tarantella's eyes flick from one corner of the room to the other, rise to the ceiling as if in prayer. Soon he must leave the stage amidst boos and hisses which continue for fifteen long minutes.

(freeze-frame: a large man, overweight and in bad need of a haircut, stands in a back alley leaning against a concrete wall. His Hawaiian print shirt is hanging out over his loud chequered pants, his greying head hangs heavily forward. Behind him is a door strung with lights: at his feet, a pile of leaves and a couple of empty beer cans)

Tarantella's third show is, not surprisingly, a media sell-out; reviewers and journos hang on their barstools like vultures. No sooner has Tarantella walked on stage and started a routine than he falters and falls back on one-liners. The room is full of gleeful disappointment. *Loss of an idol, loss of face.*

After his spectacular fall from grace at the Alhambra and his trashing by the critics, Philly Tarantella is spotted by *OK!* magazine indulging in a Rodeo Drive spending spree. His purchases are reported to be:

– seven identical grey suits by Armani
– fourteen identical white shirts
– seven pairs of matching black loafers, and
– three black bowties.

A few days later Tarantella announces his retirement from comedy. He starts up an IT consultancy firm with his sharp-tongued red-headed ex-wife and from this point on is rarely seen in public. When he is, he is wearing grey flannel, white cotton, and dull leather loafers. *Lost: one long-standing career and a larger than life personality.*

Spaghetti

'That Tarantella, he's an arrogant son of a bitch,' Jay had said admiringly, when Tarantella had first blazed on to the small screen. 'He could teach you a thing or two, Lena.'

'We have different styles,' said Lena mildly. 'Try to please every man and you end up as No Man.'

'But it has nothing to do with him being a man,' said Jay blankly.

'He sure is sexy,' said Bella, and she had looked over in a critical way at small bristling Ken who was doing the crossword with a neat blue pen.

Now Bella is horrified at Philly's demise. 'I picked up *OK!* in line at the checkout,' she says, 'and there he is looking like a fucking businessman!' She looks accusingly at Lena as if implying that, had Lena only given Tarantella a few tips, both his career and his sense of humour might have been saved.

'You know, even back in San Francisco,' says Lena, 'he never seemed to really *enjoy* comedy all that much.'

'Enjoy?' says Bella. 'Enjoy? He was there to make money, wasn't he? What's to enjoy?'

'In that case,' says Lena, 'he's made the smartest move of his life.'

February wanders into LA, trailing some showers behind it, so that Lena wakes to the soft tap of water above her face. She puts on a waterproof coat when she goes out, allows raindrops to sit on the camera lens so that when she develops her photos there are pleasing blurred circles on their surface. Davey hires a removal truck to take away his finished prototype, Jay signs up both Donna and Cindy but sleeps with only one of them, and Bella gets a commission to stuff her first ever Barbary sheep.

The grey clouds remind Lena of departure, and she goes to the sales looking for Arctic clothing.

'You're in the wrong city for thermals, lady,' says the store clerk. But then he remembers a shipment from several years ago, delivered by mistake. 'I've got a feeling it was never returned,' he says. After a long time he comes back brandishing several long-sleeved tops and several pairs of long underwear. 'It's kid's sizing,' he says, eyeing up Lena in a professional way, 'but you're pretty small.'

'You've got yourself a deal,' says Lena, and she gets him to put them in a yellow plastic bag for her. As she leaves the store she feels the skin on her leg bristle at the prospect of contact with wool. But—

We still have some time, she says to it.

Jay invites her over to what was once her home and cooks pasta for her, seriously, as if she is a real guest. After the tiramisu, when Jay begins clearing the table in a businesslike way, the purpose for the visit becomes clear.

'You remember that publisher friend of mine in New York?' he asks Lena. 'Well, I put out the bait and he's interested!' He takes the photos Lena has brought with her and proceeds to deal them out in long straight lines. His head moves along with his eyes, up and down, in a methodical way.

Minutes pass. Jay's face remains impassive. Lena looks at Jay looking at her shots and she wonders what it is, exactly, that he is seeing.

Suddenly Jay seizes a photo. 'Now, that's more like it!' he says with a beam. His fingers twitch as if they are longing to reach for the phone and dial New York, even though there it is four in the morning.

'You like that one?' asks Lena.

'Most of these are a bit – how can I put it – morbid for my tastes,' says Jay. 'No offence, Lena. But this! Christ, what a nosedive that guy took!' As he looks at the sight of Tarantella's drooping head, his smile broadens. 'The only thing is,' he adds, holding it out at arm's length, 'it could be clearer that it actually *is* Philly Tarantella. His face is kind of hidden here.'

'That's what I was aiming for,' agrees Lena. 'I'm not after celebrity shots.'

'You're not?' says Jay. He looks concerned, standing there with a small dried trail of spaghetti sauce straggling down his chin. 'But honey,' he says from force of habit, 'stars sell!'

'I'm not interested in that sort of market,' says Lena, and she starts to tidy the photos away so that Philly's large, mainly obscured face becomes completely obscured. 'If it's too evident who it is,' she says, sliding them into an envelope, 'that shot will have to go.'

Jay looks despondent. 'I'm gonna call the publisher anyway,' he says. 'I'm sure we can come to some compromise.' He seems slightly confused by Lena's decisions, but then this is nothing new.

Lena is at the bottom of the stairs, stepping out into the soft rain, when she hears the door open again behind her.

'Hey Lena,' Jay is calling.

'Yes?' she says, turning around.

'Y'know what? I didn't even notice that damn scar tonight,' says Jay. 'Just thought I'd tell you.'

'Thanks,' says Lena. 'But that's probably because I'm wearing a bandanna.'

'Oh,' says Jay. 'So you are.'

The third story of loss

Down in South Central, on the corner of Main and McTavity, is a scrap metal yard owned by a man named Mikey Mike. Mikey Mike carries a handgun with him at all times: in the glove compartment of his car, when he's walking around the yard, even when he's sitting on the john in his lunch hour reading the paper. 'Ya never know who's going to roll in through these gates,' he says philosophically. 'I've had all sorts here and they're usually fresh from the scrape.'

There comes a day when Mikey Mike is hailed from a car as he stands on the sidewalk outside his very own yard (run by his brother for thirteen years and another thirteen by himself), talking to an old golfing buddy.

'Yo, Mikey!' he hears. 'Yo, Mikey Mike!' And when he turns around he sees a carload of men, and the men are hanging out the windows calling to him. 'You wanna buy this thing?' they call to Mikey Mike, and they point to their roof.

'I'm not buying that!' says Mikey Mike. 'It's still got glass in it.' He looks more closely. 'And concrete,' he says. 'And some rusty crap.'

'We'll clean it up,' promise the men.

(freeze-frame: four men, two black and two white, sit in a car and gesture out of the windows to a small stocky guy on the side of the road. On the roof of the car is a phone box, bound around with ropes like a treasure chest. Its base is attached to a solid slab of concrete as if it has recently been uprooted from the sidewalk; rusty girders stick out from the bottom of the slab like feet)

'Yeah, man,' the men say. 'That's cool. We'll clean it up first.' They pull into the yard and pull out hammers, and then they start smashing up the phone box they have dragged out of the pavement and brought along to sell to Mikey Mike, king of scrap metal and generally known as an all-round good guy.

In the meantime Mikey Mike's trigger finger is at the ready, but his instinct tells him these guys just want some money and no funny business. The thing is, Mikey Mike's golfing buddy is an off-duty cop and he takes Mikey Mike into the office and looks out through the one-way glass and says, 'Gotta do an arrest here.'

'Hey, give them a break,' says Mikey Mike. 'They just need some money for crack.' And he laughs *heh heh heh*, because he knows that his buddy's a realist and he won't be chasing them for *that*.

'No can do,' says the sheriff. 'This is a fed.' By which Mikey Mike knows that his friend means a federal offence and there will be no blind eye around here today. And the off-duty sheriff calls for back-up, and soon four cop cars scream into the yard and the men are surrounded, and they are taken away (along with their phone box still on its big concrete foot but minus its smaller rust-covered ones). Mikey Mike is left alone in his office with his unused gun, left in peace to eat his ham and mustard sandwich and rue the day he learned to play golf.

'Shit,' he says. 'Best hunk of metal I've been offered in a long time.' *Lost: revenue for a straight dealer who knows when not to be.*

'I bet no one puts the phone box back neither,' says Mikey Mike to himself. He is right, no one does. *Lost: one working payphone from a poor black neighbourhood.*

Transport

'But Lena,' says Jay plaintively over lunch. 'These aren't even funny.'

Lena stares at him, spears a rocket leaf and dangles it from her fork in front of her. 'I know,' she says. She frames Jay's large face between the swaying greenery and the two shining prongs of the fork.

Jay continues to flip through the photos, searching in vain for something to make him laugh. He looks as if he has had sex recently: as recently as this morning, thinks Lena. His cheeks have a healthy glow and in spite of his puzzlement he draws wine through his teeth with a slow seductive pull.

'They're not meant to be funny,' says Lena finally, taking pity on him, cramming the rocket into her mouth.

'But you said—' says Jay, sounding slightly peeved. 'But I thought we were doing a book here!'

'I,' says Lena, 'am doing a book. But it is not going to be a humorous book.' She looks across the table and sees a black and white image of Mikey Mike, gesturing wildly with a tiny cellphone while a man-size phone box is dismantled at high speed in front of him. 'On the other hand,' she says with a shrug, 'humour will not be entirely absent.'

Jay also looks down at Mikey Mike but it seems that he sees only the graffiti-splashed fence and the bulge of a handgun on the off-duty cop's skinny ankle. 'You know what?' he says. 'You really shouldn't go to places like that alone.'

(*Look for me there too!* calls the bullet from its dark bed in a drawer of the SFPD forensics department. *I know places like that, although I have never been there myself!*)

157

'You shouldn't tell me where not to go,' Lena says to Jay. 'We're not together any more, remember?' She doesn't want to hurt Jay but she forces her heart to harden up. Only a few hours ago (she reminds her heart) Jay was easing himself from between someone else's legs, leaving that person to doze in the bed shared not so long ago with Lena.

Jay flushes. 'I could get you a good deal with this guy in New York,' he points out. 'Play your cards right and you could have the biggest stocking-filler this side of Christmas.'

Lena bends her head to look at the tomato in her salad: seeds suspended under the transparent surface like bodies in ice, veins spreading from the central core. These details shout out to her in the middle of the clinking, shifting café, and when she looks back at Jay he is slightly blurred.

'Just tell me you'll think about it,' he is saying, but his voice is already distanced from her, and the white cloth between them is like the huge snowy tabletop of a mountain.

'I'll get you some prints and you can send them where you like,' she says. 'Nothing can happen before I get back from Alaska, anyway.'

'What if my guy loves them?' says Jay, with relief in his voice at what he interprets as cooperation. 'What if he wants to snap them up?'

Lena shrugs. 'Publishers don't move that fast,' she says. She leads the way out into the street, hears a car backfire and instinctively ducks and turns to the distant mountains for support. They are always there like a purple-brown wall at her back, although they are beginning to waver in the March haze.

'Where are you headed now?' asks Jay responsibly. Although he has not proved fast enough to get between Lena and a silver bullet, he has always offered rides and glasses of water, and has opened car doors for her.

'To Fairfax,' she says, 'but I'm planning to catch the bus.'

'Are you sure?' says Jay dubiously. He has been out of San Francisco long enough to have developed a healthy mistrust of public transport although, strangely, he began his life on a train, was pushed out suddenly into the hot darkness somewhere near Daly City with his mother tended to by a ticket inspector. 'No,' he says decisively. 'I'll take you. Where exactly in Fairfax did you want to go?'

Exactly, Lena has no idea; she has simply intended to hang around outside temples and butcher shops and wait for a good shot to turn up. When she tries to explain this to Jay—

'Oh, I *see*,' he says, and now he sounds pleased. 'You're looking for more losers! Well, you can't go wrong with the Jewish folk.'

Lena gives up all plans and gets Jay to drop her back at the hangar. She feels jumbled, her photos smudged with Jay's large thumbprints and his misunderstanding of what they are about. There is a dusty space left by the removal of Davey's satellite, which has been snapped up not by a university but by a private corporation cashing in on the space boom, and she lies down in the middle of that space. Small shavings of metal scratch at the tops of her ears. Correction: the top of her ear, singular, and where her other ear used to be.

She feels her head creak with the constant effort of repairing itself. A tear escapes and runs quickly, ashamedly, into her hair.

The fourth story of loss

There was once a girl called Lena Domanski, and then called Lena McLeonard, who got on the wrong side of a gun and had her ear shot out. When this girl Lena looks in the reflection of a soup spoon – a trick that her estranged mother taught her a long time ago – she turns her head this way and that, looking for her old self.

(freeze-frame: a small slim girl sits bolt upright on a paint-spattered box. Her age is difficult to determine: her skin and her body are young, but her eyes look as if they have lived forever. She is looking directly into the lens. One hand holds the lead to the camera, the other is raised. The first finger of that raised hand points to the shiny mangled side of her head like a gun)

Her old self is not to be found, of course: it is not in the bowl of the spoon or outside of it. Nor does this girl, this Lena Domanski-McLeonard, really expect it to be. For if she has learnt one thing, this girl, it is that every time you step onto the street you may come back in the door a few hours later changed beyond recognition.

What has this girl lost? She has lost:
– *a mother*
– *a significant amount of blood and skin*
– *a certain sense of immunity*, and
– *a brand-new pair of red vinyl shoes.*

Ten-gallon drum

Davey arrives at the hangar slightly later than usual the next morning but Lena is still there. She is on her knees in the middle of a heap of clothes and books, throwing some stuff one way and some the other.

'Keep,' she is murmuring. 'Out. Keep. Out.'

Davey stands there watching for a while, preparing to speak. 'You're not packing for Alaska already, are you?' he says finally.

'No, I'm not that organized,' says Lena, surrounded by the waving octopus arms of old sweaters.

'What then?' says Davey, quite curiously for him.

'I'm sieving my life,' says Lena. She has lain awake thinking about this for a long time, through the dead night hours until the time when the sky turned white and the hum of generators started up around her. She has thought about Elroy rushing into the Tenderloin house bearing jokes written on scraps of newspaper, has thought of the years of hearing the phrase 'Tell Lena so she can get it down!', and of the lead, dead weight of Material lying in a notebook at the bottom of her bag.

'What are these?' says Davey, picking up one of the books from the pile of the doomed.

'My comedy books,' says Lena. 'All my routines, from Time Immemorial.' The old phrase slips easily into her mouth and rolls off her tongue. She has carried these notebooks from house to house and from city to city, like talismans guarding against the possibility that, one day, she might lose her funniness. And now

– because of an accident, because of an accidental moment – she is done with them.

'Give me a hand, will you?' she says to Davey.

Davey brings a sack barrow over and together they wheel two cartons of old jokes out the back of the hangar. Davey throws them into a barrel and douses them with kerosene, and Lena lights the match. The books burn slowly at first, with a sullen reluctance, as if not wanting to let Lena out of their sight. But then the heat takes hold, and thick black smoke begins to pour out of the barrel, and the flames leap.

'I'll be inside,' says Davey.

Lena stays out in the yard, breathing in the acrid air so that her nostrils burn and sting. Her career floats past her in small flakes of ash. And at that moment, just for a moment, she sees the balancing of a see-saw world.

'Every cloud has a silver lining,' she hears her mother – victim, victor – say, while her Polish father flips an American dime, and says, 'There can be no heads without tails.'

Lena stands there for a bit longer, watching the dust and the ash mingle. Once the inferno has lost its fierceness she goes back inside, but for the rest of the day she feels somehow lighter.

('These are amazing!' says Jay's New York publisher contact, turning the photos to the light of a hazy Brooklyn evening.

'Searingly honest portrayals of grief,' intones his assistant.

'Not entirely without humour, though,' says the publisher.

'Humour is present,' agrees the assistant solemnly.

'I don't want to lose these to anyone else,' says the publisher. 'Get on to this, pronto.')

The morning of departure is messy, as mornings of departure always are. There are a hundred small things to do – the washing of sheets, the throwing away of milk, the packing of toothbrushes – that cannot be done until the hours just before the airport. When Lena crosses the hanger she feels that she is walking on a slant, as if all the shearing and replacing of skin has left her body slightly lopsided.

'What is it?' asks Davey, carrying suitcases. Under his boots the floor looks perfectly level.

'Nothing,' says Lena, and she doesn't say much else until they are on the plane and the engines have settled into a steady hum. She looks down at her hands, opening and closing on the arm rests. 'I wish it was yesterday,' she says. 'Or tomorrow.' She opens the tinfoil lid of her lunch and realizes she has forgotten to request a vegetarian meal.

'Huh?' says Davey, sitting stolidly beside her, making inroads into creamed carrots and roast beef.

'I don't think I like limbo,' says Lena. She looks out on to the wing, shining and tilting below her.

'Can I have your beef?' asks Davey, through a mouthful of his.

'Sure,' says Lena, passing it over. She lies back and lets her head roll on the dirty headrest, using this motion to sneak looks at Davey, hoping to catch a similar nervousness in his profile. There is none. From time to time his freckled nose wrinkles as he pores over his location map.

'They're taking us somewhere west of Fairbanks,' he says. There is a pause. 'I don't know any more than that,' he says.

'Why won't they tell you?' asks Lena. 'Security reasons again?'

The engines swallow and the plane banks to the left. There beneath them, lying on a strange angle, is the grey and white landscape of southern Alaska. Soon two Domanskis – almost certainly the only Domanskis ever to land here – will be set down in the middle of that snow-bound wilderness, on a ground frozen as hard as that of their native Poland.

'I guess so,' replies Davey, surprising Lena, who by now has forgotten her question. 'My hunch is they've put the pod up the Yukon River somewhere,' he says. 'But if we don't know where we are, there's less temptation to escape.'

'You're allowed outside though, aren't you?' asks Lena. She feels the plane's skeleton creak under their feet, sees the landing gear unfold from the pockets of the wings. After a while—

'Not for too long,' says Davey. 'And only in spacesuits, with ski gloves and helmets.'

'Not so different from what your average Alaskan wears,' says Lena.

'Ha!' says Davey. His magpie mouth opens and he gives a short cough of laughter. 'You're funny, Lena,' he says. There is slight surprise in his voice as if he has never noticed this before: perhaps Lena's twenty-year career has got lost amidst the spinning galaxies in his head. Even now, as they lean together watching Fairbanks rush up to meet them, he doesn't ask her what she will do while he is incarcerated for eight weeks in a twenty-six-foot habitation pod. He just points out what he thinks is the university campus and marvels at how much snow there is for April.

The airport at Fairbanks is so plain and prosaic and flat-roofed that it seems an unlikely launching pad for great astronauts and earthly explorers.

'But don't forget gold was dragged out of the ground around here,' says Lena the Explorer (who has read Davey's guidebook).

'Mined from the permafrost,' adds Davey the Astronaut, stamping his foot on the hard asphalt.

They catch a bus into town, along Airport Road. 'Imagination is a great thing,' says Lena in the voice of a professor. 'The names we bestow speak volumes about the state of post-modern America.'

'The forty-ninth state of modern America,' agrees Davey, missing Lena completely. 'Here we are.' Instead of looking out the window at the real thing he turns again to his guidebook, reads the facts with his lips moving silently as if telling himself a bedtime story.

They get off the bus near the centre of Fairbanks and then there is less than twenty minutes before Davey must catch another bus, which will take him on his mystery tour. He and Lena stand on the corner of Sixth and Cushman with their bags heaped at their feet, and talk about how cold the air is and how clean.

'No haze!' says Lena. Her lungs feel as if they have never breathed until now.

'And no Hollywood,' says Davey, staring at the low clear hills covered only by the spikes of spruce trees.

The minibus pulls up right on time. Behind the tinted glass

are the faces of maybe-astronauts, topped by peaked caps and incongruous woollen beanies.

'I guess you'll get to know those hats pretty well,' says Lena. She reaches out to hug Davey goodbye and then he is looking at her with a sudden anxiety on his face. 'Are you sure you'll be OK?' he asks. 'You'll find somewhere to stay?'

Lena takes a quick look along the main road out of town. 'Somewhere cosy,' she agrees, but she knows already that she will go farther north than this, and soon. She calls, 'See you in eight weeks,' although the muffler on the bus has seen too many unsealed roads and roars so loudly that she cannot even hear her own voice. And then Davey is gone, and Lena's feet drag a little on the footpath as she takes her first steps all alone since the day she was born. She has always had too many people around her; now, suddenly, there are too few.

She goes into a gift shop and buys postcards, takes them to the high window ledge that looks over the empty street. She writes cards to her mother in Warsaw, to her father in San Francisco, to Bella in the Tenderloin, and to Jay in her own ex-apartment in Venice for, in spite of the twins, he has proved a true and loyal friend. After a moment's hesitation, she returns to the counter and buys one more view of Fairbanks to send to the surgeon, but she keeps her greetings short so he will have time to read to the end.

Pork

By way of an information centre, Lena finds herself a temporary home. The Applesauce Inn stands on the outskirts of Fairbanks, on stilts; it looks as if at any moment it will spread its shutters and soar to the top of the Alaskan mountains. From the deck outside her room Lena can close her eyes and be surrounded by the musky smell of real spruce, nothing like the stuff Jay used to spray around their plastic Christmas tree every December.

That first night before dinner she runs a deep bath and lies in it for a long time. Sliding down and opening her eyes under water, she sees the orb of the bathroom light far above her, wavering like an uncertain sun.

'How much sun will I get while I'm here?' she asks Seidensal, the owner of the inn.

'That depends on how far north you go,' he says. 'If you travel as far as Barrow, soon you will be able to sunbathe at midnight.' He looks at Lena and smiles. 'But in winter,' he says, 'the town is plunged into total darkness. How you would say, the other side of the coin.'

Seidensal is German and he still has a slow and polite rhythm to his speech, even though it is twenty-five years since he first came to Alaska to climb mountains. 'I damaged my knee beyond repair the first season I arrived,' he says, 'but I stayed on anyway.' When he gets up to help with the plates, he walks with a slight but noticeable limp. 'Now I get my kicks from playing golf,' he says with a straight face.

Just as Lena appreciates Seidensal's deadpan style of joke-telling, so does Seidensal appreciate Lena's blood origins. 'Domanski, huh?' he says, and after dinner he offers her a special glass of ruby wine.

'He must *really* like you, Lena,' says his wife Chipper significantly. 'That port is usually hidden away from the guests.'

'Chipper, please!' says Seidensal, his moustache drooping in disapproval. 'I am merely being polite.'

Chipper winks at Lena. Her plump all-American hands dart over the table, her diamond rings clink against what looks like family china. 'My husband isn't polite unless he wants to be,' she says. 'Beats me why he ever got into the hospitality trade.'

'To stop you from losing a small fortune, woman,' Seidensal says to her. 'Chipper would give away the shirt off her back if I were not here to stop her,' he says to Lena.

After the table is cleared Seidensal pulls out old photo albums and talks of places like Franken and the Moselle Valley, while Chipper brings out hot chocolate and chocolate chip cookies and chocolate-covered ants. 'Home-grown right here in Fairbanks, these critters,' she says proudly. 'The Japanese buy them in truckloads.'

'Oh, I can't,' says Lena, slightly embarrassed.

'Corn-fed,' says Chipper, waving an ant enticingly in the air so that its small brown head waggles at Lena.

Lena shakes her own head. 'I'm sorry,' she says. 'I'm vegetarian.'

'But you ate up all your pork chop at dinner,' says Chipper, looking puzzled.

'Well,' says Lena, looking down at the springer spaniel who has gone to sleep on her foot. '*He* ate pork chop,' she admits, giving a tiny grimace.

For the first time Seidensal bellows with laughter. The ends of his moustache rise up and out to the sides of his face like the water wings of a plane. 'We don't see too many vegetarians around here,' he says, wiping his eyes with the corner of the tablecloth. His *vee* comes out as a *w*, so it sounds like 'wegetarian'; and this is so like something Mr Domanski might say, in spite of Bella's constant nagging, that Lena's eyes smart. She takes a huge gulp of hot chocolate, burning her tongue.

If Seidensal notices her sudden silence, he pretends not to. 'You know who Lena Domanski should pay a visit to, Chipper?' he says, slapping his hand down on his map of Alaska.

'No, honey,' says Chipper obediently. 'Who?'

Seidensal clears his throat and puts his feet up on the fire irons as if readying himself for a political address.

'Who, honey?' says Chipper again, stoking up the fire so that the wood crackles.

'Jimmy!' says Seidensal. 'Lena should go north and stay with Jimmy.'

'With who?' says Lena, uncertainly. 'Where?' The side of her head clenches at the sound of someone else telling her what to do: she has not stepped out of the large, capable hands of Jay and Mr Domanski only to step into somebody else's.

'Jimmy!' says Chipper. 'Of course!' But her voice doesn't ring quite as loudly as Seidensal's, and when Lena glances across at her there is an odd look of conflict on Chipper's face.

'Jimmy is a friend of mine,' says Seidensal, rolling up the map like an expedition leader and pointing through the north-facing wall with it.

'If you can call him a friend of anybody's,' says Chipper.

'He lives all the way up in Barrow,' says Seidensal, ignoring this interjection. 'That is where you said you might go, yes? To get some twenty-four-hour daylight?'

'I might as well,' says Lena. 'You think I could get some good shots there?' In spite of her wariness, she leans forward and her fingers start to trace small roads on the rough green tablecloth.

'It's hard in Barrow,' says Chipper worriedly. 'It's never been an easy place, the Northern Slope.'

'They have real wilderness up there,' says Seidensal, and his voice takes on a wistful note. 'None of this log cabin shit, and this riverboat crap.'

'Frank!' says Chipper, looking shocked. 'Please mind your language. Lena is a *guest*.'

Seidensal subsides into his chair, but his left leg – his injured one – taps restlessly on the green carpet. 'It has been a while since I have been up to that coast,' he says. 'It reminds me of the Baltic Sea.'

'Does it?' says Lena. For a second the room fades and she sees a smaller Lena Domanski, sitting at another table with quite another map in front of her, searching for her very own outpost of the world. She shakes her head and Chipper and Seidensal come back into focus. 'Does he have a guesthouse, your friend?' she asks.

'He has only a small home,' says Seidensal, 'but sometimes he will have people to stay to bring in some extra money. Jimmy is a tracker so his work is not always regular.'

'A tracker?' asks Lena. 'What's that?' All her comments seem to be coming out as questions, but Seidensal doesn't seem to mind.

'He tracks people, mostly,' he says. 'He is one of the best. He picks up most of his work from the state troopers but he will do a job for anyone as long as they will pay him.'

'But what,' says Lena, groping, 'what does he actually *do*?'

'He finds things,' says Seidensal simply. 'People, animals, you name it. Anything that is lost, Jimmy is guaranteed to find it.'

'Perfect,' says Lena, and she feels her own face falling into a resolution similar to Seidensal's. 'That sounds perfect.'

'Oh honey,' says Chipper, and it's not clear whether she's talking to Seidensal or to Lena. 'It's not all fun and games up there.'

'Lena is not looking for fun,' says Seidensal dismissively. 'You do not travel through the heart of Alaska for fun.'

'I'll be careful, I promise,' says Lena. 'I've been through things—' She stops. 'Things that have made me take care,' she says finally. Under her baseball cap, under the protective layers of her still-wet hair, her head lies dark and hidden.

'She will be all right with Jimmy,' says Seidensal, and he limps over to Chipper and kneels awkwardly by her chair with his good leg sticking out the back, like a skater on a green shagpile pond.

'He may not have the room,' says Chipper, looking into the fire. 'I heard he found some kid out the back of Mt Doonerak, a while back.' She stops then, although Lena senses this is not all Chipper wants to say.

'I have heard that too,' says Seidensal. 'Well, if there is no bed for Lena, Jimmy will be the first to say so. He does not waste words, that man, but he says what needs to be said.'

There is a pause and a log shifts in the fire, sending out a shower of gold like a poker machine. Seidensal remains beside Chipper's chair but he looks over at Lena and gives a small nod. 'Think about it,' he says. 'There is no hurry.'

And this is true. Eight weeks of time stretch before Lena and this is only the first frost-rimmed night of it. She takes Seidensal's map to bed with her, lies between floral sheets looking at dotted trails and the solid black lines of rivers. When she wakes later in the night, the peaked map is glowing on the bedside cabinet beside her, a paper mountain lit by the moon.

It turns out that Fairbanks is nothing like Lena's expectations and everything like a town back home. Jay is wrong: there are shopping malls here, there are also visitors' centres, and laundromats, and office blocks made of glass and steel. Only when Lena steps off the sealed road does she feel the difference. Then she can sense the frozen earth reeling away beneath her feet, two thousand feet of it, shot through with the iron veins of frost.

'Even so,' she says to Seidensal, 'it doesn't feel quite real.' She knows he will understand: won't become defensive in the way that Chipper might, even though Chipper is originally from Oklahoma City.

'I tend to agree with you,' says Seidensal. He tugs thoughtfully at his moustache, twirling the ends so they finish in points as neat as his sentences. 'However,' he says, 'it is enough reality for most people.'

'Seidensal,' says Lena, 'do you think I could take some photos of you before I go?' Whether or not they can get hold of Jimmy, who has not been at the end of his phone line for days, she is planning to leave Fairbanks. She is filled with a restlessness which Seidensal says comes from breathing the Alaskan air, but which Lena knows has been growing inside of her for months.

'We would be honoured,' says Seidensal. 'We would like copies for our visitors' album, also.'

Lena takes the photos in the late afternoon, when the outlines are sharp and shadows topple against the house. Chipper takes twenty minutes to get ready, and emerges with her hair freshly flicked and her lips gleaming in the sunlight. 'How about a shot from below?' she suggests, licking her finger, arching it over her eyebrows.

'We can give it a try,' says Lena. She has never liked discounting anyone's well-meaning suggestions. She goes down below the veranda, crunching into drifts of snow, and in fact the angle is good. There the house stands on its spindly legs, straddling a pool of mud, and high in its wooden arms are small Chipper and her tall lanky husband. Their bodies are cut in half by the wooden rail, and their top halves are halved again by the long line of shadow from the hills.

'It's perfect,' she shouts and she gives the thumbs-up to her friends, purveyors of local information and fine apple sauce.

She uses up half her film on Seidensal and Chipper and then, providentially, Chipper must hurry away to the phone. After that Lena is able to shoot Seidensal for her own purposes. There is a resonance about him which she has recognized since she arrived.

The fifth story of loss

There was once a lean and tanned German, younger than thirty but harbouring ambitions as old as the hills. Turning his back on the village in which he grew up, nestled in a southern wooded valley, he packed his bags and farewelled his parents, who none the less hoped he would return to run the family inn once he had got rid of the mountaineering bug that had bitten him hard. (*Lost: an eldest son.*)

This twenty-something German travelled long distances: into the Himalayan mountains which he found wanting (they were strewn with litter, and too many people were swarming there); and to the face of the great Aoraki in the southern island of New Zealand (but the top of this mountain shivered in week-long mist, and he was forced to leave without scaling it).

And then this German man – we will call him Frank – left the bottom of the world and headed north once more to arrive in America, land of the free and home of the homeless. Picking up what work he could, he made his way through the heartlands but he stopped for a while in Oklahoma City, because it was here that he fell in love for the very first time.

The German flipped burgers in a diner in this city for a number of months but he was always conscious of the mountains of the forty-ninth state looming ahead of him. Eventually he hitched on up to British Columbia, although thinking often of the girl who had bought a chocolate shake from him and stayed for hours, and he entered a land that – although he did not know it yet – would take him in its mouth and never let him go.

And now, with his loping even stride, the German heads for the foothills of the Brooks Mountain Range, where the Arctic Divide runs through the cold tundra. Camping here he can see the bare desert earth of the north and the spindly trees of the south. He can feel the sun touching but not warming the rocks beneath him. He is farther north than he has ever been, and he climbs peaks many times older than the Rockies and more daunting than life itself. But before his beard is fully grown, dazzled by the low light he slips on a descent, and he hears his knee crack like a twig beneath him.

(freeze-frame: a tall tanned man of middle to late years raises his head towards the disappearing sun. A bold second sun is reflected

*in the ranch slider behind him. He leans on a stick and that stick
looks like a third leg, and the vertical lines of the man's three legs
are echoed below by the thin shanks of the house, built many years
earlier by his own hands)*

The German returns south in a helicopter and lies in Fairbanks
Hospital for many weeks. *Loss of a steady gait.* Much of his time
is spent writing letters to Oklahoma City; on very clear days he
turns his head on the pillow and can see the distant, friendly faces
of mountains. *Lost: ambition, arrogance, and a lifelong anxiety.*

The yodel

Lena remains in Fairbanks for seven and a half long, slow days.
On the eighth day she must pack her bags in the space of twenty
minutes, for Jimmy has been sighted in the bookstore of the
university campus, and rumour has it he will be heading north
again before evening.

'I will take you up there,' says Seidensal, 'and introduce you.'
He seems eager to escape the peeling and skinning of several
cases of apples, flown in that morning from California. Saucepans
are bubbling, the stovetop is hissing with sugar, and Chipper is
singing so loudly that the ring of the phone is hardly audible. 'It
is as restful in that kitchen,' says Seidensal to Lena, 'as it would
be in Dante's Inferno.'

Lena throws her bag into the back of Seidensal's ancient but
spotless Mercedes. 'What if Jimmy has no room for me?' she asks.
'What if there is no bed for me in Barrow?'

'In that case I will bring you home again,' says Seidensal, starting the engine. 'And we will have dinner.' It is hard to tell if he
is joking but Lena waves goodbye to Chipper as if it really is the
last time, for a while at least, and not as if she will be back in
the hot kitchen that evening eating over-sweetened apple sauce
and ice cream.

'Do you think Jimmy will still be there?' she asks. After the
highways of LA, their progress along the main road seems sedate
in the extreme.

'He will still be in the bookstore,' says Seidensal confidently. 'He is a great reader, that Jimmy, he could read the hind leg off a horse.'

'You mean a donkey,' says Lena.

'That too,' says Seidensal. 'A whole menagerie of animals. All would become lame, like me, once Jimmy started to read.'

Lena laughs and pulls her hat down. She has bought a new wool one – cream and blue, colours to remind her of the Pacific – for although it is spring the temperatures are still hovering somewhere around freezing.

Seidensal flicks on his indicator and turns up towards the campus. 'Lena,' he says.

'Hmm?' she says.

'If you do not mind me asking,' says Seidensal, 'do you find it cold in our house?'

'Cold?' says Lena. 'Not at all!' Despite the chilly air creeping in through the car doors, she is still sweating slightly under her many thermal layers from the effect of Chipper's well-radiated rooms. 'Your home is as warm as toast,' she says reassuringly. 'Why?'

'It is just that you wear your cap inside the house all the time,' says Seidensal. 'Chipper and I were worried you might be chilly, coming from California as you do.'

The orange sun blazes in through the windscreen and under the visor, smashes straight through Lena's eyeballs and into her head. Instantly she shuts her eyes but her skull is full of heat: bursting, breaking. 'Where I come from everyone wears baseball caps,' she says faintly, still with her eyes closed. 'Baseball is like a religion there.'

'You Americans!' says Seidensal in what sounds like a perfect Chipper drawl. 'You are a very odd race,' he says fondly, sounding more American by the minute, his voice no longer holding any trace of wooded valleys and wooden churches and dusty furrows of Riesling grapes. Lena sits back in her seat and opens her eyes. But her palms are slick with sweat.

By the time they reach the campus she has steadied herself, and she sees Mt McKinley in the distance, raising its snow-cap

to the afternoon sun. 'I hope Jimmy's been reading an encyclopaedia,' she says slightly anxiously. But when she and Seidensal
walk into the bookstore it is quiet, and empty except for an assistant sitting with her feet up reading back copies of celebrity magazines.

'Greetings,' says Seidensal, looking over the assistant's shoulder. 'Who is Philly Ta-ran-tella?' he asks.

'Some sad dude from LA,' says the assistant, 'who looks like
he's got more money than clothes sense.'

'Certainly that is a very dull suit,' agrees Seidensal.

'What can I help you with?' asks the assistant. 'Are you after
anything special?'

'Nothing that you have here,' says Seidensal, looking around
at the bright vacant aisles.

He and Lena go outside and walk around the campus for a
while, lowering their heads into the breeze like sniffer dogs. But
Lena has no idea who they are looking for, and she stamps her
feet on the hard ground to keep warm.

'What's that building with the satellite dish on it?' she asks, as
the clouds begin to draw in over their heads.

'That,' says Seidensal, as proudly as if he has erected it himself,
'is the Geophysical Institute. And that—' He peers at the base of
the concrete tower, then limps forward a few paces and lets out
an ear-splitting yodel. Lena jumps.

'I learned that as a boy,' says Seidensal modestly, over his shoulder. 'They called me the Honorary Austrian.'

'Is it Jimmy?' says Lena, as an answering yodel comes from the
direction of the Institute.

'It is,' says Seidensal. 'Come on.'

By the time Seidensal has harangued Jimmy for being elusive
and Jimmy has suggested that Seidensal's best yodelling years are
over, by the time they have discussed the weather and the possibility of a fresh dump of snow, Lena has had a chance to size up
the situation. So that when Seidensal raises his eyebrows in a
questioning way behind Jimmy's back she gives a tiny nod and
hopes for the best.

'Lena is wanting to visit Barrow for a few days,' says Seidensal.

'We were wondering whether you have any room to rent?'

There is a silence as Jimmy pulls out a pack of cigarettes. Lena is used to pauses now, having lived with Davey, but she has never been one to crash in where she might not be wanted so she scrunches her toes inside her boots and stares out across the forested ridges and scattered buildings, and she also says nothing.

'Smoke?' asks Jimmy politely. His long hair swings over his shoulder, as straight and dark as an Inuit's, but his eyes are blue and his cheekbones are narrow. He offers the cigarettes to Lena with one gloved hand.

'No,' says Lena. 'Thank you.'

'Yes,' says Seidensal. 'I thought you would never offer.' He takes a cigarette and there is another pause while Jimmy flicks his lighter into life, and the flame is put out by the wind, and Jimmy coaxes it back to life again. The two men stand looking at the view while Lena looks down at the ground, looks ahead to spending the rest of her time in Alaska reading old *National Geographics* and peeling apples.

'I'd be happy for you to come,' says Jimmy finally, as if it has taken him a while to decide this. He bites back on a mouthful of smoke, lifts his head to the greying sky. 'The only thing is,' he says, exhaling, 'I've got this kid staying with me. Moses.'

'We have heard,' says Seidensal. 'Have you uncovered any leads on where he is from?'

Jimmy shakes his head. 'I'll be staying at Deadhorse for a night or two on the way through,' he says. 'I'll make some enquiries there.' He lowers his head and looks at Lena. His light eyes are quite expressionless. 'You been to the Far North before?' he asks.

'No,' she says. 'And that's why I want to go there.' She pulls her coat more firmly around her, turns the collar up against the wind.

Jimmy laughs at that. 'It's a bit rough, my place,' he says. 'Nothing like Frank's palace.'

'I don't need luxury,' says Lena. 'Just a place to stay for a week or two.'

'Well, if you don't mind four-year-olds,' says Jimmy, with a shrug, 'and you don't mind the cold, then you're welcome.' Although he doesn't sound particularly welcoming, nor does he sound off-putting; he simply talks about the long drive ahead and how he intends to travel right through the night as far as Deadhorse.

'You might already know,' he says to Lena, 'that there's no through road to Barrow. But my friend Norm's got a helicopter so we can catch a ride with him.'

'Inaccessibility,' says Seidensal. 'It appeals to Jimmy.' He gives a laugh and limps away to get the car. But as Lena stands and watches Jimmy smoke, and listens to his brief remarks, she thinks that Seidensal might have hit the nail on the head.

When Jimmy sees how little gear Lena has, he raises his eyebrows. 'Travelling light,' he says. 'We'll make a tracker out of you yet.'

Seidensal slams the boot of the Mercedes, and looks pityingly at Jimmy's truck. 'Still driving that heap of American junk,' he says. 'You should get yourself a quality vehicle.'

Jimmy turns to Lena. 'You'll find that Seidensal has the best of both worlds,' he says. 'Here he is living in the most beautiful state of America, and has been for twenty-five years, but he still claims to be German when it suits him.'

Seidensal huffs and puffs in a mock-offended way. 'If Jimmy is rude to you,' he says to Lena, 'you must come straight back to Chipper and me. Our door is always open.' Although he is joking about Jimmy, clearly he means the rest of what he says. 'In fact,' he says, 'Fairbanks would be a good base for you. You can travel south from here, or east – you would get many good photos.'

'Give her a chance,' says Jimmy. 'Barrow's an OK place. It just takes some getting used to.' He grinds his cigarette butt under his heel and swings himself into the truck and Lena must say goodbye to Seidensal even though she doesn't want to.

'Let us know what your plans are,' he says. 'We will see you when you come back to meet your brother, if not before.' He shakes her hand formally. 'But you will be fine with Jimmy,' he says. It sounds like a promise but, even so, after they have driven in convoy to the main road and Lena sees the station wagon peel off in the opposite direction, she feels a slight catch in her throat.

It seems as if Jimmy has talked himself out because he drives for a long time without saying anything. But the engine is loud enough to cover his silence, and Lena slides down in her seat and watches the flatlands fall away behind them. There is so much empty space out here and the surface of the road is so rough and pitted that she starts to think of moon craters, and rockets lurching skywards. 'My brother is working somewhere up the Yukon River,' she says to Jimmy. 'At least, I think he is.'

'What's he doing out there?' asks Jimmy.

'He's on a training mission,' says Lena. 'A mission to Mars.'

'A spaceman, eh?' says Jimmy. 'Alaska attracts all sorts.' He doesn't ask any more, just drives on in silence until they pass a signpost and then he clears his throat. 'Welcome to the Dalton Highway,' he says, swerving to avoid a particularly large pothole. 'Though some people don't think it's worthy of the title.'

'How often do you drive this road?' says Lena.

'Often as I need to,' says Jimmy. 'My work takes me all over.'

'Seidensal says you're a tracker?' says Lena.

'That's right,' says Jimmy, and he changes gear and falls silent again.

They drive on and on, and the late sunlight slants through the windows of the car. Back in California, thinks Lena, the light would be fading; here the snow still lies like bright glinting pools on the rising ground.

'The cold and the sun,' she says. 'It's a good combination.'

'Like ice cream and apple sauce,' says Jimmy. The fact that he and Lena have Chipper and Seidensal in common takes away Lena's slightly draughty feeling, caused by memories of Venice Beach and of shouting children being called in off the sand.

'Won't you get tired?' she asks. 'Driving for so long?'

Jimmy pushes his hair back, twists it and tucks it into his collar. 'I can go for days without sleep,' he says. 'Sometimes it's a curse but it means I can cover the miles.'

The journey up the Dalton Highway is so long that, for Lena, it takes on a dreamlike quality. There is flying gravel, there are forested foot hills, and always there is the vast streaked sky, pink

176

and then grey and then finally, much later, darkening so that the dim ground pulls away from the headlights.

'You sleepy?' asks Jimmy, and he pulls a sleeping bag over from the back seat and offers it to her.

'I'm all right,' says Lena. She feels she should try to stay awake and talk. But the grinding of the gravel road makes her drowsy, and she lays her head down in the hammock of the seatbelt and closes her eyes. She wakes only once, when the truck pulls off the road: sees a moon and harsh electric light, smells petrol and freezing air.

'Coldfoot,' says Jimmy, briefly. 'Gas stop.' She can hear him arguing with the owner of the truck stop. 'Yeah, I know you've stopped serving,' he is saying. 'But for what you charge it should be twenty-four hours.' Then he is jumping back in, making the truck lurch, and he throws a packet of sandwiches on the seat beside Lena. 'Cheese and mayo,' he says. 'Help yourself.'

But Lena only wants sleep again, and the next time she wakes the sky is light once more and it is morning. They have come right through the Brooks Mountains and out the other side, and the land is a rich grey and patched with snow. There are no trees, nothing but miles and miles of open tundra.

'The North,' says Jimmy. 'It's like nowhere else.'

'How long have you lived here?' asks Lena in a voice croaky with sleep.

'About twenty years,' says Jimmy, and in the morning light there are lines around his eyes that Lena hasn't noticed before. 'Though they still think of me as a newcomer,' he says, turning up his collar in a slightly defensive, slightly sarky way.

The chill

Deadhorse is a cold and lonely place. Oil-rigs loom up from the permafrost, stark and threatening in the late grey afternoon. Jimmy has fallen into a brooding silence once more and Lena slithers down in her seat and starts to wonder if she has made a mistake. *One week*, she promises her doubtful head and her reluctant, blemished leg. *One week for some photos, and we'll head for the south again.*

Jimmy pulls up a driveway beside a gas station and the wheels of the truck spin on the loose snow and mud. 'We'll stay the night here,' he says, speaking for the first time in what seems like hours.

'Here?' says Lena, faintly. There is not a lot to be seen: a couple of diesel pumps, an outhouse with its door hanging open on broken hinges, and some old tyres frozen together in tilting stacks.

'There,' says Jimmy, not looking at her, gesturing at the blank concrete side of the house next door. 'Annie,' he says. 'She works at the gas station.' His voice is slightly thick and he clears his throat. 'I leave the truck here,' he says, 'because there's no through road to Barrow. But you know that already.'

'Yes,' says Lena.

There's a pause. 'I stay over sometimes,' says Jimmy.

'Oh right,' says Lena.

Annie is already standing in the doorway, smoking. She is part Inupiat, and has long black hair in a braid down her back that gives her a youthful look, but up close her skin is marked by wind and the sun.

'I heard the truck,' she says, kissing Jimmy on the mouth and then taking another drag on her cigarette. 'You never say when you're coming back.'

Jimmy shrugs. 'I don't usually know myself,' he says. 'We'll only stay tonight, I've got to get back to pick up the kid.'

'Whatever,' says Annie, exhaling. 'I don't know where Lisa's gonna sleep, though.' Her eyes flick briefly over Lena, fall away again.

'Her name's Lena,' says Jimmy. 'There's no problem, is there? She can have the spare room and I'll take the couch.'

Annie turns away, scuffs inside in her moccasins. 'What brings you all the way up here?' she says to Lena. 'Godforsaken hole that it is.' As she moves around her small cold kitchen, though, getting cups and peppermint tea from the cupboard, her feet have a sureness about them. *This is home*, they say in their muffled but definite tread.

'I'm here to take some photos,' says Lena neutrally. She casts a look over her shoulder to the dark bedroom doorway where Jimmy has dumped her bag, thinks she would rather sleep cold in the back of the truck than step on anyone's toes. But she notices that Jimmy is careful around Annie: before they have finished their tea, he has already put money under the teapot to cover a night's lodging.

'Photos?' says Annie. Although she is addressing Lena, her dark eyes stray constantly towards Jimmy, fix on his face. 'What, wildlife?' she says. 'You'll find plenty of that up the coast.'

'Not wildlife,' says Lena. 'Mainly people that I meet.'

'I'm going to go talk to the oil riggers,' says Jimmy abruptly. 'See if anyone knows anything about Moses.'

Lena doesn't want to be left with Annie's curiosity, would rather be left alone. But as soon as Jimmy has put on his coat and is out the door, Annie steps up the questioning.

'You know Jimmy's history, do you?' she says, not looking at Lena, lighting another cigarette without offering one.

'I don't know him at all,' says Lena. Without a solid night's sleep at its back, the day has been a long one; and the truck's engine churns on in her bones. She raises her cup to her lips using both hands.

'Is that right,' says Annie. 'You're just renting a room from him, are you?' Something in her face settles, and she looks at Lena properly for the first time. 'Smoke?' she asks.

'No,' says Lena. 'But thanks.'

Annie pulls the band out of her braid and combs her hair through with her fingers. 'Jimmy's had his share of problems,' she says, glancing over her shoulder as if to check that he really is gone. 'His wife died,' she says. 'A long time ago. They were hitching out of Anchorage together and she got hit by a car.'

'Oh no,' says Lena, shocked.

'Hit and run,' says Annie. 'Apparently she lay there dead by the side of the road for hours before anyone found them, and Jimmy just sat beside her holding her hand. He didn't start walking for help until she was stone cold.' There is an odd tone in Annie's voice, a dull hardness in it like the sky before rain. 'And he hasn't left Alaska since,' she says.

Lena puts her head forward on the table and rests her face on it. 'Why?' she says, into the wood.

'Who knows?' says Annie. 'He never talks about it. His wife was a Native American from some reservation in Wyoming so the body had to go back. But Jimmy just went on.'

'Went where?' says Lena. The flat wood on her cheek, the smell of detergent, Annie's long dark hair at the edge of her vision: these things remind her of some long-ago thing and she gropes through her memory but can't find it, feels comfortless.

'He just carried on north, as far as he could go,' says Annie, 'bumming jobs here and there until he ended up in Barrow. End of story.'

'It's a terrible story,' says Lena. Her mouth feels like an open wound; it moves slowly and painfully against the table.

Annie talks on to the top of Lena's head. 'No relationship since then,' she says. 'Maybe there have been women, but no one living with him until this kid. This Moses.' Her voice becomes sharp and wary again, just as it was an hour ago when she saw Jimmy walking up the path with Lena in tow.

Lena raises her head tiredly. 'Where did he find him? Moses, I mean,' she says.

'At the bottom of Mt Doonerak,' says Annie. 'Just wandering round in the snow with the weather closing in. No one knows where he came from or who took him up there.' She drags on her cigarette. 'Some dumb cheechako, I bet,' she says.

'Cheechako?' says Lena.

'A tenderfoot,' says Annie dismissively, as if she thinks a clichéd definition is the only sort Lena will understand. 'We get them all the time up here,' she says, 'thinking they can read the weather, wandering off, getting lost. Next thing you know the state troopers are being called in and it's another goddamn missing person case.' She sounds as if she would like to close off the borders between Alaska and the rest of America, breed a tough pure race with strong arms for pumping gas and strong tobacco in their pockets.

'Seidensal said that Jimmy could find anyone,' ventures Lena.

'Seidensal?' says Annie uncomprehendingly. 'Well, I don't know about that. Jimmy might be a good tracker but he's not a fucking miracle worker. He can't just pull people out of thin air, you know.' She pulls her hair over her shoulder, combs her fingers through it compulsively, again and again. 'Doonerak's a native word for supernatural being,' she says. 'It's a weird place. A lot of people have gotten lost out there and not even Jimmy's been able to find them.'

Lena feels the hair on her arms lift under her three layers of clothing. She looks around to see if a window is open or if Jimmy is coming back in the door, but the kitchen is still sealed up and the air is close with smoke.

Annie taps a narrow pillar of ash into her saucer. 'You have to take care of yourself in a place like this,' she says. It is unclear whether she is referring to the Alaskan wilderness or to a more intimate, equally cold, world. 'No one else is gonna look out for you,' she says.

And Lena, who is beginning to reel with tiredness, sees images flicking before her eyes like a slide-show on a faulty machine. There is:

– her mother, her missing mother, juggling golden coins and donuts in the faraway corner of a cold stony square
– a woman, a missing woman, lying on a grass verge with a blood-red mouth, her throat thrown back to the sky
– a boy astride a spinning red planet, singing screen after screen of soundless data
—and Lena herself lying on a sidewalk, dying, with a light dusting of snow on her hair.

Somewhere, far at the back of her mind, she remembers a onetime certainty, reaches for it. (Something about loss, something about release.) But in front of her and through the haze Annie talks on, seeming not to notice her tilting chair or the fact that the room is lurching around them.

'There's a lot of people don't like Jimmy,' she is saying. Her voice sounds stretched and uneven, and she releases a slow thick mouthful of smoke. 'They think he has no business finding bodies,' she says, 'and dragging them out from under the snow. They think the dead should be left to the mountains.'

'Annie,' says Lena, managing to stand up.

'Hmmm?' says Annie.

'Would you excuse me?' says Lena.

'Sure,' says Annie, looking slightly surprised. 'You need the bathroom?'

Lena goes into her room and closes the door. She pulls the curtains against the glaring grey evening and lies flat on the top of the bed. The room is bare, as small as a closet, and a wooden crucifix hangs at the head of the bed. The eyes of the Jesus figure are tight shut, lids stretched over swollen eyeballs; but Lena keeps her own eyes open and she stares into the semi-darkness. Every now and then she hears the swish of a car on the road, its heavy body sweeping past the house like a searchlight.

After a while she hears Jimmy come in. She can hear him talking with Annie, hears the clink of dishes and the scrape of a match, but she continues to lie. Eventually she hears a knock at the door.

'Lena?' It's Jimmy's voice, and he sounds uncertain. 'You OK?'

Lena sits up and looks at the slit of electric light on the wall. The shadow of Jimmy's hair swings across it, joins up with the larger dark of the room. 'I am,' she says, but her voice sounds weak and uncertain.

'Come have some dinner,' says Jimmy. 'We'll go to the hotel.'

'But Annie—' says Lena, in a lying-down kind of voice.

'Annie's fine,' says Jimmy, sounding more certain. 'You and I are going to the hotel.'

And they do, passing through the grey eye of the evening to the one hotel in town. They sit under swinging fluorescent lights and eat baked beans (Lena) and baked smoked halibut (Jimmy), and they talk about Moses.

'Did you find out anything about him?' asks Lena. 'From the riggers?'

Jimmy shakes his head. 'It was a long shot anyway,' he says. 'The workers here don't stay around too long, they fly in for a couple of weeks at a time and then they can't wait to leave again.'

For dessert they have fruit salad out of a tin. ('Nothing grows here but ice,' says Jimmy.) And then they are joined by some oil riggers who, although they know nothing about a small lost kid, know plenty about having a good time. Outside the windows the night is getting colder but inside the glass mists up with jokes and stories, and whisky starts to flow.

An old grizzled guy hauls out a piano accordion. 'I'm escaping tomorrow,' he says to Lena, as he adjusts the straps over his shoulder. 'Gotta get back to the wife and the bright lights.'

'Plenty of bright lights in Anchorage,' says Jimmy, with the hint of a wink at Lena.

'Where are you from, sweetheart?' the piano accordion player asks Lena.

Lena has to think. 'Los Angeles,' she says. 'But San Francisco before that. And my parents are Polish.'

'I knew it!' says the piano accordion player. 'You've got something erotic about you.'

'Erotic?' says Lena, slightly startled.

'You know,' says the guy. 'Foreign.' He picks up his battered instrument and starts into a slow, wheezing Chopin waltz that is familiar to Lena.

'My mother swears by that tune!' she says. 'She played it all the time when we were kids and now she makes her clients listen to it because she thinks it relaxes their pores.'

'Pores?' says the player in an intrigued sing-song voice. 'What does your mother do for a job?'

'She sells beauty products to people who are already beautiful,' says Lena.

'And your father?' says the player, swaying under the flickering tube.

'My father sells fatty food to people who are fat,' says Lena.

Everyone roars with laughter, and the accordion player starts in on some country and western, and Jimmy's friend Norm, the helicopter pilot, asks Lena to dance with him. 'I've got orders to fly you out of here at the crack of dawn,' he says. 'But if I had any sense I'd keep you right here in Deadhorse.' His curved stomach gyrates in a comfortable way. 'I wish my wife would wear a nice hat like yours,' he says.

Jimmy plays a tune on some beer glasses and Norm persuades

Lena to stand on the table for a solo performance, as if sensing the illicit trace of stage blood that remains in her narrow veins. Lena reaches far, far back into a distant past and her audience laughs so much that the light-fittings shake. Finally she is allowed down off her rickety wooden platform to make way for Norm, who sings a number from *Carmen* in a rich baritone. When he is finished—

'Thank you, my fans,' he says, and he bows low over his stomach. 'You may call me Don José, a man scorned.'

'I'd call you a poor sucker who's gonna have a bad hangover tomorrow,' says Jimmy.

These words jolt Norm out of his reverie. 'I've got a group of geologists to pick up in the morning,' he says in a slurry horrified way. 'And I have to take you guys to Barrow first.' He jumps down from the table so that the wooden floor shudders.

'I guess that's closing time,' says Jimmy.

Outside it is midnight and darkness has finally arrived in Deadhorse. Lena and Jimmy walk home on the long black road, their feet crunching in the cold ridged gravel.

'You were good!' says Jimmy, turning up his coat collar in an already familiar way, though this time his defensiveness is simply towards the cold. 'You could do that professionally, if you had to.' From behind the checked wool his breath emerges in dragon plumes.

'Actually,' admits Lena, 'I used to.'

'You were a comedian?' says Jimmy. 'Why did you stop?'

'I guess you could say I saw right through it,' says Lena. 'Though it was a long time coming.'

'How long?' asks Jimmy.

'Since I was seven,' says Lena, and she starts to laugh. 'Telling jokes is a very dubious way to spend your childhood,' she says when she can speak again. 'Let alone to make a living.'

'Reminds me of a word I learned,' says Jimmy, 'when we were in—' He stops short. 'When I was in Tibet,' he says lamely, finishing his sentence but not his story. He walks along with his hands stuck in his pockets and his head down.

'What was it?' asks Lena after a while, tentatively.

'Huh?' says Jimmy, looking right through her for a minute, then looking at her. 'Oh, the word,' he says. 'It was *dudzi*. Basically it means entertainment. But if a Tibetan told you he was in the *dudzi* business it'd be like saying he spends his life wasting his own time and other people's.'

'There's something in that,' says Lena, and she thinks again of the female Dudie. ('Do you dance?' that supposedly entertaining Dudie is chirping to Lena: in a trailer, in a beachside settlement, in the past. 'Do you sing?' chirps that blond, unblemished, professional waster of other people's lives.) And suddenly Lena marches into the middle of the iron-hard street and there, in the strip where the slush and the snow have been pushed aside by cars, she starts to dance. She tap-dances there on the crest of midnight, her feet hammering out a song of farewell. *No more dudzi!* they promise. *No more dudzi!*

'Lena,' says Jimmy, when she has finished, 'that was magnificent.'

And he is right. Lena has just done something trivial in a truly magnificent way, she has danced the dance of her life in elastic-sided boots and two pairs of socks, has made a silk purse out of a sow's ear.

'I'd like to be able to do that,' says Jimmy as they walk up the path to the dark house. 'But there isn't much call for it in my line of work.'

'I guess it would startle your prey,' Lena agrees.

Now they are outside the house, walking up the path for the second time that night, and now they are inside. They say goodnight very quietly in whispers, but Annie appears at her bedroom door in a dressing gown, her hair spread over her shoulders.

'Have a good night?' she asks, looking hard at them both, scanning their faces.

'Not bad,' says Jimmy. He turns away to where his bag lies unpacked on the sofa. 'No news on the boy,' he says, rummaging through the bag, 'but Lena danced.'

'Lena danced?' says Annie.

'I'm going outside for a while,' says Jimmy and, taking a new pack of cigarettes with him, he walks straight past both Annie and

185

Lena without looking at either one of them, and straight out the door. Annie glances over at Lena and shrugs, and for a moment there is a fellow feeling between them.

'So you had an OK time, did you?' she says, standing in bare feet. 'I can't say Deadhorse has much to offer in the way of entertainment.'

Lena looks out the window, sees the light falling on Jimmy's head as he stands on the front step, and a thin line of smoke drifting into the night. 'I enjoyed it,' she says truthfully.

'I guess I won't see you in the morning,' says Annie. 'If you're catching a lift with Norm you'll be leaving at sparrow's fart.' She turns away, and then she turns back again and gives Lena a rough pat on the shoulder. 'If you're passing through this way again,' she says, 'you know where I am.'

Lena's sleep is a quiet one, marked only by the occasional bark of a dog and the ticking of the clock beside her. She knocks her head on the pillow in the way she used to back in Tenderloin days and, even after whisky, it still works; she wakes up just before the alarm goes off, goes to the window and looks out at the deserted street. Stars are still poking their fingers through the pale sky but it is morning, and in a couple of hours she will be heading north again – as far north as she has ever been.

In the main room Jimmy sits at the kitchen table lacing up his boots. He nods at her when she comes in, but says nothing.

'I feel terrible,' says Lena. There is a whisky taste in her mouth and when she bends down to pick up her bag she almost retches. 'Why did I drink so much?' she says.

'You'll be all right in Barrow,' says Jimmy, without smiling. 'It's a dry town.'

Norm is also the worse for wear: he appears diminished, a mere shadow of his former operatic self. Although his eyes are bloodshot, he remembers promising to detour Lena over the Brooks Range.

'Really,' she says, 'you don't have to.' She can't think of anything she feels less like than being whirled at high altitude over high mountain peaks.

'A promise,' says Norm solemnly, 'is a promise.'

Lena doesn't want to seem ungrateful and so she sits doggedly in her seat with her teeth clenched and peers obediently out the window. As Norm sweeps them up a narrow tree-filled valley her stomach churns, but once she sees peaks below them, bare grey mountainsides and untouched snow, she starts to feel slightly better.

'See that one shaped like the Matterhorn?' Norm calls over the roar of the engine. 'That's Doonerak.'

Up until now Jimmy has been sitting silently in his seat but as they turn and bank over the mountain he moves forward and looks down intently. 'Slow,' he says to Norm.

Obediently, Norm drops to a thousand feet and hovers. 'See anything?' he says.

'Not yet,' says Jimmy. His face is pressed so close to the window that his breath makes small circles on the glass. 'Nothing,' he says. 'Shit.' He leans back in his seat again.

'Come back when there's a melt,' advises Norm. 'It's a needle in a haystack right now.'

'Finding needles is my job,' says Jimmy. 'It's about all I'm good for.'

'So who's paying you for this one?' Norm asks shrewdly.

Jimmy doesn't answer. For the rest of the trip through to Barrow he sits still and silent in his seat, and his face is set like the side of a mountain.

Home base

The first thing that strikes Lena about Jimmy's house is the cold. Although it is below freezing in the Barrow streets, it feels even colder inside Jimmy's living room where her breath hangs in the air.

'Welcome,' says Jimmy, and for the first time he sounds awkward. He stands in the middle of the one main room and gestures with stiff arms, like a novice cop directing the traffic. 'The fridge is over there,' he says, waving vaguely at the kitchen area. 'The bathroom's in there, coats hang here, and this—' He walks over and opens a creaking wooden door. 'This is your bedroom,' he says.

Lena sees bare floorboards, a bare mattress, and a view of a high back fence. There is a photo of a woman on the bedside cabinet, and a paperback book lying beside it.

'But I can't take this!' she says. 'This is your room.'

Quickly, Jimmy grabs up the photo and the book, stuffs them in his coat pocket, and looks around. 'That's all,' he says. 'Now it's yours.'

For someone who makes a living out of remaining motionless for hours on end, he seems unable to stay still. He roams restlessly through the house, fetches Lena some sheets, throws his bag down on the sofa but doesn't bother to unpack it. 'I'll be sleeping up there,' he says, gesturing to a loft built into the rafters of the living room. 'I want to let Moses keep the bunk-room for as long as he's here. A bit of stability for him.'

'Of course,' says Lena, although she is sure of nothing as far as Moses is concerned: how long he has been here, how he will like her, and even where he is at this particular moment.

'I've got to go pick him up now,' says Jimmy, as if he is mind-reading. 'If you'll excuse me,' he adds formally.

'I'll come,' says Lena quickly. She doesn't want to be left alone in this cold creaking house, where the wind has blown up from the piles and in through the cracks, driving the dust into small heaps against the skirting boards.

'Don't you want to unpack?' says Jimmy, sounding surprised. 'Freshen up or something?'

'I'm used to living out of a bag,' says Lena, avoiding the issue. She pulls down her hat more securely. 'Ready,' she says.

Outside the sun is blazing, though it has little effect on the thin cold air. Lena follows in Jimmy's footsteps, and they wade through a snowy paddock, climb over a low wire fence, and emerge into a street lined with shops. 'Down there,' says Jimmy, and his footsteps quicken so that snow flies from his boots, forming small vees behind him.

'Who's been looking after him?' says Lena. By now Jimmy is walking so fast that she can hardly keep up and she breaks into a jog.

'Brenda and Po,' says Jimmy over his shoulder. 'They let him help out behind the counter. He likes that.' They are striding up the steps of a general store – 'The General's Store' – and the bell on the door tings, and the next second Jimmy is being throttled by a tiny figure in a red snow suit.

'You're back,' says a large woman who is stocking a shelf with beans. Even though she is addressing Jimmy, she doesn't stop work for him: she keeps bending and straightening, bending and straightening, piling up the cans.

'Got back just now,' says Jimmy. His voice is muffled because he is still being crushed by padded red arms. 'This is Lena,' he says, over what Lena assumes is Moses' head. 'Lena, Brenda.'

Brenda pushes back her shaggy dark hair and holds out her hand over a pyramid of black-eyed beans. 'Hallo,' she says. She doesn't smile and Lena wonders if this is an Alaskan thing, this impassivity, learnt in the face of eight-month winters and a darkness that lasts sixty-seven days. But she does give Lena a not-unfriendly nod. 'You around long?' she asks.

'Just a week,' says Lena. 'No more.'

Brenda takes a step back, stands with her sturdy denim legs apart like a second pyramid. 'Po!' she roars. 'Hey, Po! Come say hello to Jimmy and Lena.'

With a flick and a flack, Po appears through a plastic strip curtain behind the shop counter. She has a blond perm and is about half Brenda's height, but she is dressed identically to her. There they stand, side by side, wearing matching blue jeans with pink stitching, matching denim jackets, and exactly the same style of tan sheepskin boots.

'Hi, Lena!' says Po. 'Welcome to Barrow!' Po does give a smile, a huge one that lights up her face, and she comes up and shakes Lena's hand with her warm sweaty one. Then she turns to Jimmy, who is standing there holding Moses in a semi-awkward way as if he is a sack of flour. 'That boy!' she beams. 'He's been a gem. He's real handy at weighing the carrots.'

'We've worked him twelve-hour days,' says Brenda. 'It was either that or charge nursery fees.' She looks sternly across at Jimmy and then she gives a great blast of laughter so that the cans rattle behind her. 'Kidding,' she says to Lena, just in case Lena has no sense of humour.

Jimmy extricates himself from the red arms and legs, and sets Moses down on the floor. 'This is Lena,' he says. 'She's going to be staying with us for a while so she can take some photos.'

Moses turns and stares at Lena. His face is round and his skin is light olive, and his eyes are slanted but not in the Inuit way.

'Hi, Moses,' says Lena.

'Photos!' says Po, interestedly. 'I don't suppose you take people, do you?' She smooths her curls. 'Or is it just animals and the like?' she says. 'You know, wildlife.'

'I do take people,' says Lena. 'I'm working on a book of people. People who have lost things.' She looks back at Moses. 'So you're good at weighing vegetables?' she says. 'My Uncle Larry could use you in his shop.'

Still Moses says nothing. He keeps on looking at Lena with his opaque brown eyes, but he reaches back with one hand and holds on to Jimmy's leg.

'Hear that, Brenda?' says Po. 'She photographs people! Not that we've lost anything, of course. Not that I can think of.' For a moment she looks puzzled – even slightly lost – at the concept, but then she brightens again. 'Maybe we could finally get our portraits done?' she says, bending to look at her reflection in the side of a huge kerosene tin. 'We've been meaning to for the longest time.'

'If you want,' says Lena. Moses' stare is making her slightly uncomfortable. 'I've just seen your room back at the house,' she says to him. 'Do you sleep in the top bunkbed or the bottom one?'

Moses bites his lip in a considering way but says nothing. Lena starts to wonder if he is deaf.

'I hope you don't mind me staying,' she says in a louder voice. 'Maybe you could show me some of your special places in Barrow?' A slight sweat breaks out on her top lip and suddenly the shop seems very warm. Almost, she pulls her hat off, but stops herself automatically.

'Um, Lena,' says Jimmy. 'Could I have a quick word?' He transfers Moses' starfish hand to Brenda's leg, and steps away behind a shelf of cereal. Lena follows. She stares anxiously at him, at his tired hungover eyes and his long dark hair framed around by large colourful boxes of Froot Loops.

'What is it?' she says in an almost-whisper.

'He can't talk,' says Jimmy, gesturing through the cardboard wall.

'He can't talk?' repeats Lena, parrot-like.

'Can't, or won't,' says Jimmy in a low voice. 'He hasn't spoken a word since I picked him up that day in the snow.'

Lena shakes her head, puts her hands up to her hat. Through the wool she traces the sides of her skull. Their unevenness is already familiar: on one side an ear, on the other a flattened prairie of skin. 'Can we still talk to him?' she says, floundering.

'Of course,' says Jimmy, looking slightly surprised. 'He's not deaf.'

'Does he make any sound at all?' says Lena.

'Not that I've heard,' says Jimmy. 'Maybe you'll be able to get through to him.'

'Me?' says Lena. 'But I don't know anything about him.'

'You know as much as any of us,' shrugs Jimmy. 'For the time being, anyway.'

They step back into the next aisle to find Brenda and Po fussing over Moses like two mismatched mother hens. Brenda quickly straightens up and clears her throat. 'Just giving the boy some candy,' she says in a businesslike way. 'Energy for the walk home.'

'Yeah, it's such a long way,' says Jimmy. 'Must be all of seven minutes.' But he leans forward and kisses first Brenda and then Po. 'Thanks, guys,' he says. His hair brushes over their cheeks gently and leaves just as gently, like the stroke of smooth feathers.

'You're welcome!' says Po, whose smile seems to be as permanent as her curls.

'It's been our pleasure,' says Brenda gruffly, and it looks as if there is a faint blush rising in her cheeks, though it could also be the light reflecting off the shelf of canned salmon next to her.

Lena follows Jimmy's large checked back to the door and then stops and turns, looking for Moses. But he is right behind her, so close that she could touch him, and he looks up at her silently.

He follows her out the door and down the steps, rustling slightly in his padded suit but making no other sound.

The dog

'You can use the phone,' says Jimmy, 'if you want to call anyone.'

'I have a cellphone,' says Lena, 'but I don't feel like using it right now.' This is true: for now she prefers the cobweb ties of writing, opts for the thin trails of recounted adventures that, by the time they reach their destination, will be as delayed as the radio instructions beamed to Davey's pod.

So she sits at the kitchen table with a pen and paper, and she writes to her mother of snow. Tells of clearing it away from the doorstep after a windy night, of seeing it lying on the frozen lagoon like crystallized sugar coating. Her own tales of snow, her first, and they will be unlocked and read in a distant city where the cold cobblestones might just be starting to accept the sun.

And to her father (for Lena has always been aware of the needs of an audience, and this was so long before she first stepped on to a stage) – to her father she writes of the Midnight Sun Baseball game that, Chipper has told her, has been played in Fairbanks every June solstice for decades. 'Davey and I might just catch it before we leave for home again,' she writes. It is not until she is licking the envelope that she realizes she has no home right now, not in LA or anywhere else, and she looks objectively around Jimmy's dusty kitchen and notices the almost total absence of plants and pictures and personal clutter.

She takes a picture that Moses has drawn of Jimmy's truck and pins it up on the wall alongside Jimmy's area map. The red straggles of Moses' pencil perfectly complement the contour lines of the map, but Jimmy doesn't appear to notice, although he looks at the map several times that first week to check the location of possible tracking work.

Lena goes to buy envelopes off Po. 'You do have a post office here, don't you?' she says, for suddenly she has remembered that she is in a place completely locked around by mountains and sea.

192

'Honey,' says Po with pride, 'we've had one since 1901.' She sounds as if she was not only around then, but that she also helped to lay the foundation stone of the institution.

'You could always mail them when you get back to Fairbanks,' says Jimmy. 'They'd probably get there just as fast – things don't get done in a hurry round here.' He shrugs. 'Depends how long you want to stay,' he says. He is a generous but undemanding host, heats up beans in one pan and coffee in another and doesn't bother with much else.

Lena looks at him. 'We said a week,' she says. But already she has seen faces in this town that she wants to explore, and she has no time constraints except the wide parameters of Davey's schedule.

'It makes no difference to me,' says Jimmy. 'Stay as long as you want.'

Moses comes with Lena to the post office. Even standing on tiptoe he is not tall enough to reach the letter slot in the wall outside, so he steps back and stands on the tops of Lena's boots. Although he is padded and sturdy to look at, his weight on Lena's feet is surprisingly light: a bird weight, the weight of a drift of snow that lies on a branch without bending it.

'You know where that letter's going?' Lena says to him. 'All the way to Warsaw. You know where that is?' It is not in Lena's nature to ask questions and in this she is similar to Jimmy, whose conversations seem to rest almost entirely on short unequivocal statements. But *nothing comes from nothing* she tells herself, and so when she is with Moses she makes a point of asking him things, although her questions fall on to his small blank face and fall to the ground unanswered.

'And this letter,' she says, 'this one's going to San Francisco. Ever been there?'

Moses ignores her. He stretches up his arm to the slot and is about to post Mr Domanski's letter when suddenly there is a snarl beside them, a rushing and a growling, and a huge wolf is leaping at Moses' hand.

Without stopping to think, Lena grabs Moses up off the ground and lifts him on to a planter box, and then she shouts and shouts at the wolf (which turns out to be no wolf but simply an Alsatian dog). It continues to snarl and bark and Lena continues to shout until, after many long noisy minutes, an old Inuit man shambles up and says something unintelligible to the dog, and instantly it falls silent.

Now Lena shouts at the man instead. 'A child could have been hurt!' she shouts at him. (Echoes start up in her head, the crowd roars, but nobody here is laughing.)

'He wouldn't hurt you,' mumbles the old man. 'He wouldn't hurt a fly. Keep your hair on, lady.'

After he has led the dog away, the street seems very quiet. A truck crosses at the next intersection down and a bee buzzes somewhere in the planter box by Moses' feet. But Lena, still holding on to Moses, can hear something else: she can hear Moses panting. As she stands there in the sunshine looking at the letter lying blue and muddy on the ground, she listens to his tiny pants of fear.

'It's OK,' she says to him, and to herself, sternly. 'Nothing would have happened to you. I never would have let it.'

She lifts Moses down and together they march back to Jimmy's house and heat up some refried beans flown in from Wisconsin. Later that night, as Jimmy refries the refried beans, Lena tells him she thinks she'll stay a bit longer.

The first week:

After a week with Jimmy and Moses, Lena knows their sounds:
– Jimmy: whistles through his teeth when he is shaving.
– Moses: taps on the side of the plate with his knife before he butters his toast.
– Jimmy: breathes in an uneven way when he sleeps (heard when Lena creeps to the bathroom in the middle of the night).
– Moses: makes an odd two-step knocking high on the adjoining bedroom wall early in the morning. ('What on earth are you doing?' says Lena, cautiously opening the bunk-room door to find Moses lying on his back in the top bunk. He turns his head to look at her but continues to walk his feet up the wall in a series

of thuds, all the way to the ceiling. 'Oh, you're *mountain climbing!*' says Lena. 'You're very good at it too.')

The second week:

After the second week Lena is no longer a stranger in Barrow, though she is still stared at by the Inupiat men who sit on the benches in the main street. She has learnt how many sweaters to put on in the morning, has seen Norm buzzing overhead, has watched newcomers arrive at the airfield and the sky fall with gulls at the end of the day.

During this week she sees the snow melt to slush and she becomes accustomed to the low restless wheeling of the sun outside her bedroom window. She stands on the shores of the Arctic Ocean and looks out from the northernmost point of America, but she turns away from the whale hunters and the reek of guts dumped on the beaches.

'It's a ritual,' says Jimmy, looking at her curiously. 'And it's controlled. It's not like they'll become extinct.'

But Moses also turns his face away from the whale meat that Jimmy brings home. 'See?' says Lena. 'He's got an old head on his young shoulders.' Moses' reaction reminds her of Bella and herself, and the bedroom in the Tenderloin well stocked with carcasses. 'It was like sleeping in a natural history museum,' she says.

Jimmy laughs, but Moses stares at her with a puzzled look on his face. Lena wonders whether he has ever been to a museum, if he has grown up surrounded by grey concrete buildings or green prairies or wide marshy flatlands. She sees Jimmy wondering this too, and quickly she wrestles Moses to the ground and rolls him around a bit until he smiles. She doesn't want to think too long about what Moses might have seen.

The third week:

By the third week the sun is up all the time, but Lena no longer expects the air to be warm when she steps out into the yard with her camera in her hand. Nor does she look for the swoop of palm trees against the sky.

'Though it takes some getting used to, this not having trees,' she says to Jimmy.

'We have bushes,' he says, by way of an offering. 'We have lots and lots of mud. And best of all—'

'What?' she says.

'We have imported avocado!' he says. 'Direct from the southern states.' He runs a knife around the case until it is clean and brown, and he hands Lena a cracker piled with pale green flesh from her home territory.

The fourth week:

In the fourth week, Lena and Jimmy sit on the veranda with their feet dangling over the edge and talk about Moses, whom Lena hopes to photograph and Jimmy hopes to solve.

'They're talking about placing him with a family,' says Jimmy. 'I'll have to get on to it soon.'

'Do you want to keep him?' asks Lena.

'Sometimes I have to go away for weeks at a time,' shrugs Jimmy. 'I've got a job lined up in July down in Denali, with some biologists from Canada. I can't keep asking Brenda and Po to look after him.'

'That wasn't what I asked,' says Lena.

'I want to find out what happened, anyway,' says Jimmy, which is not really an answer either. 'I'm going to go back to Doonerak, have another look around. There must be something there.'

'Did you learn to track in Alaska?' asks Lena.

'No, I was brought up on a reserve in Wyoming,' says Jimmy, and for a second his face closes, clenches around the words like a hand. 'I can hardly remember learning,' he says. 'I could recognize the prints of a prairie dog before I could say its name.'

'So was there nothing to show where Moses had come from?' asks Lena.

'It was snowing when I found him,' says Jimmy, leaning back against the wall of the house. 'It had been for a while. Another hour out in that and he wouldn't be here now.'

'And when you go back you'll be looking for – what?' says Lena, forcing herself to ask, though she isn't ready to hear the word.

'Well, bodies,' says Jimmy, as if this is a given.

'Of course,' says Lena.

'Someone must have taken him out there,' shrugs Jimmy. 'Much as the locals like to believe there's some mystery surrounding that mountain, he didn't just appear out of nowhere. The thing is, he could have walked a long way before I found him – you've seen how much energy he's got.'

There's a silence.

'If we could just get him to talk,' says Jimmy. 'Just a few goddamn words.'

'How did you know what his name was?' says Lena.

'I didn't,' says Jimmy. 'I made it up.' He sticks a cigarette in his mouth, searches through his pockets and then gets up and disappears inside. 'Well, I didn't literally make it up,' he calls indistinctly from the kitchen. 'It's from the Bible.'

'I know *that*,' says Lena, as Jimmy reappears with a box of matches. 'Everyone knows the story of Moses being found in the bulrushes.' She pauses and looks uncertain, realizes that, in spite of all those years kneeling by her Tenderloin bed murmuring her small and hopeful prayers, she'd never got to the source of it all.

'I haven't actually read the Bible,' she admits.

'It's not a bad read,' says Jimmy in a considering way. 'It goes on a bit, though.'

Lena laughs and leans back against the wall, and then she takes off her hat. Here in Barrow, where the cold is like a common enemy, it is possible to wear a hat inside and out, day and night, no questions asked. But she feels it is time.

The May sun is still watery and weak, but Lena's scar has not seen the light of day for a long time and it flinches and stings. Lena sees Jimmy looking at it and she looks away, wills him not to say the wrong thing.

He takes a drag on his cigarette, exhales. After a while he speaks. 'How did that happen?' he asks.

'I went to buy donuts,' says Lena. She shuts her eyes, feels the warm blood cupped once more in her hands and the desire to drink it to save herself.

'Not usually a dangerous occupation,' says Jimmy. His tone is casual, lies easily on her eyelids.

'I got shot in the street,' she says, still with her eyes shut. 'I got caught in crossfire.'

'In LA?' says Jimmy's voice.

'No, in San Francisco,' she says. 'Just a few blocks from where I grew up.'

'Maybe that was what saved you,' Jimmy suggests.

'Maybe,' says Lena. 'Though other people seem to think that going back was what got me into trouble.'

'There's usually a good reason for revisiting the past,' says Jimmy. There's a pause. 'Did they catch the guys who did it?' he asks.

'Yes, though it took them a while,' says Lena. 'Some feud over drug money, apparently.'

'So not even an important issue,' says Jimmy. 'Not like saving the whales.' He laughs then and Lena opens her eyes, and the world seems slightly brighter.

Behind them, behind the house, the children are straggling down Madison Street on their way home from school. Their voices rise out of the crunching gravel, over the roof, to fall lightly on the heads of Jimmy and Lena sitting there talking about shootouts in a casual kind of way on a May afternoon.

'The only thing is, it left me looking like this,' says Lena. Her voice is as light as the children's, but carefully so: it lifts itself into the air and holds itself there on slightly shaking arms.

'There's nothing wrong with the way you look,' says Jimmy. 'You look just fine to me.'

('And this—' says another New York publisher, the arch-enemy of Jay's publishing contact, 'this appears to be a self-portrait.' Seventy floors above Madison Avenue he leans against the plate-glass wall of his office, and Manhattan spreads out behind him like a cape.

'Striking, isn't she,' says his nephew, who has filched the photos from the office where he works after a falling-out with his boss over the length of his lunch hours. 'I like the pose,' he muses, 'the suggestion of gun culture. Pity about the deformity, though.'

'I think that's the idea,' says his publishing-magnate uncle drily, immediately discounting the idea of stealing his nephew away from his rival and offering him a job. 'Where did you say these came from?' he asks.

'Some guy in LA, Jay something,' says his nephew. 'I forget, it was one of those long wop names. He was this chick's manager when she was performing.'

'And where is she now?' says the rival publisher. 'How can I get ahold of her?'

'You can't,' says the nephew. 'Not for a while; she's in Alaska or some godforsaken place. I forget.'

'I want prints of these,' says the publisher, throwing the envelope at him. 'And for God's sake stop picking at that rubber plant.')

Just as the sun is content to stay around in Barrow, so is Lena. There is no further discussion about whether she should leave; at the beginning of each new week she gives Jimmy board money, and in the meantime Moses starts to creep into her bed in the morning for stories.

Letters arrive for her: from Mr Domanski who has achieved a long-held ambition and penetrated the glossy depths of Palm Springs with a Polish Sausage; from Bella who sends a photo of Mitchell on display beside a python destined for the Boston Natural History Museum; and from Mrs Domanski, excited about launching a new range of nail varnish into the untapped market of France.

'Why is everyone I know an entrepreneur?' Lena complains.

'They're not,' says Jimmy. 'You know me now.' He is due to disappear for a few days to the Mendenhall Glacier to look for a lost climber. 'Away down south,' he says to Lena. 'Your side of the Arctic Circle.'

His house is no longer as cold as it was, but it feels empty with just Lena and Moses in it. Po and Brenda come for a meal, turning up in purple denim dungarees with leftovers from the shop: shrivelled pies, day-old sausage rolls, and a packet of cupcakes that Brenda has sat on by mistake.

'Now you've stayed this long,' says Po to Lena, 'you really should hang around for the Fourth of July. It's a total blast.'

'The whole town gets booked up,' says Brenda. 'People come from all over for the games we have here.'

Lena has no desire for more people, but she is quite happy to stay with the people she is with. 'I'm due back in Fairbanks before the end of June, though,' she says regretfully.

'Why's that?' Brenda demands through a mouth full of flattened sponge and squashed mock cream.

'I have to meet up with my brother,' explains Lena. 'We've got flights back to Los Angeles.'

'Planes go to the Lower 48 all the time,' says Brenda. 'There's no rush, is there?' This could be her way of saying she would like Lena to stay, but she washes away any possible sentimentality with a huge gulp of milky coffee.

'I guess Seidensal could get a message to Davey,' says Lena, torn. Then she remembers something else. 'Oh, but Jay's lined up an appointment for me in New York,' she says.

'About your book, is it?' says Po, and her face immediately turns photogenic as it always does when she speaks of Lena's work: cheeks smooth, eyes wide. 'Got some good pitchers, have you?' she asks interestedly.

Lena has, though the urgency felt in Los Angeles has faded along with the rush of that city. Here in Barrow she takes photos only when she feels like it; the rest of the time she just concentrates on living. 'There are still a few important ones I want to get, though,' she says, and although she is talking to Po she looks down at the top of Moses' smooth black head.

'You getting on well with Jimmy?' asks Po, with a hopeful spark in her eye.

But Lena just laughs. 'You're incurable,' she says.

'About what?' says Po, extracting a new paperback romance from her bag and placing it casually at the end of the table. 'You can borrow that if you want,' she says to Lena. 'If you don't bend the spine too much we can put it back in the shop.'

After their guests have left, Lena and Moses lie on the couch together, eating jellybeans and staring at the ceiling. Lena notices a thick layer of grey dust lying on every rafter. 'We'll have to spring clean,' she says to Moses. 'You want to help?'

Moses nods.

'Even though it's nearly midsummer?' says Lena.

Moses smiles.

Lena offers him a rag and the skirting boards, and tackles the rest herself. In the kitchen cupboard are pots of mouldy jam and unopened boxes of cereal years past their expiry date. In the bathroom cabinet are tubes of toothpaste that are set solid, and old razor blades with remnants of Jimmy's chin on them. For three days Lena cleans, finishing late at night long after Moses is in bed. She sits out on the veranda, smelling of cleaning fluids that remind her of her mother, and she closes her eyes to the pink night sun.

When Jimmy gets home he stands and stares around him. 'Something's different,' he says. 'Have you swept or something?' That week and the next he refuses to take Lena's board money. 'You look after Moses,' he says, 'and you eradicate bad jam. Seems like a fair deal to me.'

'But you might need a bit for a rainy day,' says Lena.

'Doesn't rain much up here,' says Jimmy. 'The Northern Slope's classified as a desert.'

Lena hesitates.

'Seriously,' says Jimmy, who hardly needs to use the word because almost everything he says is serious, 'I don't set much store by saving. Seems to me that when you need money, that's the time to go out and do something about it.' He has found the missing Mendenhall climber, has tracked his footprints over furrowed plains and across high snowfields to find him huddled in a gully, half frozen. 'But still alive,' says Jimmy. 'So I earned my keep this week.'

'You mean you don't get paid if you don't come up with the goods?' asks Lena.

'Yeah, I do,' says Jimmy. 'But I don't feel as if I deserve it if I come back empty-handed.' He looks more serious than ever, responsibility sitting heavily on his checked wool shoulders. 'This guy's gonna be OK,' he says. 'He might lose a few toes but at least he'll get to see his wife again.' He looks over at the closed door of the bunk-room, behind which Moses might or might not be sleeping. 'Speaking of tracking—' he says.

Lena grips the edges of the table, waits for the dates and times that will bring about Moses' departure. But Jimmy doesn't go any farther. He gets up and goes to the fridge, pulls out butter and pickles and cheese. 'Want a sandwich?' he says. 'I forgot to have dinner.'

And so Lena breathes easy that night, and Moses gets to keep his silence for a little longer, and Jimmy says goodnight and takes his sandwich up the ladder to the loft. Lena hears him lie down, hears the wooden beams of the house he has lived in for nineteen years accept the weight of his body. And she lays her head down too, flat on the table in her old thinking way. For there is something else she must do, more important than sweeping away cobwebs and more difficult than getting Moses to sleep while the night sun shines. She knows she must do it before she leaves this place of gravel and snow and circling light, but she is daunted by it.

'You could take pictures of us instead,' wheedles Po. Every time Lena goes to the store now, to buy bread or film or dishwashing liquid, Po rushes for her compact, and her hands fly to her hair as if Lena is a celebrity photographer. 'Nobody here is getting any younger,' she says. 'I don't know about you, Brenda, but God knows I'm starting to show my age.' Po is at least ten years younger than Brenda, having once been one of her students at a local high school in Anchorage.

'I do want to take pictures of you, Po,' says Lena. 'The thing is, I have to be able to shoot you—' She stops short.

(*I have enabled you to see language in a different way!* babbles the bullet, as it is tossed into a file box labelled 'Polk Street Shooting'. *I have given you the gift to think around the cliché and beyond the square!*)

'I have to be able to *shoot* you,' Lena goes on firmly, 'just the way I want to.'

'Of course you can!' says Po.

'No posing,' says Lena, 'no studio shots, just you.' She finds directness is easy with Po; it lies on her in the way that oil lies on water, not sinking in, never causing offence.

'Of course you can, Lena!' says Po again. 'You can choose where, you can choose how – hell, you can even choose who!' She stops and giggles. 'Just kidding,' she says, and she rushes across the store and puts her arm around Brenda's great waist, and plants a smacking kiss on Brenda's shoulder.

'Come off it,' says Brenda. She turns to Lena. 'All my friends were surprised when I hooked up with Po,' she says. 'She's far more emotional than me.'

'Where do you want us?' asks Po, reverting to the task in hand. The eagerness in her voice reminds Lena of Mitchell rushing towards his salad bowl. 'Should we set up our living room?' she asks.

'I'd rather use a backdrop that's more unexpected,' says Lena.

'How about over in Browerville?' says Brenda, offhandedly. 'That's where we first got together.'

'Away over there?' says Po, as if Browerville is in another county rather than just across the main road, beyond the lagoon.

'Sounds good to me,' says Lena.

Brenda puts up the 'Back in Five Minutes' sign and leads the way out into the windy day, and they walk down gravel roads to where Brenda and Po began. They end up in the video store where – according to Po – Brenda's feelings first became obvious.

'She chose a romantic comedy,' says Po to Lena, in a low voice. 'I took it as a sign.'

Lena cracks jokes to make Po relax and to wipe the stern look off Brenda's face, and she takes shots under bright yellow lights against bright red carpet. 'When we get back to the store,' she says, 'I'd like to take some more there.'

By the time they return there are several old men sitting grumpy and tobacco-less on the steps. 'Don't start your photographing till we've dealt with the customers, now,' Po orders.

But Lena sets up her tripod and, while the old men are occupying

Po, she starts to shoot. Every time there is a quiet patch Po begins to preen and pose, and Lena waits. And every time the bell on the shop door rings, Lena can start work again. Po darts about fetching dried pasta and Double A batteries, ducking under Brenda's arms like a small car hurrying under a bridge. And Brenda reaches up to the top shelf for ice-cream cones, and puts her large hand on Po's head to steady herself, and Lena *clicks* and captures something – something that emerges later in the sealed dark of her temporary workroom, but has also existed for a long time now.

The sixth story of loss

Two middle-aged women named Po and Brenda, who used to know each other many years ago, are trapped. Po is trapped in a marriage which for some reason she cannot fathom has stopped working. Brenda is trapped in a bad mood that has lasted nearly fifteen years.

When they meet up again in Barrow, where Po is on a bird-watching tour, there is a recognition that has nothing to do with the fact that, long ago, Brenda taught grammar and spelling to Po. Brenda – who for some years now has been living in Browerville – invites Po back to her house for an evening of catching up and conversation. They watch a video and eat some salmon bake. In the morning they are in love with each other.

(freeze-frame: two women, one tall and one short, roar with laughter in the aisle of a video store. So narrow and cramped is the aisle that the women's bodies are pushed close together and the stomach of the tall woman rests on the smaller woman's breasts. The two women wear identical clothing)

Love does not often arrive this fast or this certainly, so Brenda and Po are aware that this is their real life. They pack up their respective pasts (*lost: loneliness*) and they buy a store just across the road from the place where they first slept together. They run this store for many years, with few arguments.

204

(freeze-frame: two store owners, one big and one small, are clean-ing up some strawberry milk spilt on their front counter. The dark woman's head is bent as she scrubs milk out of the cracks in the counter; the blond woman holds the dark one's hair out of the milk, pulling it up into the air like a trophy. They are wearing identical clothes)

After a year together, these two middle-aged women named Po and Brenda notice that, most mornings, they pull similar clothes out of their wardrobe. Every time they coincide on red shirts or chequered pants, the teller in the bank says to them, 'You guys look so great in your matching outfits!'

Brenda and Po come to a decision. From this point on they will buy one Small and one Large of each new garment, and in this way they will build up an entire collection of matching outfits. They take it in turns to decide what they will wear each day. Their favourite outfit is the purple sateen shirt with the white denim flares.

One day they hope to make it into the Guinness Book of Records as the longest-matching couple in North American History. *Lost: the fear of not fitting in.*

Digging

'A book?' says Po breathlessly. 'You want to put us in a *book*?'

'That's if you don't mind,' says Lena. But knowing they will not, she has already sent prints away. She has packaged up Brenda and Po along with the tobacco-spitting men and the cleaner from the Top of the World hotel and the chef from the Mexican restau-rant, all of whom have lived through as much as your average person or more. And she has sent them away to Jay, and to Jay's publishing contact in New York, and to another publisher who has approached her, via Jay, via the 1901 Barrow Post Office.

'Hear that, Brenda?' says Po, with excitement. 'You want to be in Lena's book?'

'It's all right with me,' says Brenda with a shrug. 'As long as we can get prints for our Christmas card mail-out this year.'

'Lena, I'm honoured,' says Po. 'Honoured,' she says again, and her eyes shine with tears.

'Oh for God's sake, Po,' says Brenda. 'Pull yourself together, would you.' But she gives Lena a not-unfriendly pinch on the arm as she goes out the back to answer the phone. When she comes back Po is serving a customer, and Brenda takes Lena into the cereal hideout.

'You want to know something?' she says. 'I haven't been apart from Po any longer than a weekend. Last year, when she went down to Anchorage for a class reunion? I couldn't sleep a wink the whole two days.'

'I won't tell,' promises Lena, boxes of Lucky Charms at her back for good measure.

'She's ruined solitude for me,' says Brenda seriously.

Taking her camera, Lena goes outside to look for Moses. She finds him sitting on the front steps watching the Ditch Witch trundle along the road on its way to the graveyard, where it will carve out a new resting place for an old local. Gravel spurts from its wheels, is turned to sharp grey glitter by the sun.

'Hey, Moses,' says Lena. She pauses; she always does, just in case one day he will answer. 'Moses,' she says, and she takes a deep breath. (It is never easy embarking on something you have procrastinated over for weeks.) 'You know how I've been taking pictures of the people round here?' she says. 'Well, I thought I might take some of you. You think you could handle that?' In fact she feels as if she should be asking herself that question: it is quite possible that she will not be up to the job.

Moses opens his mouth as if he is about to say something, and his small front teeth show like two rows of milky corn kernels.

'You think yes?' says Lena.

There is silence.

'Or you think no,' she says, snapping the lens cap on to her camera as if there will be a corresponding click in Moses' brain and he will instantly start to speak again.

But Moses simply sits and stares after the machine. It is as if he is mesmerized by the turning of its wheels, and the great blade used to saw the frozen earth.

Lena shivers. 'Come on,' she says, and she takes Moses' hand and pulls him up off the steps, though his head still cranes to look down the street. 'Let's go home,' she says, although it is neither of their homes, it is a cold and draughty house belonging to someone she and Moses have known for a matter of weeks, and soon might never see again.

Even so, there is a shared sense of relief when they step into the battered house and close the door on the world. Jimmy is not there, is helping the neighbour install a new water pump. But his stained old coffee cup sits on the table, and the newspaper lies in a relaxed way beside it, and Lena and Moses have only to look around to remember their own small comforting routines.

'Hot chocolate?' says Lena. She looks at Moses' smooth violet-veined wrists, at his tiny socked feet on the floorboards, and suddenly she hopes that Jimmy will be able to track down the mystery in Moses' past. Until he does, she thinks, Moses will remain slightly ghostly, a small wispy figure able to be snatched up by a passing machine and carried away down long gravel roads.

Over the next few days she hangs out with Moses: walks around the lagoon with him, hunts for bugs, sits in the background while he plays with the kids from next door. She carries her camera with her like a baby, always at her back or her front, ready. But it is impossible. Asleep or awake, Moses eludes her.

In the middle of June there is a warm spell that thaws the top layer of the permafrost, and brings honking clouds of geese on to the lagoon. Lena's feet uncurl in her boots like small pale plants, Moses runs around in short sleeves. Po calls round for a chat and while she is there the phone rings.

'It's for you, Lena,' says Jimmy, holding out the receiver.

Lena is startled: no one has called her since she arrived, and her cellphone has long gone flat. Slightly anxiously, she takes the phone and hears Davey's voice emerge: faint, staccato. 'Allowed two calls,' the voice says. 'Team morale. Few minutes.'

'You're OK,' says Lena with relief, but her voice gets dragged down into layers of static.

'Checking,' says Davey. 'Glad. You.'

'Did you get the number from Da?' says Lena loudly.

'Far,' agrees crackling Davey. 'Middle of nowhere.'

Lena tries to smooth out Davey's tinfoil sentences. 'So I'll see you in ten days?' she says, clamping the phone to her ear, straining to hear.

'Then,' says Davey's voice, and the line goes dead.

'My brother,' says Lena, looking over at Jimmy and Po. 'Confirming that there really is life up the Yukon River.' She is sweating slightly from the effort of the call, goes over to the calendar and counts with her finger. 'That's the day I'm due to meet him,' she says. Her words fall flat into the quiet room. She begins to think of medical centres and tax returns, of appointment diaries and checkups and the scar therapist's card lying unused in the bottom of her bag.

Po steps in. 'Can't you persuade her to stay a bit longer, Jimmy?' she says in a businesslike way. 'It's not often that a person gets all the way up to Barrow.'

'She's welcome to,' says Jimmy seriously. 'Of course she is.'

'There you go, Lena!' says Po, as if this is all that's needed.

'But Davey's expecting me,' says Lena lamely.

'If it suits you to stay,' says Jimmy again, 'you're very welcome.'

This is the closest he has ever come to offering an opinion, and Lena's scalp prickles with embarrassment and indecision. 'Thanks,' she says. 'But I shouldn't. I have a life somewhere else.' She looks at Moses sitting in the window seat, his face screwed up against the sun, and her stomach twists.

'So what do you guys plan to do with all this warm weather?' asks Po, who is adept at filling in awkward gaps without realizing it.

'I was thinking,' says Jimmy, 'that Lena and Moses might like to try some tracking.'

'Tracking?' says Lena with faint alarm.

'Not people,' says Jimmy. 'Just animals.'

'Animals?' says Lena, with more definite alarm. She has faced down sniggering firemen and street kids with hens, she has met bullets and plastic surgeons with equanimity. But she has had no experience with wolverines or grizzly bears.

'Only on a small scale,' says Jimmy, seeing her face. 'Promise.'

They leave early the next morning, the three of them, in the truck Jimmy keeps in Barrow. 'My run-about-towner,' he quips, and he drives them south in it, bumping along dirt tracks and across the wide marshy tundra. Moses sits between them, leaning against Lena's arm. With every bump of the truck the breath is jolted out of him, and Lena holds her hand up in front of his mouth so his small hot puffs land on her palm.

'What on earth are you doing?' asks Jimmy looking sideways at them.

'I'm catching his breath,' says Lena. She laughs and can feel, though not hear, Moses giving a little laugh too. His small body shakes against hers, and together they absorb the rough road.

By the time they have jolted to a stop, they can see shadowy foothills in the distance and once the engine is turned off they stand with the silence pressing on their heads. 'Huge,' says Lena, although she hardly knows which aspect she is referring to.

'Let the tracking begin,' says Jimmy. He walks a way off from the truck and starts casting over the ground, like a hound hunting for a scent. Then he beckons them over to where there is a tiny indentation in the grass, and they sit down beside it and stay there for a long time. Lena lies back and looks at the sky, wonders if it is getting tired of the sun's constant attention.

'Just a bit longer,' says Jimmy. Moses goes over and lies down right in front of him, but Jimmy pays no attention until a mosquito hovers over Moses' cheek and Moses bats it away, waving his hand in the air like a drowning swimmer. 'Keep still, would you,' says Jimmy but still he doesn't look at Moses, focusing instead on the ground and the sky.

Moses looks gravely at Jimmy, then he crawls on his hands and knees like a tiny child over to Lena, and lies down across her feet.

'I hate these bugs,' Lena says to him, swatting away a swarm of blackflies. She fishes out some repellent, smears it over Moses' exposed hands and feet and then over her own. The musky smell reminds her of heat and holidays, and of lying too close to a snoring Jay in the glow of a small orange tent.

'Jimmy?' she says, holding out the tube to him. 'Want some?'

Jimmy doesn't answer.

Lena sits with her knees crooked up and Moses' red padded weight like a sinker on her feet, pulling them towards the centre of the earth. After Jimmy's reprimand, Moses is taking care to lie still: so still that after a while Lena thinks he has gone to sleep. But when she peers around into his face, his eyes are still open.

He lies there on Lena's feet, and Lena sits there, and the sun trawls steadily through the blue sky. Jimmy stays completely motionless, crouched back on his heels. Eventually—

'Got it!' he says.

'Got what?' asks Lena.

'The angle of the sun,' says Jimmy, and he puts his head low to the earth. 'Perfect,' he says.

'What exactly are we following?' asks Lena.

'A mouse,' says Jimmy. He is looking sideways across imprints so small that, even when he points them out, Lena can hardly see them.

'A *mouse*?' she says, thinking he is joking.

'I'm not joking,' says Jimmy. 'You of all people should know when someone isn't joking.'

'Hear that, Moses?' says Lena. 'We're looking for a mouse. We're hunting a musk-mouse.'

'Not a musk-mouse,' says Jimmy, who is being more than usually serious today. 'Just an ordinary one. Don't confuse him.'

They move slowly across the lichen and the campion: more slowly even than the languid sun. Moses becomes heavy with tiredness but Jimmy doesn't appear to notice. He is busy interpreting the ground, reading the blades of grass as clearly as written words. 'This one's been bent, see?' he says, but to Lena only, since Moses has long since lost interest. 'And this one – there's no moisture on this. Something's gone past and knocked against it.' He looks at Moses who is flopping around on the ground like a bored seal. 'Don't lie on that!' he says, moving him out of the way.

'I think Moses needs a rest,' says Lena, torn between interest and responsibility. 'Maybe we should do this another day?'

'See this!' says Jimmy, ignoring her suggestion. 'See this row of holes?' There is an unaccustomed lift in his voice, and he points to another blade of grass that looks exactly the same as all the other thousands surrounding it. But when Lena lies down and eyes the grass up close, she sees tiny holes on its green surface.

'What are they?' she asks, lying there on the rough ground.

'They're nail marks,' says Jimmy. He is lying only a foot away from Lena and when she looks past the grass at him his face comes into sharp focus: small lines around his mouth, dust in his eyebrows, and an absorption in his eyes that is total.

'I can't believe anyone can track a mouse!' says Lena, and it gives her hope, the fact that, in all this space, one small particular creature can be located.

When they come to a narrow creek a flock of Canadian geese rises up in alarm. Their wings make a metallic noise, a persistent rise and fall that sounds like a siren. And then the noise fades and the geese are gone, disappearing towards the north in one elegant winged eyebrow.

Jimmy seems to remember about Moses then. 'You tired?' he asks. Even though there are purple shadows under Moses' eyes, he shakes his head. 'OK,' says Jimmy, who obviously wants to believe him. 'We'll go on.'

On the other side of the creek is a bed of rock. 'How can you follow something over rock?' says Lena. But Jimmy tells her that rock is no easier or harder than any other ground.

'Dust is taken,' he says, 'or dust is compressed.' And he leads them on, until he stops on a patch of ground that again looks no different from the rest of that vast, wide, grassy land. 'Hmm,' he says.

'What?' says Lena.

'He's been taken,' says Jimmy, kneeling and looking. 'The mouse. He's been snatched.'

'By what?' says Lena, taking hold of Moses' hand just in case.

But Jimmy is standing up, and dusting his knees off. 'An eagle,' he says. 'Scuffle right there, see?'

'No,' says Lena. 'I don't.'

'What about this?' says Jimmy, and he bends and picks up a miniscule feather which he gives to Lena.

'Amazing,' says Lena. She stands like a small straight Maypole in the middle of the tundra and Moses spins around her. 'Poor mouse,' she says.

On the way back to the truck they walk like Indians, in one straight line: Jimmy, Moses, Lena. When Moses lags behind, Jimmy puts him up on his shoulders and tells stories about the reserve he grew up on: stories of tracking foxes and bears, and deer, not to mention human beings.

'It was a bit like Alaska,' he says. Because he is facing forward, his voice floats back to Lena with a few words missing here and there. 'A – – of wanderers,' he says. 'Sometimes people want to – – lost. But they don't think about—'

'What?' says Lena, closing the gap. Perhaps because she has been made newly aware of tracks, she sees that Jimmy walks with his feet pointing straight ahead, heel to toe. 'What don't they think about?' she asks.

'About the people left behind,' says Jimmy, as they reach the truck. He lowers Moses to the ground, straightens up, rubs his neck. 'That's why I'm a tracker, I guess,' he says. 'Things that are lost need to be found. No messy endings.'

They sit in the cab of the truck to eat their sandwiches, and they drink orange juice out of a thermos. It could be lunchtime, or later: Lena has no watch and no idea, for the hours spin and reel into each other, encouraged into anarchy by the constant sun.

Before they have even finished eating Moses falls into a doze. He lies sprawled on the seat, curled fingers twitching in sleep like tiny sea-anemones. 'Any luck with him?' asks Jimmy quietly. 'With the photos?'

'None,' says Lena. Every day this problem bites her as persistently as the mosquitos down by the lagoon. 'I don't know why,' she says. 'I guess I don't know enough about him yet.'

(freeze-frame: a small boy is playing with a yellow bulldozer. He looks like any small boy)

'You've seen the photos,' she says, a little despondently. 'They're no good.'

212

'Not as good as your other ones,' agrees Jimmy. He never chooses his words simply to make someone feel better: something that causes unease in a person like Po, who prefers life to be agreeable at all times.

'True,' says Lena with a sigh. She now has enough material for one or even two books, has photos of sufficient quality to satisfy one New York publisher, or two. She has young truck-drivers and old men playing dominoes, she has whores and nuns and a lesbian couple (loving and much-loved) with different personalities and identical clothes. But she cannot crack Moses.

(freeze-frame: a small Asian-American boy stands on a stool by a sink, brushing his teeth. Out of the cracked mirror his face is reflected back at him like a small pale moon. He is about four years old. It is impossible to tell what he is thinking)

'I got another phone call from child welfare yesterday,' says Jimmy. 'They want him in Anchorage.'

'What did you say?' asks Lena. Her voice bounces in a slightly panicked way off the windscreen.

'That I'm going back to Doonerak next week,' says Jimmy.

'Are you?' says Lena.

'Of course,' says Jimmy, sounding slightly surprised.

'And then what?' says Lena. She feels Moses' hand drift against her leg and, unhappily, she closes her eyes against her own contradictions.

'I told them that if I don't find anything,' says Jimmy, 'I'll bring him in after that.' His voice is like an official piece of paper, conveying a message but no particular emotion.

Bring him in, thinks Lena inside her hot, angry, conflicted head. *As if Moses is some maverick needing to be corralled!*

'Lena?' says Jimmy, and suddenly he is taking her hand.

She opens her eyes and sees that his face is anything but expressionless. 'I have to find out,' says Jimmy. 'It's the least I can do for him.' His dry, rough fingers move on Lena's as if they are working a piece of wood. 'Sometimes I don't know how to treat him,' he says. 'I feel all at sea.'

'You do fine,' says Lena.

Jimmy looks at her. 'No, I do OK,' he says. 'You do fine.'

'But I don't know anything about children!' says Lena.

'Sometimes you're like a child yourself,' says Jimmy. 'You always will be.' He drops her hand suddenly as if he has only just become aware that he is holding it. 'I say that in the best possible way,' he says hastily.

Lena looks at her wrist. The quilted pattern of Moses' snow-suit is imprinted on her skin. Jimmy starts up the truck, and Lena puts on her seatbelt out of long habit although Jimmy always drives without one, and Moses sleeps on. They drive home in silence but every now and then Lena takes a quick look at Jimmy. Beyond his profile, out the truck window, the sky is as huge and as light as ever but there is no lightness to be found in Jimmy's face. It has been left behind somewhere in the wide tundra, has fallen and rolled into the cracks in the lichen, leaving no tracks.

Back

In her last week in Barrow Lena has odd moments of panic: moments when she stands in the middle of a gravel street with the dust rising around her and hears the world muffled. Although she has become used to listening through a layer of scar tissue, during these moments she cannot even hear properly inside her head. She must feel for her pulse to check that her heart is still beating; her wrist, unlike her head, never betrays her.

Moses seems as unsettled as she is. Through half-sleep Lena hears him, sneaking outside at 3 a.m. to play in the sandy yard. Each time she is about to get up, but Jimmy is already there.

'How do you think you're gonna stay awake in the day,' she hears him saying to Moses, 'if you play all night?' But he sounds sympathetic as if he, too, is finding the midnight sun slightly disconcerting.

Even when on the surface things appear to be shifting, tradi-tions have a way of keeping afloat. And so Lena continues to fix grapefruit for breakfast. Every morning she slices the fruit in half and carves carefully around the edges so that each segment can be lifted out separately (this is what Mr Domanski used to do). Next, she spreads white sugar on the top of each half – as Mr D used to do – and leaves them standing so the juice at the bottom becomes thick and sweet. Yes, this is what Mr Domanski once did for Lena and Bella and Davey, and now Lena does it for Moses in what might well be the last days of their acquaintance.

There is a morning when Jimmy gets up earlier than usual and Lena gets up later. A trail of toast crumbs shows that Jimmy has already eaten and gone, but Moses' special bowl and cup sit untouched on the bench and so Lena calls him when the grapefruit is done.

'Moses!' she calls, and she turns back to the coffee on the stove and waits and counts to ten: for this is another morning routine that has become as regular as clockwork. Sometimes she might get to count to eight or nine, but she never makes it to ten because before she does Moses will be running in through the door and up to the table. (Lena counts, she waits, she looks forward to Moses' rushing feet and his small, silent, anticipatory face.)

Now she calls again, and she counts *one three five seven* on grapefruit fingers. Moses does not appear. *Eight.* The coffee hisses. *Nine.* Moses is not there.

'Moses?' Lena calls. She lifts the coffee off the stove, hears a noise, turns around. And Moses is standing behind her, pointing a gun at her head.

There is a loud crack.

Lena is flooded with red. Her body fills with dark red heat, there is red in front of her eyes and spreading through her chest so she cannot draw a breath.

(*this is what it's like, remember?* crows the bullet from its dark cardboard coffin. *This is what it is like to be shot!*)

Lena has been shot. She cannot breathe and she cannot scream. She is falling, falling down, and there is blood red all around her.

Forward

Jimmy finds her. Although she has been lying there for a very long time, it may also only be seconds for, when she hears Jimmy's voice and opens her eyes, she sees Moses still standing there with the gun in his hands.

'Oh Christ!' Jimmy is saying. His voice is frantic but faraway, like the sound of strong emotion on a television set playing in another room. 'Oh Christ!' he says. 'Are you hurt, Lena? Are you OK?' And then he is unfurling her fingers, which are somehow still wrapped around the knife, and she is being lifted up off the floor although a part of her wants to stay there, curled up against the kitchen cupboards with her back to the Tenderloin wall (for memory has a way of cutting corners, just as history repeats itself).

As soon as Jimmy sees that Lena has not been shot, that the *crack* was a plate knocked to the floor by Moses' small gun-toting elbow, he starts to shout. Lena has never heard Jimmy shout before, and this is almost more upsetting than what has just happened. He strides over and pulls the gun out of Moses' tiny gripping hands, and then he begins to pace around the kitchen, his boots booming on the floor and his voice echoing off the bare walls. 'How could you be so stupid!' he is shouting, over and over at Moses. 'I've told you never, never to touch the gun!'

Lena leans on the arm of the chair. 'Don't,' she tries to say. 'Please don't.' But her voice is not working properly: even she can hardly hear it. So she sits like a mute in her chair, unwilling audience of one to an unexpected scene.

Moses, too, stands mute, although for him this is now habitual. He stands and stares at Jimmy, and after a while Jimmy realizes he is the only one making any sound and he also falls silent. The three of them form an awkward triangle, one sitting, two standing, with the table floating like a wooden island in the middle of them.

'God, Moses,' says Jimmy eventually. 'Don't ever, ever do that again.' He carries the gun right away out of sight, putting it outside on the veranda, and then he comes back inside and sighs. 'I'm sorry I shouted,' he says to Moses, giving him an awkward kind of hug. He looks across at Lena. 'And you,' he says. 'Are you all right?'

Lena takes a deep breath and wipes her hand across her forehead. When she brings her hand away there is blood there, and underneath the blood is a tiny serrated mark across her palm, like the tracks of a mouse.

'You're hurt?' says Jimmy. He comes over and helps her out of the chair, and he holds her hand under the tap until it aches with the cold. Then he puts his arms around her and holds on to her for quite a long time. 'I heard you scream,' he says against the top of her head.

'But I didn't,' says Lena.

'You did,' says Jimmy. 'I heard you all the way across the yard.' He sounds perfectly normal again but as he stands there holding her Lena feels a slight tremor, as if the earth is turning over inside him.

The sheet

Waiting and watching. That is what tracking is all about, according to Jimmy, and he makes it sound like a good thing. But that night Lena watches and waits, and she feels that the night will never end. Beside her the clock ticks like a time bomb: she waits for an explosion that never comes. After three hours of waiting – after one hundred and eighty minutes, after ten thousand eight hundred seconds – she feels so nauseous that she can no longer lie still. Getting out of bed she makes her way to the door, hand over hand, using the wall for support like an old woman.

The night sun stares in through the windows, filling the living room with yellow light. Until now, Lena has not realized that Jimmy must sleep without curtains and she feels guilty as she creeps to the kitchen sink for water.

'Why are you up?' says Jimmy's voice, from somewhere in the rafters.

Lena starts. 'Did I wake you?' she says.

There is a small laugh. 'I thought you were Moses,' says Jimmy, and he looks over the edge of the loft bed. 'Well, the question stands,' he says. 'Why are *you* up? It must be after two.'

'I don't know how to sleep,' says Lena, exhaustedly.

'How to sleep!' says Jimmy, with another laugh. 'If anyone could crack that one, they'd be a multi-millionaire by now.'

Lena goes to the foot of the ladder. 'Can I come up?' she says politely.

'Sure,' says Jimmy, though his voice is guarded. 'I've got a sheet on,' he says.

Lena puts one foot on the ladder. The dowelling rung sits hard in the bare arch of her foot. 'Ow,' she says, and she climbs on. 'Ow,' she says again. 'Ow. Ow.' By the time she reaches the top, she collapses on to the end of the mattress. 'I hope you keep your boots on when you come to bed,' she says.

'That would be about all,' says Jimmy, and sure enough he is sitting there against the wall bare-chested, though the sheet is tucked firmly around his waist. Lena sits with her back against the other wall so that her legs and Jimmy's meet at right angles, one set under the sheet, one above.

'Welcome,' says Jimmy formally, just as he had on the day of Lena's arrival in Barrow. His arms are bigger than Lena had thought they would be, his shoulders wider.

'Thank you,' says Lena, just as she had on her first day. She looks at the white bumps in the sheet that are Jimmy's feet. 'Did you know that your feet point straight ahead when you walk?' she asks him.

'That's because I grew up with Native Americans,' says Jimmy. 'The Inuits walk like that too.'

'I hadn't noticed,' says Lena.

'Only white men splay their feet out,' says Jimmy, as if he isn't one of them. 'It comes from living in cities too long, from walking on pavements instead of trails.' He tilts his head back against the wall, looks across at her, looks tired.

'Did I wake you?' asks Lena again.

'I don't sleep much,' says Jimmy. 'I'm not very good at it.'

They sit for a while and talk about Lena's self-imposed work and Jimmy's irregular work, and every now and then they stop and look out at the orange sun rolling along the horizon.

'Do you ever get used to it?' says Lena. 'The lack of night?'

'I still feel jet-lagged,' says Jimmy. 'And it's been nineteen years.'

'Nineteen years,' says Lena. She stops and thinks. 'That's the same amount of time I lived in the Tenderloin,' she says. 'So this must feel like home to you now?' She also lays her head back against the wall, and feels the wood catch gently at her hair and at her new-old, year-old scar.

'I don't know if I believe in home,' says Jimmy. 'You just make a foothold somewhere and you stay.'

Lena thinks of her father enthusiastically spreading his small Polish domains across the west coast of America; thinks of Davey, most secure when looking into vast empty space. 'Maybe,' she says. 'But at least people know you here. You belong.'

Jimmy looks at her. In the yellow light his eyes look very dark and not only weary, but wary. 'They don't accept me, though,' he says. 'You've seen those old guys who sit in the main street and the way they look at me.'

'Even though you walk just like them!' says Lena. It is not the right time for jokes: Lena McLeonard would never have allowed this. But right now Lena Domanski would say anything to take the tiredness out of the eyes opposite.

And partially, it works. Jimmy gives a small smile. 'Sure, I walk the walk,' he says. 'I know the lingo. But when it comes down to it there's no getting away from the fact that I'm from the Lower 48.' This, too, is said as a kind of joke, but then he lifts his hair away from his neck. 'Got the scars to prove it,' he says, and Lena sees a jagged white line running down below his ear.

'How did *that* happen?' she asks, shocked.

'I got mouthy at a party one night,' says Jimmy. 'Got smart, got glassed.'

'But they know you!' says Lena again.

'In a way,' says Jimmy, 'you can't blame them. They've got a long history of grievances and I come somewhere at the end of it.'

'What about Po and Brenda?' objects Lena. 'They're not native – they haven't even been in Barrow as long as you have.'

'They're both second-generation Alaskans,' says Jimmy. 'Born and bred. It makes a difference.' He shrugs. 'Don't feel sorry for me, Lena,' he says. There is a slight defensiveness in his voice and Lena knows that if he were wearing any clothes at all, he would be turning his collar up right about now. 'Some people are born to be outsiders,' he says. 'It has its advantages.'

Down by the lagoon a bird is calling, on and on without fall like a woman held at the height of orgasm. After a while, Jimmy speaks again. 'You can try to sleep here,' he says. 'If you want.' He says it casually, as if he is offering nothing more than a cup of his usual muddy black coffee.

'All right,' says Lena, also casually. 'Thanks.' She shuffles over and lies down on top of the sheet, with her head on the very edge of the pillow. Jimmy slides down under the sheet and for a time they both lie completely still. Neither of them says anything but the sheet over Jimmy's chest is rustling loudly. Finally—

'Goddamn heart,' says Jimmy. 'Always gives me away.'

Lena sits up then and takes off her pyjamas, first the top and then the pants. Jimmy traces the square on her thigh with his finger: it looks calm in the diffuse light, lies calmly and submits to his touch without flinching.

'You've been through a lot,' he says. He takes his hand away again.

Lena gets under the sheets. She keeps the lower half of her body away from Jimmy, but leans inwards so her arm will reach over his shoulder. Jimmy puts an arm under her neck. Their other arms lie at awkward angles between them.

'The spare arm syndrome,' says Jimmy.

'What?' says Lena.

'That's what we used to call it,' says Jimmy. He coughs. 'Sorry,' he says. 'I shouldn't talk about someone else when I'm in bed with—' He coughs again. 'With you,' he says.

'You're talking about your wife,' says Lena.

'That's right,' says Jimmy. His voice is quiet but it vibrates through his shoulders and runs up into Lena's arm.

'I heard what happened,' she says. 'You don't have to explain.'

'It might sound dramatic,' says Jimmy, 'but I haven't been happy since she died.'

Lena moves her body into his then, and they twine their legs together and stop talking. Jimmy's hand cradles Lena's head, moves up to rest quietly on her scar. The direct contact is as startling and as safe as darkness.

The towel

Lena is in an earthquake. She is running down a street looking for a church, looking for a scuttling crab. A plate spins past her head and the roaring sky falls like water. She is running she is falling she is—

awake, with a start, to find herself in the loft bed, and she hears a loud rattling coming from the ladder.

Jimmy's hand has moved in its sleep. It has crept away from her head and now lies cupped over her right breast. Under his loose fingers her nipple rises and falls, keeping time with her breathing.

The ladder continues to rattle.

'Jimmy?' says Lena softly.

He is awake instantly, sitting up so fast that it is probable he will never realize how his hand has betrayed him in the night. 'It's Moses,' he says in a low voice. 'Sometimes he still wants to be taken to the bathroom.' He pushes the sheet back and stands up, then realizes he's naked and quickly wraps a towel round his waist. 'Sorry,' he says. He ducks his head so that his long hair falls over his face.

Then he is gone, disappearing down the ladder. 'Morning, Moses,' Lena hears him say. There is an answering silence, and then footsteps, and the closing of the bathroom door.

Lena lies in the vacated bed. She pulls the sheet up over her face and breathes in the cotton: warm, and as thin as skin.

'It will not happen this way again,' she says. The sheet rises and falls with her breath like a shroud over the living.

Height

The week disintegrates, falling away into a mass of cloud. Huge purple billows gather out at sea, and the old men outside the store spit tobacco and mumble of freak storms. But Jimmy remains intent on going to Doonerak.

'Next Tuesday,' he says, 'if no emergency work comes up.' He goes to the stove where the coffee has been sitting, stewing, for the past twenty minutes. 'Do you want to come?' he asks Lena, with his back to her.

'I don't know,' says Lena. 'Maybe I should stay with Moses?'

'Moses is coming,' says Jimmy, pouring the coffee. 'He was always coming.'

'Are you sure you should take him?' says Lena, alarmed. 'What if something terrible happened out there?'

'Lena,' says Jimmy, putting a cup down in front of her. 'Of course something terrible happened. Why do you think he won't speak a word? Why can't he even tell us his name?'

Lena spoons sugar into her coffee and stirs so hard that the thick black syrup slops into the saucer. 'All right,' she says eventually. 'We'll all go.'

'Good,' says Jimmy. 'Because I want you to come.'

Lena tips the coffee from her saucer into her mouth in a careless kind of way. But her stomach clenches and the side of her head, more often than not quiet and painless, starts to ache.

I have had enough of change for now, she thinks.

Jimmy walks around the kitchen, looking out at the grey sky. 'Let's hope the storm blows through before then,' he says.

Overnight there is thunder and lightning, and then the rain arrives. On Sunday morning Lena wakes to a torrential downpour; before long the streets have turned to rivers, and the backyard is a pool. On Monday the rain clears to a drizzle but the air remains humid and heavy, making the skin on Lena's scar tighten. All day Moses carries his bucket and spade between the veranda and the yard, making vast batches of mudpies, while inside Jimmy makes plans.

'This is weird shit,' he says, looking out the window and at the barometer. 'The weather's always crazy here, but this—' He stops to answer the phone. 'Yep,' he says. 'Yep, I know.'

Lena can hear Norm's voice on the other end, arguing and then stopping. Jimmy doesn't reply straight away. He lights a cigarette, inhales slowly, exhales through his mouth and nose. Only when the smoke is out of his lungs and hanging above his head does he speak again.

'It'll be OK,' he says. 'Ice, maybe, but only surface snow.' He pauses, and Norm's voice comes crackling down the line again.

'If there's anything to see,' says Jimmy, and his mouth goes into a stubborn line, 'you can bet that I'll see it.'

Lena has almost hoped for another storm but when she wakes the next day the light is sharp and bright, and the sky has been rinsed as clean as a white china bowl. In silence, they drive out to the airfield where Norm and his helicopter are already waiting for them.

'Why is it always so early?' asks Lena plaintively. 'Don't pilots sleep like normal people?'

Norm chuckles so that his bulk shakes in his seatbelt. 'Ain't no normal folk all the way up here,' he says. 'If you're wanting that, you'd better go back to LA.'

'You've got to be kidding,' says Lena. 'In California people pay millions just to be told they have a complex.'

'Listen to you guys!' says Jimmy. 'Anyone would think you'd done a song and dance together.' He looks quite relaxed, sitting there with one arm around Moses who is still half asleep, but his fingers are moving compulsively on Moses' shoulder.

As they get closer to the mountains the fresh snow is clearly visible, running thickly down the crevasses. Even the willows in the creek beds are dusted with white.

'This is a whole lot of snow for June,' says Norm. 'Hasn't happened since – well, I dunno. When would it be, Jimmy?'

'Huh?' says Jimmy, who is dividing his time between looking intently out the window and looking intently at Moses. Suddenly he is taut like a rope that has been pulled tight.

'The last big summer dump,' says Norm expectantly.

'Oh. Yeah,' says Jimmy. 'Yeah, you get it all here.'

Norm looks over his shoulder at Lena, takes his left hand off the controls and loops his finger at the side of his head. 'Crazy,' he says. 'Cracked.'

He does the circle that Jimmy has asked him to, sweeping them low over the Arctic Divide. Lena can see icy turquoise water running over stones, and on one side of the valley—

'Trees!' she says, and they really are trees, although they are spindly, wind-swept ones.

'You're just a *southern girl at heart*,' sings Norm in his best baritone voice.

He drops them at the bottom of another long river valley, lowering the helicopter on to a small gravel strip. 'This is about as far up as I can get a flat landing,' he says.

'We want to start here anyway,' says Jimmy. 'You don't solve a puzzle by starting halfway through.' He unclips Moses' seatbelt, lifts him out and sets him on the ground. 'Do you remember any of this?' he asks. 'Have you been here before?'

Moses stares up at him with solemn eyes. Lena remembers the dog trainer she and Bella once watched in Golden Gate Park. ('It's not cruel,' Bella had said authoritatively. 'It's in the dog's best interests.') But Lena doesn't want Moses to be obedient and fall into line. She wants him to remain stubbornly silent and for them all to go home, so that she can go back to Fairbanks leaving Jimmy and Moses intact, a complete unit. She turns her sleeves down over her hands, walks away a few steps.

'I'll see you back here this afternoon,' says Norm in a cheery voice. 'Happy hunting.' But the look he gives Lena is a sympathetic one.

'I'll fix you up for this when we get back to Barrow,' Jimmy says to Norm, dragging his attention away from Moses for a second. He reaches out and shakes Norm's hand in his familiar, oddly formal way.

'Hell, no, you won't,' says Norm. 'It's been a real good season for me so far. Damned if I can't afford the odd run into the mountains for a friend.' Hastily, he gets back into his bubble and lifts off. Even though Lena moves away, the wind from the rotorwash blows through her hair and snatches the breath out of her mouth.

But then, just as suddenly, Norm is back, hovering low, shouting out the door.

'You forgot this!' he is shouting to her, and he is holding her camera bag.

'Drop it!' shouts Lena. With a *whoomph* the bag is in her hands, and her arms drop to accommodate the weight.

'Just as well you got it,' says Jimmy. 'You might never get another chance like today.'

Lena looks around. The helicopter disappears over the side of the mountain in a flash of silver; the sky is a rich blue. There is perfect silence apart from the background sound of the water. 'Never,' she says.

Jimmy takes Moses to the edge of the stream and Lena crunches around on the gravel to drown out the words. She gazes through a few different lenses at the steep sides of Doonerak, and then looks with her naked eye at the real thing.

'It does look a bit like the Matterhorn,' she calls out. But her voice falls on to the shingle, sinks down amongst the stones and is gone before Jimmy and Moses can hear it. The peak soars above them all, silent, secretive. There is a strange twist to its top that reminds Lena of a lopsided body.

The stone

Once Jimmy has finished examining the ground around the banks, he leads the way up the riverbed, hitching his daypack to one side so he can put Moses on his back. Lena follows behind. For as long as possible they keep to the side of the creek, but the banks get steeper and soon they are having to step, and sometimes jump, from boulder to boulder. Fresh snow lies on the surface of the bigger rocks; first Lena slips into the water, and then Jimmy.

'Lucky we brought spare socks,' says Jimmy, over his shoulder, over Moses' small clinging body.

With squelching feet, they leave the river and head off through some low willows. When they reach the bottom of another steep gully, Jimmy stops and puts Moses down. 'What is it?' he says.

Moses takes a few uncertain steps forward, kicks at a stone, looks up at the mountain and then down at the ground. And all the time Jimmy remains perfectly silent, watching him.

After a while—

'I think we've got something here,' he says, gazing up the gully, squinting against the sun.

'How can you tell?' asks Lena.

'Something's different,' Jimmy says vaguely, nodding at Moses. 'If you stand close to him you can feel a kind of – I dunno – a thrumming.' He takes Moses' arm, not gently, not roughly, and he holds onto it for a while as if it is a kind of a navigational instrument. 'Yep,' he says, dropping Moses' unprotesting arm again. 'Definitely.' He points over to a big flat rock. 'If you sit right there and watch hard,' he says to Moses, 'you might just see a golden eagle.'

He takes Lena a short distance away. 'This is about where I found him,' he says in a low voice. 'His clothes were almost iced up so he must have come some distance.' He stares up the gully again. 'Just past that S-bend,' he says. 'That's where I suspect it'll be.' He doesn't specify what. Lena looks over at Moses, a small red figure gazing obediently at the sky. She bites her lip and tastes blood.

'The only thing is—' says Jimmy, and two frown lines like tyre tracks appear between his eyebrows. 'The thing is, I don't like the look of that surface,' he says. 'Most of the new snow's blown down into the gully.'

'Maybe we should wait?' says Lena. 'Come back when it's melted?' There is a tiny note of hope in her voice.

Jimmy shakes his head. 'It'll turn to ice before it melts,' he says. 'I should really go now.' Although Lena is unaware of any change in Moses, she is acutely aware of one in Jimmy: he is newly sharpened, attuned, and his eyes are narrowed against the white glare around them. 'Oh,' she says. 'Right.' Her voice flattens out and she doesn't know what else to say.

'You'll be all right here,' says Jimmy, focusing on her for a minute. 'Put on all your extra clothes and stay in the sun. I'll be back as quick as I can.' He adjusts the pack on his back, tightening the straps, and then he goes over to Moses and bends down in front of him. 'Hey you!' he says in a friendly way. 'Look after Lena, will you?'

Moses looks at Jimmy and his eyelashes lower in a kind of nod. Then he resumes his watch of the sky, his small palms placed firmly, flatly, one each side of him on the rock.

Jimmy turns back to Lena. 'It'll be better when this is over,' he says. 'For him.'

'I know that,' says Lena, and she does but all the same she feels anxious. 'Trackers don't like loose ends,' she quotes, trying to convince herself that what is happening is not only right but inevitable.

'That's right,' says Jimmy. 'Things should always be finished.'

(For a second his voice sounds immensely tired, and under its stretched surface are:
– the screech of brakes
– an argument never resolved
– and a woman's crooked body lying on the side of a road just out of Anchorage.)

'Seidensal said you can find anything,' says Lena, by way of encouragement.

'Did he?' says Jimmy. 'That German peg-leg. He talks a lot of crap.' But he looks pleased as he pulls his hat down over his long hair.

Lena goes and sits beside Moses, and together they watch Jimmy heading up the gully, slipping sometimes on the loose snow. Soon he is out of sight around the first bend and Lena and Moses start playing a game with pebbles, arranging them in patterns on the large flat rock; but then they see Jimmy emerge into view again. He is much higher now, and he zigzags slowly across the gully, a black-beetle figure crawling on snow.

'See Jimmy?' Lena says to Moses (waiting for, not expecting an answer). As she watches, Jimmy stops in a narrow point of the gully and bends over to examine something. He stays in the same place for minutes on end. A small cold wind creeps under the ear flaps of Lena's hat, making her head ache.

It is very quiet. No insects, no birds. Jimmy's figure is bending and straightening, now his arms are outstretched. Now he is dragging a long dark shape up the side of the gully, something that looks like one of the dead seals on the beach at Point Barrow; now he slips and lets the thing fall. It is like watching a silent movie. But then there is a sound – though a tiny one – and it comes from beside Lena.

It is Moses. His eyes are fixed on the gully: he is rocking back and forwards on the rock, and an odd moaning is coming from his lips. 'Moses!' says Lena in alarm. This is the first sound she has ever heard him make, and it is nothing like what she has hoped for. 'Oh, Moses, don't,' she pleads. 'We'll look after you, I promise. You'll be OK.'

Nothing she can say can stop him. Even as she presses him against her coat, he moans on, sounding more elemental than human.

Rope

After a long time Moses falls heavily into sleep, and Lena's feet start to go numb. At last she sees Jimmy emerge from the gully. He is descending by the same route as he climbed up by, but now his progress is much quicker. Before the blood has returned to Lena's feet, he is on the slope in front of her, slipping fast in the loose scree.

He is breathing hard, and there is sweat on his face. He nods at Lena but for a second has no breath to speak.

'Is it?' asks Lena, almost in a whisper.

'Yes,' says Jimmy when he has caught his breath. His voice is so low that Lena can hardly hear it. 'It's what I thought.'

'Only one?' says Lena. Against her ribs Moses' small body stirs, his memory returning from wherever it has been.

'Yes,' says Jimmy again. 'But I've gotta go back up – I need another rope to secure him.'

'Shouldn't we wait for Norm?' asks Lena worriedly.

'Don't want to wait,' says Jimmy briefly. 'There's a snow slab up there a couple of inches thick. A few hours and the whole face of the gully could shift.' He nods towards Moses, still half wrapped in Lena's coat. 'Is he doing OK?'

'Not too badly,' says Lena. 'He cried.' She doesn't know if this word goes close to describing the sound Moses has made.

Jimmy seems to think this is a good thing. 'A step in the right direction,' he says. 'It's gotta be.' He is on edge, bends and rummages in the second backpack for the other rope. 'What I want you to do now,' he says to Lena, 'is go back down to the drop-off point. You know how to get back?'

'Sure,' says Lena. She unfolds her arms from around Moses and he emerges a little rumpled, though the calm of sleep is still in his face. His hat has ridden up to the top of his head and Jimmy pulls it down again.

'You're gonna do just fine,' he says to Moses. 'You want to go back down the hill with Lena now?'

Moses nods, reaches for Lena's leg and holds on to it the same way as he did with Jimmy on Lena's first day in the store. Tears come to Lena's eyes but there is a relief in Moses reaching for her, a comfort in providing comfort.

Jimmy coils the rope around his waist, looks back up at the mountain. The summit stands far above them, stark as a paper cut-out against the blue sky. 'Glad I don't have to go all that way,' he says. 'But I'd better get going.' He turns to go and crunches a few steps across the snowy shingle. But then he turns around again, coming back to Lena as she sits there with Moses at her side. 'Lena?' he says. And now he is so close that she can see a pulse in his neck, and the end of the tiny thread-like scar emerging from his hair.

Bending down towards her a little stiffly, he kisses her: an awkward kiss that lands somewhere near the side of her mouth. For a second she feels his breath merging with hers, a current of warmth in the cold air. He steps back.

'You're sure you know how to get back?' he says for the second time. His eyes stay on her face: they are so dark that the reflected sun in them appears to be shining from far inside, like the pinpoint entrance to a cave.

Now Lena feels a pull inside her that is almost like a pain: it is as if the ache in her head is spreading through her and running into her bones. She stands up and reaches out for Jimmy, takes hold of his hand. His arm is as stiff as a piece of wood, but as she runs her fingers over the small callus on his palm the ridged skin feels almost like her own. She has to force herself to let go of his hand.

'I won't be long,' says Jimmy, as if he's going to the corner store for milk.

'And then,' says Lena, 'we can all get on with being happy.'

'Happy!' says Jimmy. 'You think so?' But as Lena watches him go she sees a certainty in him, in the angle of his feet and the way he uses his arms to balance his body.

As Jimmy heads steadily upwards, Lena and Moses slither and slip downhill. They reach the river and wade across the shallows, not worrying anymore about wet feet. 'Who cares about a bit of water?' says Lena. She watches Moses' face and sees the glimmer of a smile, and they continue on their slow way. By the time they get to the gravel patch imprinted with helicopter tracks, they are both sweating inside their coats.

Lena changes Moses into dry socks and ski pants, and makes a bed for him out of Jimmy's spare sweater. Within minutes he has fallen heavily into sleep. Lena walks back to the edge of the river, sees the gully like a thin thread of cotton against the stark white hillside. Can she see Jimmy halfway up the gully? She thinks she can, then thinks she cannot. The distance moves stationary objects, turns rocks into climbers and makes the still air shiver. She tries so hard to pick Jimmy out of that vast land-scape that black spots being to dance like midges in front of her eyes.

Behind her Moses sleeps, for a while forgets. And Lena waits there by the river, eyes shielded against the glare. Waits for Jimmy, waits for Norm, waits for something that she has half expected all along in the ache of her head and her bones.

A falcon flashes low overhead. Lena looks up and, for a sharp and shining moment, looks straight into its eyes. (She is seven years old again, is standing on a pavement in San Francisco, is anticipating something in the hurting of her head and the holding of her breath.) In the darkness of the falcon's eyes she sees the earth laid bare: the hollow hearts of mountains, the vaults of underwater lakes that have never seen the sun. Through the soles of her feet she can feel the layers of rock and soil stretching away beneath her, but in that moment they are no more than thin skin protecting the beating, heated core of the earth.

She stands there on the skeleton of the world, and she waits.

She sees Jimmy then, a tiny figure high in the snow gully, held still by her stilled vision. 'Jimmy,' she says, as she catches sight of him. But she is speaking to herself. 'Jimmy,' she says again, although he is far from earshot.

Behind her Moses moves. Lena turns, the sun catches in her eyelashes and, for a second, she is blinded. All these things happen at once. And then

Lena's sight returns.

There is a huge crack that splits her hearing

(yes, Lena says later to the bullet, *it was as loud as you*)

and a supersonic boom, like two express trains colliding, or the particularly loud beat of a heart.

Opposite her, the world is falling. The gully is shifting before her eyes, turning to a sliding river of snow. Great white slabs overlap and then overtake each other, like loose tiles racing down a roof.

Lena cries. She cries out but her voice is lost in the roar of snow. She catches at each sliding moment but there is nothing to be done. She replays the white blur over and over in her mind, sees all its possible endings even as the avalanche rolls to a halt.

There is no more. Silence settles on the mountain and there is no sound other than the quiet one of Moses breathing.

Cracks

Norm comes back earlier than arranged to find them sitting by the river. Sitting with their backs to the huge arc of debris spewing from the mouth of the gully, Moses building small dams in the shallow water and Lena watching quietly. He is swift to organize a course of action, radios for help even as the tears pour down his face. 'Send a Pave Hawk helicopter,' he says urgently, 'and some paramedics.'

But there is no point, says Lena inside her quiet snow head. It is for Norm's sake that she remains silent, listens to him confirming their location and telling the rescue team to be quick and to bring oxygen.

Norm puts his arms around Lena and Moses. 'I was worried about you all,' he says. 'That's why I came back early. I knew it was avalanche weather.' He looks at the changed face of the mountain. 'I hope they hurry,' he says, but his tears drop hot on Lena's head so it is obvious that he also knows speed is irrelevant.

After the rescue helicopter has arrived, after the river valley has become a busy place swarming with stretcher-bearers and running dogs, Lena leaves Moses safe with Norm and forms part of the procession to the bottom of the avalanche. During this time there are no pictures in her head: only white noise that falls and merges with the crunching of feet in the snow.

Jimmy lies in an arc of scattered rocks and ice. He is on his back, arms stretched wider than they ever were in life. His legs are twisted at a strange angle underneath him, but his eyes are closed and his face looks perfectly peaceful, even though it is covered in long deep scratches and flecked with blood.

Lena reaches out, combs her fingers through Jimmy's hair. The long strands are filled with grit.

'Must have lost his hat in the fall,' says one of the team members. He clears his throat and looks at Lena crouching there beside Jimmy, camera swaying round her neck. 'Take your time,' he says gruffly, over his shoulder.

The other body lies half buried in icy debris, not far from Jimmy, already bound up in Jimmy's rope. Lena hardly looks at it: she takes a glance, for Moses' sake, and turns away again. While the rescue team dig and carry and curse, she sits on her heels beside Jimmy. His hair looks very black and his fingers quite white, and these are the two main things she remembers afterwards, even though she has some time to look at him. When she finally takes her camera out she tilts it upwards, towards the mountain.

The authorities must take Jimmy in the end, while Norm flies Lena and Moses out of the valley. The two of them sit close together behind Norm's bulky back, while Norm talks backwards over his shoulder, loudly, as if building up a wall of words.

'You'd be welcome at our place,' he says. 'For as long as you wanted. Or you could go stay with Annie. You know her, don't you?'

And it is this that brings the first tears to Lena's eyes: the image of Annie, pumping gas, swearing at the customers, and refusing to look at Jimmy's truck or think about Jimmy.

'I do know Annie,' she says, 'but I think we should go home.' She doesn't think this, she knows it, and she has never been more grateful for the certainty.

When they reach Barrow Norm lifts Moses out of the helicopter and sets him gently on the ground.

'He didn't see anything, did he?' he asks in a low voice, over Moses' head.

Lena looks at Moses, who is bending and pulling at his trailing bootlace. He looks grave but not particularly perturbed. 'No,' she says. 'Jimmy made sure I took him off the mountain.'

'He knows the risks damn well,' says Norm, talking about Jimmy as if he is still alive. 'He's a stubborn bastard – always thinks he knows best.'

He pauses. Lena feels again the faint remembered twang of warning, pulling at her stomach, stretching her ribs, making it hard to take a breath.

'He knew the risks and he took them,' amended Norm, wiping his eyes. 'That was just the way Jimmy was.' With one breath he assigns Jimmy to the past, and this too is the way things must be.

Twenty-four hours later Norm is back in Barrow. He returns

the following evening, arriving on the doorstep of Jimmy's house with a quiet grey-haired stranger in tow.

'Detective Scott,' says the grey-haired, plain-clothes stranger, and he shakes hands with Lena and accepts a root beer, and politely avoids looking too closely at the echoing empty shell that is Jimmy's house.

'I thought I'd stay while you get filled in on the facts,' says Norm. He takes his own root beer and moves his chair a short distance away to sit like a stolid gatekeeper outside Moses' bedroom door. 'Kid asleep, is he?' he asks gruffly.

Lena sits at the table with the detective (a patient man who suffers from hay fever and an overload of work) and she listens to him talk for a long time. After the detective has finished his story and his drink, has sneezed four times and blown his nose and left for a much needed night's sleep at the nearby motel, Norm clears his throat but doesn't speak. Lena stares so hard at Moses' bedroom door that the cracks in the wood bleed into each other, and when she looks back at Norm for a second all she can see is black.

'Some people shouldn't be allowed to be parents,' she says, with an angry catch in her voice.

'Some people just don't take care,' says Norm. 'It's nothing to do with being a parent.' He sets his empty bottle down on the floor. 'Moses was lucky being picked up by Jimmy,' he says. 'Now he's lucky with you.'

'Oh, Norm,' says Lena. 'How are we going to go on.' But she knows, even as she and Norm look at each other and begin to cry, that somehow they will keep waking and sleeping, and life will keep happening to them whether they want it to or not, just as it did to Jimmy.

'I should get going,' says Norm. 'Got to fly the sarge back to Anchorage in the morning, early.' But he sits on for an hour or so, small puffs of dust swirling around his feet, until he can see that Lena is so tired she will sleep, even if only in her chair.

Once he has gone, though, Lena remains at the table. Pulling her chair in closer, she lays her head down with her good ear against the wood, and she listens for her thoughts. There is no

234

Mrs Domanski to tell her to move along, no Mr Domanski to interrupt her or Davey to hunt for or Bella to hide from, and she stays sitting there for a long time. Finally she moves as if sleep-walking to the bottom of the ladder. She puts her hand on it as if she is about to climb up to the loft, then takes her hand away again and rests her head on the seventh rung. 'Coming ready or not,' she says under her breath.

The seventh story of loss

A small boy of four years and seven months lives in the State of California with his father. This father, who works as a scientist in the UC Berkeley nuclear research lab in Livermore, is kindly but vague; he is constantly headhunted by universities all over the world on account of his skills as a researcher, which are far more highly developed than his parenting skills.

In the early days of a San Francisco spring, when the wind is scattering light green leaves over the East Bay suburbs, the father of the four-year-old boy is told to take a break. 'You have worked for twenty months without a vacation!' says the head honcho, the big cheese, the leader of the Livermore nuclear research group. Although this man would split an atom without a thought for the future, he is now thinking of this father's small son. It is high time, he thinks, that the father spent some time with the boy, particularly considering the tragic loss of the mother in child-birth.

'Oh, sure,' says the father-researcher vaguely. 'I'm sure you're right,' he says, vaguely guilty. And he decides to take his son (aged four years, seven months and twenty-nine days) all the way up to Alaska, that most romantic and far-flung of the American states. 'It will be an experience for you!' he says to the boy but, secretly, having been brought up on a diet of Jack London books, he has always had a hankering to go there himself.

The father and son take a tent and a primus stove, and they end up sleeping two freezing nights in the wilderness of north-ern Alaska; the father never notices the cold, and the boy never complains. But on the exact same day that the boy turns four years and eight months, the sky is brilliant blue, the sun smiles down on them, and the mountains call to them in friendly voices. 'Hey, lab rat!' they call to the father. 'Escape the cage!'

The father hears the calling, and he looks at the legs of the son, grown strong from the climbing frames of the UC Berkeley crèche. 'Let's go for a hike,' says the father to the four-year-old boy with the straight black hair. They leave their campsite in the middle of nowhere and they hitch a ride with a grizzled old hunter to the base of what some would say is the wildest and most mysterious mountain in the North.

When the boy gets tired and the sky clouds over, the father is not ready to leave. *Lost: one all-consuming work ethic.* The call of the wild has entered his blood, the anxiety of recycled nuclear waste lies at his back. 'Twenty minutes,' he promises. 'That's all I'll be.' And he climbs, in his thin plimsolls and his thin thread-bare sweatpants, all the way up to the edge of a gully and looks for a second towards the crooked top of the mountain. There, in the blind of the disappearing sun, he recaptures for the first time the bright beautiful face of his boy's dead Japanese mother and in that moment loses *four years and eight months of grief and regret*.

He falls ten meters into the gully, that father, and his skull is smashed in before he can utter a sound. He hangs from a rock face caught by the straps of his backpack, and the first snow falls softly on his shattered head. When he is found many weeks later by a renowned tracker from Barrow, his body is frozen to the core.

House calls

'Of course I will get a message to your brother,' Seidensal says. Chipper's voice breaks in from somewhere in the background, crackling through an already crackling phone line.

'We are wondering what will happen to the little boy?' repeats Seidensal obediently.

'We're still waiting to find out,' says Lena. 'There don't seem to be any living relatives.' She hears Chipper's voice exclaiming in sympathy, and then Chipper's quick busy footsteps hurrying off to the kitchen where she will start baking cookies for motherless Moses.

'Now,' says Seidensal instantly. 'Now tell me the rest of the story.'

Lena tells him. Of the long slow way to the bottom of the avalanche, of Jimmy's grazed hands, white against white, and of the camera hanging round her neck: dead-weight, anchor.

'I would not tell Chipper this,' says Seidensal in a low voice, 'she would think I am sacrilegious. But just between you, me and the fencepost—' He hesitates. 'Do I have that right?' he queries. 'What I mean to say, Lena, between friends, is that it is not a bad thing to die on a mountain. That is the right way to go.' There is an almost wistful note in his voice as if he hopes that, when his time is up, his face will also be turned towards an Alaskan peak rather than a fringed floral lightshade.

'Jimmy probably thought that too,' says Lena slowly.

'But we will miss him,' says Seidensal. 'Oh yes, we will miss him, you and I.' Chipper's footsteps get close again and, quickly, Seidensal's voice changes. 'I will let your brother know you will follow at a later date,' he says like a kindly but impersonal travel agent.

And so the day marked on the calendar as Lena's departure date brings no kind of departure and it passes quietly by, although as Lena helps Moses through the bath and puts him to bed she looks at his small closed face and thinks of Davey's pale freckled one, turning towards the airport bus, turned towards home.

They stay there, Lena and Moses, living on in Jimmy's house for a number of weeks. Sometimes they cry. In that quiet waiting time several official visitors come from Anchorage. They ask many questions of Lena and Moses, some of which Lena does not know how to answer while Moses can answer none.

A real estate board goes up in front of the house and Brenda comes round to dismantle the bed in the loft. (Lena has been up there only once, and this will not change.) Brenda thunders up the ladder, making the house shudder and plates rattle in the cupboard; she bundles up sheets and pillows and loads them into the back of their van, and then she single-handedly wrestles the mattress down the ladder.

'We're having a yard sale in a few weeks,' she says. 'Might as well swell the numbers.' She is matter of fact, almost hard, the whole time she is working, and her sweater is knotted round her waist in a businesslike way. But when she finally pauses for a cup of coffee, she looks at Lena and her face twists.

'It was probably for the best,' she says. She puts her arms around Lena, strokes her head. 'He had that look about him,' she says. 'Same look I've seen with deer I've hit on the road.'

Lena lays her face against Brenda's shoulder, breathes in the smell of washing powder and artificial strawberry flavouring. 'I know that,' she says in a muffled voice. 'I just miss him, that's all.'

Po comes in from the yard where she has been having a one-sided chat with Moses. She goes over to Brenda's chair, smoothes Brenda's shaggy hair back with both hands. 'Have you got a rubber band?' she asks Lena. 'Brenda's hair's grown like wildfire this summer.'

'Get away with you!' says Brenda, leaving her head unresistingly in Po's hands.

'How's your picture book going, Lena?' asks Po, smoothing and shaping.

'I just have to sort through the prints once more and I'm done,' says Lena, finding Po some string and pouring out the coffee. 'You want to see the final shots?' she asks. She lays them out on the table, waits a little anxiously. ('That routine was useless!' she hears a teenage Bella scoff in her head.)

'It's Moses! He's beautiful!' breathes Po. 'Almost as good as the real thing!'

'That's him, all right,' says Brenda, poring over the black and white images backed by stained table-top. 'You've got him to a tee.' (Brenda, like Jimmy, would never say something she doesn't mean, any more than she would warm instantly to a newcomer intending to stay in Barrow for only a few days.) 'Playing in the dust like that,' she adds. 'It almost looks like he's tracking. Jimmy would approve.'

'I like that one of the mountain,' says Po with admiration and a slight covetousness in her voice. 'That's real pretty. I wouldn't mind a copy of that for the den.'

Brenda looks at her watch. 'Po!' she says, and she pushes her chair back. 'We've got to get back to the store.'

She and Po clash cups into the sink, bundle up bags and sweaters, and head for the door. But when they reach it they turn in unison, like well-rehearsed performers in a vaudeville act, and they march back and put their arms around Lena so that she is covered, smothered, by the two of them.

'We're going to miss you,' they say, into Lena's hair.

Dividing lines

The sun still strides along the coastline but it is no longer as bold as it once was. Lena senses winter waiting somewhere out to sea, ready to rush back in and take over where it left off. The lime-green chill in the air reminds her of Mrs Domanski, happy in her faraway landscape which is also frosted for eight months of every year.

Jimmy's house, which hardly feels like Jimmy's any more, is almost empty. There were few things in it to start with, and now there are fewer. Its blank windows and booming floorboards speak of departure, but even so Lena must wait. She tries to keep busy, sorting out the last batches of negatives, replying to Jay's always urgent calls. ('This could be a bidding war, Lena!' says Jay in an important voice. 'Don't hang around too much longer up there.')

Before she sends the final photos away, Lena takes one out of its covers and looks at it for a long time. She traces its shape with her finger, leaving a smudge that fades even as she watches. After a while she calls Bella.

'You think I should include it?' she says. 'It's different from the others.'

'Different in what way?' queries Bella. She sounds preoccupied. 'Oh *shit*!' she says.

'What's the matter?' asks Lena, alarmed.

'I just dropped a fucking tray of eyes all over the floor,' says Bella. 'Cost me a fortune. Sorry, what were you saying?'

'About this photo,' says Lena. 'What do you think? Some people might think that it doesn't fit.'

'There's always one that doesn't fit,' says Bella. 'Take Delayed Davey, for example.' Her voice, made loud from years of rowdy Domanski dinners and tough from battling through the streets of the Tenderloin, blasts down the phone; by the time it reaches Lena, in spite of having travelled all the way from the west coast of America to the far North, it is still almost a shout.

'Davey fits,' objects Lena, holding the phone slightly away from her ear. 'In his own way.'

'Listen to me, Lena,' says Bella with authority. 'When your mother lives in Poland and your father lives in fast food joints and your brother lives in fucken dreamland, well, I don't think you should get too hung up on *belonging*.'

When Bella comes to say goodbye, though, her voice softens a little round the edges like plastic left in the hot sun. 'Hey kiddo,' she says, Uncle-Larry style. But there is no bad joke to follow. 'We miss you here,' she says. 'Whatever happens with Boy Moses, you should come on home.'

After Lena hangs up she leans on the windowsill, still holding the phone to her ear, and she listens to the odd sound of an empty line: a tunnel with no traffic in, the imagined roar of the sea. Suddenly she senses the long arms of California reaching out for her. She goes to the table and picks up the photo. 'You can tell your own story,' she says to it. 'Or not.'

She divides the negatives into two piles, packs them in two envelopes with New York addresses, and posts them on her way to the store. Far away on the tundra, the caribou begin their long migration south.

('The photos have arrived!' says Jay's publishing contact. 'I love them! When's the girl due back?'

'Soon, her agent keeps promising,' says the assistant. 'The thing is, I've had some bad news.'

240

'What?' says Jay's publisher pal in a suspicious voice.

'You know that Hotshot on Madison?' says the assistant nervously. 'He's on to her too.')

('I love them!' says the rival publisher, otherwise known as the Hotshot on Madison. 'Sheer fucking genius.'

'I don't know about this one, though,' says the Nephew peevishly. He has recently been fired for pilfering and is waiting for his Uncle to offer him an internship. 'This one sucks,' he says.

'The mountain?' queries the Uncle-Publisher. 'I think that got in by mistake – it's more of a wilderness shot.'

His Nephew picks his teeth with the wilderness shot. 'And the rest?' he says. 'What category?'

'Human interest, of course,' says the Hotshot Publisher, wishing the Nephew would leave. 'Dump that, would you,' he says irritably. 'We don't want nature. Nature doesn't sell.'

'No,' echoes the Nephew obediently. 'Nature doesn't sell.')

Early one morning there is a phone call that splits the quiet Barrow house in two. Lena stumbles out of bed, crashes into the door, opens it, and makes it to the phone before it stops ringing. Moses appears in his pyjamas at the bunk-room door.

'Thank you,' says Lena, a little breathlessly. She watches Moses' face as she listens. 'Thanks,' she says again. 'Goodbye.'

She puts down the phone and goes over to Moses and holds on to him so hard that a loose button falls off his pyjama jacket and spins away over the floor. Moses makes a small crushed noise.

'Sorry,' says Lena to Moses. She kisses him and lets him go, picks up the button and closes her hand hard around it. 'They said yes!' she says. But her voice comes out slightly crushed too, as if it has been flattened at the bottom of a box for some time. It is a heavy burden, this: the fact that sometimes you can do nothing but wait for other people's decisions before making any of your own.

Cookies

In the first week of August the sun dips below the horizon for the first time and immediately Barrow feels different. It takes on a plainer and more sensible face: the dust no longer whirls and dances, but lies quietly on the surface of the streets.

Lena folds clothes and packs bags, and thinks of the darkness that will soon clamp down on Barrow, grabbing the town with its cold hard teeth and holding on hard for months on end. Beside her Moses' red snow suit hangs over the edge of the bunkbed, along with the rest of his small donated collection of clothes. The new stains and holes in them tell stories that Moses cannot. *When?* thinks Lena. She folds and packs, folds and packs, but now tries to concentrate only on what her hands are doing rather than the future.

As she leaves to fetch Moses from the store, she feels her anxiety growing. *When*, she thinks again, as if with an old and tired routine she can't get out of her head. *And how?* She crosses the yard (remembering Jimmy on the first day), trudges over the muddy empty lot (remembering the first day), climbs the fence and sets off down the road to the store.

She is still two blocks away when, suddenly, Po comes bursting out of the store, leaping down the steps and into the street like a small gazelle in pink leggings. The screen door bangs behind her like a gun; Lena marches steadily on.

'Lena!' Po is crying out. 'Come quick, Lena!' Now she is running as fast as she can towards Lena, silver trainers flashing.

'Are you OK, Po?' calls Lena in alarm. 'Is Moses OK?'

Po's face is streaked, her makeup running. She reaches Lena. 'Moses said—' she gasps, but the rest of her sentence is lost in a sob.

'He *said*?' repeats Lena, and now she also starts to run. She flies up the steps of the store and through the door, where she sees nothing out of the ordinary: simply Moses stacking cookies into perfectly shaped tower blocks, as he often does.

Brenda is at her post behind the counter and she looks up at Lena's sudden entry. 'Moses was just telling me,' she says conversationally, 'that chocolate chip cookies are his favourite kind.' Her eyes are dry: after all, she has not cried over Jimmy or the break-up of her fourteen-and-a-half-year marriage, so why shed tears over a small boy who has been wordless for a while and has now begun to speak again? None the less Brenda's cheeks are red, and there is a slight flush on her neck.

Lena kneels down beside Moses. She looks at his cluster of box-buildings, and at his small careful hands placing another storey on what looks like a Californian beachfront hotel. 'You like chocolate chip, do you?' she says. 'I think they're pretty good too. But you know what I *really* like? Donuts.'

'Donuts?' repeats Moses. His voice is small and cloudy, higher than Lena has imagined.

'Donuts are the best!' says Lena. She waits for a minute. 'And next to donuts,' she goes on, 'I like cats. Do you like cats?'

Moses looks at her consideringly, nods. Lena feels a moment of acute anxiety before realizing that, even if you can talk, you have the choice not to. 'I've got a cat called Mitchell back home,' she says. 'He lives in San Francisco, in a place called the Tenderloin.'

'Tenderloin?' says Moses, and he gives a small laugh.

'Have you been there?' asks Lena.

'Maybe,' says Moses vaguely. He turns back to his cardboard city and puts the finishing touch to a short skyscraper.

On the way back to the house Lena and Moses walk slowly in the sunshine, close but not touching. As if taking part in an awards ceremony, they parade before a row of old Inuit men dozing on benches, only here they are followed by snores instead of by applause.

They walk on, past the bank and the barber's shop.

'What's your real name?' asks Lena, after a while.

'Miles,' answers Moses. His voice has an odd creak to it, like a piece of machinery that has been lying around in a dark shed for a long time. He and Lena pass the bicycle repair shop, and dust gathers on the tops of their shoes.

'I like Moses better, though,' says Moses, as if he has been thinking about this for some time.

'Well, that's OK,' says Lena. 'Everyone should get to change their name if they want to.'

'Did you ever do that?' asks Moses, as if Lena is a hundred years old and her life is almost at its end.

'Actually, I did,' says Lena, and there is surprise in her voice. 'Twice.'

('I hear you've also got your eye on this fabulous photographer,' says the Madison Avenue Magnate down the phone. 'This comedian, this funny woman, this girl extraordinaire.'

'That's correct,' says Jay's publishing acquaintance cagily. 'I didn't know she was a comedian, though.'

'Ex-comedian – worked under a different name then,' says the doyen of New York publishing who always knows more. 'She might be retired,' he says, 'but the humour's still there.'

'You think?' says Jay's publishing buddy in surprise. 'I find the pictures grave.'

'I guess that depends on whether you've got a sense of humour,' the Hotshot Publisher says to the not-so-hot East Coast contact of West Coast middle-man Jay Antonelli. 'What I mean, of course,' he amends smoothly, 'is what sort of a sense of humour you might have.')

The time before a departure does not always need to be a restless time, and on the final night the kitchen in Barrow is peaceful and quiet. Lena is frying onions and Moses is cracking eggs into a bowl; every now and then they exchange the odd comment, in a laconic but still slightly surprised way. And every now and then one of them looks towards the door, as if hoping it will open and a third person will walk in.

The phone rings instead, making Lena jump and Moses drop the egg-whisk. It is Mr Domanski on the line.

'I was sorry to hear about the loss of your friend,' he says gravely. 'Alaska is a dangerous place, make no mistake.'

'The world can be a dangerous place,' says Lena. 'It's not just Alaska.'

'Well, it is good you are finally coming home, Pie,' says Mr

Domanski. 'I was beginning to think that all my women had deserted me.' From the tone in his voice it is clear that another letter has recently arrived from Poland.

'Da, don't start,' says Lena, with a laugh and a sigh.

'I have been preoccupied with a new menu for the fall,' says Mr Domanski, changing the subject. 'I am wondering, do you think chilli dogs could be made to seem Polish?'

'I'm probably the last person you should ask,' says Lena mildly. 'About hotdogs or about Poland.'

'If only your mother would take an interest in these matters,' says Mr Domanski, reverting instantly to what is on his mind. 'She could be of great value to me, but her head is always full of lip-shadow and eye-gloss.'

'You mean lip gloss—' begins Lena.

'Yes, yes, whatever,' interrupts Mr Domanski. 'Has the little boy begun to talk yet?'

'Actually, yes!' says Lena. 'He—'

'It's about time, too,' says Mr Domanski. 'It is the quiet ones that cause all the problems. Think of your mother.' A small hope springs up in his voice. 'If you get to keep the boy,' he says, 'perhaps we could persuade your mother to come back and look after him?'

'No!' says Lena. (Moses looks up, drops an egg. 'No problem,' says Lena, scooping it up off the floor with a fish slice.)

'She was a good mother to you children,' says Mr Domanski challengingly. 'Until that dancing nonsense took her away from us, away from her proper home.'

'She's home now,' says Lena firmly. 'In Poland. You know it.'

'At least she is making good money,' says Mr Domanski, realizing that he is beaten. And now a familiar note of guilt creeps into his voice, reminding Lena of cracked linoleum floors and hard kitchen cupboards and the smell of burnt meatloaf. 'I must go to Pasadena tomorrow,' he says. 'I wish to check out a location for a new Polish Sausage.'

'Oh,' says Lena, with another small laugh. 'I see. So you'll leave the house key with Uncle Larry?'

'Yes, you can collect the key from Larry,' says Mr Domanski

hastily, 'and I will be back the very next day! You understand, don't you, Pie? This could be the location of a lifetime.'

'You want to tell me about it?' asks Lena.

'Oh, certainly I will!' says Mr Domanski. His voice becomes loud with relief and enthusiasm, and soon site details are booming from the phone and mingling with the more mundane sounds of hot oil spitting and pans clattering.

When Lena is finally allowed to say goodbye—

'Well, some things never change,' she says, putting down the receiver. The scarred skin over her left ear gives a slight remembering twitch. 'Though some things,' she says, looking at Moses stirring the pan, whispering to himself as if practising a newly remembered joke, 'some things change dramatically.'

She and Moses sit at the table eating crunchy scrambled egg and slightly blackened onions, and they talk for a bit about Jimmy, and then fall into a companionable silence. After that the only sounds are those of Moses gulping milk, and the squeak of cutlery on plates, and the soft chirping of the fridge in the corner of the kitchen. Lena breathes out and the skin on the side of her head settles back, quietly.

(*But I thought you were coming back to me, Lena!* cries the bullet disappointedly, from its dull dark box in a dull dark file room.

No, says Lena to the bullet.

I've missed you so, wheedles the bullet, from its dark box in a dark file room in a small police station in a southern precinct of San Francisco. *Please say you'll come back to me, Lena, my friend!*

No, says Lena loudly, *never again*)

There is a stillness to the house that night which is surprising. Lena lies awake in the bed that was once Jimmy's and then has been hers for a while and after tomorrow will be sold, and she listens for any sound. It has always been quiet here but tonight the silence is so deep that it is like a snow-drift without end, so wide it is a sea without landfall. Even when Lena closes her eyes all she can hear is the sound of her own heart sending blood around her body, and her bones stretching long and easy on the mattress.

She sleeps then, and in the moment before sleep she is aware of a rare thing: she is aware of rest.

('Lena Domanski?' says the Madison Magnate, Uncle to the Nephew. 'She's flying out of Alaska tomorrow.'

'About time,' says the Nephew in a moody voice. 'God knows why anyone would want to stay in that hellhole.' Longingly he looks down seventy floors into the cauldron of New York: a swirling mass of barstools and highballs and girls.

'You look like you need something to do,' says the Uncle, who has relented and given the Nephew a job. (It is the Nephew, after all, who has delivered some of the most innovative photography the Uncle has seen in years to his very door.)

'Oh, all right,' says the Nephew reluctantly. 'If I have to.'

'You can take a look at this,' says the Uncle, who trusts the Nephew with reading work only and keeps a close eye on all manuscripts. (It was the Nephew, after all, who stole the innovative photos in the first place.)

'What is it?' asks the Nephew, a distinct lack of curiosity in his voice.

'It's by an ambulance driver in San Francisco,' says the Uncle. 'The story of some chick who took a bullet through the head in a drive-by shooting.'

'Non-fiction, is it?' asks the Nephew, who always prefers things to be categorized for him.

'Looks more like reality-based fantasy,' says the Uncle, flicking through the manuscript. 'The story of what could have happened to this babe after she hit the dust.' He flicks again with sharpened eyes, ignoring the Nephew's outstretched hand. 'Philly Tarantella!' he says, flicking and reading, flicking and reading. 'Talking bullets!'

'Yeah?' says the Nephew with enthusiasm. 'Give it here!'

'For God's sake,' says the Uncle, and there is a touch of alarm in his voice. 'Just keep this one under your hat, would you?')

The asking

Norm arrives on the airfield at the crack of dawn to pick up Lena and Moses. This time, though, he is not in his helicopter but in a Cessna. 'My second set of wheels,' he jokes. But when he looks at Lena and Moses, there is a wateriness to his eyes. 'The morning air,' he says, by way of an excuse. 'It's chilly.'

'Chilly billy,' says Moses.

A tear runs quickly and ashamedly down Norm's face. 'Jimmy was a friend,' he says, with a sob and a cough.

'He was,' says Lena. 'The best.'

She looks at Norm for a moment, then leans forward and kisses him on the cheek, making him blush.

'Oh, get on with it would you,' says Brenda, who has turned out before breakfast to say goodbye. Her hair stands up on one side like the comb of a rooster, while one side is still pillow-flat.

'Brenda!' says Po. 'Please!' Her apricot mouth glimmers in the early light. 'They won't see each other for a while,' she says reprovingly, pinching Brenda on the arm with her tiny gloved hand. 'Give them some time.'

But Norm has already become businesslike again. He picks up Moses' small bag and stows it in the plane, and then places Lena's beside it. 'I guess that's it,' he says. 'We'd better get going.'

'Looks like the wind's changing,' says Brenda, looking up into the clear white sky. 'It'll be a head one all the way to Fairbanks.'

'Let's go!' says Moses, running in excited circles. 'Let's go, Lena! I wanna meet Mitchell.'

'Mitchell?' says Po to Lena. 'I thought your brother was called Davey.'

'My cat,' explains Lena. 'He'll be waiting for Moses to hand-feed him lettuce, become his salad-slave.' As she looks towards Brenda and Po she suddenly experiences something closer to stage fright than she has ever felt in her life. 'I don't know what to say,' she says. 'I'm no good at goodbyes.'

She and Brenda and Po stand close and lean their heads together in a three-cornered pyramid, arms at their sides, foreheads the only point of contact. Their collective breathing sounds solid and reliable under the thin whistling of the wind. When they straighten up—

'I remember something Jimmy once said to me,' says Lena slowly.

'What's that?' asks Po, with a small crack in her voice.

'That even though most of the time people walk forwards,' says Lena, 'it's always possible to follow the same tracks back. If you need to.'

And then it is time, and Lena and Moses are helped into the plane by Norm and buckled into their seats, and they look out through smeared glass at the two familiar figures standing in front of the truck. Norm settles his bulk into the seat so that the plane shudders.

'You're meeting someone in Fairbanks, right?' he says over his shoulder as the engine leaps into life.

'My brother,' replies Lena. 'He's coming out from California to meet us.' The roughness of the wheels on the grass shake the three of them around and Moses reaches excitedly for Lena's hand.

'That's good,' says Norm in an approving way. 'Family's important.'

With a lurch and an upwards swoop, they are lifting into the thin and whining air. Lena looks resolutely at the back of Norm's neck.

'Davey was up the Yukon over summer,' she says. 'On a mission to Mars.'

'Space,' says Norm admiringly. 'Must be magnificent.' He points the plane's nose towards the sky and then levels out; in front of them the mountains are turned to salmon pink by the sun. 'Though you know,' he says, 'I'll bet even in space you couldn't get a better view than this.'

The peaks get bigger and more silvery, and then the plane is flicking past the sunny peak of Doonerak and emerging like a sigh over the vast sweep of the tundra. Lena leans her head against the glass, cranes back for a last look at the mountains. The vibrations from the window enter her head through her scar, feel like fingers.

'And where are you headed after Fairbanks?' asks Norm conversationally.

The paradox

Tucked away in the heart of San Francisco is an area called the Tenderloin. It is an odd place: crammed with people and buildings, rife with crime. You might not choose to live there but if you happen to grow up in the Tenderloin, you might also find yourself returning there.

Seen from a distance – say from the air, or from the even farther-away place of memory – the Tenderloin might seem difficult to know. Draw closer, and its face also gets closer, becoming sharper, more in focus, as if seen through the lens of a camera. Now there are city blocks, now individual streets. Now black cars and blue cars, and pointed silver bullets. And now you can make out girls with hens, and genial donut-makers, and sisters striding about in sandals; now women sweeping or weeping on their front steps and store owners sitting in back alleys and Vietnamese restaurants with windows lit by lime-green fish tanks. Yes, this is the Tenderloin.

Sometimes this area can shatter people's lives, and sometimes it can help put them back together. Occasionally, it does both. And it may be – it is likely, it is probable even – that Lena will get to keep Moses and vice versa. For just as snow falls in summer and jokes are not always funny, loss can sometimes lead to a finding.

Acknowledgements and thanks

to Creative New Zealand, the DAAD Institut, the Goethe Institut, and Kunst-Werke Berlin; and in particular to Barbara Richter and Gerrit Bretzler for their kind help.

Many thanks to David Hatcher and Olivia Lory Kay for their close readings and advice; and to Sean Gallagher, Tom Hanratty, Neil Pardington, Leighton Pace, Antoinette Wilson and John Wilson for their help in the writing of this book.

Special thanks to Simon Trewin and Jill Foulston

and to Margie and Rach for their continued love and support.

Now you can order superb titles directly from Virago

☐	A Rhinestone Button	Gail Anderson-Dargatz	£10.99
☐	The Woman Who Gave Birth to Rabbits	Emma Donoghue	£7.99
☐	The Mineral Palace	Heidi Julavits	£6.99
☐	Tempting Faith DiNapoli	Lisa Gabriele	£6.99
☐	The Falling Woman	Shaena Lambert	£6.99
☐	The Leader of the Swans	Linda Lee Welch	£6.99

Please allow for postage and packing: **Free UK Delivery**
Europe; add 25% of retail price; Rest of World; 45% of retail price.

To order any of the above or any other Virago titles, please call our credit card orderline or fill in this coupon and send/fax it to:

Virago, P.O. Box 121, Kettering, Northants NN14 4ZQ
Fax: 01832 733076   Tel: 01832 737526
Email: aspenhouse@FSBDial.co.uk

☐ I enclose a UK bank cheque made payable to Virago for £.......

☐ Please charge £ .... to my Access, Visa, Delta, Switch Card No.

☐☐☐☐☐☐☐☐☐☐☐☐☐☐☐☐

Expiry Date ☐☐☐☐   Switch Issue No. ☐☐

Name (Block Letters please) _____

Address _____

_____

_____

Post/zip code:_____   Telephone: _____

Signature:_____

Please allow 28 days for delivery within the UK. Offer subject to price and availability.
Please do not send any further mailings from companies carefully selected by Virago   ☐

Word 2003
POUR
LES NULS
2ᵉ édition